WAR AMONG THE CROCODILES

THE SHADOW WARS TRILOGY: BOOK THREE

LEAH R CUTTER

KNOTTED ROAD PRESS

CONTENTS

Also by Leah R Cutter

Urban/Contemporary Fantasy Series

The Witch's Progress

Circle of Air

Circle of Fire

Circle of Water

Circle of Earth

Seattle Trolls

The Changeling Troll

The Princess Troll

The Fairy-Bridge Troll

The Troll-Demon War

The Troll-Human War

The Troll-Troll War

The Cassie Stories

Poisoned Pearls

Tainted Waters

Spoiled Harvest

Bloodied Ice

The Shadow Wars Trilogy

The Raven and the Dancing Tiger

The Guardian Hound

War Among the Crocodiles

The Clockwork Fairy Kingdom

The Clockwork Fairy Kingdom

The Maker, the Teacher, and the Monster

The Dwarven Wars

The Chronicles of Franklin

Franklin Versus The Popcorn Thief

Franklin Versus The Soul Thief

Franklin Versus The Child Thief

Epic Fantasy Series

Houses of the Dead

Houses Divided

Houses Fallen

Houses Reborn

Forgotten Gods

A Wind Blown Torment

A Stone Strewn Clash

A Sea Washed Victory

The Tanesh Empire Trilogy

The Glass Magician

The Desert Heart

The Ghost Dog

Huli Intergalactic: Science/Space Fantasy

Origins

The Strawberry Girl

Mysteries

The Purloined Letter Opener

Dancer in Darkness

Trophy Hunters

The Alvin Goodfellow Case Files

The Rabbit Mysteries

The Shredded Veil Mysteries

Mystery, Crime, and Mayhem

PART ONE
BECOMING

YVETTE

"But Mama, it's cold outside!" Yvette complained.

The snow had come early that year, and stayed, piled high around their little cottage. It was over eight-year-old Yvette's head! That night, it sparkled under the half-moon, like the sugar sprinkled on shortbread, frozen and beautiful. Their sleigh stood in the center of the front yard, and beyond that, columns of dark, grand pines. Even the trees couldn't escape the garlands of snow, though they'd tried to shake themselves free, shivering in the winter winds.

"Tsk," Mama said, scolding. "It's the *fin de siècle*. The end of the century. With that kind of attitude, you might not see the next."

Yvette sighed and turned away so Mama wouldn't see her roll her eyes. "*Oui*, Mama."

Mama had seen the previous century change—from 1799 to 1800—when she'd been younger than Yvette, merely five. However, Mama still seemed to be a woman in her late fifties, with long gray hair braided into a crown around her head, beautiful pale white skin, a tiny nose and wide dark eyes.

At least after Yvette sighed again, Mama went back to the trunks in the storage room of their tiny cottage and pulled out two more quilts. She handed them without a word to Yvette, just a sharp look.

Yvette carried the quilts out, across the front room and past the roaring fire in the fireplace that took up most of one wall, to the door where their bags were piled. She held the soft and warm quits in place with her chin as she carried them, breathing in the cedar, lavender, and mint that Mama used to keep the moths away. Being wrapped in them would be like walking in Mama's garden.

But it wouldn't be enough. Yvette would be *cold*. Which was just awful. And Mama wouldn't teach Yvette any spells for keeping herself warm. Claimed she was too young.

Mama would drive them in their sleigh from their cottage on the mountain down to the village of Lamoura that evening. The sun left the mountains early that time of year, so it was dark as night outside, though it wasn't that late—just after supper.

The carriage was open, not closed in. Nasty winds would seek Yvette out, burrowing in and finding her skin no matter how tightly she wrapped up. They always found Yvette, were always bothering her.

Finally, Mama finished gathering everything together by the door, all their bags and blankets and gifts. It was time to get dressed. Mama helped Yvette into her layers of stockings and petticoats and skirts and blouses and sweaters. Yvette felt caged in, unable to move. She walked stiffly, like a wooden doll. She felt ridiculous.

When she saw her friend Thierry, down in the village, he'd make fun of her.

It was still better than freezing.

Yvette knew better than to complain any more about the cold as she helped Mama carry everything out to the sleigh: the blankets, their bags, Mama's bag of magical sachets to sell to the village women, the little jams and jellies they'd give as New Years' gifts, and whatever was in the strange lumpy satchel that Mama had kept hidden under her bed and had worked on next to the large hearth with the fire banked low after Yvette had supposedly gone to sleep.

The cold bit into everything not covered up, stinging the skin around her eyes above the muffler drawn tightly across her face. She breathed in the scene of lanolin and wet wool. The piece over her mouth froze quickly, moistened by her breath. At least Mama had let her draw her fur cap well down over her ears, mashing her dark curls.

She'd cut them all off if Mama would let her. Shear them off like the shepherds sheared the sheep every spring.

Mama tucked Yvette into the sleigh, making her a nest of furs and quilts, tucked in behind her and around her, surrounding her with their warmth.

The sleigh wouldn't move on its own, unlike those new horseless carriages that the boys in the village were all talking about. Yvette didn't agree with Mama that the new vehicles would be the ruin of them. She wasn't exactly sure why Mama felt that. Mama liked trains. She'd even promised to take Yvette to Geneva by train the next spring.

The secrets of the internal combustion engine fascinated Yvette. How did they go? What made them move? How did all the parts work together?

Even Yvette knew those engines were important.

Mama got free use of the neighbors' horses in exchange for overseeing the births of all their animals, making sure their cattle and sheep were healthy. She had a way with animals, could get the shyest of mice to creep out from the hedge and feed from her hand. Yvette hadn't inherited her gift—she didn't know what her magic was.

However, Mama hadn't borrowed any animals that night.

Yvette sat, curious, wondering what Mama would do. She wouldn't pull the sleigh all the way into the village on her own, with her magic, would she? That was too far away. And the path was very steep in places. Mama's magic wasn't that strong.

Instead, Mama stepped in front of the sleigh and started conjuring. Yvette paid careful attention to the words, even though Mama wasn't speaking French but Latin, mixed with some language Yvette didn't know. Mama was slowly teaching Yvette spells and potions, herbs and healing, but Yvette always wanted to know more.

Mama raised her arms up to the half-moon just peeking over the pines. She wore her great, shaggy, brown-fur cloak, the one that made her look like a bear. Her skin looked as pale and white as the snow, her small nose and sharp chin catching the light. The words swirled out of her delicate mouth like the lightest frost, there and gone, carried away by the winds.

When Mama stopped, the silence of the mountain rushed back in, filling the small yard. Yvette was afraid to move, afraid she might accidentally break the spell.

From her perch on the sleigh, she saw the snow start rippling. The clean white surface moved as if it was being blown by strong winds. A sifting sound came, like freshly falling snow.

Suddenly, snow weasels popped up out of the snow near Mama's feet. One, two, a half-dozen!

Their fur wasn't truly white, but more golden. It shimmered in the pale moonlight. They were the same size as the weasels who lived in the woods. Their dark eyes burned like coals as they came to sit on their hind legs, looking up at Mama.

Yvette forgot about being cold for the moment. Thierry had made fun of Yvette when she'd told him about the snow weasels. Said they were just a fairy tale.

He was wrong.

Yvette hadn't known that Mama could call snow weasels to her.

Yvette was absolutely going to have to learn *that* spell.

Then Mama started the next spell. The language sounded older to Yvette, with less French and Latin, with more words she didn't know.

The weasels swayed back and forth in time with Mama's words, as if she was singing to them, though Yvette didn't think the spell was musical at all. Finally, two of the weasels dropped down and went to stand in front of the sleigh, while the other four slid back under the snow, the ripples on top showing them swimming away quickly.

Again, Mama raised her arms to the sky, throwing her head back as well. This time, instead of her words and the steam from her breath flowing out, light poured down, a silver cone, as if Mama had her own personal snowstorm raining down on her.

She gathered the light together, then directed it, her arms moving in circles, as if she was fluffing the light up.

The snow weasels started to grow. Their legs got longer, while their bodies and tails shortened. Their fur grew as white as the moonlight and shorter as well.

They were turning into horses!

Yvette remembered to shiver in the cold. But it didn't matter as much.

Mama *never* did big magic like this.

Maybe the coming of the year 1900 was as important as Mama said it was.

Finally, by the time Mama was finished, two handsome white horses stood where the weasels had been, already harnessed to the sleigh. They looked as fancy as the horses of the English Queen, Victoria, in the postcards the master stonecutter in the village had up on the wall of his shop. Red leather harnesses tied the pair together. They had silver bits, and more red leather made up the reins.

If Yvette squinted just right, she could kind of see the snow weasels underneath, puffed up huge with magic, their golden fur glowing. Mama wanted Yvette to develop her sight more, and now, Yvette understood why.

If her mama could do this kind of magic, and she'd always claimed to be just a minor magician, what could someone really powerful do? How would Yvette be able to see through their spells?

Mama climbed slowly into the sleigh beside Yvette. She seemed very tired. Yvette helped tuck quilts in around Mama, sharing her own.

"Mama," Yvette started, "that was, that was…magnificent!"

Mama smiled tiredly up at Yvette. "Couldn't have done it without the snow weasels," she murmured, then yawned. "Always easier to start with a magical creature, or to use some part of one, nail clippings or hair or something."

"Yes, Mama," Yvette said, nodding. "I remember." Mama had taught her that a while ago about the clans, the people who could change shape into boars or hounds, tigers or crocodiles, vipers or ravens. There had been a whole family of boars just to the south of them, farther down the mountain, but they'd moved from their vineyard recently and Mama hadn't bothered to find them again.

"You're a good girl," Mama said eventually, shaking herself, then picking up the reins.

"*Merci*," Yvette said proudly. "I am trying," she couldn't help but add.

"*Mai oui*," Mama said with a sly smile. "And after tonight, you will try even more."

With that, Mama flicked the reins and they were off, dashing across the top of the snow.

What did Mama mean by that? Yvette knew better than to ask. Mama would never reply until she thought it was the right time.

But maybe, tonight, it would be time for answers and teaching.

And more magic.

When Mama reached the end of the lane to their cottage, instead of directing the horses down the mountain, she turned up.

"Where are we going?" Yvette asked. They weren't going to give a neighbor a ride into the village, were they? There wasn't really room for anyone else on the seat of their tiny sleigh. They were all tucked in together, wrapped in quilts and furs, their gifts and bags and that one mysterious satchel wedged in under their legs and beside their feet.

"You'll see," Mama said. She sat back and held the reins loosely in her hands. The horses didn't really need much direction, as they weren't really horses.

They flew up the lane, the horses dancing daintily across the top of the snow. The cold wasn't too horrible, though the wind did blow on them constantly. Yvette stayed snuggled into her quilts, breathing in the scents they carried, the lavender and mint. The pines stood back from the road in places, letting in the pale light.

Not too far up the mountain, Mama tugged on the right rein. The horses leaped off the road, racing down a path Yvette hadn't seen. It was dark under the trees. The wind whistled sharply here. It would have been scary if Mama hadn't been there, going so fast and barely able to see.

Why were they in such a hurry? Were they late?

The horses ran faster now. Yvette could see more of the weasel about them here in the dark tunnel made by the trees, their front legs stretching out, their long bodies curving up as their hind legs then hit. The gold of their fur shone, brighter than the half-moon.

Suddenly, they burst out of the woods into a large clearing. Yvette recognized it as the place Mama had taken her that summer, for the solstice, for them to sing in new sun.

It was much brighter here, as though after the moon had spilled her light into the meadow, the snow had captured it and now softly glowed. Under the top of the smooth surface ripples played out—the other snow weasels, keeping up with their brothers.

The horses slowed and came to a halt in the middle of the meadow.

"*Merci*! *Merci*!" Mama called out as she got off the sleigh. She was still moving slowly, as if the winter cold had crept into her bones.

"Come," she said, holding out her hand to Yvette.

Yvette bit her lip. It was going to be *cold* out there, out from under the quilts. Her boots would get full of snow and her toes would be wet for hours.

But Mama had that sparkle in her eye, that gleam that

meant fun. Like the time she'd conjured ice for them in the middle of the summer so they could have cherry-flavored cold treats, or the time she'd made madeleine cookies that were like real clam shells, so they could open their mouths and sing Happy Birthday to Yvette.

With a barely concealed sigh, Yvette shoved off the quilts and furs on top of her, one by one, until the cold could get at her. She stood, ready to hop off the sleigh, when Mama said, "Get the big bag."

Yvette's heart started racing. Did Mama mean the mysterious bag with the bulky thing she'd been working on all fall?

"*Oui*," Mama said to Yvette's unasked question. "The bag you're not supposed to know about."

Yvette grinned and bent down, her hand going straight to the bag in question. It was heavier than she'd expected. The satchel itself was plain, made of heavy black cloth, with two wooden pieces forming the handles and a brass latch locking it tightly. It was longer than Yvette's arm and as big as Mama's wooden cutting board, the one she used to make long loaves of bread on.

Yvette picked it up with both hands and sniffed it before she handed it over to Mama. It smelled smoky, which made sense, because Mama often worked on it next to the hearth fire. It also smelled like dandelions, warmly bitter and full of sunshine.

Mama took the bag and set it in the snow. It gleamed with its own dark light against the whiteness. Then she held out her hand for Yvette.

Even through her mittens, Yvette could feel Mama's inner fire burning her hands. Someday, Mama would have to teach Yvette how to keep herself warm like that. Mama said it wasn't healthy for her, but Yvette *hated* being cold.

Which was also why Mama wouldn't teach her yet—she claimed Yvette would overuse her power.

Yvette jumped down from the sleigh. The weasels stayed as horses but they drew away, ambling to the edge of the meadow. Their brothers joined them there. The non-changed ones stood on their hind legs so they could touch noses with their horsy brothers. They chittered quietly to one another. Yvette imagined they were telling each other about their adventures.

Thierry wouldn't believe her, but Yvette might still try to tell him about the snow weasels.

Mama left the bag where it was, sitting in the snow, then unlatched it. Light spilled from the inside of it, golden light, as if it was lit by summer fireflies.

Using both hands, Mama scooped up the item from inside the bag. It grew in the air, now that it was no longer confined, as Yvette expected it would: The bag really had been heavier than she'd expected it to be.

The rolled up thing stretched out until it was about a meter wide. Then Mama put it down on the snow, where it continued to unroll itself.

Yvette clapped her mittens together in delight when she realized it was a rug, maybe a meter wide and twice as long.

Was it a flying rug? Would it take them around the world?

Golden thread twisted and knotted along all the edges of the rug, like the beautiful ancient crosses that she saw in the old graveyard. Brown vines with large red and green leaves snaked across the body of the rug, like the ivy that covered the ruined church and hid the cheerful larks and mourning doves. In between the leaves were huge yellow blossoms, each one bigger than Yvette's outstretched hand.

She didn't know what kind of flower it was, though the petals were shaggy, like a petunia.

"It's wonderful, Mama!" Yvette said, taking her mother's hand again.

"And it is yours, my darling," Mama said, wrapping both of her warm hands around Yvette's.

"Mine?" Yvette asked, surprised. They'd already exchanged their *Noël* gifts. Yvette didn't have anything more for Mama for *fin de siècle*. "Thank you, Mama," Yvette said.

Mama drew Yvette forward, urging her to step onto the rug.

The magic swirled up around them, golden dust motes dancing in pale moonlight.

"What's it for, Mama?" Yvette asked, stopping, afraid to make the magic swirl up any higher.

"To help you in your studies," Mama said. "It will be your focal point while you are learning."

"Oh," Yvette said. She couldn't help but be a little disappointed. She'd really hoped the rug would fly.

Still, it was a wonderful gift.

It meant that she could learn more magic now. Maybe without Mama always saying *no, too young*.

"Tonight, the rug will bring you to your focus," Mama said, letting go of Yvette's hand and stepping back.

"What do you mean?" Yvette said. She stayed where she was, but she did turn to see Mama better.

"Sit in the middle of the rug," Mama instructed. "Then listen to all that the rug has to say."

Yvette bit back her sigh. Why couldn't Mama just *tell* her things? What was she supposed to hear? How would the rug speak to her?

Still, she did as Mama said. As she sat down, more

golden dust motes rose up, then floated back down, dotting her tights and skirt.

At least the rug felt warm under her butt. It would have been awful if it was cold.

Yvette looked around the clearing. The weasel horses and their brother snow weasels were still off to the side, standing under the lone oak still bravely holding onto its brown leaves. She couldn't hear them chittering anymore, but they weren't paying any attention to her.

Mama stood someplace behind Yvette, as she'd done in the past when she wanted Yvette to learn something on her own.

But what was Yvette supposed to learn?

The half-moon had already gone past the center of the sky and was setting. Stars glittered in the thick black sky. Even in the dim light, the snow still sparkled. The wind carried the sounds of the snow shifting, flakes blown against one another, a quiet, peaceful sound. The air smelled tangy, as though a thunderstorm was on the way.

Then the winds came.

The first one merely brushed across Yvette's shoulders, sending a chill down her spine. Then another came, fluffing the curls that had escaped from where she'd smooshed them down with her hat.

Then another, and another, all lightly touching her in different places, like her knee, the back of her hand, her nose, her cheeks, her toes, and her lips.

Winds had always sought her out, determined to steal away her heat and make her cold. The rug wasn't letting them do that, though.

Or was it?

Cracks had formed around the edges of the golden looping knots that surrounded the rug. The winds flowed through those holes, like dark vines seeking the sun.

Why was the rug letting them through? Wasn't this supposed to be her focus place, where she could study and learn? The winds were just distracting.

Yvette tried hard to listen to the rug. Mama had said she had to listen, right?

However, the rug wasn't saying anything, at least, not anything she could hear.

Yvette was about to look over her shoulder, to ask Mama for advice, when she heard a soft sigh.

The wind on her right. Was it trying to tell her something? Did the winds talk? Mama's animals could, Yvette was certain, though they'd never had anything to say to her.

"Go on," Yvette whispered to it.

The wind sighed again, then told her of an avalanche higher up the mountain. It carried the last breath of the three mountain goats who'd been caught in it.

Yvette shivered, feeling their deaths but not mourning them. That was just the way of things, life and death. At least the wind remembered them, for a short while.

The wind that kept tickling Yvette's curls spoke up next. It told of the fireworks to the east of them, in the countries already celebrating the New Year. Yvette suddenly smelled the sulfur the wind carried with it and felt the grainy soot from the blown-apart explosives.

Then the next wind came, carrying news of the bears sleeping deeply in their caves, the wind having brushed lightly across the tops of the rocks, unable to dive any deeper.

And more.

Stories of squirrels stirring in their nests, the fight a newly married couple had had, the way the brilliant diamonds in the town of Lamoura shone after the master gem cutter had finished with them, how happily the birds to the south sang, waiting for the spring and the chance to return to the mountain.

Yvette caught her breath when she finally realized what was happening.

She didn't have a way with animals—not that they'd bite her, she was more skilled than that. But they didn't come to her calling, not like Mama. She could see when a cow was distressed in birth. Everyone could see that. But she didn't know before it got dangerous, couldn't ease a calf out.

The winds, though. They spoke to her in a way she was certain they didn't speak to Mama. Did the animals carry news to Mama? Maybe the birds did, in the summer, when Mama fed them and they came and sang sweetly, perched on her shoulders, whispering in her ear.

It was marvelous, all the things the winds knew. All the things they'd tell her. All that she could learn. She could know everything in the world!

This was her magic. This was what Mama had meant, that Yvette would find her focus. That she'd try even harder now.

Mama had been right. Yvette would happily sit and study and listen to the winds for hours on end.

Still, Yvette couldn't help but sigh.

It also meant that she was going to always be cold, the winds constantly blowing on her.

But such was her fate.

山 山

T he man was there again. He stood just across the lane, opposite the great round gate to Li Li's family complex. Not many people were in the street that early that morning: two older women taking their morning stroll for their health and gossiping about everything, a businessman hurrying to his office, and three workers in their paint-stained tunics sauntering along.

Li Li tugged on Auntie Fu's sleeve. "There's a man over there, watching us," she said quietly. Though she was only eight, she knew better than to point at him. Not because it wasn't polite, but because she didn't want to call attention to herself.

Calling attention to herself or her family was bad. Being noticed was bad. Bad things could happen. Had happened to more than one of her friends and their families.

The man stood as still as a statue, leaning against the gray stone gate to the *hu tong*. He wore an older, longer tunic in a bland, light brown color, with matching pants, not the usual outfit of Mao and his Red Guard. A straw hat perched on top of his long, gray hair, peaked, like what the farmers in the market wore.

His face was broad and wide and plain. The only thing interesting about it were his dark eyes, which shone wetly like a rabbit's. He didn't look like any of her cousins or uncles, but he still reminded Li Li of someone, like he should be family.

Auntie Fu looked up from tying her bag shut. "Hmmm, dear?"

Though Li Li loved her auntie, she sometimes wondered if the chickens in the yard were less scatterbrained.

"There's a man over there," Li Li insisted. "He's been there every day this week. Watching."

Auntie Fu looked up and over. "I don't see anyone, dear," she said.

Li Li looked back. The man *was* more difficult to see than he had been. It was like his clothes blended into the wall now, the brown fading into the gray stone archway.

But Li Li could still see him. Some part of her just *knew* he was there.

She didn't insist that they go and ask the man what he was doing. Again, that would be calling too much attention to herself and her auntie.

Instead, she took her aunt's arm, protectively leading the way to the market. *She* would defend them if anything happened, if anyone came after them. She wasn't exactly sure how she would do it, but she had a sense that she *could* do it, better than anyone else in her family.

Something deep inside her soul nudged up against her, waves of agreement flowing from it.

Li Li didn't know what that was either, though she'd felt it before.

It was yet another thing that she didn't bring up, didn't tell anyone. Wasn't about to draw attention to it, to herself.

Bad things could happen if she did, she knew. They already had. Papa couldn't work anymore, and last week Mama had gotten yelled at in the market for being too proud.

It was a scary time, and Li Li never wanted to cause more shame for her family.

L i Li didn't know what to expect when Mama came and got her late one night. Her two sisters still slept on either side of her, all of three of them piled together on the one big bed. Only Li Li had woken when Mama had opened the door, the light from her candle casting a soft glow.

Had Mama known that Li Li would wake first? Li Li didn't know, but she assumed so.

Mama stayed in the doorway and beckoned to Li Li with her other hand. She wore her long hair down, as if she'd been getting ready for bed.

What did she want?

This was different. Unusual. It had never happened before.

Different was almost always bad.

Li Li wished for a moment that she could close her eyes, pretend to be asleep like her sisters.

But even though Mama couldn't see in the dark like Li Li (none of her family could), it was already too late. Mama knew she was awake, and obviously wanted Li Li to crawl out of the bed and come with her.

With a sigh, Li Li did just that, sneaking out of the warm, sour smell of the nest she and her sisters had made and walking silently across the room to where Mama stood.

Mama lifted the candle a little higher and peered at Li Li, as if trying to find a spot on her face or her top that Li Li had neglected to wash away.

"*Shenme*?" Li Li whispered. What was wrong?

"Come," Mama merely said.

Li Li followed Mama out of the sleeping quarters, across the courtyard, and into the Hall of Greeting. Many candles burned brightly in the hall, though it had electric lights as well. The hall itself wasn't that big or grand—just a square room with the family poem done in her father's flowing calligraphy on the wall, proud lists of her ancestors hanging beside it, a small statue of *Shin Lo*, a god of good fortune, in the corner with faded purple peonies and a bowl of rice at his feet.

She hadn't known what to expect, but it certainly hadn't been the man who'd been watching their family complex for the last week.

He knelt in the place of honor behind the formal ebony table in the center of the room. Tea had been served, the cups sitting empty, the musty scent of Mama's good chrysanthemum tea still lingering. Papa knelt uncomfortably beside the man. He, at least, had put on a good robe, brown and green, while Mama still wore her red robe from the day before.

"Li Li, this is Han Zhe," Papa said, introducing them.

Li Li gave the man a formal bow. Was he actually family? She still thought he looked familiar, or felt familiar, or something.

"Do you recognize me?" Han Zhe asked.

Instead of replying, Li Li looked at Papa first.

Papa gave Li Li a tight smile. "You can answer him," he said. "Truthfully," he added.

When Papa said that, it meant that Li Li should not lie about who she was. Papa had told her that sometimes it was okay to lie, particularly if someone was trying to hurt her. And too many strangers asked too many questions in the market these days.

"Are you a cousin?" Li Li asked Han Zhe. "Or an uncle?"

She didn't like the smile of triumph that the man gave Papa and Mama.

"Not exactly," he said. "I'm part of your *shizu*, though."

The word he'd used for *clan* seemed to echo through the room.

It meant more than just her family's ancestors, she knew that.

The *other* who now swam inside her, who twined around her soul, nudged her again, making Li Li look down.

She, this sister, this twin inside her, also recognized this man.

When Li Li looked back up, the man had golden eyes with merely slits for pupils. His skin had a green sheen and was patterned, like scales.

The sharp smell of Papa and Mama's fear spiked through the room.

Li Li stepped forward, ready to defend them against this man. "Stop it," she growled.

Her own voice was surprisingly low. She found that she'd already raised her hands up, ready to claw at this man, tear him to pieces.

He would *not* hurt her family.

Han Zhe merely chuckled. "You see?" he said, spreading his hands wide, like a priest giving a benediction, his eyes already returned to their normal, piercing black.

Mama and Papa's fear hadn't gone away, though. Now they were looking at *her*, afraid.

"What?" Li Li asked. She knew she wasn't being polite. But she was also scared, and tired, and she didn't like any of this at all.

"Your eyes are like his," Mama whispered.

"Oh. *Oh*," Li Li said, suddenly understanding.

This man also had another who swam inside him. That was what made them kin.

"Do you want to go with this man?" Mama asked abruptly.

Li Li looked at the man, then back at Mama. The ties she felt to this man ran deep, deeper than those she had to her own family.

She still wouldn't abandon Mama and Papa. Not just yet. "Do I have to?" she asked.

"Not now," Mama said, her own smile triumphant.

"But soon," the man said. "She needs training, or she could be a danger, not just to herself but to others."

Li Li nodded. She understood what the man was saying. This other who had come much closer to the surface now didn't understand the need to blend in, how dangerous standing out could be. She didn't care much, either, certain that her claws and fangs and great crocodile scales could protect her.

"I will keep her tame," Li Li assured the man.

He just smiled at her, that indulgent smile that adults gave children all the time, that smile that said he knew better.

But this Han Zhe didn't know Li Li. He didn't understand that despite being only eight, once she'd set her mind to something, she would do it.

They arranged for Li Li and Mama to go to the compound where Han Zhe and the others lived. She would start her lessons with them, while still living with her family.

After Han Zhe left, Mama pulled Li Li to her, holding her tight against her chest.

"I'm not leaving yet," Li Li complained as she started to feel stifled.

"I know," Mama said, letting Li Li go and wiping her own eyes. "But you'll be gone soon."

Li Li didn't say anything, but she was more determined than ever to keep control of herself, of this other, and not bring any shame to either her family or her clan.

Long after Li Li had crawled back into bed, her sisters close around her and breathing in time with their soft snores, she stayed awake, thinking about her differences, thinking about her ancestors, thinking about how she might keep everyone safe.

As Papa said, these were trying times. Mao was calling for a revolution. There were demonstrations and people punished in the street every day.

That just meant Li Li would also have to try even harder.

CARLOS

Carlos always bragged that when he was an infant, snakes had come to visit his cradle. They'd formed long ropes to tug on it, rocking him to sleep. His room kept getting bigger as the years went on, the snake ropes longer and longer so they could have a firm anchor from which to pull on the (now) hand-carved wooden cradle that his grandfather had slept in, that rose five feet above the just-polished wooden floor.

Of course, it wasn't true.

Carlos never talked about his real mother, who'd been addicted to crack cocaine. The kitchen had been squalid, and Carlos didn't learn until much later that rice wasn't alive and it didn't usually wiggle on its own. The cracked linoleum floor from that room haunted him, its green and black splotches spreading like a curse. His nightmares involved him crawling over the same spot over and over again, never able to get away from it.

When he was eight and his mother died, the snakes really did come for him—the viper clan, his brothers.

They took him from Mexico City and up into the

mountains of Guatemala, to one of the hidden temples there. The pyramid stood as tall as his former apartment block, the top just poking out above the trees, made out of carved stones, each taller than he was. The paint that covered the pyramid was as faded as the greatness of the viper clan, Carlos felt. The jungle that crept up on all sides scared him at first: There was no place to hide, or maybe too many places.

Instead of the sound of the freeway and the honking of cars, Carlos only heard bird song, the rustling of the vines, and the chanting of the viper priests. The air was clean and even the water tasted sweet.

However, Carlos never fell in love with the temple. The priests were all very nice, but pimps drove better cars, had better clothes, ate better food. He didn't get the whole vow of chastity thing either. Wasn't he supposed to feel good? Why be ashamed of his strong body? It was easy enough to be careful, to never deposit living seed in a woman, particularly once the priests had taught him how to control his body.

So, though the priests raised Carlos and he learned the songs, stories, and recitations of the viper clan, he always knew that the temple was too small to hold him.

Until he was fourteen and had his first vision.

ARIEL

Ariel sat in the school's reception, just outside of the principal's office, kicking her heels against the old wooden chair. The air conditioning unit smooshed into the window wheezed, but didn't help make the room cooler, not one lick. A wooden counter thicker than the old wall down by the levee ran between the three chairs lined against the wall and the rest of the office, like a great brick wall, keeping the kids on one side and the adults on the other.

Mrs. Grady, the large black woman who ran the office, sat at her desk like a queen and ruled over the two other secretaries. She'd finished with her typing and was talking on the phone now while she filed her long blue nails and shot nasty looks at Ariel now and again.

With a sigh, Ariel leaned back further in her chair. But she kept drumming her heels, mainly 'cause she knew Mrs. Grady hated it. Any minute now, Mrs. Grady would blow up. She'd slam the phone down and tell Ariel to stop making that confounded racket, and Ariel would say she was sorry and she would stop.

For about two minutes.

Then she'd start right back up again.

It was like everything else that happened at that school. Ariel just didn't fit there and the kids knew it. It wasn't that her skin was a different color or something: At least three-fourths of the school were black, like her. But they'd all grown up knowing each other, and she was still the new girl, the hick come from the backwaters of Mississippi to the big city of New Orleans.

She knew Mama was disappointed when Ariel got into fights—she was only nine, not yet ten—but she couldn't help it. There was just something inside her that wanted to fight. She tried to control it, to not give in to this angry thing inside of her, but she couldn't help it.

Everything was all unfair: the new school, the tiny apartment, the winds that snuck through the tiny streets and into her bedroom at night carrying smells that just about made her crazy with longing to run.

Plus, Ariel was getting stronger, too. She couldn't tear those boys apart, not yet, but she'd left her mark but good on old Theo Wilie. Scratched his skin until it bled. That sight of blood had been like a jolt of electricity through her, making her howl and clench her teeth so she wouldn't bite him.

Took three of the bigger boys to pull her off him.

Next time, she might actually carry through on her threat and choke him to death.

She didn't have to put up with disrespect. That place inside her that was always boiling mad made sure of that.

When the door to the office opened, Ariel couldn't contain her surprise when she saw Aunt Mabel come walking through. "What are you doing here?" she asked.

"I'll see to you in a minute, dear," Aunt Mabel replied in that prissy, white-woman tone of hers that would have even the school board shaking in their loafers.

Ariel sighed again as Aunt Mabel marched directly into the principal's office. Mrs. Grady looked up from her nails but didn't actually try to stop Aunt Mabel. She seemed to recognize a force of nature when she saw one.

Instead, Mrs. Grady just smirked at Ariel and went back to her phone call.

Aunt Mabel wasn't really an aunt. She was a friend of the family, had evidently looked after Mama back in Mississippi as a little girl. She was as old as the hills, and looked it some days, too, her white skin as pale as the white roses she grew in her yard, age spots scattered across her broad forehead, wrinkles fixed and solid. Her hair was so white it was nearly blue, done up in perfect curls. Her eyes were what marked her as different, though, as green as the pond scum back in Mississippi.

It wasn't necessarily a good sign that Aunt Mabel had come to get Ariel instead of Mama. Her aunt didn't understand what life was like for Ariel, being uprooted from her home, Mama still looking for work. Dad had split long before. Ariel didn't even have a picture of him.

Just a minute or so passed before Aunt Mabel came out. Her eyes flared dark and stormy. She paused in front of Ariel as she straightened her white-and-blue floral dress, setting her matching purse on her arm just so.

Ariel gulped and sat up straighter in her chair.

"You're coming with me," Aunt Mabel said in those clipped tones of hers.

Ariel paused, just for a moment, the urge to disobey, to stomp her foot and say *no*, surging through her.

She shook herself, hard. That wasn't really her, was it? Mama had raised her to be a good girl. And she tried to be. Mostly. Why was she so set on having her own way?

Ariel got out of the chair and quietly followed Aunt Mabel out.

She didn't think the old white woman would be able to help her figure out what was going on inside her own head.

But maybe Ariel should ask anyway. If there was anyone who'd keep her secrets, it would be Aunt Mabel.

* * *

A riel's next surprise came when Aunt Mabel drove them straight to the freeway and started heading out of town. "Where we going?" Ariel asked, unable to contain herself.

Aunt Mabel's car was nicer than most any Ariel had ever sat in. The outside wasn't anything to look at: It was an old Mercedes, painted a plain brown color that had faded. But the inside was cream-colored leather, smooth and soft, and smelling like money.

"First, I should apologize to you. I know that I've waited too long. I should have done this a while ago," Aunt Mabel said. "But I wanted to make sure before I introduced you to the sisterhood."

Ariel raised her eyebrows at that. Sisterhood?

One of their neighbors, back in Mississippi, had called Aunt Mabel a witch and accused her of doing spells out in the swamps.

Aunt Mabel had just laughed and laughed, a throaty kind of funny growl, but she hadn't paid any more heed than that.

"What kind of sisterhood?" Ariel asked. It wasn't going to be lame, like a bridge group or something, was it?

"You'll see," Aunt Mabel said with a smile that didn't reassure Ariel at all.

When had Aunt Mabel gotten sly and hard? Was she really a witch? Or just a crazy old white lady?

"Does Mama know where you're taking me?" Ariel asked.

Aunt Mabel gave a bark of a laugh. "That she does, honey. Though she's part of the reason why I waited so long. She had to be sure as well."

"Sure of what?" Ariel asked. Could she just open the car door and throw herself out? Aunt Mabel was sounding crazier and crazier. Or was that a sure way to get herself killed?

"Who you truly are," Aunt Mabel said. "Now sleep. It will take some time to get there."

Where? Ariel wanted to ask. However, her eyes were already closing and she was drifting away with the steady hum of the wheels on the interstate.

She shouldn't feel safe. Part of her knew that. Aunt Mabel really had gone around the bend.

Yet, she still trusted her aunt. Aunt Mabel had always kept her word. Never told any of Ariel's secrets.

And that dark place inside of Ariel, the part of her that wanted to fight all the time, and rend and tear, was comforted by her aunt's presence.

Ariel woke with the late afternoon sun bathing her face through the windshield of the car. They'd stopped, and some part of Ariel, deep inside of her, knew they'd been resting for a while.

Cypress trees and blackberry brambles surrounded the car. Ariel couldn't even see a road behind them. It felt to her like they were deep in the bayou. Water pooled to her right, covered with swamp grass and tall cattails. Even through the closed windows of the car the chorus of insects screamed loudly, cycling up and down. Birds called out, waking from their afternoon nap, about to go hunt up their dinners.

Aunt Mabel stood in front of the car, resting against the hood, her head tilted back and her face lifted up. Was she enjoying the sunshine? That didn't seem right. She was the whitest white person Ariel knew. She always went outside wearing a fancy hat that kept her face in the shade, as well as gloves, protecting her fair skin.

So what was she doing?

That thing inside of Ariel stirred. Aunt Mabel was doing *something else*.

Somehow, Ariel recognized that Aunt Mabel was scenting the air.

Ariel lifted her head too. There were too many unknown scents for her to track—that sour smell, maybe humans, about a mile to the west; the brackish water, trapped by the reeds; a sweeter scent that was almost like flowers, that seemed familiar, somehow.

Aunt Mabel didn't change her position any, just lifted one lily-white hand and beckoned for Ariel to come out and join her.

Ariel sighed. She wasn't scared, not exactly. That dark place inside her could defend her from a skinny old white lady. But she was a long, *long* way from home. Nothing but wilderness surrounded her.

And maybe her aunt was a witch. Ariel sure had fallen asleep fast on the way there.

Ariel stepped out of the car, the sound of the insects as overwhelming as the drilling noise got at home, from where they were tearing up the street just a few houses up from hers. The air was wet and hot, but that didn't seem to bother her as much as the emptiness of the bayou.

Sure, there were probably people around somewhere. But Aunt Mabel had chosen a spot where they were well hidden.

No one would find Ariel's body for days. If ever.

Ariel strode around to the front of the car, then deliberately mimicked the way Aunt Mabel was standing, head back, eyes closed, taking in deep snoutfuls of air.

Something inside Ariel stirred. She realized that it was like a second soul, swimming around her own.

That wasn't normal, was it? She tried to push it down, but it was like an oil slick on water, and just oozed the other way.

Aunt Mabel started humming. It sounded like one of those old-time ballads. A sea shanty, maybe. It had that kind of soft sway to it, of waves and currents.

The *other* inside Ariel swam more peacefully. Ariel stopped trying to push it down. Aunt Mabel started singing. Though Ariel didn't know the language, she still understood it. The song suggested they, she and this *other* who called herself Gret, were both meant to be. The sound of it was like spring rain in the garden, full of quiet and that fresh rain scent, relaxing.

"You can feel it, can't you?" Aunt Mabel asked when she finished.

Ariel wasn't sure what she was asking about. The heat of the sun? The amazing way the air smelled, carrying a hundred different scents? That dark twin of hers, deep inside, named Gret?

When Aunt Mabel turned to face Ariel, her eyes had changed. Instead of that bright green they were more brown and golden, shining with light.

Ariel felt something *shift* inside of herself. Though she didn't know for certain, she would have bet good money that her eyes now matched her aunt's.

"Are you a witch?" Ariel felt compelled to ask. Was *she* also a witch?

Aunt Mabel's snorting laugh came in reply. "Oh, no, dear. Nothing as mundane as that."

Her aunt started to transform.

Ariel stepped back, terrified and amazed. Was her aunt a werewolf? Her jaw elongated and wicked tusks sprang up out of it. Her hands changed, her fingers fusing into black hooves with sharp edges. Thick, curly brown hair laced with gray sprang up across her forehead, arms, and chest. Her nose turned into a pig-like snout, though ridged with bones.

She didn't fall to all fours, though. She remained upright, taller than she'd been, proud and strong.

She gave a great roar of greeting. Ariel found herself roaring back, that *other* inside of her recognizing this being in front of her as *kin*.

"I am a warrior of the boar clan," Aunt Mabel announced. Her voice was gruff, but it still held the prissiness of the old white lady.

"And so are you."

Li Li

A crowd had gathered outside the gateway to Li Li's family complex. They wouldn't let anyone leave, though Mama had spent some time pleading with the leader there, trying to send her daughters away.

She never specified which daughters, how many were in the compound. Li Li admired how careful Mama was with her language, so the crowd would never be certain how many people were still inside at that point.

But the leader—the butcher's son from down the lane—merely jeered at her. "Better they should learn their proletariat lessons now, while they're young. They will be raised by the State." He wore a black Mao jacket with a student's cap, though he wasn't smart enough to pass the exams.

Li Li didn't like the sound of that threat at all from her carefully chosen seat, just inside the gate, out of sight of everyone. She also didn't like how angrily the crowd growled. They reminded her of the mad dog that had tried to come into the market the week before, the one with red eyes and foam around its mouth, how the only thing they could do with it was to shoot it.

Li Li alternated between being very scared and very angry. These people were dangerous. Her twin, who swam very close to the surface, was ready to defend her with great crocodile teeth and claws. She found she was growling.

Li Li tried to stop. She was the one in control.

But it was very, very hard. Particularly when there was such a threat.

Mama pulled Li Li away from the door and back to the rest of the family gathered in the courtyard.

Papa knelt in front of all the children, Li Li, her two older sisters, and her eldest brother. He wore his formal teacher's robe, brown and green. Maybe he was trying to remind the crowd that they should respect him.

Li Li doubted this crowd respected much of anything.

"The crowd will break down the gate, soon," Papa said gravely.

"We will fight them," Li Li replied. She folded her arms over her chest so her hands wouldn't form into claws. While Mama and Papa knew her true nature, her sisters and brother didn't. All they knew was that she was getting special training twice a week.

None of them knew about the crocodile clan, or the magic.

"You will *not*," Papa said.

"But—" Li Li started to protest.

"I said you will not," Papa said firmly. "You will *not* fight them. You cannot. They will kill you, instead."

Ice-cold *shouzhi* walked down Li Li's spine.

Her sisters and brother didn't seem to notice what Papa was actually saying. That the crowd would kill someone that day.

And that he was prepared to die for them.

Papa took Li Li by her bare arm and led her over to the Hall of Greeting. "Hide there," he instructed her, pointing to the small gap under the hall, that only someone her size could crawl into and hide if they stayed on their belly and lay very still.

It would ruin her pretty blue blouse, the one that Mama had bought special for her at the market.

Li Li looked over her shoulder at her eldest brother, her two sisters, and Mama standing there with her arms around them, holding them close, tears sparkling in her eyes. Auntie Fu had stayed in her bed, hiding.

It wouldn't do any good. Even Li Li knew this. If this crowd would harm her brother or sisters, they'd hurt someone like her aunt as well.

Li Li threw her arms around her Papa, giving him a fierce hug. "I won't forget," she said softly.

Papa kissed the top of her head. "Burn incense for us during the *qingming* festival this fall," Papa said.

Li Li nodded, though that hadn't been what she'd meant.

Of course she'd remember her parents, and how they gave their lives so that she, and probably her brother and sisters could live.

But she'd also remember their attackers. Every single one of them.

And get her revenge.

YVETTE

The long, tooting whistle sounded again.

"Here comes the train!" Yvette told Mama excitedly. Neither of them could see it. The station was just past a bend, and the pines, blackberries, and tall grasses that had crowded up next to the track hid the train further.

The cheery whistle sounded again, echoing through the mountainous crevice the tracks rolled along. Yes, it was definitely closer.

Then Yvette's winds rushed up, letting her know exactly how far away the train was.

"*Oui*," Mama said absently. She coughed suddenly, holding her gloved hand over her mouth. She doubled over with the strength of her cough.

Yvette went directly to Mama's side, taking hold of Mama's elbow, holding her steady as the fit passed. When Mama straightened up, she was pale, much too pale. She wheezed loudly, trying to catch her breath.

"Are you all right?" Yvette asked, worried as always. Mama had gotten sick that winter and developed a hacking cough that hadn't gone away, despite the long, warm summer.

"I'm fine, I'm fine," Mama insisted, as she always did. She drew in another long, shaky breath, then pasted a bright smile on her face. "See?"

Yvette knew that Mama was lying, but she held her tongue. The doctor in the village hadn't been able to do much for Mama except to tell Yvette to keep her warm and make her drink sugared-vinegar water, which Mama had thrown out the first chance she'd gotten.

Even Yvette's winds couldn't tell her what was wrong.

Would they find a cure in Paris? Yvette hoped so. Mama had insisted they were going merely to introduce Yvette to *société*, as they'd just celebrated Yvette's eighteenth birthday, as well as further Yvette's studies in the *mystères*. They would be in Paris for at least two years before they returned.

They stood alone on the broad wooden walkway next to the tracks, three large steamer trunks full of dresses, petticoats, and shoes resting behind them. Their bags for their train journey seemed deceptively small but were quite heavy, stuffed to the brim with magically folded items.

No one else waited with them on the platform—it was late summer, and the local shepherds and farmers were all too busy with the harvest and their herds. The tiny station behind them was merely a waiting room, square and plain, with a few benches and a large hearth to keep away the mountain chill.

Mama wore a very fashionable dress, of course, with the waist just under her bosom and the skirt long and flared out. It was the color of her favorite gray doves, with a white collar and bib down the front, and delicate white lace edging the top layers of her skirt as well as the cuffs on her long sleeves. She'd powdered her face to give it the palest sheen, while her lips were painted a daring red.

Even with her illness, Mama still burned warm. Yvette didn't know how she could stand it. While she hadn't ever gotten used to being cold, not exactly, she didn't like overheating, and rarely used any kind of warming spell for herself.

Yvette also wore a fashionable dress, though it wasn't cinched under her breasts as tightly as Mama's—Yvette hated being caged in. It had a high waist and was made of simple cotton, white with the palest of green stripes running down it.

Yvette had adored the material when she'd seen it in the dressmaker's shop in Geneva. They'd taken their annual trip to Switzerland earlier that year to get ready for their trip to Paris.

The dressmaker had sniffed when Yvette had praised the material and said, "*Mademoiselle* should consider another fabric, perhaps. Something more…elegant."

Yvette knew what he was actually saying—that she shouldn't get vertical stripes, as they'd make her look even taller than her 1.8 meters.

So she ordered not just one dress made with vertical stripes, but half a dozen.

Mama had warned Yvette about waiting to have an heir. They'd talked late one summer night after Yvette had turned sixteen, Mama maudlin and drunk. Mama had told Yvette to have an heir when she was young, then go on with the rest of her life. Mama thought she'd waited too long, past her first century, before she'd had Yvette.

Yvette had thought about the conversation long and hard. However, she wasn't interested in boys, not in the least. They were so boring, and none of them had anything half as interesting to say as the winds. Even her old friend

Thierry had turned to the two careers most men had in the village: farming in the summer, lapidary in the winter. Though they'd remained friends, she sometimes swore that he was as dense as the stones and gems he carved.

It didn't matter to Yvette if the boys didn't like how tall she was, or that she towered over almost everyone she knew. There really wasn't any way for her to hide it. She wasn't about to live her life cloaked under some sort of illusion spell.

The train whistled again as it came around the final bend. Black soot poured from its chimney, staining the air and the winds. The cowcatcher in the front no longer gleamed, but was spattered with bugs. A large, steam-powered light stared out from the center of engine car, baleful and cold.

With much squealing of brakes, the train slowed to a stop. Henri the conductor jumped out: a stout and hearty man, dressed in a black coat, waistcoat, trousers, and hat. His black mustache formed a perfect curl on either end under his large nose. Blue eyes twinkled out at them from beneath bushy brows.

"*Bonjour!*" he called merrily. "Madame Lyon! Mademoiselle! Welcome!" He rushed to Mama's side to give her his arm and help lift her into the train while two workmen carried their trunks into the luggage car.

Yvette would have wondered about Henri, if he had a crush on Mama, except that the winds had whispered to her once of his true love, Jean-Paul. She thought it a shame how the two men had to keep such affection hidden.

She'd never told anyone, of course. Such secrets were not hers to tell. She merely reveled in the knowing.

They'd purchased tickets for the finest sleeping cabin they could. Yvette had wondered once whether Mama called money to her on the winds, if the weasels carried coins to her that had been buried, or if the great hawks hatched her eggs of gold.

The answer had turned out to be much more mundane. That spring, Yvette had finally been introduced to the family banker in Switzerland. His family had been employed by her family for centuries, with two goals: To keep both of their families wealthy, and to be very, *very* discreet about it.

Mama had asked the banker about his latest grandchild, expressing concern over his wife's recent cough, knowing as many details about his life as if she'd seen him every day. Yvette later learned that Mama's birds kept very close track of this man—one of the ways to insure he stayed honest.

Yvette was still learning to control and direct her winds. Generally, they just brought her whatever random bit of information they carried.

Sometimes, though, they went where she told them to go.

She focused on this banker, then kept a straight, stern face when they swirled around him, instead of clapping her hands with joy.

She wasn't yet able to keep track of him whenever he left the office, but she knew it was just a matter of time and training.

Their cabin on the train still smelled of the linseed oil used to polish the wood that covered the walls. The seats had been folded down, with bright red-and-white striped cushions. Their bags had already been placed on the clever table that folded down below the window. The brass that protected the ends of the seats and made up the handles shone, even in the shaded light.

"*Merci*," Mama said as she sank down onto the cushion, leaned back, and closed her eyes.

Yvette caught Henri's eye. He nodded, his jovial smile replaced for a moment by a very serious look. Then his smile came back.

"Don't you worry, *mademoiselle*. I will see to it personally that your journey is the smoothest we've ever made," he assured Yvette.

She also knew that he'd speak with the cooks, urge them to produce their finest meals, with wholesome chicken soup and fluffy eggs, two of Mama's favorites.

"Thank you, Henri," Yvette said. She pressed a gold coin into his hand, the first of many that she planned to gift him with, particularly if they arrived in Paris on time, or even a little early.

Then Yvette sat beside Mama, taking her hand. Was it fever that was burning Mama up so? Yvette longed to open the window, to let the fresh air and breezes in, but she knew Mama would complain if she did.

Mama quietly started to snore just as the train smoothly pulled away from the station.

The sunlight blinked into their cabin, now there, then gone again, blocked by the tall trees. The engine chugged along, the rhythm soothing.

Just how sick was Mama? In the dim light, Yvette could see how Mama's skin had changed. It now had many fine lines, wrinkled like a crêpe mourning gown.

Was Mama dying? Yvette knew that while magicians like them generally lived longer than humans, Mama was the oldest of their kind. At least as far as her winds knew.

So Yvette held Mama's hand, drawing out some of the fire so Mama would maybe feel better, hoping this wasn't their last journey together, but knowing in her heart that it probably was.

Ⅱ Ⅱ

L i Li lay on her belly under the Hall of Greeting, her hands over her ears. An ant crawled over her bare arm. She wanted to shoo it away, to scratch where its feet tickled her skin, but she stayed perfectly still, as Papa had instructed her.

No one could find her. She had to live.

She still flinched every time Mama cried out in pain. When Li Li realized she was shivering, she tried to tighten all her muscles and grow as stiff as a board.

And be just as quiet and unnoticed.

The attack stirred something in Li Li's soul, that *other* who had recently come to the surface and mirrored her. It wasn't the right time for her sister to come out, though. Not yet time for claws and fangs, scales and magic.

Soon, this other voice promised her.

Li Li shivered again. Soon.

She couldn't see the attackers from where she was hidden. And she didn't really understand their jeers about her parents being *bourgeoisie*, how her family had too much while others went without.

She didn't like Mao and his cultural warriors, even if they had set out to right all the injustices of the world.

This other, though, this twin of hers, could smell the people attacking her parents. The butcher's son, who always had the scent of blood and envy, the leader of the group. The old man who sharpened knives in the market and watched people go by with greedy eyes. The auntie from up the street who whispered false things about everyone in the neighborhood.

Li Li marked all of them, even the ones she didn't know, vowing to remember them, despite how desperate her older brother was now pleading with the crowd, trying to save Mama and Papa.

"Come," came a whispered voice from behind Li Li.

Li Li was proud of herself for not starting. She turned her head slowly, looking over her shoulder.

No one was there.

"Come," came the voice again.

Li Li recognized the *type* of voice, though not the bearer of it.

It was one of them, from her *shizu*, the crocodile clan. They would hide her with greater magic than hers as she crept out, help her get away from those hurting her family.

For a moment, Li Li paused. She wanted her revenge *now*. Why couldn't she help Mama and Papa? Save Auntie Fu? Make sure that her brother and sisters got away?

But she knew she couldn't. Papa had said no fighting. Plus, even though she was only eight, she was a big enough girl to realize that this crowd was too wild, now. They had the scent of blood in their nose. Nothing would deter them from more.

Nothing would stop these people but death.

And her claws and fangs weren't mighty enough.

Not yet.

So Li Li inched away, smearing more dirt across her beautiful blue shirt, following the whispering voice, out from under the hall, then hiding in the shadows as best she could, slipping over the back wall of her family's compound.

She almost regretted not being there until the end, not witnessing Mama and Papa's deaths.

She didn't have to be there, though, to know the truth. They would die poorly, at the hands of amateurs.

The people who had done it would die just as badly someday.

ARIEL

A riel sank back into the seat of Aunt Mabel's fine car, exhausted by all the training they'd done that afternoon but also pleased. The rich smell of leather wrapped around her, comforting her.

It seemed Aunt Mabel wasn't completely crazy. Not unless Ariel had also gone round the bend.

But it didn't feel that way. Gret—her twin, her boar soul—didn't feel that way either. Ariel felt as solid as the earth under her hooves, more dangerous than the shifting land and water of the bayou, and more at peace with herself than she'd ever been before.

Aunt Mabel also sighed as she sank into her seat. She started up the car and drove it out of the grove like there was a paved, four-lane highway in front of her.

Ariel had no idea how her aunt had done that, but she was gonna have to learn.

"Now, what is the first recitation?" Aunt Mabel asked.

"Never tell a soul what we just did," Ariel said, not giving Aunt Mabel back the exact words but instead, the gist of the rule.

Aunt Mabel glanced over at Ariel and gave a sharp nod. "That's correct. If you tell anyone, ever, it won't be just me who'll come looking for you."

Ariel shivered in the cool air conditioning pumping through the vents in the dashboard. "Who are the others? Where are they?"

Aunt Mabel gave another nod. "They're here. Close by. I'll take you there some weekend. Introduce you to your Aunt Belle and the rest of the clan." She paused, then added, "It's why your Mama moved from Mississippi, you know. So that you could be raised in the families."

Ariel blinked, too surprised to reply. "She what?" she eventually said. "All the way from Mississippi to here? Just for me?" She'd thought Mama had lost her job as a hotel maid. Again.

"She suspected you were clan, like her oldest sister, Crystal, had been," Aunt Mabel said. "Knew you should be raised closer to us."

Ariel nodded slowly. Mama's sister Crystal had died in a car crash just after Ariel had been born. Mama still missed her sister, and had commented more than once how much Ariel resembled her.

"How did Mama know about the clans?" Ariel wasn't supposed to tell anyone, was she? Even if she had a sister, she was still supposed to keep it a secret. She was glad, though, that she'd be able to tell Mama, that she didn't have to keep the secret from her.

"Crystal didn't tell your mother," Aunt Mabel said firmly. "Your mother was a curious child, though. And she followed her sister to my house, more than once." Aunt Mabel gave an old-lady laugh. "Thought I was dealing drugs to your family or something."

Ariel snorted. That would be the thing Mama would suspect—she was always going on about how dangerous drugs were, how Ariel couldn't even think about getting involved with such things. Mama had even once threatened to kick Ariel out of the house if she ever discovered any drugs in her room. She'd been teasing at the time…probably.

But Ariel had never even been tempted. She'd always felt like she was too much of the earth to go tripping through the skies.

And now she knew why.

"Your family has been part of the boar clan for generations," Aunt Mabel said proudly.

"Then why's we so poor?" Ariel couldn't help but ask. The boar clan took care of their own, didn't they? That was another of the rules that Aunt Mabel had taught her that afternoon.

"Your mother's a proud woman," Aunt Mabel said gently. "Don't you think I've tried?"

Unfortunately, that made all kinds of sense. Mama would only ever go on food stamps as a last resort, and only after Ariel had complained about being hungry and getting tired of rice and beans.

She was now gonna have to take better care of Mama.

Gret agreed, sort of. Though Mama wasn't *kin*, not like Aunt Mabel, she was still *family*. And family mattered.

A riel tugged at her long skirt again and fidgeted. Aunt Mabel shot her a hard look, but Ariel couldn't help it.

Ariel had *never* worn something as fancy as that before. Not even to church. It was like a christening gown, with fine white satin under delicate white lace. The outfit was actually loose on her, with a pale-green sash made out of a wide, satin ribbon tied around her waist. Her arms were bare as well, just little caplets over her shoulders.

The lace itself was in the pattern of roses and thorns. Ariel knew better than to tell Aunt Mabel that it looked *goth* and reminded her of those silly white tourists who wore black and skulls all the time.

They waited in a narrow hallway in an old plantation house. Aunt Belle was holding court in the front sitting room that day. Wooden paneling went from the floor to about halfway up the walls. Then the walls shot up, and up, until they reached that extra-tall ceiling that the old houses here in New Orleans all seemed to have. They were covered in old-fashioned paintings, portraits of the important women of the clan.

On either side of the hallway stood wooden cupboards, full of fine china and glassware. Was it all as old as the house? Ariel was afraid to touch anything, afraid she'd break it.

It all gave her the impression of age. And power. And money, the kind that she figured mostly old white folks had. But there were just as many black faces in the pictures.

The door to the front parlor opened. A woman stood there. She reminded Ariel of the two old spinster sisters at her old church who always acted as greeters. She wore proper church clothes—a green suit with a white floral blouse, and matching hat and gloves.

"Aunt Belle will see you now," she announced. While her voice was as sweet as honey, it still held those proper Southern overtones that implied Ariel wasn't worth the audience.

Ariel bristled, but kept it under control. She wouldn't be shaming either Aunt Mabel or Gret by losing control of herself, not that morning.

The room was just as fancy and old as the rest of the house. Tall windows fanned up, almost to the top of the tall ceiling. More pictures hung here, not just portraits but modern photos too. As well as fancy cross-stich samplers that had been framed, the recitations of the boar clan carefully spelled out, like, "Leave the battle in order to fight another day," and "Mourn the dead with good food," and "Be of the earth."

A group of wooden folding chairs made a semicircle in the middle of the room, open to the door. Beautiful gold and red rugs covered the scarred wooden floor. A glass and crystal chandelier hung from the ceiling.

While some of the chairs were wood and slatted, like the kind of chairs that were in the community room at Ariel's church, others were stuffed, like living-room chairs.

In the middle of the line of chairs was an extra-large one. It wasn't a throne, not quite. But it had a large round back to it, taller than all the others, with carved wood scrollwork around the edges of it. It was made of some kind of shiny, black material, with arms that were also made of wood; the bottom of each leg was carved into shiny hooves.

Ariel did what was expected of her, what Aunt Mabel had trained her to do—to walk in front of Aunt Belle and give her a curtsey.

Ariel had never been taught how to curtsey before. She was pretty sure she was still doing it wrong.

But Aunt Belle gave her an approving nod when Ariel looked up.

"Welcome," Aunt Belle said. "I welcome you to the boar clan." Her skin was as dark as the aged wood in the parlor, while her eyes glowed and weren't really human. Her face was round and she had dimples in her fat cheeks.

Her nose was flat and broad, spread out across her face, but her lips were thin, extended in a sharp smile.

She wore a red-and-white floral dress that covered her from her neck to her feet, with long sleeves as well. It wasn't a church-going dress, more like a fancy dinner dress.

"Thank you, Aunt Belle," Ariel replied. "I am happy to be among sisters."

The other women all murmured and nodded. They were mostly dressed in church outfits, but some were more fancy, like Aunt Belle.

"I understand that Aunt Mabel is your sponsor," Aunt Belle said.

Aunt Mabel came and stood next to Ariel. "I am," she said proudly. "I will look after Ariel, train her, help her become a proud warrior of the boar clan."

The other ladies murmured more at that. They seemed surprised.

Ariel was confused. Wasn't that what she was supposed to be? Aunt Mabel had called her that the first day she'd changed.

Weren't they all warriors of the boar clan?

"Do you think that's strictly necessary?" Aunt Belle asked.

"As necessary as it was with me," Aunt Mabel told her. "Maybe even more so."

The other ladies now all peered closely at Ariel. She wanted to fidget but knew that showing any sign of weakness right now might be deadly. Instead, she straightened her back and stood up even taller.

That seemed to satisfy Aunt Belle. "Make sure that you see to every aspect of her training, then. And you," she added, her piercing gaze returning to Ariel. "You make sure to listen to everything your aunt tells you. Or else."

Ariel still wasn't sure what all of this meant. "Or else what?" she asked stubbornly, though she knew she wasn't really supposed to say anything more.

"Or else you'll have the rest of the clan to deal with," Aunt Belle said, her incisors suddenly lengthening and tusks starting to sprout out of her lower jaw.

"Yes, ma'am," Ariel said, knowing that was the correct response, though she didn't feel like saying that at all.

Gret wasn't cowed either. What she'd really wanted to say was, *Come and get me.*

YVETTE

Yvette stomped down the Paris street, angry with Mama, with all of *société*, but mostly with herself. The night was cool and wet, the autumn rains turning everything gray and dreary. Even the bright street lights couldn't burn away the encroaching shadows.

A lone carriage came the opposite direction up the street, the echoes of the horse's hooves bouncing off the tall, elegant row houses on either side. The wood smoke of the hearths added another layer of fog to the air. Witty laughter and gay repartee was surely going on in each parlor she passed, *société* at play.

Yvette walked alone—the nineteenth district was generally a safe place, even if she was a woman walking by herself at night. She knew how to take care of herself, and had enough magic to protect her from most.

How dare Maurice take that attitude with her? Claiming to be smarter than all women, just because he was a man? She might be the fairer sex, but she was fully educated—she knew her Latin and the classics better than him.

And yes, he might be handsome with fine dark eyes and a wicked smile, and his cologne might be finely crafted with just the right blend of spice and masculine warmth, but she'd smother him with a pillow if she ever woke up beside him and he started speaking.

How could she have been so fooled by his good looks and charm? She should know better than that.

But worse, how could Mama think they might be a match? Or did she expect Yvette to just use him to breed, to make an heir with him and then forget him, as Mama had with Yvette's father?

Mama had never hidden the fact that she had no idea who Yvette's father had been—he'd been passing through, and she'd decided it was time for her to have an heir. Yvette had never set her winds to finding out, either: He'd never known he had a child.

Yvette shivered, but not from the cold. She wasn't like that, couldn't just call a man to her, use him, and send him away.

Mama was, though. Yvette had known it all her life, but the differences between them hadn't come into such sharp relief until they'd moved to Paris, three years before.

Perhaps Yvette would change her mind, later, when she was much, much older and really needed an heir. Maybe then she could just use someone, as well as herself, that way.

She doubted it, though. While Mama had a coldness to her that even her warming spells couldn't touch, Yvette felt empathy. Maybe it was her winds, whispering other people's secrets to her all her life, that made her feel so connected. She certainly hadn't learned it from Mama and her birds.

Yvette turned the corner, slowing down more as she walked, though she kept her long stride. At least she had the sense not to wear those stupid hobble skirts that Anna Marie was so found of. Yvette still hated being constricted. She'd go back to being a barefoot *fille sauvage* in the mountains in a heartbeat if she could.

Yvette slowed further. The tall stone houses with their elegant lintels, leaded glass windows, and steep roofs suddenly loomed above her. There were no trees on this street, nothing green or natural anywhere. Yvette suddenly missed the woods, Mama's garden, the fresh mountain air, the heart-stopping cold of the spring behind their cottage.

The previous month, the *Assemblée* had voted to increase the length of military service from two to three years.

War was coming.

Maurice was stupid if he thought otherwise. How dare he pat her hand and tell her that politics wasn't a woman's place? Didn't he understand that not just men would suffer and die?

Yvette didn't know exactly where the war would start. It wouldn't just be a civil war, started by those dissatisfied and left behind by all the modern conveniences that Yvette and her mother and *société* shared, or even a political war between dissatisfied nations. Germany was already looking for an excuse to invade.

And Paris would be a horrible place to live in during a war.

They must leave. Not before *Noël*, no, or the new year. But in the spring. She would see to it.

Decision made, Yvette turned to go back to parlor games and charades and drama that Mama loved so well.

A dark cloud floated behind her, an independent shadow carved out of the night.

Yvette stopped short, pulling herself up to her full

height. What was this? She'd never seen such a thing before.

It wasn't human, but it wasn't fully magic, either. Yvette peered hard at it, trying to see beyond its darkness.

What type of creature was this?

Her winds didn't know. They'd never seen such a thing, either.

The darkness licked the air between them, a single tendril of disgusting smoke, undulating unnaturally.

What did it want? Was it trying to determine her strength?

"Be gone! *Allez*!" Yvette commanded.

The wind pushed at the smoke, but it curled away, undeterred.

The shadow was very strong, much stronger than it looked. Yvette would need a storm blast, maybe a gale wind, to make an impression. And even then, that might not be enough to do more than merely push it away for a minute or two.

"What do you want?" Yvette asked.

The shadow didn't have words, not really. It had hunger, though. Hunger for her magic. Maybe even her soul.

Where had such a thing come from?

Yvette probed it with her magic, trying to trace its origins. Was it being directed by a rival magician gone rogue? But she couldn't find any connections between this dark cloud and anyone nearby. It appeared to be autonomous.

And it had to be relatively new, or had always stayed hidden. Yvette was confident that her winds would have told her about such a creature before now.

"*Non*," Yvette told it simply. "Now go." She started to

gather the winds to her, harsh gales that would tear this shadow into strips.

She had no illusions that she'd destroy it. But her winds could probably distract it long enough for her to get away. The wind whistled in her ear, rising in pitch. Her skirt flowed out behind her, and her blouse tightened across her chest.

The shadow shrank back, gathering its strength together, poising itself, getting ready to spring.

Yvette braced herself for the attack. She was *damned* if this thing was going to take her. She gathered more winds in her hand, the force tearing at her glove. Her hat flew from her head and her curls sprang up, the hours her maid had spent straightening them lost in a moment.

Suddenly, a fire appeared inside the shadow itself. It started, surprised.

Mama appeared behind the shadow, growling. Blue flame burned in her palms. She'd grown as tall as Yvette, puffed up with magic, though she was far, far bulkier, like a bear.

Yvette recovered quickly and threw her wind at the shadow as well, tearing it to shreds. Mama's flames burned the weaker ends while Yvette's winds shredded the parts that remained intact.

The shadows retreated slowly. Now wasn't the time for it to fight.

But a promise of its return hung in the air long after it had left, the stench worse than the Seine in the spring.

"What was that thing, Mama?" Yvette asked as she stripped her tattered gloves from her hands. Nothing could be done about her curls now. Maybe she could start a new trend, the opposite of the hobbled, stupid girl—the wild, intelligent one.

"I don't know," Mama said.

"It—they—will come back," Yvette warned. That thing —those shadows—*hungered*. They wanted her soul, the souls of everything on earth. They were small now, but they'd grow greater with time.

They needed to be stopped. Soon. Before they got too strong.

Mama tilted her head to the side as if Yvette had spoken her thoughts out loud. "The shadows, *oui*, they may become a problem later. But they are not your concern."

Yvette blinked, surprised. Mama sounded so odd, as if another voice spoke through her. She'd heard Madame Lafitte speak similarly when she foretold the future.

Then Mama cleared her throat and drew a wheezing breath.

Yvette looked at Mama sharply. She'd stopped coughing so badly once they'd arrived in Paris and she'd seen a healer, but sometimes Yvette still wondered if Mama had actually gotten well or if she'd just learned to hide her illness better.

Mama shook off her shambling shape, shrinking down to normal size. She looked up at Yvette and said, "We should go home now, *non*?"

"*Oui*," Yvette said. She would set her winds to find out everything she could about the shadows in the morning.

Maybe they weren't worth the bother, and ultimately, wouldn't be her concern, but she still wanted to learn about them.

For now, she linked arms with Mama and continued up the street, toward the main intersection where Mama would call a horse-drawn cab, the horse irresistibly drawn to her, the cab driver confused but generally willing to take such an expensive fare.

"You don't want to go back to the party?" Yvette asked after a moment.

"Oh, no," Mama said, her laughter tinkling like toasting champagne glasses. "It was much, much more dramatic to just storm out of there. They'll be talking about my exit for weeks!"

Yvette shook her head, not surprised. Mama loved her dramas, just like she loved the lights of Paris, the warmth and gay parties, all of *société*.

Just as Yvette loved her quiet and her winds and missed the mountains so much.

They couldn't stay here. Not with the war coming.

But maybe when it was over, they could return, at least for a little while.

ARIEL

"So why did they all seem so surprised when you said you'd train me?" Ariel finally asked Aunt Mabel as they were driving away.

The sun was only partway to the horizon, and the heat beating at them. The air conditioner in the car was working overtime. The scent of warm leather from the seats made Gret calm down for the first time that day.

Aunt Mabel gave her barking laugh. "They aren't all warriors, honey. In fact, only a few of them know the in-between stage of warrior versus boar."

Now it was Ariel's turn to be surprised. "Really? Why?" The way Aunt Mabel had taught her, she assumed being a warrior was one of her three natural states: fully human, fully boar, or warrior, which was a mix of the two.

"It ain't genteel," Aunt Mabel said, her voice returning to its prissy, old-white-lady tones.

Ariel snorted in return. She didn't really do *genteel*. That wasn't something Mama had taught her, or ever expected her to be.

"While I'm certain that you don't believe I understand

your modern age," Aunt Mabel said, glancing over at Ariel with a sly smile, "I'm equally certain I understand *you* quite a bit."

"Okay," Ariel replied slowly. She was equally certain that this old white lady didn't have a clue.

"You need to be respected," Aunt Mabel said. "Your pride will get in the way of you trying new things, looking ridiculous. But you *must* try. And you will fail. So you *must* try again. And again."

"So you're saying if I just work hard enough I can do anything," Ariel said cynically. She'd heard all that before.

It only worked if you had money. And privilege. And power.

Now, being a member of the boar clan was a leg up, one she hadn't known she had before. It would help.

But she was still a black girl from Mississippi. The world was set against her from the start.

"Oh, no, honey. I'm not saying that at all," Aunt Mabel said. Her eyes were even twinkling with her laughter. "What I *am* saying is that you've got to try. The world don't owe you anything at all. Working hard won't necessarily bring you any kind of success."

"Then why should I even try?" Ariel asked, confused. This wasn't the kind of talk she'd been expecting at all.

"Because the trying is what's important," Aunt Mabel said. "Not the succeeding."

"You're only saying that because you *have* succeeded," Ariel said, unable to keep the words back. *And you're an old white lady.*

Aunt Mabel shook her head. "You might think that, now. But it isn't true. You'll see."

Ariel shook her head. Just trying wasn't ever gonna be enough.

Not for her. Or for Gret.

The great, golden *jin yu* swimming in the pond made a plopping noise as he dove for the small ball of rice Li Li had just thrown into the water. Large green lotus leaves floated around the edges of the pond. A single pink blossom reached up to the sky from the depths, a symbol of hope that Li Li no longer believed in.

Not after listening to her parents being attacked. Not after the clan had told her of their deaths.

Li Li watched with interest as the fish scooped up its prize. The others came closer, like the one with the red and white blotches that was as long as Li Li's arm.

But the first goldfish gobbled up its prize, as lucky as all fish were supposed to be.

The spring sky shone down brightly blue from above the tall halls surrounding the courtyard and the pond. It would have been a day that made Mama sing while she swept the garden stones.

But Mama wasn't there anymore. Or Papa.

Li Li's new clan had made sure that her brother and sisters had found good homes, where they'd be protected and kept safe. Auntie Fu had only survived a few days after the attack, dying of a broken heart rather than her injuries.

No one was looking for Li Li. The rumor that the clan had spread was that she'd already been sent into the countryside, to work in the fields there, to make up for her *bourgeoisie* past. A rumor that she was certain her siblings would always agree with if it meant hiding her.

It had been a little over a week since the attack. Li Li's new family had let her be, sitting next to the pond and feeding the fish. They assumed she was in shock, or in mourning, or something.

They didn't realized that from Li Li's carefully chosen seat she could hear *everything* that went on in the compound—in the Hall of Teaching, the Hall of Greeting, as well as the kitchen to her left: the whispered concerns about her, the fights about whether they needed to leave China until the current madness worked its way out, whether their cover as part of the Red Guard was blown, if there would be enough food that winter.

"Listening, I see," came a sly voice from close beside Li Li.

She didn't start, but made herself turn slowly. That was something Li Li worked hard at, controlling her actions. It was part of making sure that *she*, that is, Li Li, was the one always in control, not the twin swimming inside of her.

Han Zhe sat beside her. He was the only one who had ever been able to sneak up on her. No one else even in this new family could surprise her.

He was also the only male of the crocodile clan that she knew of. Almost all the members of the crocodile clan were female, just like all those from the hound clan were male.

Han Zhe wore his usual plain brown tunic, though he

wore a student cap, too. It wasn't because he thought much of their Glorious Leader: It was just to fit in.

Li Li knew about fitting in, blending, staying hidden. Father had taught her that, too.

Han Zhe's long gray hair was tied into a braid, hidden up under his cap. His face was still broad and bland, with his dark eyes the only two points of interest.

"You'd make a good *shouwang zhe*," he commented, tearing off a tiny bit of moss from under the lip of the steps and tossing it into the pond.

The fish darted toward the falling piece, picking at it, probably hoping it was food.

"A watcher?" Li Li asked after a moment. "What is that?"

Everything here was new and different. Or maybe old and the same, how things used to be, before Mao and the changes. Before the revolution.

Her new teachers had assured Li Li that she'd be able to continue her English studies—something she knew her parents would be pleased with. Plus she'd be learning calligraphy, math, *joss* folding, and magic, of course.

No one had mentioned *watching*.

Han Zhe shrugged, a movement as graceful as everything he did. "People from the clan are born outside the *zu* all the time. With so much disruption in the country, more will be lost. The watchers go out and find the wild ones, try to bring them back to the clan."

"You're a watcher," Li Li said after a moment. "You found me. Tried to get me to come to the clan compound early." Before the attacks. Had he known they were coming?

Han Zhe nodded, giving her a broad smile. "And here you are."

Li Li pressed her lips together, not wanting to point out

that the only reason she was there was because her family had been killed. Otherwise, she might never have come.

It took a lot of focus, but she'd already proved Han Zhe wrong once: She'd been able to control her sister, her crocodile soul. It had been difficult sometimes, to stay human, to not give in to claws and fangs. Particularly when her brother teased her, or her sisters pulled her hair.

But she'd never put her original family in danger.

After a moment, Li Li asked, "Every clan has watchers, don't they?" Because that only made sense. That the ravens, the hounds, and the tigers certainly would. Probably the boars and the vipers would as well.

"I suppose they do," Han Zhe said. "I hadn't really thought about it before."

Li Li studied the fish in the pond, thinking. Mama and Papa had been happy with her staying with them, even after she'd learned about the crocodile clan. They'd whispered about it late at night, but Li Li had still heard them talk about how important it was that she stayed human and not just *other*. They wanted her to experience the world outside of the Middle Kingdom, not just her own clan.

As far as Li Li knew, the crocodile clan rarely met with the other clans. The clans stayed separate, in part so they could never be betrayed again, as the ravens had done to them so long ago.

If she was a watcher, though, she'd stay outside. Watching. Learning not just about her own people, but the other clans as well.

Was that why Han Zhe was a watcher? Because he was the only male, and needed to stay be apart from the rest of the crocodile clan?

"I will do this," Li Li announced to Han Zhe. "I will become a watcher."

Han Zhe laughed, as everyone who was older than Li Li tended to do when she made her decisions. Even though she'd already proved him wrong once.

He would learn, as they all did, that when Li Li made up her mind, nothing on earth could stop her.

YVETTE

"Mama!" Yvette called up the stairs. "*Vite*! We must hurry!"

She paced across the entrance hall, from the stairs to the door, sticking her head out again. "*Un moment!*" she called to the impatient taxi driver. It had already taken the servants far too long to carry out their hastily packed trunks, loading them into the automobile. While Mama would have preferred a horse-driven carriage, Yvette knew they needed the speed of a car.

The train going back east would be leaving soon. They had to get out of Paris, now. Before the war started. Before all the trains would be commandeered by the army.

Before the Germans pushed into France.

When Yvette turned, she was stunned to see Mama coming down the stairs in a regular dress, not her travel clothes. She looked beautiful, of course. Mama always looked beautiful. Her dress was made from a fine pale-green silk, with an over-tunic of white lace. She wasn't wearing a jacket, gloves, or even a hat.

"I'm not going with you," Mama announced from the stairs.

Yvette bit her lips together to prevent herself from saying the first things that came to mind. She knew she couldn't make her mother do anything. Though Mama might call Yvette stubborn, she'd learned it at the feet of a master.

Of course, Mama hadn't said anything before then—she loved her stage dramas. She'd gotten so much worse since she could watch them every week. Yvette was glad they hadn't come to Paris any earlier. Mama might have been unbearable if Yvette had had to put up with this sort of thing growing up.

Finally, Yvette managed to ask, somewhat politely, "Why not?" Was it Mama's health, still? Yvette still didn't know if Mama was well or just more skilled at hiding her cough.

Mama laughed, sounding more gay and free than she had since they'd left the mountains. "I am old, dear—"

"But—" Yvette started to say. She stopped when Mama held up her hand.

"I *am* old, my dear. Older than I let on."

Yvette nodded. So it was her health.

"I've waited all my life to do something important," Mama continued. "You've heard it mentioned before. The Merlin-complex. Living so long—there must be a reason. I learned, soon enough, that it wasn't you."

Yvette nodded, swallowing down her bitterness. Was this why Mama had been so insistent that Yvette have an heir sooner rather than later? So that she wouldn't be expecting too much from her heir?

"That meant it had to be something else," Mama continued blithely. "Some other cause that was keeping me alive. Something I still needed to do."

"So this war is your *raison d'être*?" Yvette asked. She couldn't keep the anger out of her voice. Mama had stepped back, putting distance between herself and Yvette when Yvette had been much younger, making Yvette find her own way with her magic and her life, while Mama focused on her garden. In many ways, Yvette had felt like the adult between the pair of them, particularly since they'd arrived in Paris.

Mama gave a very typical shrug. "Who knows?" she said gaily. "I feel it is, though. It's time for me to do something grand, and important, and very foolish."

"You're going to give your life to this war. A war you don't believe in," Yvette said flatly. The war wouldn't bring anything but death to millions. Yvette didn't need her winds to tell her that.

Mama shrugged again. "It is *my* life. Not yours. And it is very nearly at its end. But you—ah, you have much more living to do."

"No, Mama, I don't," Yvette said. "I will go back up to the mountains, and I won't come back out." She'd never hidden from Mama just how much she missed their cottage, how the winds here carried the stench of the *bidonvilles*, the children living in the street with no sanitation and no hope.

Mama just gave Yvette a smile. "We'll see," she said coyly. "I predict that when the time is right, you will come down off your mountain." Then she stood up straighter, marching to the bottom of the grand staircase. "Come. Give your mother a kiss goodbye. Let's not be too sentimental."

"*Oui*, Mama," Yvette said with a sigh. She walked closer and kissed her mother's cheeks. Mama still smelled of lavender and rosewater, of her summer gardens full of rosemary and mint.

Yvette would cry later, when the winds brought her the news of her mother's actual death, how she'd been killed during the Battle of the Marne.

Had Mama been responsible for the miracle that happened during the battle? Had her birds distracted the German generals, so that they exposed their right flank to the French?

Yvette's winds couldn't tell her.

For now, Yvette walked out the door of their Paris apartments alone, determined never to return to the "civilized" world again.

And she wouldn't. For almost a century.

CARLOS

"And then I told her, 'You're doing great!' and I took, like, a dozen more pictures. The flash showed her boobs *every time*," Stevie told them.

"And she didn't realize her shirt went see-through?" Patrick asked.

"Nope. Not at all," Stevie said solemnly.

Carlos nodded with the other boys gathered around the table in the kitchen area. This was *awesome*. That girls had shirts that went see-through when you took a picture!

Not that Carlos had a camera or anything, nor could he buy one. The temple sure didn't have that kind of money. And it wasn't as if he saw many girls up here.

But Carlos wouldn't be at the temple his entire life. He had places to go. Things to do. Greatness to achieve.

"Do you have the pictures?" Francisco asked, practical as always.

"Yeah," Stevie said, with a sly grin. "And I can mail copies to you. For a price."

Carlos sat back as the other boys bargained with Stevie. It wasn't as if Carlos had any money. He wasn't a rich American like the rest of them. Besides, Carlos wasn't certain Stevie was telling the truth.

He already had Stevie's mailing address, however. As well as the addresses of many of the other boys.

This year would be different. This year, they'd all reply to Carlos' letters.

A buzzing noise started, loud and obnoxious, as though the generators that provided the backup electricity for the temple had just shorted out. Carlos looked up, trying to see where it was coming from.

Then he realized the other boys didn't hear it. Patrick had asked another question, and they were all listening to Stevie's reply.

What was that? What was happening?

Suddenly, Carlos' stomach rolled. His breakfast—the cornmeal pancakes sweetened with honey, runny eggs that were half fresh from the hens out back, half made from a dehydrated mix, and plenty of *xocolati*, a cold chocolate drink made with vanilla and pepper—threatened to come back up.

"You okay?" one of the boys asked.

Carlos could barely hear him over the buzzing in his head. His skull throbbed in time with the noise. Then, the pain hit him. It was like someone with a dull blade was trying to section his head apart, one piece at a time.

"Yeah, I'm fine," Carlos lied, standing. "I'll catch up with you guys later," he said.

The boys were used to Carlos going off to do chores every morning after breakfast while they attended classes in recitations and viper lore. Carlos was the only one their age who lived at the temple full time, while they just came for a couple of weeks every summer, like camp.

Carlos kept his head down as he raced out the back, behind the kitchen cooking area to the small cabin that only his. It sat tucked in just under the edge of the jungle, so it was always in the shade. It was made from solid timbers that would rot in weeks if Carlos and the priests didn't keep up the protection spells.

The jungle was hard on anything that wasn't a part of it.

Most of the time, Carlos bitterly complained about how cold his cabin was, but right now, he blessed the cool darkness when he got inside.

His stomach rolled again, but before he got to the bathroom out back, his right leg gave out. Carlos dropped heavily onto the wooden floor.

Had one of the boys slipped him something? Because Carlos would swear his leg had just turned to smoke.

Seizures struck Carlos, his body convulsing in ways that he knew were not normal.

Then the vision started.

Carlos kept his face down as he went to go see Father Pablo, the head priest of the temple. Carlos didn't know Father Pablo well. He didn't teach any of the classes for the boys, just led the chanting in the evenings sometimes.

The priests' quarters were back behind the tall stone pyramid temple. There were rooms inside the temple, at the bottom of it. However, they were cool all the time, the stone shaded by the tall jungle surrounding it. Those were the teaching and meditation cells, not living quarters.

The priests, like all of the viper clan, preferred being warm and in the sunlight. So their row of rooms was in a clearing just past the temple. It looked little better than slum housing to Carlos. There were maybe a dozen doors in the row, each leading to a single room. They shared showers and toilets.

Each room did have a screened-in porch, back behind it, so the priests could sit in the afternoon sunlight and not be bothered with bugs, or pray outside at night and not worry. But that was the only advantage Carlos could see.

Father Pablo lived in the shack on the far end, closest to the jungle. He opened the door at Carlos' first knock, inviting him into the tiny space. He was dressed in a brown T-shirt and jeans. He glanced down at Carlos' feet.

Carlos noticed the priest was barefoot and hastily toed off his sneakers.

The room was neat and clean, like one of those Japanese houses that Carlos had seen in the movies. It seemed bigger than Carlos was expecting. The floor was made from a dark wood that had been polished so hard it practically glowed. The walls were painted the same orange as the baked pottery pieces that were popular with the tourists. A single bed covered in a colorful striped blanket lay in one corner. The rest of the room was empty, except for a few very small pictures hanging on the wall, paintings of cactus and fruits.

"Come," Father Pablo said, walking through the small room and out the back door, just past the foot of the bed.

Carlos followed. Outside, the screened porch was almost as big as the room. There were chairs here, two sturdy wood ones, with cushions tied to them. A wooden table stood between them with a clear glass pitcher of water, the heat of the day already making droplets form along its curved sides.

Beyond the two chairs was a desk with its front folded closed. A portable heater stood in one corner, currently not turned on. Plants in plain brown pots grew all along the far wall. Some of the plants were tiny, in pots smaller than a teacup, sitting on a re-purposed bookshelf. Carlos recognized some of the bigger plants, like the rosemary and pepper bushes, the rubber tree and the great oak. But he had no idea what at least half the plants were.

Father Pablo indicated that Carlos should sit in one of the chairs, then sat himself down in the other. "Water?" he asked.

"Please," Carlos said. He wasn't sure how to begin, now, how to talk about what he'd seen.

The father seemed content to wait, sitting back in his chair, sipping his water.

He had the same sharp features as most of the priests, his nose larger than the others, dark eyes peering out from a projecting brow. His cheekbones were still prominent, even when he wasn't smiling. Though his thin lips always looked as though he was about to smile.

His chest was well developed and he had visible muscles along his darkly tanned arms. All of the fathers trained in the ancient fighting arts and were capable warriors. Every time a new class of students started in the summer, they gave a demonstration of just how strong and fast they were.

Carlos never tired of watching them perform.

But how good would those muscles and reflexes be against what he'd seen coming?

"I had a dream," Carlos started with, taking another sip of his water. Why had this vision come to him? It should have gone to one of the older priests. They'd at least know what to do.

Father Pablo merely nodded his head. He didn't look at Carlos, but continued to watch his potted garden.

That made it a little easier for Carlos to continue.

"Darkness rose up, corrupting us," Carlos said. He shivered despite the warm sunshine coming into the porch.

"Stripping us of our power, our souls." The priests moved like zombies, no longer under their own power, their strings pulled by shadowy figures. A golden web of lies contained them, constrained them, directed them.

Carlos glanced at the father, who nodded again, indicating he should continue. "They flood the temple, then they spread out from there, taking over the towns and villages of the mountain." Soon, no one in the world would have free will. They'd all be controlled by those others.

"The shadows," Father Pablo said.

"No," Carlos said almost immediately. There had been figures in the shadows who had attacked. The shadows themselves had just hidden them for a long while. The figures were all connected by a golden spiderweb, not by fog.

"The coming battles with the shadows have been predicted for a long time," Father Pablo continued as if Carlos hadn't disagreed.

Carlos felt his back stiffen in alarm. Though what he'd seen hadn't involved the shadows themselves, but something worse, hiding in them, he still let it go. Surely the father knew what he was talking about. "You already know about them, these shadows?" Carlos asked. "Why haven't you done anything about them?"

Father Pablo gave a dry laugh. "We tried. We failed to stop them the first time. We won't fail the second time."

"So my vision is worthless," Carlos said, bitterness rising up in him. Even if his vision hadn't been directly about the shadows.

Though Carlos wouldn't stay at the temple—not even knowing that he had visions like some of the other priests could make him stay—he'd at least thought he might become important enough that they'd write his name on the temple stairs, with the names of the other heroes of the clan.

"No knowledge is worthless," Father Pablo said sternly. "You know what to look for, now. What to guard against. You won't be corrupted."

Carlos swallowed down the rest of his angry words. It wasn't the father's fault that Carlos' vision wasn't bigger. Or that he couldn't convince the father that his vision involved something other than what had been predicted. Something that came after the shadows. Something worse.

It was because he was up here, in the temple, and not in the city. His visions would be grander, more important, once he returned to civilization. He was too isolated here to have much influence.

"Thank you, Father," Carlos said, standing abruptly.

The father stood more slowly, keeping his steady gaze on Carlos. "Stay true to your visions," he said. "Always let their light guide you."

"Yes, Father," Carlos said. He bowed his head, then left, heading back to his room.

Soon, he would dream big. Much bigger than anyone here.

He had a destiny to fulfill. And no one was going to stop him.

FU RAN

F u Ran wanted to do everything that her father did. She followed him around (like a puppy, according to eldest brother).

Father liked to sit in the afternoons and read his paper. The wan San Francisco sun would peer through the windows at them, the summer as cold as the winters. The sitting room was generally reserved for Father on Sunday afternoons, but he would allow Fu Ran beside him if she was good and sat quietly and didn't disturb him.

So Fu Ran sat with her school books, reading happily (though she'd turn the page of her book more often than he would turn the pages of his paper). But she was reading about dinosaurs and talking cats, not the fine long lines of Chinese characters in his newspapers.

Father would swirl the ice in his glass before drinking the special tea that Mother made him of ginseng and *bo he*. Fu Ran would do the same with her glass of watery lemon drink that Mother made for her.

Fu Ran would never admit that there was another person there in the sunroom with them.

Though *person* wasn't the right term. She was like the sister that Fu Ran never had, who liked the magical animal stories the best and always held Fu Ran's hand during the scary parts.

One afternoon while Fu Ran read to her invisible friend/sister, she noticed that Mother had come into the room. She was looking at Fu Ran strangely.

"Who are you talking to?" Mother asked.

Father looked up over the edge of his paper at Fu Ran, as if he was curious as well.

"No one," Fu Ran said immediately, closing her book.

Her friend growled, that rumbling sound that no longer scared Fu Ran.

Mother and Father looked at each other, saying words with their eyes that Fu Ran could only guess at.

The next Sunday, Aunt Leeda came for lunch. She was ancient, with wrinkles that crinkled around her eyes when she smiled. She wasn't really related to the family, but she had been a friend of Mother's for years.

After they'd eaten cool cucumber salad and warm chicken dumplings, Aunt Leeda served everyone a smelly, herbal tea that she'd brought with her. Then she insisted that they drink that, instead of the usual drinks in the sunroom.

Why was she changing things? Fu Ran wanted to yell at her mom for letting Aunt Leeda have her way.

But Fu Ran was a good girl. Both Mother and Father told her that often. So she gathered her books and lay on the sunroom floor and read.

Aunt Leeda made Fu Ran's sister/friend nervous, but she at least liked the tea. It made Fu Ran sleepy, so she let her friend read instead. The world they read about was so interesting! It was filled with talking tortoises and ships that could fly. Her friend was much better at making all the animal noises.

"What are you reading?" Aunt Leeda asked suddenly.

Fu Ran started. When she turned to look back, she realized Father was no longer there. Just Aunt Leeda.

How dare she sit in Father's chair?

Fu Ran put both her hands over her mouth after the growl had erupted.

But Aunt Leeda didn't yell at her. Instead, she gave a toothy grin. "Your mother was right to call me," she said, nodding. "You are different than they are."

Fu Ran wasn't sure she liked that.

In fact, if she had her way, she wasn't ever going to be different than anyone.

When Fu Ran first went to college, she enrolled in premed. She was determined to be a doctor, just like Father. It didn't matter that Father was human and she was of the crocodile clan. Father was a plastic surgeon. One of the best.

She would be the best too. Make both her father and her clan proud of her, particularly Aunt Leeda, the one who taught her about being in the crocodile clan, who raised her according to the tenets of their kind, taught her the recitations, promised to take her to China one day.

Then came Fu Ran's first ER rotation.

Her father had arranged everything. Fu Ran was supposed to have a nice, quiet rotation, in a hospital down in Daly City, south of San Francisco.

Instead, she ended up reporting to a hospital in downtown Oakland.

And fell in love with the excitement, chaos, and general *rush*.

She was never going to become a plastic surgeon in a nice, safe, clean office.

Instead, she'd wage battle every day against all the bad things and become the head of the ER

INTERLUDE

FROM "THE GUARDIAN HOUND"

Virmal

Sun poured through the old-fashioned leaded-glass windows, baking Virmal and his twin sister, Harita, where they lay on their blankets for their afternoon nap. Gold-painted radiators with fancy scrolled tops hissed and clanked under the windows. The wood floor pushed up against Virmal, uncomfortable and not giving under the soft fur blankets. Virmal liked burying his face into the fur, the musky smell soothing.

Harita, of course, had more of the sunshine. She always got more of everything.

Virmal grumbled and rolled closer to his sister so his right arm wouldn't be in the shadows. He pulled at his blue jumper, tugging down the sleeve. It was always too cold here in England, especially compared to his home in New Delhi. He never felt truly warm.

A cloud passed over the sun. Virmal opened his eyes and glared up at the gray cover.

It would probably start raining again or, because

England was cruel, it would wait until it was time for them to go out to the park and play.

Virmal growled softly, deep in his throat. Grandma Irita had said he shouldn't growl like that, not out loud; it was disrespectful.

But sometimes the growls crowded his throat, forcing their way out.

It was like something else lived under his skin. Something fierce and wild and *glad* that he could make his grandmother shiver.

The sun peeked out from behind the clouds. Virmal stretched his hand up to it, wanting to capture every last drop of warmth.

Harita pushed at Virmal, shoving him away and out of the light.

Without thinking, Virmal slashed at her, growling loudly.

Harita grabbed hold of her bleeding arm, staring at Virmal with wide, scared eyes.

Everything was silent and still in the front room. Virmal scrambled up to his knees. What had he done?

Then Harita screamed. The sound ran claws up Virmal's back and he snarled in response. She needed to shut up, shut up, *shut up*.

If she wouldn't shut up, he would make her.

Virmal rocked closer and growled again, low and deep, a noise that rumbled wonderfully through his chest. Color fled the world, and the smell of blood, of small things wounded, of *prey*, took over everything else. He could taste it on his tongue, lap it up like cream.

A tiny voice in the back of Virmal's head said no, he shouldn't do this. She was his *sister*, his fraternal twin.

The other didn't care and leaned closer still, filling

itself with the complex scent of fear and family, blood and home.

At least the girl had stopped screaming. Her rabbit-large eyes darted around the room, seeking escape.

Maybe they could let her run. At least toward the door. Then they'd trap her again.

They snarled and showed their teeth, big and sharp.

Before they could reach up their paw/hand and bat at the girl, a commanding voice ordered, "No. Don't. Virmal. Don't."

At the mention of his name, Virmal shook himself and blinked, the world returning to normal as if he'd just woken from a dream.

But Harita's fear was real, and so were her wounds.

"Grandma?" Virmal said, turning toward her, tears springing to his eyes. He'd been bad. He'd hurt Harita. And everyone always loved her more.

"Hush now," Grandmother Irita said, looking sternly from Virmal to Harita and back again. "Harita, can you growl back?"

Harita shook her head.

"Not even a little?" Grandmother asked.

"No!" Harita said, trembling despite her strong denial.

Grandmother Irita sighed and tugged on her blue and gold sari, pulling the material down. "Ah well. I'd hoped you'd share this, like you've shared everything. But it's not to be." She pressed her lips together and put her fists on her waist.

The clouds covered the sun again, making Grandmother Irita's sari suddenly look black, stealing all the light from the room. She looked like a terrible, angry goddess as she pronounced their fate.

"You will stay here, with me," she announced. "And not return to India."

Virmal turned from Grandmother to Harita. "I'm sorry," he whispered. Sorry for hurting her. Sorry for trapping them both here in England.

That broke the spell that seemed to hold Harita. She wailed loudly, scrambling up from the floor and throwing herself at their grandmother.

Virmal twisted back to look at them. Grandmother Irita had bent down and was stroking Harita's head, but her eyes were full of sorrow as she stared at Virmal.

"Why does she have to be here?" Virmal whined when Harita stood in the doorway to their classroom, her notebook pressed hard against her chest by her crossed arms.

"She has to learn the recitations, too, in case she births a girl who comes to power," Grandmother Irita said dismissively as she walked to the front of the room. Beyond the tall window, red and orange leaves twirled in the autumn wind. Grandmother Irita laid her books down on the desk, then sat behind it, facing them.

Virmal sighed, but he didn't say anything more. He'd liked spending time alone with his grandmother, learning the stories and history of the tiger clan. It was so unfair that Harita got to be there. *He* was the one with the power. He was the tiger warrior, not her. He was the one with the tiger soul: She wandered near to his human soul, then away again, but always within reach.

But Harita still got everything.

Virmal planted his elbows on the hard wooden table that served as his desk, pressing his heels down on the worn rungs of the chair. Scents of *dahl* and sweet tea floated up from the kitchen along with the smell of rain that always rode the wind. He didn't look at his sister when she sat down, but he also didn't growl at her—Grandmother Irita had trained them both out of that.

"And more than that, she's family," Grandmother Irita added. "Maybe we'll start with that recitation today."

Virmal knew better than to groan. While some of the recitations were cool and had neat stories associated with them, too many of them listed all the things he couldn't do, like *don't show yourself to other people, don't transform in public, don't use your claws against an unarmed human,* and on and on.

Grandmother Irita put the recitation notebooks on their desks. Since they were here in England and not at any of the tiger temples, every page of the recitations that they wrote had to be destroyed at the end of their lessons.

Virmal liked putting the pages in the flames of the hearth downstairs in the parlor. But, knowing his luck, that would be something else Harita would get to do today.

The sound of Harita unzipping her pencil case made Virmal look over at her. It was pink with some kind of Japanese anime cat on it. If Grandmother Irita hadn't been there, he would have made retching sounds. How could she be from the tiger clan and still like such cute, girly things? Virmal would never understand his twin.

Then Harita grimaced as she reached up and put the pencil case at the top of the desk.

Was that a bruise on her arm?

Virmal got out his own pencil and tried to sniff the air without Grandmother or Harita noticing. His nose told him astonishing things.

There was the milky porridge they'd had for breakfast, and the thin trace of dirt from when Harita had gone outside to check the bird feeders, and just there, before she'd come down, underneath the kitchen smells, were salty tears.

What did Harita have to cry about?

Virmal wrote the first recitation as Grandmother Irita recited it: *The tiger clan comes first.*

First before family, though? Harita was family, but wasn't clan.

Hurt one. Hurt all.

Many in the tiger clan were solitary in nature. Some of the recitations, like this one, were a way to bring them together. Virmal didn't like being with many other people, but he didn't mind being with his sister if she was quiet. She mostly didn't set his back up.

Temper revenge with wisdom.

Virmal didn't like the story that went with that one. It made him shiver, just thinking about how the tiger clan families had attacked and wiped each other out for generations.

It was one of the good things to come after the treachery of the ravens. The clan had stopped turning against each other and had united as one, instead.

Defend the others in the tiger clan, the ambush of tigers.

That one was harder, actually, for Virmal. He was never sure what was the right way to defend the ambush. Was it to be like Sree, and attack with claws and fangs? Or to be like Ansuya, and talk everyone into agreeing? He never saw himself like Soniya, who sacrificed herself, drawing away the hunters and their dogs so her family could escape.

Harita shifted in her seat, and Virmal could smell tears coming closer.

Was Harita defending the clan in some way? A way that was hurting her?

She'd never tell if she was in trouble. She might be a spoiled brat, but she kept secrets better than the goddess Surina, who knew the end of everyone's life but carried the burden alone and would never tell the pilgrims who came to worship at her temples, no matter how much gold they left or how they pleaded.

Surina could be tricked into revealing what she knew, though.

Virmal wrote the next recitation without really hearing it. How could he trick his sister into telling him?

Though Grandmother Irita didn't say it, Virmal wrote the first recitation of their lesson again.

Hurt one, hurt all.

Virmal had never been so aware of his sister before. He kept track of Harita all the time, following her by scent when he couldn't be close enough for sight or sound.

It surprised Virmal how gentle Harita was. All his female cousins, tiger warrior or not, had a cruel side to them. They'd put their dolls into paper prisons, denying them food while they had tea parties sitting outside the gates, or they'd make up long, involved stories about their teddy bear generals and pony captains and the war they'd bring and how the farmers would suffer and curse them.

The stories Harita told with her dolls involved playing house and taking care of their children, or starring in a Bollywood movie, or even holding a pageant show.

In the corner of the playroom, Virmal drew pictures of spaceships exploding, ninja warriors with cat-like features, or creepy voodoo ravens with Xs for eyes, doodling as he always did, but also listening like never before.

On Tuesdays and Thursdays, Virmal and Harita went to the big school, with the other kids; they were homeschooled only on the other days. Virmal had friends he walked with from homeroom to history class, down the loud hallways filled with kids and lockers. That Tuesday, he finally noticed that Harita only had two friends, and all three of them looked and smelled wary, carrying their books tightly.

Harita always wrapped her arms across her chest, carrying her books. So did the other girls.

Virmal wasn't stupid. He knew what that meant.

Someone was bullying his sister, and she'd had her books pulled out of her arms on a regular enough basis for her to be defensive all the time.

His tiger soul growled at that. She didn't like it. Not one bit.

Hurt one, hurt all.

"Sorry, I can't go," Virmal said as he shut his locker.

Vijay, Sal, and Eric all complained. "Come on, you promised!"

"Look, just play three-person footie," Virmal suggested.

"Lame," Eric replied.

"I'll play next week," Virmal promised, hurrying out of the dim school hallway and into the autumn cold. God, he hated England. He quickly buttoned his heavy, blue wool peacoat up to his neck, then pulled his gray hat down more snugly over his ears. He took the stairs from the school two at a time, then raced up the block, trying to catch up with Harita.

Nasty wind pushed at him, blowing through the thick

wool as well as the sweater Virmal wore underneath. Maybe he should switch to his winter down jacket; at least that resisted the wind. But the guys would make fun of him. Ornate metal fences enclosed the gardens to his left. Only a few brave, colorful leaves dangled from the trees. The smell of rain was in the air, but the wind *always* smelled like rain.

Ahead of Virmal, Harita walked alone. She walked quickly, like a rabbit scurrying across a field. Even from a block away, the wind carried the scent of her fear. She turned the corner, and Virmal hurried.

Three boys had surrounded Harita by the time Virmal caught sight of her again.

"Going home so fast, little mouse," the tall white boy in the dark green coat said.

"Did you bring us the money?" a dark Indian boy asked, in a black coat that looked very much like Virmal's.

Harita bared her teeth at them. "Never," she said.

At least she was standing up to them. But there were three of them and only one of her. Plus, they were all bigger than she was.

Why hadn't she told anyone, though?

"Leave me alone," Harita said loudly.

"Or you'll scream?" the last one sneered. He was short and white. He shoved Harita's shoulder. "You know what happened last time you did that."

The Indian boy pushed Harita next, hard enough that she almost stumbled and fell. Then he yanked on her backpack, trying to strip her of her books.

Virmal couldn't hold back. His tiger soul growled as he hurried forward. "Leave her alone," he ordered as he pushed through the boys to stand beside his sister.

"Oh, a big bad knight in shining armor," the tall white boy mocked.

"I can take care of this," Harita hissed at Virmal.

Virmal's tiger soul pushed at him. *Brave*, she purred.

Harita shoved Virmal back, behind her.

No wonder she hadn't told anyone. She thought she needed to deal with the boys all by herself, as a matter of honor.

"*An ambush is stronger than each warrior, alone*," Virmal quoted to Harita in Hindi, one of the recitations.

"*Each warrior makes her own way*," Harita quoted back.

"Bored now," the smaller white boy said. He reached beyond Harita and pushed at Virmal.

"Together?" Virmal suggested, for the first time happy that both of them had taken some warrior training, learning to fight. Harita hadn't taken as much, but he'd ask for her at every class, now.

They took off their backpacks and turned their backs to each other. Virmal spread his legs wider, one a little in front of the other, his weight on his toes, rooting himself in the earth, his hands up in loose claws. Though Virmal couldn't see her, he knew Harita did the same. Then Virmal let out a low growl. Harita echoed him: a human sound, but eerily accurate nonetheless.

The three boys seemed uncertain, suddenly. Then the tall white boy in the green coat sneered. "She can't really fight. I bet you can't either. They're bluffing." His voice gained strength.

"You're bigger than we are," Virmal told him calmly. "And there are three of you. But together, we're stronger."

"What, you and your girlfriend?"

"She's my sister," Virmal declared. A sudden pride filled him. "And we have greater heart than you do."

With a second snarl, both Virmal and Harita attacked.

Virmal exploded forward. He couldn't use his claws or teeth—Grandmother Irita would skin him alive for that.

However, he could still use the speed of a tiger warrior.

He drove the heel of his palm directly into the lower chest of the Indian boy, making him gasp and stagger back.

Down! cried his tiger soul.

Virmal ducked.

A wild swing of the tall white boy whizzed over Virmal's head.

Virmal grinned at the white boy, showing all his teeth. Then he *slammed* into the other boy, coming in low and extending up, driving his shoulder into the boy's chest and his elbow into the boy's stomach, pushing him away.

The tall white boy recovered quickly and tackled Virmal, driving them both to the ground. Then he reared up and smashed Virmal in the face.

Virmal howled, wrapped his legs around the boy's waist, and flipped them so he was on top. Blood pounded in his skull and dripped from his nose. He didn't bite the boy's shoulder, even though he wanted to. Instead, he brought his knee up into the boy's groin, then, using both hands, slammed the boy's head against the ground, once, twice.

Stop, his tiger soul warned before he did it again.

Virmal lifted himself up and away. The boy groaned but didn't try to get up. Virmal quickly looked over to his sister.

Harita's opponent was also on the ground. She grinned at him, one eye already bruising, her hair pulled out of its neat braid, her knees as muddy as his.

The Indian boy had run away, deserting his companions.

Harita and Virmal silently picked up their backpacks and walked away. Virmal's face hurt, and he knew he'd have a shiner that matched Harita's. But his tiger soul was content. Honor and duty had both been served.

"Why didn't you tell me?" Virmal asked as they turned the next block.

"I could have handled it," Harita said hotly.

Careful, now, his tiger soul warned.

"I couldn't have fought all three, not by myself," Virmal told her. Of course, like his sister, he would have tried to at first.

"Why did you help me?" Harita asked.

The wind blew at Virmal. He was suddenly tired and cold. "You're my sister."

"But you hate me."

Virmal thought about it for a moment. Harita always got the best of everything. Even though he was the tiger warrior, Mama and Papa always asked about her first when they called, always talked with her first. She got better grades than he did both at school and at home. Grandmother Irita liked her better.

"You're my sister," Virmal finally said.

His tiger soul gave a comforting growl, as close to a purr as she could.

"But—"

"No. You're my sister. You're clan. You're family."

Nothing else mattered, not really.

"Those boys might be back," Virmal warned as they neared their flat. "With their friends."

"Grandmother Irita is going to ask about that," Harita pointed out, gesturing toward his throbbing eye.

"*The ambush takes care of its own*," Virmal quoted.

If more boys came, and Virmal and Harita couldn't handle them, they could get help.

Neither of them had to stand alone.

PART TWO
CATALYST

YVETTE

The early spring night was dark, moonless, and clouded, but Yvette didn't mind: She didn't really need light to see. She knew the borders of her property up in the mountains well enough to circumnavigate it without stumbling. Plus, she could *feel* it, the edge as distinct as the borders of a lake, shifting occasionally with the seasons but still as diverse as rock versus water.

When Yvette had been a young woman in Paris, first learning the *mystères*, she'd worn gowns specifically for doing magic. They'd been severely black, voluminous silks. Getting dressed in them had been part of the ceremony for Yvette, with all the hooks and buttons, the underskirts and boning.

After the ritual of dressing, Yvette would meet with the other magicians living in Paris at the time—six in all. They each called forth a magical flame to light their way, then walked stiffly from the drawing room where they'd gathered through a hidden door beside the mantel and into the magical practice space hidden behind.

Here, doing magic in such formal gowns seemed silly.

As well as impractical. Too many brambles blocked the path. Though they usually listened to her, that wouldn't stop them from reaching out and snagging her clothes occasionally.

Instead, Yvette wore the more modern slacks that had become the fashion since the war. Mama would have been scandalized, but then again, Mama was no longer there.

Four times a year—for the equinoxes and the solstices—Yvette walked her borders, strengthening the barrier there. Not too many had ever challenged it over the years. The locals knew better. But there were more and more tourists, hikers taking in the idyllic views the Jura mountains presented.

Plus, sometimes shadows slid along it, seeking weaknesses.

No matter what Mama said about the shadows, how they weren't Yvette's concern, she still kept an eye on them.

The winds told Yvette of how the shadows had corrupted the hound court, in Germany. They didn't have a foothold yet in any of the other clans, but Yvette suspected it was just a matter of time.

The shadows were evil. They would destroy everything once they got the strength, taking over the clans first, then moving on to humans.

However, neither Yvette nor her winds had a clue how to defeat them.

She'd never had to face down another shadow, not since that time in Paris. Then again, she was protected in her land, and on the mountain, and rarely left it. Of course, she made the occasional trip to Geneva, to visit her banker and to see the latest fashions, buying herself a bracelet or maybe some earrings.

Yvette found herself less and less interested in actually

visiting the outside world. She preferred to merely listen to it with her winds, not directing them, but just letting them carry what news they thought she needed, like de Gaulle being elected president and the new states that America had absorbed, Hawaii and Alaska.

Yvette always started her path around her border at the front, past the yard and the dark pines that rustled with her winds to the edge of the lane, where it intersected with the main road that went up the mountain. It wasn't paved yet. She knew that was just a matter of time, as more and more automobiles came into the region.

Most people would never notice her little lane. She kept it open so she could leave easily with a carriage or sleigh, and someday, probably, a car. She hung teardrops of glass from the trees on either side of the lane, enspelled with distraction magic, so if someone did notice the entrance to her lane, they'd be distracted by something else and forget it soon enough. It was much more efficient than trying to hide the lane.

A bulbous, dark mirror hung from the trees there as well. It was a bit larger than her palm, in an eight-sided frame, painted black. It wouldn't stop any shadows as far as she knew, or distract any humans.

One of Yvette's friends from Paris had sent it to her, telling her it would protect her against demons. She'd scoffed at the message—there were no such things as demons, at least not as far as her winds were concerned. Man was by far the worst creature on the planet.

Still, when the winds reported some months later her friend's unexpected death, Yvette hung the mirror by the lane, the main entrance to her land, in the memory of her friend. The mirror had some magic to it, though not much, mainly a spell to keep the glass from cracking. The wood wasn't magic, which she thought was odd—it was much more likely to weather badly. But maybe such mirrors weren't normally kept outside, exposed to the elements.

Yvette caught the mirror in her winds, checking it first that night. It seemed perfectly fine. She still wasn't sure it was necessary, but better safe than sorry.

She'd thought about taking the mirror down more than once. However, caution had always stayed her hand. The mirror, for all its lack of magic, was more than it seemed.

And maybe someday Yvette would learn its secrets, and why it was supposed to keep demons at bay.

Then Yvette started to walk her land. She wrote her name on the stones that made up the lane, each one recognizing her and only her. The brambles and their thorns turned toward her, sharpening in her presence. Early purple and white crocus quivered as she passed, dreaming of the noonday sun.

It took several hours for Yvette to walk around her entire border. The birds stirred uneasily in their nests, chirping in their sleep, ready to sing her name in the morning. The mice and voles and other small animals, too, all recognized her, acknowledged her right to the territory they shared.

The night was starting to loosen its hold by the time Yvette made it back to the start of her lane. The trail she'd left behind didn't flare up like the magic in the rug Mama had made for her. It was more subtle than that, a soft glow, diffuse, that rolled across the land like a carpet of fog.

Yvette felt a deep sense of satisfaction flowing over her as she walked back to her small cottage. Her property was safe. Her winds would keep her informed of the world while she stayed behind her borders.

She would sleep well for a few hours before the sun would peek through her curtains and wake her. Then she could start another day of learning about everything in the world.

***

Yvette woke suddenly from her deep sleep. Summer nights were short in the mountain, but it was still many hours until the sunrise.

Something was wrong.

She rose from her bed at the back of the cottage. She'd replaced Mama's bed with a beautiful hand-carved wooden sleigh bed and a heavenly modern mattress and box spring. The quilts still smelled of Mama's lavender, which continued to grow wild in the backyard, but also of Yvette's roses, plants that Mama had never had the patience to raise.

The thick cottage walls didn't allow the winds in, something Yvette appreciated more and more over the years. They could come when she invited them, and not bother her all the time with their gossip and news of the world.

Yvette didn't change out of her sleeping gown. While she'd never quite gone back to being the wild girl after returning from Paris, living barefoot and free in her pantaloons, she still had a looser sense of propriety than her neighbors.

If she shocked them by being outside and dressed like this, that was their problem, not hers.

Besides, it hadn't been a human calling to her who had woken her. Or one of those who called themselves the flower children—the hippies—who would frequently get lost in the woods, tripping on mushrooms or some drug.

No, this was something else.

Yvette slipped on her work clogs and stepped outside.

They weren't the most graceful of shoes, but they'd save her feet from the raspberry brambles and nettles that she encouraged to grow at the edges of her property.

The dew soaked the hem of her sleeping gown. She'd have to dry it with her winds later. Or maybe just go shockingly nude for the night—she'd done it before, when the moon was too full and the winds too wild—dancing like a dervish on the front lane, the dark pines silently swaying in time with the music she heard in her head.

Her winds had told her about the flower children, who danced in just paint on the beaches of California. Maybe someday she'd go join them, shock them all that such an old lady would come dance, though she didn't look that old, maybe in her thirties, despite being over seventy now.

The wrongness lay at the front of her property, near the lane. Her border was secure, that much she knew. Nothing was trying to break through. However, it was still being... tested, perhaps.

Yvette gathered winds to her, keeping them at the ready. They weren't her only defense, but they were still her best.

A young Indian woman stood at the lane to Yvette's property. She peered quizzically at the teardrops of glass hanging from the trees, distracted, but not enough to stop noticing the property.

It was obvious to Yvette that the young woman wanted to step across the border. However, she couldn't.

What did she want? Why was her presence strong enough to wake Yvette from a deep sleep?

Yvette stepped out of the shadows and directly into the middle of the lane. She knew that she appeared abruptly before the young woman. Her white sleeping gown would make her seem ghostly, along with her height. She now let her hair curl naturally, like a mane around her head. She'd stopped wearing makeup years before. No matter how much sunlight she got, she still stayed naturally pale, with bright green eyes, a haughty nose and a broad forehead.

"*Bonsoir*," Yvette said.

The woman didn't start. She appeared to have sensed Yvette coming. She didn't bother even glancing at Yvette but continued to stare, instead, at the little glass pieces.

"Those aren't enough to keep me here," the woman—no, teenaged girl—said. She spoke in soft French with an unusual accent. Her hair was long and black, held in the back by a silver brooch decorated with chunks of amber. She wore the modern uniform that all the teens seemed to favor these days, the new bellbottom jeans, with a pale blue blouse under a heavier, navy-blue pea coat.

"You are correct. Those aren't what are keeping you on that side of my border," Yvette told the girl. She peered closely, finally determining that the girl was one of the tiger clan. Her tiger soul sparked brightly inside her, then just as abruptly disappeared again, making her look normal. Yvette might have missed it if she hadn't been looking for it.

When Yvette looked again, she realized that the human girl was puffed up, her bulging muscles straining her jacket and her jeans, looking ready to fight, the tips of her fingers already bearing claws.

The girl should have been able to step onto Yvette's lands. She had enough of her own innate magic, being one of the tiger clan. Why couldn't she cross?

The girl made a swiping motion, like a cat batting at a toy.

Yvette's border lit up. A golden curtain shone for an instant, running along the edges of her property. The winds stirred, swirling around Yvette and making the pines beside her rustle, needles slithering to the ground.

One of the clan had *never* elicited that sort of reaction before.

Was there something wrong with this girl?

"I could break through, you know," she boasted to Yvette.

"Then we would fight," Yvette told her simply. Any being that caused her border to flare up so couldn't be regarded as a friend. "And you wouldn't win." She didn't know that for certain, but the girl wouldn't be able to engage in a fight with Yvette without being severely hurt, that much Yvette could guarantee.

The girl snarled at Yvette, baring her teeth. "*Hurt one. Hurt all,*" she recited.

Yvette nodded. Every clan had sayings such as that one. She didn't know all the sayings of all the clans, but she'd heard many over the years. "However, the clan would then declare you foolish for tweaking the nose of a magician. They would not come to your defense." Though Yvette didn't know that for certain, she still spoke with conviction.

There weren't any formal agreements between the clans and the magicians. Informally, clan members would seek out magicians now and again for help with something. They'd pay for the help with clippings of their nails or hair—it was always easier for a magician to do magic starting with magical ingredients.

Any magician who attacked a clan member unprovoked would die, the vengeance of the clan terribly quick.

Any clan member who attacked a magician unprovoked got what they deserved at the hands of the magician. There was more than one story of a magician clashing with a member of the clan—and the clan member losing.

While Yvette wasn't the strongest magician she knew, she could protect herself.

The girl batted at the border again, growling, as if it were a physical thing that she could see.

Maybe she could.

Yvette caught a glimpse, suddenly, of the dark shadow the girl cast. Her back stiffened.

The girl was infected with the shadows, those things that had tested her borders now and again.

It was far, far worse than the hound court. The shadows were intertwined with the girl's tiger soul.

What had happened to this girl? Or was it the entire tiger clan?

In the morning, Yvette would have to direct her winds toward both the India court, as well as the new one set up in Britain, to try to find out.

Was this why the tiger clan had split back in 1947? Into two proper courts? She'd always assumed it was because the British had left India to its independence then.

"Why do you want to come onto my property?" Yvette asked.

The girl focused her burning gaze on Yvette. "They say you know things."

Yvette couldn't help but laugh. "I'm old, *ma chérie*. Of course I know things."

"You work with the winds," the girl said. She sighed suddenly, deflating. Instead of a fierce warrior, she seemed like a lost teen. "I want to learn."

"Surely you have more powerful teachers who have greater magic than I," Yvette said, puzzled. The tiger clan were known for being the most magical of all the clans. Why would this girl seek her out?

Or was it because of the corruption of her soul?

"But none of them can teach me things like you can,"

the girl whined. "The winds know everything. I want to learn to hear them."

The girl suddenly reminded Yvette of herself when she'd been young, yearning to know *everything*. It didn't matter what she did with the knowledge, just that she have it. "I'm not sure I can teach you," Yvette said slowly. "Listening to the winds is a natural ability. It wasn't something I had to learn." She had learned to call up some winds, but others still came to her without her doing anything.

"You *will* teach me," the girl insisted. She tried to take a step forward.

The golden curtain sprang up again, dazzling and sharp.

Yvette had always imagined her barrier as a solid wall, not something as diaphanous and flowing as it now appeared. However, it would still cut the girl to shreds if she tried to force herself through .

Yvette enhanced the image she saw, adding piercing spires of glass to the curtain, sparkling and deadly.

The girl took a step back and shook her head, frustrated.

"No, *ma chérie*, I will not teach you anything beyond respecting my boundaries," Yvette said. She couldn't help but be amused by the tiresome kit. "Now, go. I am an old woman. I need my rest. *Allez.*"

Yvette called her winds up and sent them dancing around the girl. They twirled around her, spinning her around.

The girl helplessly struck out, clawing at the wind. However, there wasn't anything physical for her to connect with. The winds were bodiless, but forceful just the same.

She looked over her shoulder at Yvette. "I will be back," she warned.

Yvette gave her a shrug, the one that Mama had always used, the one that she'd been told marked her as purely French. "My answer will be the same."

"No. Someday, you will change your mind," the girl prophesied. With that, she gave a sharp nod to Yvette and marched down the lane, the wind still nipping at her heels.

Yvette stayed where she was, watching the girl disappear around the bend. What a strange encounter. Why did this youngster—this Tiger Lily—think she could force Yvette into doing anything she didn't want to do?

Nevertheless, Yvette spent the rest of the night strengthening her borders, adding glass spires and spears to the solid wall, making sure that not just the shadows but also those infected by them couldn't pass through.

CARLOS

Carlos nearly choked when he saw his first zombie.

It was the middle of the day in Mexico City. The sun shone down harshly on the crowded street. Hundreds of people pushed along, going one direction on the sidewalk, while hundreds more pushed by the other way. A very typical Saturday in the heart of the city, just outside the farmer's market held at the stadium. The sidewalks were too crowded for buskers, though a few brave souls still begged, sitting on the front step of a row house. Even over the smell of so many warm bodies came the delicious smells of chicken on skewers and pork frying in garlic and onions.

It was the perfect location for a pickpocket. The mark wouldn't even know he'd been hit for blocks as he left the market. And these tourist women who thought clutching their handbags would stop him. Instead, the more tightly they held on, the more tempted he was to take from them.

Maybe he used just a touch of magic to ease his hand into tight places, a slight numbing so that the mark wouldn't feel his hand.

Of course, Carlos could be doing other things with his gifts. But working a crowd always amused him.

Plus, it passed the time between visions.

The American doctors labeled his episodes seizures, *grand mal*, and accused him of epilepsy and other mind diseases.

Carlos knew he wasn't sick. It was just the price he had to pay for his gift.

There was a reason why those who had a lot of visions were ensconced at the temple, where they could be looked after. Interacting with the regular, modern world was... difficult at best.

But Carlos stubbornly wouldn't go back to the temple to live. Only to visit.

He made his own way, visions be damned. Sure, he committed petty crime to support himself. Jail—even jail in Mexico City—was better than being trapped at the temple.

But then, in full daylight, Carlos saw the zombie. Like what his visions always showed him.

However, this wasn't a vision. He was fully awake, aware.

The zombie moved like it was alive. It walked like a normal person, not a shambling mess. It wore a nice shirt and jeans and even sneakers. It used to be a young man, Mexican, maybe a little older than Carlos' twenty-eight years. It didn't drool.

But there was no soul left behind its eyes.

Carlos didn't know if it could talk. Why was it walking down the street? What did it want?

Carlos followed after it, keeping himself to the shadows and with many people between them, though the zombie never looked over his shoulder once, was never suspicious. For as little soul as it had, it still had a sense of direction.

The zombie walked to one of the nearby apartment blocks mainly inhabited by students. The neighborhood wasn't dangerous, though it wasn't safe either. The apartment blocks all needed to be repainted, the bright sunlight fading the coral colors of the bricks.

At the door, the thing paused.

Carlos shrank back. Was there someone pulling the thing's strings? Watching to make sure its puppet arrived? That had always been part of his visions as well, that golden web of connected masters.

Slowly, very slowly, the zombie reached into its pockets and pulled out its keys.

Now there was drool, dripping from its lower lip down onto its shirt, as it bent its head, searching for the right key. Its hand shook with the effort to remember, to tackle this mundane task.

The door opened. Reflex, not thought, made the zombie reach out and hold the door open.

The girl coming out merely nodded at the zombie, not really seeing him as she skipped down the steps.

The zombie slipped inside.

Would it remember where it lived? Or would blind habit propel it to the right door? What would it do when it reached its home? Sit there and rot while it watched the game that afternoon?

Carlos turned to go, then turned back. He took a picture of the front door with his cell phone, along with the number of the place, so he would remember it later.

The zombie had been one of those creatures from Carlos' visions. He was certain of it. The fathers had all assured him that they were the creatures of the shadows.

Carlos still didn't think so. This was some other threat. Something that hid in the shadows, but was much worse.

Then Carlos started shaking. Was he so revolted by what he'd just seen?

No. Damn it. A vision was coming.

Carlos ran to a nearby park, letting his magic aid his speed, so he was somewhere cool and green when the vision hit him with the force of a sledgehammer.

Now it was Carlos' turn to drool and gibber, to curl up on his side and lose all sense of himself and where he lay as the visions took him over.

The American doctors had tried to "cure" him. They didn't understand the importance of what Carlos saw. Luckily, he knew better than to take the pills they so easily handed out at the clinic, knew better than to fall down in the middle of a crowded street and be carted off to the hospital (again).

The visions meant Carlos couldn't work a regular job, but he was okay with that. He'd rather be out in the crowds anyway.

This vision was the same, the people who had been turned into zombies, the viper priests stripped of their power, a shadowy contingent of humans operating in the darkness, their long talons dipping into every pie.

These weren't the shadows, no matter what the priests thought.

But Carlos had never dreamed of how to stop them, which was why he didn't insist the priests listen more carefully to him.

He would have to solve the problem of these zombie makers, these soul eaters, himself.

YVETTE

Yvette kept waiting for Tiger Lily to return. The girl had captured her attention. Yvette sent her winds to England, first, then to India, following her. She was a wild one, always challenging the others, always fighting. Yvette nearly called back all her winds. There was nothing interesting about the girl. Yvette must have been mistaken, the visit an aberration.

Then the winds told Yvette of Tiger Lily standing alone in her room one day, at the tiger court in India. She poked and prodded at her own face, scratching at it. She took off her sari and revealed other scratches and bruises, unusual for someone from the clans—they usually healed so quickly.

However, Tiger Lily kept tearing at her own skin, as if she was trying to get rid of something, or get at something.

Her tiger soul knew something was wrong. Perhaps she was aware of how the shadows had corrupted her soul.

Tiger Lily was the only one in the entire tiger clan who even suspected, as far as Yvette could tell.

But Tiger Lily didn't return.

Other clan members did seek Yvette out after Tiger Lily's visit, maybe one or two a year. She wasn't sure how she'd gathered such a reputation with them. It wasn't as if she left her property very often.

Still, they came. They all said she knew things, which was true.

In exchange for her knowledge, they offered trimmings —nail clippings from the hounds, a scale or two from the crocodiles, hair from boars and tigers, even a few drops of poison from a stray viper.

Never a raven, of course. They still thought they were the only magical clan—the only magical beings, even—as far as Yvette could tell. The raven clan had been separated from the rest of the clans by a great spell that even prevented them from seeing the others in their true form.

Yvette had never determined the exact cause of the raven clan's ostracism by the other clans, but she suspected it was due to the raven's betrayal back in the 1200s.

As Mama had taught Yvette, magic starting with something already magical was much easier. Yvette created potions that she sold to other magicians who came to see her, or to those whom she'd exchanged letters with for years.

The clan members never stayed long. And Yvette didn't always understand why they needed the information they did. Surely with their newspapers and TV they could find out what she knew themselves?

Shadows came as well, more and more frequently. They always tested her borders, though they didn't try to break through. Every once in a while a few would challenge her when she left her home and went to the village, but she always beat them back with Mama's flames and her winds.

Very few farmers lived in Lamoura now. Tourists

swelled the streets and took her favorite table at the pub, athletic boys and girls who hiked and skied in the mountains.

Sometimes, Yvette even made the trip into Geneva. Her banker had passed on, as had his son. However, the granddaughter was quite sharp, and had doubled Yvette's fortune—quite a feat, as Yvette already had an incredible amount of money.

She thought sometimes of creating an heir, but she just couldn't make herself go through with it.

As the years passed, and the next century started, Yvette couldn't help but wonder *why* she continued to live. Yes, magicians tended to live longer than humans, but rarely as long as Mama. All of Yvette's friends, the magicians she'd met in Paris as a girl, had already died. Yvette didn't do anything to prolong her life, no spells or potions, yet she still appeared to be a woman in her fifties, not well over one hundred and counting.

Was it just good genes? Or was it something else?

Mama had called it Merlin syndrome—the assumption that a magician made sometimes, that Yvette was living for something, some special person to walk into her life. Someone she was supposed to teach, or a great deed she was supposed to do.

Yvette had always scoffed at that. It struck her as a comfortable delusion, to imagine oneself with such grandeur.

She couldn't help but wonder as another year passed: Was there some reason for her great, long life?

$$山山$$

The primary tenet of being a watcher was to *watch*. Wait to act, to interfere, to announce the presence of the clan. Then wait again. Then wait some more.

Be certain. The clan couldn't risk exposure. Better to wait too long and clean up a mess left behind by someone who needed training than to announce too soon and have to kill those who weren't part of the clan.

Li Li liked watching. She was good at it, a natural, according to her teachers.

She knew that Papa would be proud of her for learning how to blend in, for using her magic to make herself invisible. He'd said more than once that standing out caused problems.

If only she'd had more ability when she'd been younger. Possibly she could have saved her family.

Or possibly not. Han Zhe, before he'd died, had told her that her fate was as present and as changing as the spring cherry blossoms.

Li Li wasn't sure what he'd meant, if her fate was set in stone or mutable.

Such thoughts generally chased around inside her head like geese chasing after grain. When she grew tired of such games, she'd usually go hunting.

She was good at hunting, seeking those of the clans who were born outside the known families, or whose families had been lost during the revolution. She found the threads of scent easily, tracing each thin string through the city, past the old compounds that had been turned into communes, then reverted back. Past the gardens that had been dismantled until beauty became important again. Through the slums and the shoddy construction, to the beautiful neighborhoods that remained miraculously intact.

Waiting was more difficult. The longest wait Li Li had had was also the one that made her the most proud: She'd waited until she was eighteen before she went to find those who had hurt her family.

A lot of them had also died during the revolution.

She'd taken care of the rest, as she'd promised. And she burned incense for her parents at each *qingming* festival even when it was forbidden to do so.

Though Li Li would never seek out her sisters or her brother, she was quite pleased to know that if she ever did meet them, she'd be able to tell them that their parents had been avenged.

It never surprised Li Li that the women with the most power in the crocodile clan were also the richest. Despite what Mao had said he'd bring, the world would never honor the poor or the poorly connected, no matter how virtuous they might seem.

As a watcher, Li Li had many relationships with people outside the clan: shopkeepers, cooks, gardeners, even security guards. She had eyes and ears throughout Shanghai. The clan, of course, wouldn't consider those connections important, so Li Li stood outside the primary power structure.

That was fine with Li Li. She spent her time waiting and watching the people in power, too, always accurately predicting the shifts in power and alliances, keeping herself safe.

The first time Li Li acted without waiting, and waiting, and waiting, occurred during the spring of 2005.

Pollution hazed the brilliant blue sky. Li Li wore a mask to filter the air. It made tracking scents more difficult. However, without it, her nose was completely blocked.

She maintained the appearance of a peasant woman come to the big city. Her face was broad and plain, made plainer through a simple illusion charm she always wore as a necklace. She had a sprinkling of freckles across her tiny nose despite her straw hat, and also wore gloves to keep her hands beautiful. She cut her black hair short and deliberately didn't take care of it, so it stuck out like straw around her head.

Li Li rode her solid black bicycle through the streets that morning, with the waves of other workers. She rang her bell frequently, not just to warn the other riders around her, but because she liked its tinkling tune.

She was tracking a teenager, this time. Normally, the soul of the clan made itself known when a child was eight or ten. There were a few times, though, when either the clan soul didn't manifest until much later, or when the youngster was able to hide their soul sufficiently, so that none suspected.

Li Li knew that because of the stifling culture of conformity imposed by Mao and his extremists, the wild ones of the crocodile clan who'd been born outside of the normal families had become experts at hiding.

This was a young man, hustling to make a living,

working harder than any of his compatriots. He worked as a salvager, going out to the huge dumps at the edge of the city, searching for precious metals. He seemed to be able to smell them, which was one of the clues that Li Li had that he wasn't normal.

Li Li admired the boy and took more of a personal interest in him than she had in the others. There was something special about him. He was always laughing with his friends, putting them at ease. She'd seen him help an old woman out at the market just because it was the right thing to do, not for money.

He had a good soul, which was becoming rarer these days.

However, was he part of the crocodile clan? Li Li hadn't sensed his crocodile soul circling around. He seemed to spark, instead.

Was he part of the raven or hound clan? She knew their watchers. They didn't live in the city, but only visited now and again. So few members of the other clans were born in China.

Or was he something else? Merely a magician, a human with some magical powers?

Li Li debated contacting one of the other watchers but decided against it in the end. She needed to wait, as always. Wait until she was certain.

That morning, even outside the city the pollution continued, like tendrils of seaweed clinging to the land. Eventually, though, the acrid smell of the air gave way to the overwhelming scent of the dump. There were too many scents to track: the moldy rice that a restaurant had thrown out, the rotten lemon and orange peels from one of the high-end bars, the chicken blood from the butcher's, the plastic smell of the modern Styrofoam packing materials that businesses had illegally dumped here.

The garbage was piled as high as a house in places. In others, it formed small, rolling hills. Twisting paths had been formed between the heaps, with dangerously slick trails to the tops of the taller hills.

The boy had arrived much earlier, probably with the first light. His bike leaned against a pipe that stuck out of a concrete plug, locked tightly.

Li Li nodded in approval at his caution. There were never many scavengers, at least not now. There would be by the end of the year if the predictions of the crocodile clan came true and the economy was headed into yet another economic crisis. But better to keep his transportation safe, the one way for him to get back into the city.

As Li Li pedaled around the first bend of the towering mound of garbage, she stopped abruptly.

What was a car doing there? And an expensive German car at that? The tariffs that someone would have to pay to import it would be astronomical. Never mind the cost of gas.

They must be very rich, not just in cash, but connections.

The paths through the garbage weren't wide enough for a car. Li Li looked carefully at the edges of heaps just behind her. A dull magic tinged the opening, fading fast.

They must have created that opening with magic. Magicians, then? No one from any of the clans would have been so bold or called that much attention to themselves.

No one stayed with the car. Li Li didn't try the door, but she assumed it was firmly locked and that the car itself might possibly be armed. Definitely it would be magically booby-trapped.

She copied down the license plate number, intending to have someone from the clan look it up later.

What were such people doing out here?

Li Li hid her bike, out of sight of both the boy's bike and the car, then sprang up lightly to the top of the nearest garbage mound. The ground squished unpleasantly under her feet, the soft paper and food stuff rotting. However, it was much easier to travel, leaping from one mound to the next. Plus, she'd have a much better view of everything.

The stench was overwhelming. She'd have to wash all her clothes in lemon, as well as use magic to get rid of the smell. Birds circled overhead, their shit adding to the foulness of the surface. The sky was still hazy, though wide open above her.

The mound under her feet was warm, the garbage moldering and producing methane gas.

Maybe someday, someone would start mining it. She'd read about such things being done in America. How they drew the methane from the garbage.

But she couldn't think about that now. Instead, Li Li lifted her head and focused on the boy. Where was he?

It wasn't difficult to track the boy through all the other scents that morning.

He stank of fear.

Li Li hurried along across the tops of the heaps, leaping from one to the next, until she was closer, then she dropped down to the ground and moved more cautiously through the piles of garbage.

The mounds gave way to a roughly circular opening around an abrupt corner.

The boy stood in the center of it, surrounded by a group of well-dressed businessmen. Their clothes screamed riches and power. They were all Chinese, but they wore western fashions.

They were doing…something to the boy. Li Li wasn't certain what. Magic of a type, but she'd never encountered dark magic like this before, as stinky and oily as the ground she stood on. The boy jerked from side to side, as if being bitten by large insects. But he didn't run. He couldn't get away—one of the magicians held him in one place with their magic.

Li Li found it difficult to watch. She'd liked this boy. She couldn't stop the attack, however. That wasn't her place. She was a watcher. The boy might or might not have been of her clan, or any of the clans for that matter.

She'd seen too many die unfairly to react. She'd learned at a young age that she couldn't avenge the world, much to her regret.

She still marked each of the magicians, memorizing their scents, in case she had to track them at some point.

The magicians seemed to be draining the boy. Li Li watched the spark fade from his eyes. When they'd finished, the boy's eyes were empty. No intelligence remained. No drive.

Certainly no magic. If the boy had been from one of the clans, his clan soul had just been stolen from him.

Which was a frightening thought. How could the magicians do that? Were they a threat to her and her clan?

From the way the boy swayed, Li Li doubted he had enough strength or will to return to his home. He might survive a few weeks. But there wasn't enough *there* anymore for him to live.

He'd die soon, probably by blundering into traffic.

If the magicians had left more of his soul, would the boy have turned to begging and drugs instead? Trying to gain back what he'd lost?

The magicians turned as one to go.

Li Li shrank back against the hill of garbage behind her, *fading* as she did so, confident in her ability to hide herself.

One of the men still stopped a few feet from her. His face was flushed and fat, as if he'd just had a rich meal. He didn't look directly at her, but addressed the open air. "We know you're there. You're lucky we've already fed."

Li Li didn't move, didn't react. She wasn't about to give herself away.

And they might be surprised at how strong she was. If they attacked her, they wouldn't get away without damage as well.

However, warning delivered, the group moved on.

The boy stood where he was, listing to one side. His eyes were clouded over, as if he'd developed cataracts.

Li Li turned to go, then turned back.

Though the boy possibly hadn't been of her clan, he didn't deserve this fate.

She was a watcher. She didn't get involved.

It wasn't up to her to decide. She should wait and see what happened to him. How he survived. How long he managed to live with his very soul eaten.

The boy drooled, long sticky strings hanging from his mouth to his chest.

Li Li's disgust propelled her forward.

The magicians had stolen too much of the boy's wits. He might not even make it back to the city in this state.

It was too cruel, even for her, to leave him like this.

Li Li looked all around her. Were there any others nearby? Other salvagers?

They'd all stayed away, or were working the other side of the dump that morning.

Four great running steps brought Li Li beside the boy. He didn't resist when she grabbed him, didn't make a sound when she kicked his leg hard enough to crack bone, then snapped his neck.

The illicit thrill of *acting* surged through her. She'd

never done anything like this before during her long life. She's always watched and waited. Never acted. Not like this.

Li Li left the boy there at the foot of the garbage heap. The birds were already circling. His body might be found. It might not be. He didn't have a family to mourn him, or friends who would avenge him.

Just her, the silent witness.

It wasn't fair.

But Li Li had learned far too long ago that life was never fair.

YVETTE

S pring came, and Yvette prepared to walk her borders. The night was crisp and cool. There hadn't been as much snow that winter; however, it hadn't ever gotten really warm that spring yet, either. She wore comfortable, durable jeans now, custom-tailored to fit her long legs and slender waist. Though she still had work clogs, she wore boots that night, along with a heavy wool jacket. She'd tried the new synthetic fabrics, the ones that would keep out the winds and the rain, but they'd been too constraining. They hadn't smelled right either.

Yvette walked from the front of her old cottage, across the yard and through the corridor of pines to the front of her property. No numbers hung on either side of the lane to mark her address. No postal box stood there either. She did have "No Trespassing" signs posted on the back of her property, and near the stream, though there weren't many hikers brave enough (or stupid enough) to try to hack their way through the raspberry brambles and nettles.

Glass teardrops still hung from the trees, strung up on tough fishing line that withstood the weather better than other materials Yvette had tried. She regularly strengthened the distraction spells they carried, which was enough to make most turn away from her property.

She discovered as she examined her front defenses that the mirror she'd hung there so long ago, that her friend from Paris had sent her, the one supposedly to keep out demons, had developed a crack in the wood frame.

Her winds had never told her of demons, not after even a century. Yes, there were some strange creatures in the world, magicians who practiced foreign magic. But demons were merely fairytales.

Still, she would probably replace it. She'd had it there for too long to feel comfortable without it. She'd have to remember to send her winds looking to find one, later. Though she wasn't sure where she'd direct them to start their search.

As a last resort, she could always check the internet. She hated the necessity of the huge dish she'd stashed away in the meadow to the north of the house. While her winds brought her news and more, such as the smell of the rioters in Iran, or the noise of the bankers protesting in Greece, she couldn't communicate with anyone via her winds. The children who played at being magicians all used chat rooms, now, instead of what they termed, "snail mail." None of them had real power, or at least not the ones Yvette had "met."

The stones at Yvette's feet held her name, written in a cursive that was no longer popular. Just the green spikes of daffodils had pushed above the leaves and mulch: It hadn't gotten warm enough for anything to bloom. They knew her and waved in her winds. Fewer small animals rustled in their nests as she passed, though every generation acknowledged her and her right to the land.

When Yvette finished circumnavigating her property

she felt very satisfied, as usual. Her home was protected, safe. None could bother her.

Yvette had set up a trust for stewardship of the land after she'd passed. It would never be developed, or even made public, but would be a private haven for all of Mama's birds as well as her own roses.

It would be even more centuries before her cottage would fall to ruin. It had been built when they understood such things, the exterior walls nearly a meter thick. The roof would fail first, the clay tiles that she'd replaced twice already falling apart due to the constant attacks by the weather.

Her magic wouldn't persist past her death. Her border protections would fall with her last breath. And she would never foster an heir. A few of the items she'd enchanted would persist, but that would be all that remained of her.

No, she would die here, alone. If she felt her death coming, she would try to die outside in the garden, as it would be a while before anyone discovered her, possibly months.

Yvette quite liked the idea of her body going back to the earth, to feed the soil and the small creatures. Though the lynx were now protected, not many remained in the mountains, and she hadn't seen a bear in at least a decade, though she knew a few were still around. None of the bigger creatures would find her and despoil her body.

Or maybe it would be the shadows who would take her. They'd grown much stronger lately, testing her borders regularly.

Eventually, the shadows would move past the clans, taking over more and more humans, intent on destroying the world, sucking all the life out of it. She would be dead by then, but it would still be a shame. There wasn't anything she could do about it, though. She knew of nothing to destroy them, though she'd searched long and hard when she'd been younger.

Less than a week later, Yvette woke to a day that felt clearer than any before it. There was a quality to the air, cleaner, though her mountain air wasn't polluted.

She sat up in her old feather bed. Mama's quilts had fallen apart with age and use and Yvette had replaced them with her own, sewn under the moonlight with golden thread so they'd keep her both safe and warm, holding in only the good dreams.

What had happened? Something was different.

Nothing had changed in her room, not for decades. The carved mahogany highboy still presided over the room from just beyond the foot of the bed, holding her jeans and T-shirts and sweaters. Her upholstered reading chair stood in the corner, the red and gold flowers that made up the fabric badly faded. She'd have to replace it soon.

The thick walls formed their own window seat that Yvette had covered with brightly colored pillows. The glass was new, double-paned, custom made, designed to keep the winds and elements out. But Yvette didn't see anything in her yard that told her why everything felt different.

Without changing out of her sleeping sweats and T-shirt, Yvette stepped out of her back door and into her protected garden. The roses hadn't started blooming yet— it was far too early. Snow still lay gathered in the corners, in the shadows where the spring sunshine couldn't reach. The wilted, brown remains of Yvette's herb garden filled the raised beds. A few crocus lined the path, eager to welcome the spring sunshine.

An *effet de serre* took up the whole corner of the yard. All its glass windows were fogged over as usual, making it difficult for Yvette to see the hothouse plants thriving inside. She would have to check it later, make sure the lemons and other citrus were still producing.

Before Yvette could take another step into her yard, the winds rushed up to tell her of the great battle that had taken place the night before, over in America.

The shadows had been defeated. *Eliminated*. Forced from the earth. Not just in America, but from all over the world.

Yvette blinked, surprised. How had this happened? Why? She *had* to know.

She cast her winds to the far side of the world to find out everything they could while she went back inside and made a simple breakfast of good bread, butter, cheese, fruit, and her favorite dark coffee.

Mama had told her once that the shadows hadn't been Yvette's concern. She'd been right.

Then Yvette carried it all outside, settling herself in a comfortable lounging chair in the middle of the focus rug Mama had made for her so long ago, and let the winds commence to tell her all about the young hound prince who'd been hidden for so many years, of the great warriors from all the clans that he'd gathered together, how they'd fought the shadows and defeated them.

Yvette sipped her coffee and marveled at the news.

Was this why she'd been kept alive for so long? So that she could witness this great act?

She snorted at herself. She wasn't that important. If she'd been at the battle, that would have been one thing. She was just learning about the events after they'd occurred.

She imagined that the private chat rooms for the magicians were ablaze, the children there talking of nothing but this feat.

Could she lower her borders? No, there were still too

many tourists who might stumble onto her property. But her borders didn't have to be as strong as they'd once been. That may prove useful, if she ever started showing her age and her magic started fading.

What would it mean to the clans? How strong could they grow, now, that they were no longer so constrained? What kind of power would they acquire? Would they grow too much, too big, and be forced to come out of the shadows themselves? Reveal themselves to the humans?

No, they wouldn't do that. They'd been in existence for millennia, always in hiding.

Still, in this new age of openness, one never knew.

Yvette had more questions than answers, and delicious events to watch unfold. This was so much better than any play or even TV show with its false drama.

She spent the next few days in her garden, sitting and listening to the winds and all the changes, primarily being made in the hound and the tiger courts. That the ravens knew of the other clans made her happy—maybe she could meet one of them, now. The vipers were still few, hiding in their temples, but they did celebrate the ending of the shadows. The boars never needed an excuse to party, and had been kicking up their heels in quite a few towns. The crocodiles hadn't been infected, so they didn't bother to notice.

It was probably one of the most important events in recent history, Yvette knew.

And while she'd learned as many details about it as she possibly could, most of the human race would never know about it, which made it doubly delicious.

VIRMAL

"Aunt Panita isn't getting better," Virmal told his sister Harita grimly as he walked into her room.

It was a very plain room, with none of the cushions, pillows, or soft silk drapes that abounded in the rooms of those from the tiger clan. Instead, all the surfaces were unadorned: The single bed had just a simple brown cover on it, the wide window seat beyond it was merely wood, even the chair that Harita sat on was metal without a cushion.

The walls were a light-colored stone, secure against most attacks, physical or magical. Even the pretty diamond-paned leaded window glass was bullet-proof and secure. Small balls of cotton hung from the corners of the ceiling, unnoticeable, really, the magic in them making the room soundproof as well as immune to casual scrying spells.

Harita was the most colorful thing in the entire room, dressed in a bright red and gold sari. Her makeup was impeccable, her almond eyes framed by long, perfectly curled lashes, her wide lips painted with the exact matching shade of red, with a gold *bindi* in the shape of a tiny flame centered on her forehead. She wore her long black hair pulled back in a ponytail, caught up in a gold filigreed holder that held a subtle charm of protection.

Of course, Virmal would never tell Harita how pretty she looked. She was his fraternal twin sister, after all.

And human.

He was the one with the tiger soul, one of the rare males of the clan. He tried to look as good as his sister did, in his royal blue silk tunic and pants with the gold trim, his short black hair and intense dark eyes peering out from under bushy eyebrows, his skin a lovely brown and clear, but he knew that she'd always outshine him.

Harita stayed seated at her desk, not looking up from the ancient book she was intently studying. "Of course she isn't getting better," she said. "Aunt Panita is an attention whore."

Virmal frowned. It wasn't that he disagreed—but one generally didn't state such things out loud.

Aunt Panita and all the powerful women who made up the tiger court in India had all fallen "ill" when the shadows had been defeated. They felt powerless now, used to the strength the corrupted shadows had brought them.

Many had recovered, relearning the "old" ways to do magic, bitterly complaining all the while about no longer being as strong as they'd once had been.

Only a few believed Harita and Virmal's stories about the shadows and why it had been necessary to banish them.

"No, it's something else," Virmal insisted. It was as though every time Aunt Panita got stronger and built up her magical reserves, something would siphon off that strength, drain it away.

When he received no reply from Harita, Virmal finally asked, "What *are* you reading?"

Now Harita looked up. "An old account of demons," she said eagerly. "And how they would use spells to drain the strength of those who were vulnerable."

Virmal blinked. "So you don't think Aunt Panita is looking for attention," he said, trying to clarify.

Harita shrugged. "She might not *just* be looking for attention. There might be something more to her complaints."

"But her room is magically protected. And in the center of this complex," Virmal said, gesturing widely to include the entire court of the tiger clan. "How could anyone get to her?"

India had rarely been at peace and the tiger court buildings reflected that, with tall crenulated walls protecting the complex, the buildings all made from pale yellow stone and well-guarded with magic, as well as secret tunnels both between the buildings and in and out of the complex, in case the complex went under siege. Again.

"That's what I'm trying to figure out," Harita replied. "There's supposedly a special type of mirror that will turn the demons away."

"There's no such thing as demons," Virmal pointed out. And the tiger clan would know. Their watchers were always on the lookout for magicians and magical beings, as well as any wild ones. There were many accounts of strange occurrences, miracles and blessings from the gods that couldn't easily be explained away with magic.

Harita raised one perfectly-shaped eyebrow. "There's no such thing as alien shadows either. You know, the ones who can corrupt a tiger soul."

Virmal opened his mouth to reply, then closed it again.

What could he say? She was right. The shadows had been real.

Maybe there were such things as demons.

"What does demon-turning mirror look like? What kind of spells does it require? Where can we get one? Or a dozen or more?" Virmal finally asked. It wasn't that he believed Harita necessarily, but he was willing to try anything at this point.

They had to do something. Or Aunt Panita as well as some of the other older aunts would die.

"We need to visit a local magician," Harita told him, a sly smile tugging at her lips. "One of the *dhayanai.*"

Virmal sighed and glared at his sister, but after a moment, nodded. He didn't understand Harita's fascination with the local magicians. It wasn't as if she had any magic herself.

The *dhayana* had a bad reputation for attacking the tiger clan. There had been more than one report where a *dhayana* had stolen the tiger soul from a warrior. Of course they died, badly, afterward. However, it wasn't safe to just blithely go calling on a magician.

Virmal also knew that now that Harita had finally found an excuse to go and see one, nothing would stop her.

He would just have to go along and protect her.

Woe to the magician who tried anything with his sister. She might not be a tiger warrior, but she was still family.

Hurt one. Hurt all.

FU RAN

F u Ran felt a spring creep into her walk as she
pushed open the doors of the ER. Though she
denied it to her father when she chose this path instead of
the safe, boring plastic surgery path he'd wanted her to
take, she would admit to herself that she was an
adrenaline junky.

And working in an emergency room in a hospital in
downtown Oakland fit her much better than a boring office
ever would.

There would be shootings for her to deal with.
Stabbings. Overdoses. Old people who should have seen a
doctor decades ago and now had gangrene. Gout.
Dementia. And just plain weirdness.

Sure, there had been TV shows about hospitals and the
ER. They weren't anything like the truth. It was much
more chaotic, much more disorganized, much more
painful, interspersed with long bouts of not much to do.

Fu Ran loved it.

What would she find today?

The head nurse, Patrick New Bird, tall and brown and

broad, whom people generally mistook for a security guard, caught her by her elbow as she walked past.

"Phone call waiting for you," he told her gruffly. He wore his long hair pulled back in a braid and often threatened to put feathers in it to commemorate every death, but the amount would have ended up trailing down his back and across the floor.

Another spike of adrenaline rushed through Fu Ran. "Who is it? The CDC? The FBI?"

"They're speaking Chinese," he told her. He gave her a disapproving glare.

"*Shenme*?" Fu Ran replied, teasing.

Patrick continued to frown down at her for another moment before he broke into a great, friendly grin. He gave her a lot of grief about not being a real American, even though she was ABC—American Born Chinese. It was her parents who had immigrated.

All of Patrick New Bird's ancestors had been born in the Americas, however.

Fu Ran went into the tiny office that she shared with three other doctors. They generally worked different shifts. Today, Tom was still sitting at the desk. He looked as though he'd been through hell. Maybe he had been.

"Rough night?" Fu Ran asked.

Tom merely nodded. Though his cheeks were round and fat, that morning they stood out more, making his blue eyes seem sunken. His white skin was even more pasty than usual. He kept his head shaved to hide the male pattern baldness that had set in when he'd been in his twenties. Otherwise, his head would have been fringed with auburn curls.

"They're waiting for you on line three," he said as he pushed himself out of his chair. "I'll be getting some coffee if you need me."

Fu Ran opened her mouth then closed it again, pushing her lips into a firm smile. "Thank you," she said. As opposed to saying *why the hell would I need you?*

Then again, he'd always thought himself much more important than her. She let him believe that occasionally, until his ego expanded to the point that no one else could be in the same room. Then Fu Ran would take him down a peg.

Again.

She'd never gone out to dinner with him, and generally turned him down when he asked her out for coffee as well. She kept it strictly professional between them.

She wouldn't even touch him with Patrick's dick.

"Hello?" Fu Ran said as she picked up the phone.

A string of Chinese came flowing out. It took Fu Ran a moment to switch gears, to process what they were saying.

Aunt Leeda was sick and needed her help. She was acting confused.

Fu Ran sat back, pushing against the stiff plastic of the chair. Aunt Leeda had been her mentor in the crocodile clan. Had introduced her to the *shizu*. Shouldn't the clan be taking care of her? The other aunts and sisters? People who were already *in* China?

"You must come now," the voice insisted.

"Who is this?" Fu Ran asked.

"An old friend. Come quickly. Save your aunt."

Then the line went dead.

How could Fu Ran just drop everything and fly back to China? What was really going on with *Tie-tie Li Da*? Who else could she call and ask? And what had the caller meant when she'd said Aunt Leeda was acting confused?

Fu Ran had work to do. A shift to pull. Possibly a long shift, if the day continued the way the night had been. She didn't have time to chase this down.

And she wasn't about to ask Tom to pull a double. He was already exhausted and likely to make stupid mistakes, well, more stupid mistakes.

Besides, she *definitely* didn't want him feeling as though she owed him a favor.

Fu Ran couldn't put in a call to China, not on the hospital phone. And why had they called there and not on her cell phone?

She had more questions than answers, and no time to chase down the answers.

She still found herself smiling. It meant one more thing to juggle that day. One more thread to keep track of. One more mystery to solve. One more thing to add a rush to her day.

She couldn't wait to get started.

YVETTE

Yvette lay drowsing on a comfortable, portable hammock in her front yard. The night was soft and full of crickets and buzzing flies. The frogs in the nearby stream added their bass to the night's song. A sliver of moon peered down on her, the stars peeking through the wispy, high clouds.

She should probably go inside and go to bed, but it was so pleasant there, lying and dreaming in the late summer night.

The pines sighed on the wind, mourning their cousins on the far side of the mountain being cut down.

Should she try to buy the entire mountain, so she could protect all of it? She had the money. She might even have enough money to buy the influence she'd need.

But it was too public a gesture. People would learn her name. Better to stay hidden and just mourn with the trees.

A presence walked up the now paved road winding up the mountain, stopping at the entrance of her lane.

It didn't move on.

Yvette wondered why it stayed there. Was it one of the

clans? She hadn't seen anyone since the shadows had been defeated that spring. Normally, if it was someone from the clans, they would just stride up the lane, ignoring her border and her spells.

The presence made a hesitant step across the border. It paused, as if it had been expected to be stopped. Then it took another step. And a third.

Yvette sat straight up. Someone *was* coming to see her. Someone…different.

She called her winds to her and hopped out of her hammock. The pines bristled as well, their usually droopy needles suddenly sharp and spiked, ready to protect Yvette if she needed their help.

Yvette waited in her yard, a single low flame in her hands, lighting the area so she could see better.

A girl, no, a woman, stepped out from under the trees, coming slowly up the lane. A young Indian woman, her long hair pulled back and caught in a silver brooch.

Yvette blinked and cast her light higher, floating it above her head.

It *was* Tiger Lily, the girl who had visited her back in the late Sixties.

She was no longer infected by shadows.

"*Bonsoir*," Yvette said, smiling at the woman.

As Tiger Lily drew closer, Yvette kept her smile, but made her light considerably brighter.

The woman looked old—much older than she probably was. Having the shadows ripped from her soul had aged her. Dark circles accented under her haunted brown eyes. Her fair brown skin was splotchy, as if she had a fever, and held more wrinkles than a young woman should.

Tiger Lily wore skin tight jeans now, instead of bellbottoms, and looked very fashionable. Her shirt was still a pale blue, though her coat was black leather, hanging down to her knees.

Yvette felt distinctly underdressed in her leggings and baggy sweatshirt. Then again, she hadn't been expecting visitors.

Tiger Lily silently crossed the yard, coming to stand close to Yvette. She was much shorter—most women were —barely coming up to Yvette's chest. Her eyes flared golden in the dark, burning with tiger brilliance.

"I can cross your border, now," Tiger Lily said with wonder. "Why?"

"Do you not know?" Yvette replied, curious. What did the tiger clan think had happened to them?

"A great illness has struck us, you know," Tiger Lily replied.

Yvette couldn't contain her smile. The girl remembered. Yes, Yvette was old, older now. She still knew things.

"Our magic is…weaker," Tiger Lily declared.

Yvette raised her eyebrows in a silent question. She was surprised anyone from the tiger clan would admit to any weakness.

"We still have our claws and teeth," Tiger Lily growled.

"*Mais oui*," Yvette said. The tiger clan were also great fighters. Though none of the clans were known for their patience when it came to settling an argument. They were all far too ready to grow claws and fangs and fight instead of sitting down with a bottle of good wine and talking things through.

"What happened to us?" Tiger Lily asked plainly.

"What do your elders say?" Yvette asked. She would tell Tiger Lily—she generally answered any question the clan posed. But she was still curious.

"We are sick," Tiger Lily said. "Infected with a plague. Though there are others…"

"Yes?" Yvette probed.

"Two. Come from a great battle, supposedly. Virmal, and his sister, Harita. They claim we had been infected before and are now clean. But how can that be?" Tiger Lily was obviously frustrated. "We are weaker now. Not stronger."

Yvette nodded. "Virmal and Harita speak the truth," she said softly. "You were infected by the shadows. They did increase your power. They also changed you. Made you cruel. Stripped you of your humanity. Siphoned off the true power of your tiger souls."

"But why?" Tiger Lily asked, sounding lost. "Who were the shadows? Why did they abide with us for so long?"

"That's a long story," Yvette told her. "For another time."

"But—"

"*Non*," Yvette said firmly. "Tonight, you rest. Recover from your long journey. Tomorrow we will talk."

The woman nodded and swayed suddenly, as if the will that had driven her to seek out Yvette suddenly evaporated, leaving her exhausted.

"You can sleep by my fire, Tiger Lily," Yvette said as she turned to go.

"That is not my name," Tiger Lily said, protesting. "My name is Indukala Khushi Deshmukh."

She said the name proudly, as if Yvette should recognize it.

"*Non*," Yvette said, disagreeing just as strongly. "You are Tiger Lily. And will remain so until you have earned your name with me."

The woman just stood there, blinking, surprised.

Had no one defied this woman as she was growing up? Was she so used to getting everything she wanted? Yvette was going to have to remember to tell her no on a regular basis.

"Come," Yvette said firmly. "I will make a nice nest for you by the fire."

She could see Tiger Lily wanted to protest again. She probably thought she deserved the finest linens. Or perhaps she expected Yvette to give up her own bed.

Yvette nearly snorted at the thought. This woman-child was just going to have to get used to things being different.

She also knew that the woman's inner tiger would prefer a nest of blankets beside the fire.

That was something else the shadows had tried to do—to change the essential nature of the clans' tiger soul.

Tiger Lily followed Yvette into her cabin and settled in quickly, too tired to put up much more of a fight. Yvette spread out her magical focus rug, the one Mama had made so long ago, that Yvette had repaired pieces of over the years, and let Tiger Lily sleep in the middle of that. It would help heal her magical soul as well.

After her guest had collapsed into a deep sleep, the firelight giving her skin a healthier glow, Yvette stayed up for a while, planning. She would have to make the most nutritious soups for her guest, fill her with sunshine as well as good meat.

She couldn't cure this woman—that would take years. But she might be able to teach her to listen, not to the winds but to herself, her tiger soul.

Had that been why Tiger Lily had sought her out, all those years before? Had she realized that she was missing something? That her tiger soul hadn't been complete because it had been so filled with shadows?

Was this girl why Yvette had stayed alive so long? She

couldn't contain her snort of derision, making her guest stir briefly before sliding back down into deeper sleep.

No, Merlin syndrome was just that—named for a fictional character with a fictional cause. Yvette was no hero. She'd spent her life up here, in what could be called her ivory tower. She'd likely die there, too, possibly sooner rather than later.

She'd die not knowing everything, which would be her only regret. And though she hadn't done that much with her life, she'd still die satisfied.

ARIEL

Ariel woke from her sleep with a start, Gret growling. There was someone standing just outside her tent.

"Ms. Ariel?" came a hesitant call.

"Yes, Gonzales?" Ariel called back. It was, what, 2 A.M.? What the hell did the foreman of the crew of migrant workers want? Was there a fire in the vineyard?

"There's a phone call for you. At the main house," he said.

Ariel reached into the tent pocket just over her head. *Shit.* She'd forgotten to charge her cell phone. Again.

"Be right there," she said.

She hadn't given anyone the number of the vineyard she was working at—she'd been traveling for a while. She'd stop and work now and again, pick grapes or make wine or wash dishes, then travel some more.

Only someone from the boar clan could have tracked her down.

And a call like this meant trouble.

Ariel quickly slipped her leather jacket on over her T-shirt. Not so much for warmth, but so that poor Gonzales wouldn't sprain something looking at her tits. Her flip-flops were just outside the door to her tent. She slid her feet into them, then easily stood up.

"This way," Gonzales said, politely holding the kerosene lantern up higher so she could see the path.

She didn't need the lantern—it ruined her night vision, actually. But she let him think he was helping her, walking behind him, when all she wanted to do was race up to the main house as fast as she could.

The door to the main house stood open, the pool of light from the front porch spilling out in a cool circle.

Ariel had been traveling for some time now, following the migrant workers, and electricity kind of freaked her out. Her eyes weren't used to the light at all. It seemed to buzz and stab at her, unlike the flickering light of candles or an open fire pit.

The tasting room was off to the left of the wide, open entranceway. Two staircases circled up to the first floor, broad and wide. People got married up at the vineyard and had their pictures taken there, pretty white flowers and netting draped along the deep red, cherry wood and brass bannister. A chandelier hung over the center of the space, not as fancy as the ones back in Louisiana, but nice enough for Washington state.

An old-fashioned telephone sat to the right of the entrance, with a separate handle connected to a phone body with a long, curling cord. At least it wasn't so old it had a dial instead of push buttons.

"Hello?" Ariel said into the phone. "This is Ariel."

"Dearie, this is your Aunt Mabel," came the creaking voice from the other side of the line.

Chills ran down Ariel's back, starting at her neck and going all the way down to her butt.

Aunt Mabel did *not* sound well at all. In fact, if she

hadn't told Ariel her name, Ariel would never have guessed it was her aunt.

"What's up?" Ariel asked casually.

"It's your Aunt Belle. She's sick," Aunt Mabel said. "She's even taken to her bed."

Ariel blinked in surprise. That meant Aunt Belle was *really* sick. The end of summer was when all the ladies came calling, as many of the heads of the boar clan families gathered together at the plantation and tried to outdo each other with their jams, their wines, and their good cooking.

Just because the boar clan weren't as organized or as formal as the damned hound court didn't mean they didn't keep order among themselves. It was a genteel sort of way to figure out the pecking order. Not the fight to the death way that of course the stupid ravens had.

Ariel didn't think much of the boar "court." Though she'd told Mei Ling that she wasn't an outcast from the boar clan, she'd never been part of the inner circle, either. Not exactly. Despite being Aunt Mabel's protégée. She'd never really done genteel, even less so than her aunt.

Had Aunt Mabel known that Ariel would battle the shadows someday? Was that why she'd raised her as a warrior?

Not that the boar clan were visionaries. They left that to the vipers, still clinging to their smoky temples in South America.

"Do you need me there?" Ariel asked. She wasn't exactly sure why Aunt Mabel was calling her. It wasn't as if Ariel was in line for the throne or something.

"Please," Aunt Mabel said, her tone whispery.

Something was really wrong. Ariel didn't like it. Gret didn't either.

But what choice did she have? She'd been enjoying

herself out in eastern Washington, working in a vineyard there. Though the owner hadn't trusted her at the start—what the hell did a black woman from Mississippi know about raising grapes?—he'd come to rely on her nose by the end of the season. She knew which plants needed more water, more help, could always rout out any sickness in the vines.

Her people were good with the earth and all the plants that grew there.

But they'd always been especially good with wine.

"I'll be there in a few days," Ariel promised.

"That's good, honey. See you then." Aunt Mabel hung up without saying goodbye, or even asking about how Ariel was doing.

Had that even been Aunt Mabel? Ariel didn't know.

There was nothing for it, though. Ariel would pack up and hit the road with the first light, hightailing it back across the country on her hog of a bike. Sure, she could fly, but this kind of bad news would be waiting for her no matter when she got home.

VIRMAL

Virmal had never been to this part of New Delhi before. It wasn't actually New Delhi at all, but Old Delhi. It was little better than a slum. The streets were still dirt and too narrow for a car. Shacks crowded up on either side with sagging walls and doors assembled out of scrap wood and leftover pieces of insulation. A single thick cable came into the street. From it hung dozens of illegal wires, people tapping into the system to get cable and power. Faded food wrappers and torn plastic bags cluttered the edges of the lane, piled up against the foot of the buildings.

The driver of the motorcycle cab Virmal and Harita rode in shook his head, obviously disapproving. He didn't say anything, however. He was well paid by the clan to do his job and drive members of the clan where they needed to go.

He'd also been trained in many martial arts and would protect the motorcycle cab and its passengers better than a mere security guard.

"Are you sure about this?" Virmal asked Harita as they finally slowed to a stop. They'd changed out of their court clothes into much plainer outfits, he in a light brown tunic and pants, she in a darker orange sari with no jewelry and a gauzy gray scarf covering her head.

They still stood out on a street like this, their wealth evident in their clean clothes, their clear skin, their well-fed bodies.

Harita pointed.

They weren't parked across from a door. Instead, a corridor had been built along the edge of the street. The bottom half of the manmade tunnel was built out of mismatched wooden planks, while the top was composed of stretched and faded black cloth. The roof had been formed out of corrugated green plastic, stained and moldy, held down with rocks.

Virmal looked in the direction Harita pointed in. What had caught her attention?

Dusty brown pots holding limp mast trees stood guard on either side of the entrance. There wasn't a door, just a foreboding black opening. Virmal recognized the magic surrounding it, the simple spell the magician used.

Virmal was just about to ask Harita what she was pointing at when he finally saw it.

An eight-sided wooden frame hung from one of the branches of the trees. It was about the size of both of Virmal's palms spread out, painted black, and holding a bulbous convex mirror.

Virmal stared at it, teasing apart the magic. He found a thin thread coming from the mirror itself, used to keep it from cracking.

What power did that mirror have? Was that one of the mirrors Harita had been reading about? What was so important about them?

He didn't know. But he knew that Harita would never stop until she'd unraveled its mysteries.

YVETTE

Someone stirred in Yvette's outer room. She roused from her sleep, the quilts on her bed heavy and warm. The room was dark, even the stars not daring to disturb her.

It's just the girl, her winds whispered to her.

Yvette turned over, prepared to slide back into another sweet dream.

Wait. That wasn't right.

She hadn't invited her winds into her bedroom that night. That was part of why she'd spent so much money for the new windows and frames, so they'd be secure against her winds and she might be able to sleep fully at night, undisturbed.

None of her winds were actually there in her rooms, with her.

Yvette's dream tugged at her. *Come back to the soft green hills.* She resisted, recognizing the magic for what it was: Not identical to her distraction spells, but from the same family.

Yvette's anger suffused her like a sudden flame. What

was Tiger Lily doing? Had she gained Yvette's trust merely to turn on her, possibly rob her like an ordinary thief?

No. It wasn't the girl. This distraction magic was too similar to Yvette's own. It wasn't clan magic. It was some other magician.

Certainly they knew better than to attack her in her own home. Didn't they? Even the irreverent children of today held her in awe, calling her the mage of winds.

Then who was it?

Yvette rose out of bed silently while casting her own illusion so whoever else was in her house would think she still slept. Cautiously, she crept to the door of her bedroom, opening it merely a crack and peering out.

Tiger Lily still lay sleeping in front of the fire.

A group of five others stood around her. They were human. Powerful magicians, all of them.

Were they working in concert against the tiger girl? Why?

Yvette bristled with anger. The girl was under *her* protection, under *her* roof.

How dare they?

Winds came readily to her hand. Without warning, Yvette threw them at the other magicians, attacking.

The strength of her blow should have knocked them over. Or at least forced them apart.

Instead, they withstood her attack, barely noticing it, as the mountain might laugh at her efforts.

As one, they turned slowly to face her.

They were all dressed similarly in American business suits, well made, with ties and white shirts. The two women wore their own version of the power suit, skirts and jackets of the best linen, with silk blouses, gold necklaces and earrings.

One of the men stepped forward, a short man, not fat, but with a round, red face and big, meaty hands, the kind that could easily scoop up a chicken and wring its neck without any effort. A butcher's hands.

"So glad you could join us!" the man said jovially in English.

"Get out of my house," Yvette ordered them.

The man actually seemed amused. Amused! How dare he. Yvette seethed with rage.

"Not until we have what we came for," he told her calmly.

Yvette reached out with her power. It took little effort to gather up the coals from the well-banked fire and throw them at the intruders, aiming for their faces.

That seemed to surprise the man. He hissed, deflecting the coals with a wave of his hand. The rest brushed off the flames as if they were merely drops of water and put out the small fires almost negligently, all the while staring at her.

They shouldn't have been able to do that. The flames should have burned them. This group of magicians were much better protected than Yvette had anticipated.

"That wasn't very nice," the man chided. "You shouldn't do that again."

He reached out one hand, grabbing at the air.

Suddenly, he was inside her mind, rooting around in her head for her knowledge of the fire.

The violation sickened Yvette. The last good glass of wine she'd had just before she'd slept threatened to come back up. She struggled against this damned magician, but she had no defenses against such an attack. No one had ever dared invade her mind.

He still seemed amused as his fingers riffled through

her huge store of knowledge, neatly organized so she could access whatever she needed quickly and easily.

That was now going to work against her. They'd be able to find and take what they needed without too much searching or effort.

The magician plucked out the knowledge of how to throw fire as neatly as removing a file folder.

Yvette had no choice but to give it to him, feeling violated and empty, standing there gasping.

The woman next to the man made a smacking noise, as if she'd just eaten up all the knowledge that Yvette had released.

The others licked their lips, as if they'd just tasted something lovely, like a cat with cream. They were obviously connected to one another.

These weren't normal magicians. Yvette had never met anyone like them. Her winds had never known about them, either.

"Who are you?" Yvette asked, pulling herself together. She couldn't throw her fire again. The knowledge of how to call it from her hearth was missing. It was a tiny piece of all that she knew, though it was as obvious to her as a moth-hole in her favorite quilt.

Yvette still knew how to start a fire. It wasn't the same as using an existing fire. It would be easy enough to call up another flame and set it dancing in her palm. She'd have to figure out a different way to throw it, but given time and her winds, she knew she could.

These magicians didn't realize just how deep her knowledge went. How much she knew, and how she could use it.

"We are the soul eaters," the man said proudly. "The demons from your nightmares."

"You're joking," Yvette said, disgusted. These children

—for they were all barely in their thirties—were all human. There was nothing remotely demonic about them. They weren't clan or other.

"Your mirror kept us from you, all these years," the man said with a shrug. "It broke. We were following her, but were happy enough when she led us to you."

Yvette stood up straighter. Were these the people her friend had warned about, all those decades ago? This group of rogue magicians? Why hadn't she spoken more plainly? Or had she believed their claims of otherworldliness, of demonhood?

They certainly believed it, if a plain mirror like what she'd had out on her lane had held them back.

Shaking her head, Yvette knew better than to blame someone else. This was her own fault. She should have replaced that mirror as soon as she'd seen the wood cracking, earlier that spring. But how could she have known?

What else had her winds not told her? Had they recognized these people as magicians, and not paid any more attention? Or had they been told to move on, this group deliberately hiding from her?

"What do you want?" Yvette asked, biding her time. They would make a mistake. She just had to be patient. Then she would destroy them all.

The man smacked his fat lips together. Really, he was like a butcher. "Knowledge," he said simply. "And power."

Yvette understood the need for knowledge. She'd lived all her life simply wanting to know things. She'd only settle for knowing *everything*.

"So you just take it?" she asked, as coldly as she could. She felt the ghosts of the man's fingers riffling through her brain again, seeking for what she knew.

She couldn't hide her knowledge, any more than she

could hide her great height, though at least that wasn't as noticeable in these modern days.

"It is ours for the taking," the man intoned, as if repeating part of a ritual.

It is ours for the taking. Yvette memorized that bit, filing it away deep inside her so she'd be able to send her winds searching for any who repeated that phrase.

"And what will you do with it?" Yvette asked. She barely did anything with the knowledge she had, but she still felt as though she should ask.

"*All knowledge is food,*" the man intoned.

Another bit of ritual that Yvette hoped to use against them someday.

"So you eat the knowledge, then fart it out?" Yvette said, goading them. She would not show fear to such as these, even if they could destroy her.

"Nothing so inelegant as that," the man said, showing his disappointment in her.

"But do you keep it?" Yvette asked. She thought she knew the answer, but she needed to make sure. "Keep all that knowledge you acquire?"

Not that she would ever kill another magician just to learn what they knew.

Probably.

"The knowledge comes, the knowledge goes," the man said. He suddenly tossed sparks from Yvette's fire up into the air, using the knowledge of the flame that he'd acquired earlier from Yvette.

How long would he keep that knowledge? Hours? Days? Weeks?

It didn't matter. They were fools, shitting in their own nests. They could have learned and kept their great knowledge if they'd taken the time to acquire it on their own.

But these were spoiled children, like many in this newest age, who didn't understand patience.

"I am telling you now to leave," Yvette said, drawing herself up. She wished momentarily that she was wearing her ancient black silks, the gowns she'd worn as a teenager, that she'd always associated with great magic.

"*Non*," the man said. To add insult to injury, he turned his back on Yvette, drawing the group of magicians back around Tiger Lily, still deeply sleeping on the hearth. They were *feeding* on her, on her magic and memories. They would strip her bare, then finish off Yvette. Unless she stopped them.

Yvette didn't try to call all her winds, or to call the wind in general. That knowledge was too important. Instead, she called up a single wind, the southern one that always brought her the sweet smell of grapes in late spring.

Just as quickly as it sighed into the room, the knowledge was stripped from her and the wind was banished.

Yvette drew in another wind, the one from the far alps, that always carried the cold of the glaciers, the sounds of the creaking ice.

Again, once she brought forward this ability, it was taken from her, casually, as one would steal a sweet from a baby. It wasn't the man's fingers in her brain this time, though, but one of the others, the woman on the far right, perhaps.

Yvette couldn't overpower this group. There were too many of them. If there had only been one, possibly she could have overwhelmed the rogue magician with her great, accumulated knowledge.

How was she going to get away? Any of her defensive spells took time to cast, time she didn't have.

She reached deeply, pulling out one of the earliest things she'd learned—calling Mama's bears.

But even before she could roust them from their den, the ability to call them slipped away, like salmon sliding down a stream.

Another appeared inside her head. Suddenly, her memories were being picked apart, the attack savage and ruthless.

Yvette's memories of Paris, the foul stench of the Seine each spring at the start of the previous century…and that smell was suddenly gone.

Without thinking about it, Yvette started fires burning on the backs of all the magicians in the room. The fires didn't go out immediately, and the acrid smell of burning cloth filled the room.

The magicians stopped their feeding on Tiger Lily and turned as one to her. "I took your knowledge of fire from you," the man said, the astonishment apparent on his fat face.

"I am old," Yvette bragged as she slipped in yet another call, again, one of her oldest, calling the tickling winds.

The group didn't seem to notice. Or maybe it was because Yvette hadn't really learned that as a spell—the winds that liked to ruffle her curls had always sought her out, long before she'd even realized her special abilities.

Calling that wind wasn't something she'd learned. It was a natural ability. She didn't know if these stupid magicians could take it from her.

"I have more knowledge than anyone you've met before," Yvette continued. She had to keep their attention on her.

The tickling wind stole into the room. It did what it

always did—went straight for her hair, stirring it, causing chicken flesh to rise across her nape.

It ignored the other magicians. They all wore their hair short, as was the modern style.

The only other person in the room with long hair was Tiger Lily.

Beyond the magicians, Yvette saw the tiger warrior stirring as the wind pushed its fingers across her scalp.

The man nodded. "You've always been considered a great prize."

"Why attack me now? Just because of the broken mirror?" Yvette asked. "Or is it because the shadows are now gone? And there is a hole for monsters like you to fill?"

Tiger Lily started to transform as soon as she opened her eyes. These magicians were overconfident, thinking they could control one of the clan that way. They hadn't pushed her into a deep enough sleep, just a light slumber, like they had done with Yvette.

Yvette cursed these children yet again. How she would have longed to actually watch one of the tiger clan become a warrior. She knew about it, her winds had told her of it frequently.

Not the same as being able to observe it for herself.

The man scowled at her. "The shadows were unnatural. They would have destroyed the world. We won't do that. We just want to control it. Control everyone."

For just a moment, Yvette saw the great golden web that spun out from far beyond this group to the others of their kind. The channels were thin—how much power was being shared? Or knowledge? She didn't know. But it was one more thing she *had* to learn.

Yvette still laughed at the man, knowing that her amusement was worse than a physical blow to these arrogant fools. "*Mon cher*," she said. "You are already destroying the world by not cherishing the knowledge you acquire, but spoiling it."

"Enough," the man said, reaching his hands forward, his fingers eagerly seeking her knowledge again.

"I agree. Enough," Yvette said as Tiger Lily rose to her full height behind them.

VIRMAL

Virmal growled softly, deep in his chest, as he stalked down the corridor toward the magician's door. He didn't like this place, not one bit. He didn't like the smell of rancid pork that formed another barrier to the door, he didn't like how the magic tried to dim what little light filtered through the black cloth stretched over the windows, and he really didn't like that his sister stubbornly walked right behind him.

The corridor had a dirt floor, well packed and dusty. It went on for much longer than it should have, another magical trick. At least it was slightly cooler there, out of the sun, than it had been on the street: New Delhi, or even Old Delhi, in August, was still in the grip of summer.

Finally, they arrived at a six-paneled, wooden door. It had been scavenged from a much more grand building. Intricate carvings outlined each of the panels, diamonds and curlicues. The panels themselves weren't original: They might have at one time held inlaid wood or precious stone, now they were plain, cheap plywood.

Virmal still hesitated before he knocked. Did that wood hold more magic?

Harita silently handed him one end of the scarf covering her head.

Virmal nodded his thanks, wrapping his hand in it before knocking at the door. The cloth wouldn't prevent stronger magic from getting through. However, it would block lighter spells that needed skin contact to work.

"Come in!" The voice from behind the door was high and thin, like a boy's.

Virmal turned to look at Harita. She'd told him that the magician was an older man. She shrugged.

Maybe he was out and this was his son.

Virmal opened the door, his hand still protected by her scarf.

No windows let light into the crowded space. Electric fluorescent lights buzzed and flickered overhead, yet the room still seemed dim. A plain wooden table stood in the center of the small room, rectangular and sturdy, like a table from a lab.

It was the only clear surface in the entire room. Shelves lined the walls, from floor to ceiling, completely covered with things. Virmal couldn't easily categorize what all the shelves held: books, certainly, but there was also an old-fashioned microscope, a collection of antique porcelain doll heads, as well as two jars full of cats-eye marbles, three wind-up phonographs, a box full of older, foldable cell phones with more spilling out, small red clay statues of Vishnu, Ganesh, and other gods, bundles of electric wire, and more.

Virmal was used to the crowded rooms of the tiger clan. But this was too much.

What did this magician do with all these things? Did he use them in his magic? What did he make with them?

Hidden amidst all the clutter was a tall, fleshy man. He was bald—possibly completely hairless, as his chin appeared to be as smooth as a boy's. He wore a dark brown tunic and a touch of magic that helped him blend into the background. The smile he formed with his fat lips looked hungry.

"Greetings!" he said, spreading his long arms wide. His voice rang out in the small room, high and clear, like a boy's. "I am Ekanga. I welcome you to my workshop. It's so rare that I see one of your kind here," he added addressing Virmal. "And particularly such a rare breed. What can I do for you?"

Virmal narrowed his eyes. This magician, this Ekanga, seemed far too welcoming. What tricks did he have up his voluminous sleeves?

Virmal let Harita answer. "What do you know of demons and mirrors?" she asked.

"Oh ho!" Ekanga replied. "I know much. But my knowledge does not come cheap."

Now Virmal smiled. Finally, they came to the heart of things. This magician wanted something from them. And thought because of their rich dress that they'd be fools, easy to bamboozle.

Ekanga had no idea who he dealt with. Though Virmal had been raised in England, away from the rest of the tiger clan, he'd still learned to bargain at Grandmother Irita's knee.

As had his sister.

Harita sniffed, full of disdain. "You can't have that much knowledge or you wouldn't be living here," she said pointedly.

Ekanga drew himself up to his full height. He really was tall, not quite two meters, but close. He appeared to be in his fifties, though Harita had thought he was older. "I live free of the soul eaters, those magicians who call themselves demons," he said proudly. "Can all of your clan say the same?"

The soul eaters? Virmal had never heard the term before.

It appeared that Harita had. She turned to Virmal, raising one eyebrow, as if asking a question. Though they were fraternal twins and had been raised together, they'd never developed their own special language. They'd generally needed words between them to communicate.

Still, Virmal knew what she was asking. He was the one from the tiger clan, not her. He was the one who was magical. It was his fur and nail trimmings that Ekanga would demand as payment. It was Virmal's magical essence that the magician would use for his own magic, whatever that was and whatever other parts it involved.

Virmal didn't trust this man one bit. It galled him to the core that they were going to have to deal with him.

Still, they needed answers. And Harita wouldn't ask Virmal for anything unless she considered it desperately important.

Virmal nodded once. He would let her do the bargaining for his skin, trusting that she would protect it as well, if not better, than he would. She would get good value for anything she bargained away.

She would make Grandmother Irita proud.

ARIEL

Aunt Mabel insisted on meeting Ariel out at the plantation, where Aunt Belle had taken to her bed. Ariel had ridden like hell getting there. She was tired, and sore, and even Gret was cranky.

Okay, so possibly Gret was usually cranky.

It was late enough that the road to the plantation house was empty for Louisiana—just a few semis blowing past her. The air was still thick with summer heat, smelling like hot asphalt and burning crops. Only a half-moon peered down on her between the orange street lights.

The turn-off for the plantation wasn't lit. Ariel didn't know if that was normal or not. She'd never been out here at night before. Tall, majestic oaks lined the lane leading up to the main house. Ariel downshifted her bike so she was barely puttering along, the road recently paved and smooth enough to take at high speed should she ever feel the need to.

Gret circled restlessly inside Ariel. She didn't like this. It felt like a trap.

But who would be lying in wait here for her? Who

would be stupid enough to take on the boar clan? Particularly in their seat of power?

Ariel didn't know, but she was sure willing to find out.

Half a dozen cars were parked out front of the old plantation house: Aunt Mabel's ancient Mercedes, Aunt Belle's Cadillac, even Aunt Jeremiah's little Mustang. The front of the house was dark, no porch lights on over any of the three doors, no lights in the rooms beyond. A bare crack of light shone a shaded window on the upper floor, but it went out as soon as Ariel pulled up.

Ariel rode her bike next to Aunt Mabel's car, up onto its kickstand, turned off the engine and took off her helmet, shaking her dreads free. The chorus of cicadas and crickets sounded loud. Even frogs still bellowed from the pond in the back. They were all sure awake, though maybe no one in the house was.

Ariel sat where she was for a moment, debating if she should just leave the keys in the ignition. In the end, she pocketed them, not because she thought someone would take the bike, but because she told herself she was being ridiculous.

This was supposed to be a safe place for her and her clan.

She left her helmet on her bike so it would be easy to grab if she had to take off in a hurry.

The plantation house looked solid and black in the dim light, like it was carved out of shadows. Ariel shivered. They'd defeated the damned shadows. This was her own paranoia getting to her. She stomped up the wooden stairs in her boots, the *clomping* noise sure to get her scolded by Aunt Mabel if she heard it, then went to the door on the farthest right.

Like many of the old buildings, the plantation house had three doors. The center one was traditionally reserved for animals, when the plantation house had been built. Now, it was used sometimes for ceremonial purposes, when the boars were fully changed.

At least Ariel had good enough night vision to see Aunt Mabel standing just inside the screen door, the bigger, wooden door already opened.

Ariel could smell her aunt too. She smelled as if she'd been sick recently, doused in lavender water and sucking too many peppermint drops. Her face was slack, as if all the personality there had been worn out by too many days of hard living.

"Dearie," Aunt Mabel said by way of greeting.

Ariel grabbed her aunt in as fierce a hug she felt she could give the old lady without breaking her, even lifting her off the floor once, just because she could.

Aunt Mabel gave her usual squeak. The sound warmed Ariel's heart.

Maybe it would all be okay.

"She's waiting for you," Aunt Mabel said as Ariel pulled back.

Ariel narrowed her eyes at her aunt. That wasn't the way her aunt normally spoke. She should have asked how Ariel's trip was, if she was tired, could she get her something to eat or drink. Even if she'd been sick, she still would have been more hospitable.

Unobtrusively, Ariel took a deep breath.

There were others in the house.

Humans, who weren't of the boar clan.

"I see," Ariel said, nodding. Her hands had already started transforming into hooves.

A light glowed in Aunt Mabel's eyes for a moment and her face grew more animated. "That's good, dear," was all she said, using her prissy white woman tones.

But she gave Ariel a very satisfied smile before her face fell slack again.

Ariel turned away, heading for the grand staircase leading to the second floor.

Someone was controlling her aunt. Overriding her will.

That someone was gonna pay.

VIRMAL

Virmal held perfectly still as the magician, Ekanga, trimmed the ends of his claws. Virmal had just transformed his left hand, as requested the claws, muscles, and orange-striped fur flowing neatly and blending back into skin mid-forearm. Virmal's tiger soul circled closer to the surface. She kept up a soft, continuous growl, as uneasy as he was.

It was almost funny how even she didn't care for how crowded and overrun the magician's workshop was, how she felt claustrophobic with so much clutter. If Virmal had to guess, it was partly because the magician's junk was all hard edges and mechanical parts, while the rooms at the tiger court were covered in brightly colored pillows, thick rugs, and the softest blankets.

"You asked of mirrors," Ekanga said casually, though nothing about his movements was casual. Instead, he moved cautiously, precisely, fetching surgical clippers that Virmal recognized from a specialty store in England, cleaning the table with an acrid-smelling solution, positioning a bright light to shine directly onto the spot where Virmal held his hand.

"Did you notice the mirror outside?" Ekanga asked without looking up.

"Yes," Harita said. "We did. Bulbous and bronzed."

Ekanga merely raised his eyebrows in response while maintaining his concentration on the clawed hand in front of him. "Many don't see it," he said softly.

Virmal nodded. He would have missed it if Harita hadn't pointed it out to him.

Snick. The clippers were incredibly sharp and the tip of Virmal's claw came off neatly.

"It looks like an ordinary mirror," Ekanga added, examining the next claw. He'd originally asked for blood, hair, and an actual, full claw pulled wholly. Harita had bargained him down to the clipping from one hand and three whiskers, already carefully pulled. "Very little magic, yes?" he asked.

"Yes," Virmal replied in a growl. Harita shot him a look, but Virmal didn't bother shrugging or in any other way defending himself. He was uneasy here, and this man made him doubly so.

What was it about this man that made him so different? Virmal couldn't put his nose on it, but the magician smelled…wrong.

"The mirror itself is actually full of magic," Ekanga said. "And can only be created using magic."

"How?" Virmal asked, puzzled. He would have to take another look at the mirror, see if he could tease out its power. The mirror itself had barely seemed magical at all.

"Traditionally, there are two ways to make mirrors," Ekanga said, warming to his topic as he *snicked* off the tip of another of Virmal's claws. "Simply put, polish a piece of glass and put silver behind it, or take a piece of wood or bronze, apply silver, and polish with finer and finer sandpaper or grit until you can see yourself."

"This mirror wasn't made traditionally?" Harita asked.

"Oh, no, it was. It's a flat mirror," Ekanga said. "Made with a flat piece of glass and backed with silver. The magic comes with the bending of it."

When Ekanga didn't continue, Virmal asked, "And?"

"The magician uses his force of will, as well as his fist, to bend the mirror," Ekanga said. He absent-mindedly patted Virmal's hand, as if to calm him.

That just made Virmal growl again.

The magician didn't seem to notice as he isolated the last of Virmal's claws for trimming. "The magic catches and pools in the convex shape. I don't know if you realize it, but you throw out a thread of magic when you try to determine if something is magical or not. Because of the way the magic pools in the curved shape, it gets thrown back at you."

Virmal nodded grudgingly. That made sense, actually. No wonder these mirrors were rare. It would take not just force but great skill to bend glass out of its flat plane, not shatter it, but also not spoil it, to maintain the mirror's natural properties of reflection.

"More than one magician has lost his life using impure glass or silver, or even losing his focus at a critical time," Ekanga added. "The mirrors may look simple, but they are actually incredibly difficult to make. However, they're wonderfully effective at stopping not only seeking spells, but the soul eaters as well."

"Why?" Harita asked. "Does it have a field we can't sense?"

"Exactly!" Ekanga said. "She's very good," he said conspiratorially to Virmal. "Now, as near as I can figure, the soul eaters use a particular type of magical thread to attach to their victims. That thread is always reflected by the mirrors. If one of the soul eaters tries to attach to a victim in the vicinity of one of the mirrors, they end up attaching to themselves instead, or since they always work in groups, to one of their fellow members."

"So that's how we get rid of the soul eaters?" Virmal asked. "Merely hang a bunch of these mirrors around the complex?"

Ekanga laughed, a trilling, light sound, like a boy's. "If it were that easy, don't you think the soul eaters would have been eliminated by now? As magicians, we're not very organized. But I think a cause like this might draw us together. But, no." He shook his head and clipped the last of Virmal's claws.

Virmal drew his hand back from the table, relieved that the ordeal was over with.

He didn't immediately transform back to fully human. He felt better with his claws drawn.

"Once the soul eaters have touched a soul, they can always get back in. They're like mold. You can't ever completely kill it. Not unless you destroy the fabric it's growing on."

Harita frowned. "Mold dies in sunlight. And with enough bleach."

Ekanga nodded sagely. "True enough, if you're dealing with a single bolt of cloth. But what if it's an intricately carved chair? It's going to sneak into the cushions and lie dormant until it has a chance to come back."

Virmal didn't like the implications of this. "So our people who have been infected..."

Ekanga sighed. "I will tell you the truth, though I know you won't like it. They may recover. They probably won't. Plus, whatever memories they've lost are now gone."

Memories? Aunt Panita hadn't been forgetting things,

had she? Virmal would have to test her when they returned.

"In addition, since the soul eaters already have a way into your people's heads, the mirrors won't stop them. They have a line in. The mirrors might stop new infections, but they might not, if they're not placed correctly," Ekanga said seriously. "The damage will spread and get worse, leaping from one person to the next, until they've all turned into puppets."

"How do we help those who have already been touched by the soul eaters?" Harita asked.

"You can't," Ekanga said firmly. "You can only cut off the source from the soul eaters by killing it."

"There has to be another way," Virmal said. Though he didn't always see eye to eye with his various aunts and those in charge of the tiger clan, he wasn't about to go and kill all of them. He wasn't a raven, about to attack his own clan. "What if we kill the soul eaters who are touching our people?" Virmal asked. "Kill the source?"

"You'd have to kill all of them," Ekanga said slowly. "They're all connected. Leave just one alive, and they'll come back."

Virmal smiled. That, he could do. "Better them than us," he said.

Ekanga shook his head. "You don't understand. There are too many for you to conduct such a bloodbath. The soul eaters may claim to be demons, but they're merely corrupted magicians. The only way to ever be certain that you got them all would be to kill all the magicians, everywhere in the world." He paused, then added, "Not that I'm suggesting you go ahead and do such a thing. That would mean the death of too many innocents."

Virmal pressed his lips together tightly to contain his

growl. While he might be all right with contemplating such a thing, he knew his sister would not be.

"We'll need to talk with the other clans," Harita said quietly. "Thank you," she added, picking up the mirror that Ekanga had been willing to part with.

"Even the raven clan?" the magician asked.

"Yes," Virmal said. Peter had turned out to be a worthy warrior, the time he and Virmal had sparred. Not that the ravens were trustworthy, though Peter was making changes to the entire clan, trying to bring them into the modern day, trying to win back their honor.

"Interesting," Ekanga said. He stood up from his table, his clippings gathered carefully into a modern scientific collecting dish. "Thank you for coming to see me today. It's been most educational, though I won't be such a pushover when it comes to bargaining next time. Please come back to see me if you need any more help."

Virmal hid his smile at Harita's frown. She'd done very well at bargaining. But of course, a proper merchant was always going to complain about how poor the client was leaving him.

The corridor out to the street was dim after the electric lights of the magician's room. And warm as well. Virmal went first, his hands back to normal but his claws and fangs ever ready.

There had to be a way to stop the soul eaters without destroying either the people who had been infected or killing all the magicians.

Harita and the others would find a way.

Though if there had to be some killing as well, Virmal was okay with that too. His clan had been attacked when they were at their weakest.

It was time for revenge.

Hurt one. Hurt all.

CARLOS

No one waited for Carlos when he got off the bus in the middle of nowhere. The driver checked with him, twice, making sure that he really wanted to be dropped off at the mile marker Carlos had given him.

There weren't any nearby towns or villages. No trails the *gringo* tourists hiked along. Just a solid wall of trees on either side of the narrow, recently paved road. Vines connected the trees and bushes, making the greenery even more solid. The macaws and monkeys chittered angrily at Carlos as he stood on the side of the road after the bus had left, breathing in the fresh, green smell. Heat rolled over him, heat that not even the cool mountain air could cool.

Carlos wasn't entirely surprised that no one from the temple waited for him. He hadn't told anyone he was coming. Normally, that wasn't an issue: Someone at the temple would have seen his visit and so generally, someone was always waiting.

However, Father Pablo was ill. Though the other fathers at the temple might have been expecting Carlos, there were too many other visitors for them to bother with

Carlos, the black sheep, the visionary who refused to stay at the temple, refused to become a proper priest.

Carlos hefted his backpack onto his back and walked up the road. There wasn't a single trail that led to the temple. That would have been too obvious as well as taken too much magic to hide. No, a path would just appear when the jungle was ready, or when the walker was ready. Or both.

Carlos hadn't walked more than a couple of meters when a path through the underbrush gradually opened, the vines and brambles rolling back slowly.

That was odd.

Normally, the start of the path appeared in mists and grayness. Carlos hadn't seen an opening in the trees at all and had just had to trust that the smoke would dissolve into an open trail before he got too far from the road.

Just how sick was Father Pablo? Was it affecting the entire temple? All the land the vipers held?

Carlos made his way warily under the trees. More than one path led to the temple. Boys were taught that at a young age. It was the viper way.

But was this the right trail? Carlos wouldn't know until he reached the end.

ARIEL

Ariel didn't bother creeping up the stairs. Whoever was upstairs already knew she was there, knew she was coming. Surprising them that way wasn't possible.

But these humans, these magicians, she'd bet, hadn't been dealing with a bunch of warriors. Even Aunt Belle had difficulty with that form. Instead, they'd had a bunch of wild boars on their hands. While her clan could see through most magic, and were more stubborn than Mississippi mud, they still valued being genteel. Hell, they'd probably invited their attackers in for tea, hoping to talk everything out first.

By the time Ariel reached the top of the stairs, she'd changed into her full boar warrior form. Tough hair curled over her forehead, cheeks, arms and chest. Razor-sharp tusks grew up from her lower jaw. Her hooves could cut or shatter an opponent's weapon.

And she could *see*. Aunt Mabel had always kept Ariel tied closely to the earth. Ariel was more grounded than most of the others in the boar clan.

Her eyes weren't tricked by magic, by the lights that

had shadows cast over them, by the smell of fresh grass that was supposed to hide the scent of blood.

All her sisters had keen sight as well.

Ariel's was better.

Ariel walked softly but swiftly down the narrow hall leading to Aunt Belle's bedroom. More cross-stitch sayings were framed and hung along the walls here, about kin and taking care of your own, about the pride of the boar clan, about leaving the battle alive and coming back to fight another day.

The other clans accused the boars of being undependable allies.

Ariel recognized that it wasn't that they weren't trustworthy, but their first alliance was always going to be to their sisters.

As it should be.

The door opened silently. The magicians thought they were being clever or something, hiding in the shadows. Ariel didn't roll her eyes, but she thought about it.

Aunt Belle raised her hand, as if she wanted Ariel to come to her side.

Ariel disobeyed her and stayed standing at the foot of the bed instead.

The thing lying in the bed wasn't really Aunt Belle, not really. It looked like her, wore her body.

But her soul was gone. Ariel just knew it.

Besides, if it had really been Aunt Belle lying there? She would have insisted on a proper curtsey, first, from Ariel before calling her over.

"What have you done to her?" Ariel asked when Aunt Belle's arm dropped back to the bed like the puppet strings that had been holding it up had just been cut.

"We should have known that you would see through the illusion," came a smooth man's voice.

One of the magicians hiding in the corner stepped out into the light. He was a tall man, in a black suit that screamed wealth and power. He wore a starched white dress shirt with a blood-red silk tie and a gold tie-bar across it. He was mostly white—just a trace of something other mixing in his pasty face from some ancestor a few generations ago.

He eyed her greedily. "A proper boar warrior," he said, nodding, his eyes raking up and down her.

"Here to kick your ass," Ariel promised.

"No, my dear, I don't think so," he said.

A force suddenly held Ariel, like a giant's hand wrapped carefully around her, holding her in one place.

Fools had left her arms free, just bound her legs.

"Oh, I don't think so," Ariel said. It was easy enough to see the root of the magic, the thin tendril that floated out from her side, and slash her hoof through it.

Without pausing, Ariel rushed the main magician.

He hadn't been expecting that at all. Then again, Ariel didn't do genteel.

He backed up, his arms flailing, magical blades spinning out at her.

Ariel easily blocked his poor attempts, slashing that pretty suit to shreds. That white shirt of his sure did show the blood nicely.

The other magicians joined in. But they weren't trying a physical fight, not like he was. They were attacking her brain, making her head feel as though it was gonna explode unless she backed off right now.

They didn't understand that wasn't ever gonna happen. Ariel didn't ever back off. Not from the shadows, and certainly not from these assholes.

With a sudden sweep of her leg, Ariel knocked the

magician onto his back. Then she stomped down, hard, on his neck.

The hollow *snap* of his spine breaking echoed through the room.

The pressure kept building in Ariel's head. These assholes were trying to pick her brain apart. If she wasn't careful, they'd steal her memories of Mama and the swamps of Mississippi where she'd grown up, the stale smell of the long hallways of her first school where she'd been sent to cool off, the taste and fire of sweet bourbon from one of her aunt's stills.

"What the hell are you people?" Ariel asked as she backed up. There was only her. She suspected if she went downstairs, she'd find Aunt Mabel as limp as a rag doll, whatever force the magicians had been using to power her all used up.

"We are the soul eaters," one of the women said, stepping up. She was obviously the next in the line of power.

Too bad she wasn't anywhere near as good a magician. Ariel could see the sticky lines of magic that she was trying to call up. How she was trying to build a web around Ariel. How it spread from her to the others and out, probably to the rest of her kind.

Ariel slashed away the web with sharp hooves. Gret roared inside her, angry. It took only one long step to slash the woman's face open, the blood pouring into her eyes so she couldn't see. She faltered in her casting and Ariel took the time to grab her arm and break it, twisting sharply so she couldn't cast any more.

Another magician stepped up, drawing closer to Ariel but not as close. This time, he attacked using what felt like swamp magic. He was chanting and calling up green stringy lines, like moss and reeds, set to bind her.

As soon as Ariel turned to face him she realized her mistake. The others were all ready to pounce, each using a different type of magic.

Was that what these soul eaters did? Steal other people's magic?

There were too many of them. Ariel wanted to kill them all. But they'd surrounded her.

Leave the battle to fight another day.

Aunt Mabel had told Ariel that more than once. It was one of the boar clan's main tenets.

With a desperate howl, Ariel twirled where she was, slashing at all the magic eating at her.

There was nothing she could do about the other magicians inside her head, feeling them tapping at her brain, trying to steal away her memories, sap her power.

If she stayed there, they'd get Gret.

And eat all of her alive.

Ariel broke away from the pack of soul eaters, racing out of the room, down the long hall, then tripping down the stairs.

The magic followed: Those assholes still had their fingers in her brain. Distance didn't matter. They were like leeches, stealing away her power and mind no matter how hard she tugged at them. Some part would be left behind.

She just needed some salt. That was how you dealt with leeches. And demons.

Ariel sprinted to the kitchen. To her surprise, Aunt Mabel was there ahead of her, with an iron frying pan in her hand.

"Quick!" she said, her voice whispery and barely there.

What did her aunt want her to do? Ariel grabbed for the pan, but her aunt evaded her grasp, and instead, tossed the contents of the pan into Ariel's face.

A white, powdery substance covered Ariel's face. She

breathed it in by accident and started coughing immediately.

It was a combination of powdered corn meal and cayenne, stinging her eyes and burning her lungs.

"What the hell?" Ariel asked. Was Aunt Mabel actually still under control of the magicians?

Except that the teasing twitching fingers of magic in Ariel's brain lessened abruptly.

Before Ariel could say anything more, Aunt Mabel threw another handful of something into her face.

Salt. Coarse-ground and stinging.

Ariel shook her head, her long dreads sliding across her back.

The last of the magicians' magic was gone.

Ariel turned to go fight again.

Aunt Mabel grabbed her arm. "No. Go," she panted as if she'd been the one fighting the magicians.

And maybe she had been. She suddenly twitched, as if the magical hooks that had been in Ariel's brain had been transferred to hers.

"Run," Aunt Mabel said again as she turned to the stove. Flames suddenly shot up on all the burners.

The smell of gas was overwhelming.

Ariel didn't want to leave her aunt to die, even if she was taking out all these other stupid magicians.

But her aunt's face had grown blank again.

How much of Aunt Mabel was still there? Could she ever recover?

The old white woman prided herself on her memory. How much would she hate living if she couldn't remember her first icebox and the iceman who'd delivered the straw-covered blocks in his horse-drawn cart?

Ariel turned and ran, her motorcycle already racing before she'd even gotten it off the kickstand. She'd made it to the end of the driveway before the old plantation house exploded. She was glad she was still in her leathers as the heat from the explosion enveloped her, splinters of wood driven into her back.

Tears streamed down Ariel's face as she rode along. She wasn't about to turn back and see the damage. Nothing had survived that explosion, not the damned soul eaters, not her aunts, not any of her heritage.

A big hole in her heart matched that burnt, empty space she knew was behind her.

Who the hell were these damned soul eaters? Where did they come from? Why were they attacking her clan?

Ariel would have to find her other sisters, the other aunts. Warn them about the attack. Make sure they were properly wary of all strangers.

Then she'd contact Lukas. Demand help.

That damned hound owned her big time.

CARLOS

Carlos walked along the trail through the jungle slowly, his head constantly looking left and right, making sure that he was alone. He still didn't trust this trail, though the jungle felt the same: too green after the concrete of the city, too closed in, and all the insects and animals chittering too loudly, even compared to the construction going on just up the street from his apartment.

Carlos hadn't returned to the temple since the defeat of the shadows. Like all those in the viper clan, Carlos had felt the filth pass from the world and had celebrated. Maybe on someone else's credit card, but it had still been a special night of food and wine.

That the hounds had done it with help from all the clans had made it even more special. Carlos envied Gezane: Even though he'd been the one who had failed to stop the shadows when he'd had a chance, at least he'd killed them in the end. He'd become a great sword that had beaten the shadow creatures. His name would surely join the other heroes painted on the steps of the temple.

However, after the shadows had passed, Carlos'

zombies hadn't disappeared. He still saw new ones at least once or twice a month, over the six months since the shadows had been vanquished.

The priests had been wrong. Carlos' visions hadn't been about the shadows, but those things hiding in them.

Plus, his visions hadn't lessened. If anything, they'd increased, showing the world more and more in danger from these soul eaters.

None of Carlos' visions had shown Father Pablo getting sick—that news had come through the usual channels, one of his more well-connected vipers sending a messenger to the market to track down Carlos.

When the trail Carlos walked along emptied out of the jungle at the end of the row of rooms for the priests, he took it as a sign. Normally, the trail ended at the front of the viper complex, near the front gate, though there had never been a wall around the complex.

Maybe he had been walking along the right trail, and it had led him exactly where he needed to be.

Carlos kept his pack on his back and went directly to Father Pablo's rooms. He'd go say hello to the others afterward. Laugh at the ones who sneered at him, or subtly snubbed him. The ones who thought he was wasting his gifts.

He'd have the last laugh, he was certain. His visions had certainly turned out to be true so far.

The mid-afternoon sun beat down warmly when Carlos stepped out from under the shade of the trees. The scent of chicken cooking in garlic and peppers filled the clearing, overlaid with the usual smell of sweet copal incense from the tall pyramid temple. Raucous birds called to each other, warning of yet another stranger in their territory, while the monkeys stayed further back, loudly screeching.

A man Carlos didn't recognize stood outside Father

Pablo's door. He was dressed in a nice *guayabera*, light orange in color, with fancy white embroidery running in broad lines down the front. He also wore nice gray slacks and brown leather loafers. He kept his head down, but Carlos had the impression of impeccable teeth and clear, tanned skin.

If Carlos was looking for a mark in the market, he might pick this man just for the challenge he represented. As well as the money and power he held.

The man opened the door for Carlos silently. Carlos nodded in thanks, then paused at the threshold.

The stench of decay wafted out of Father Pablo's rooms.

This was not good.

The polished wood floor reflected the many candles burning on the shelves and along the floor. Father Pablo's room had always been immaculate, now, it seemed empty, barren.

Carlos crossed himself as he stepped over the threshold, calling on Saint Laziosi to keep him from harm.

The father lay on his bed under his colorful striped blanket. He looked skeletal, pale, almost white. Carlos hurried over to his side.

The father turned blank, empty eyes up to Carlos.

Carlos froze in horror.

Father Pablo had been turned into a zombie.

This was his nightmare, made real. Why hadn't the others noticed it? Why did they just believe the father to be ill?

Maybe because they hadn't lived with Carlos' visions. They'd always assumed he was another failure, his visions showing what everyone already knew.

A skeletal hand sneaked out of the covers and gripped

Carlos' arm before he could escape. The father turned his empty eyes to him.

"The others were fooled," he whispered sharply. "You've stayed away. Still see true."

"Yes, Father," Carlos said, horrified. It was worse than he'd imagined. Father Pablo hadn't been completely taken over. He was still there, buried somewhere inside of himself. He'd held onto enough of his wits to know what was happening to him.

Who had done this to him? And why?

"You must kill me," Father Pablo commanded Carlos. A sliver of his old strength returned. "Then get away. Don't let the soul eaters take you too."

Carlos recoiled even further. He'd never killed a man. Sure, he'd stolen many things, and fought, when he'd had to.

But he'd never taken someone's life. He used his wits to get himself out of the hospitals and jails.

The strength left the old man and his hand fell from Carlos' arm. Father Pablo had enough of himself not to start drooling, but only just. Harsh lines crossed his sunken brow, making him seem ancient. His eyes grew cloudy, as if covered in cataracts.

Something else came to the forefront of Father Pablo's consciousness. A slick smile crossed his lips. "So good to see you, my son," Father Pablo said smoothly. "You must go see the others. They have so much to tell you."

Or rather, the thing controlling him said.

Was it possible to bring Father Pablo all the way back? Was there enough of his soul remaining? Or had he just used up the last of his consciousness and his strength talking to Carlos?

Carlos had to believe that the father was gone, well and

truly consumed, if he was going to do what the father had asked of him.

With a shaking hand, Carlos reached for the father's pillow. He cupped Father Pablo's naked skull and laid his head back down on the bed. The father's skin felt red-hot, his life burning away. The thing animating him still smiled inanely at him, not questioning his movements.

"Forgive me," Carlos whispered. Then he pressed the pillow over the father's face, pressing down tightly as the father weakly struggled. Carlos held his breath, keeping his mouth firmly shut, afraid he might vomit.

Finally, the act was done. Carlos stood, shaking as badly as if a vision was coming.

What had he just done? His brothers would revile him. No one would understand. No one else would see.

Quickly, before the father's keeper realized his prey had escaped, Carlos turned and raced for the door. The unknown man still stood there.

Was he even of the viper clan? Or a magician, a human, disguised?

Carlos didn't bother taking the time to find out. He merely nodded at the man as if everything was fine, then, instead of going past the temple and toward the rest of the complex, headed right, toward the jungle.

Just as Carlos reached the edge of the trees he heard shouting behind him. When he turned to look, he saw men running from the temple, toward the long row of rooms that the priests lived in.

Suddenly, light fingers of magic touched Carlos' head. They were *inside* him, trying to get at him, trying to make him stop, turn around, come back.

A path opened up before Carlos, full of the familiar smoke of the viper clan.

There was no going back for him.

Carlos stepped into the mist. Cool clouds enveloped him. The fingers of magic in his head slid away.

Carlos didn't know where this path through the jungle would take him. He suspected it would drop him off closer to a town than usual.

From there, he'd make his way back to Mexico City, then beyond, all the way to the hound court in Germany.

Carlos swallowed the bitterness that filled his mouth. His own people couldn't help against these damned soul eaters. They'd been corrupted, taken over, made into zombies.

But the hounds had taken care of the shadows. With their help, Carlos could defeat the soul eaters, earn the trust of his brothers again.

He'd been born to do great things.

He just hadn't realized that the start of his heroic journey would be so hard.

YVETTE

Yvette wasn't sure she'd remember the tiger warrior in all her glory, but she tried to notice all the details she could as Tiger Lily rose from the hearth: the orange-red fur that covered the girl's face, her brilliant golden eyes, the way her muscles rippled across her chest and arms, the deadly claws that now tipped her fingers.

At least the magicians realized their mistake quickly enough. They attacked again.

Tiger Lily jerked, as if being stung by bees. Yvette sympathized, knowing they were picking apart her memories, throwing more fire at them before they took that knowledge from her too.

However, being a tiger warrior wasn't something Tiger Lily had *learned*. It was something she was, part of her being.

It would take a lot more for them to rip that from her. Though she didn't think for a moment that the soul eaters couldn't.

The warrior attacked with claws and fangs that now

sprouted from her upper jaw. She grappled with one of the other women, trying to tear her apart.

The woman had her own defenses, a brilliant blue glass armor, similar to the raven's, that covered her.

Tiger Lily's claws weren't as effective, but she still sliced the woman's chest open.

Yvette brought in her own winds, a gale force, scooping up sparks from the hearth and throwing them into the face of another magician. He howled as loud as the coursing wind and doubled over, hands clawing at his eyes, trying to wipe away the stinging soot.

Two down. Three to go.

Then Yvette felt her power being stripped from her, the ruthless one back in her mind. She struggled to hold onto her winds, but how could she defend herself from someone mining her brain, her memories? She knew of no protection.

Yvette tried throwing useless trivia at them, of the sounds the spring made out behind her house when the ice first started cracking in the spring, the smell of freshly washed wool, the taste of the blueberries before they were fully ripe, the feel of the stinging wet snow.

One by one, her memories were taken from her, along with other tidbits, like the perfect way to cook chicken bones to make a good, solid stock, the chittering of the snow weasels the winter before last, when there had been so little snow they had come to her and complained about it, the smell of the diamond oil in the lapidary, that the master smiths used for cutting their gems.

Yvette growled and tried to attack again, but her winds were gone, at least the strong ones.

She could relearn them, but it would take time.

The rug in front of the hearth had been special to Yvette, she knew that. But she couldn't remember where she'd gotten it, why she was so fond of it. Why she still hesitated to burn it.

Though she didn't remember what the rug was for, she could still grab up a piece of it, one of the brilliant yellow flowers with the shaggy petals. She turned it into a brilliant ball of flame and set it in the chest of one of the men.

It ruined her rug, tearing a hole in it that way.

She could mourn it later, if she could remember it at all.

The rogue magicians hadn't been expecting that trick. Then again, they'd never kept anything magical or enchanted around them—always eating it all up.

Yvette would have to remember that. If she could.

The first woman that the tiger warrior had attacked was down, bleeding, hopefully dying on Yvette's hearth.

A second now faced Tiger Lily. He had forged himself a magical sword, lit with blue flames, and had cut the tiger warrior badly. Where had he gotten that knowledge? Another magician's ability to forge weapons?

The two others faced Yvette, ripping things from her, all the subtlety gone now. It was worse than any headache she'd ever experienced, her brain pulsing inside her head with pain and loss.

She had to get out or there would be nothing left of her but a mere shell.

A surprising kick from the tiger warrior slashed at one of the magicians attacking Yvette, freeing her for a moment.

The tiger warrior howled at her. "Run!"

Yvette hesitated. She couldn't let another fight her battle for her.

"Live to avenge me!" the tiger cried out as she slashed and fought the three remaining opponents.

Yvette knew the girl wouldn't survive. They'd already

taken too much of her fighting ability from her. Only one of her arms was still working. She was bleeding, badly, from her shoulder, her waist, her leg.

But she could distract all the magicians. They'd turned away from Yvette, arrogantly confident that she had little left to attack them with.

Fools.

"I will remember you," Yvette swore.

Then she turned and fled toward the door.

She paused in the doorway, looking back. The tiger warrior was already on her knees in front of her attackers.

Yvette snatched up a pair of scissors that she kept beside the door, that she usually used for snipping her roses, making beautiful bouquets in the spring. She quickly snipped off three of her curls and left them on the threshold before she slipped outside.

The big, black, sleek German car that the magicians had driven waited in the center of her yard.

That would do.

The knowledge of the workings of the internal combustion engine was something the magicians had left Yvette with—the fools had thought it wasn't worth anything.

She applied it to the curls she'd left on the doorstep. She searched for the spark, the ignition of the engine, casting it out until she replicated that explosive kick that turned the engine over.

However, in such a confined space as her doorway, using all the power Yvette could muster, instead of a small spark, it caused a mighty explosion that vaporized everything in its path.

The thick walls of Yvette's cottage contained the blast, though the whole building shook. All her brand new windows blew outward, the sound of the glass shattering loud in the quiet night. Her roof lifted briefly before settling back down, the tiles cracked.

For the first time since she'd awoken, Yvette found she could breathe deeply. She stood in the cool spring night, panting as though she'd raced up the mountain. Her mind and her thoughts were her own. No one else was in her head.

But she wasn't finished yet.

Yvette stalked back into her house. The fire was still burning—her rug, her furniture, everything feeding the flames. She didn't need to call up a light to help her see, not that she could, anyway.

The magicians had all been killed. As had Tiger Lily.

Yvette couldn't stay. The smoke was too thick and she didn't remember how to clear her lungs, though she knew there was a wind that would do that for her. She retreated back outside, tears streaming down her face.

For the first time in her life, Yvette felt old, all her decades crashing down on her.

It would take time for her to rebuild. Time to clean the blackened walls, the cracked roof, the shattered windows.

Time she probably didn't have.

She could get a new mirror to hang out at the front of her property, but how long would that hold these rogue magicians off? Would it really stop them? How did it work, anyway? There had to be more magic to it than what she'd sensed.

She was in danger now, possibly for the first time in her long life.

The shadows had always been a threat. These magicians were much more immediate and real.

She would have to stop them. She felt the weight of her decision settle onto her shoulders, like a *geas* cast by fate.

Yvette couldn't help but laugh at herself.

And yet—she had an Arthur. Or at least, had had one. One she would avenge, or die trying.

Indukala Khushi Deshmukh.

Merlin syndrome indeed.

PART THREE
DANCE

FU RAN

Though Father would deny it, China was *made* for people like Fu Ran. It was loud and chaotic and crazy.

She loved it.

Maybe she'd have to come back more often. That would make her family happy, as well as the *shizu*.

As she walked down one of the main streets of Beijing —filled with hundreds of people all living their own individual lives—she kept pausing, the mixture of Mandarin and Cantonese and other languages catching her ear, making her want to figure out where they were from, what they were saying. The smells were rich, much richer than the streets of San Francisco, roasted chicken with garlic and fennel, *conji* made with chicken fat and rice, *ho li* buns filled with sweet almond paste.

The Chinese natives could tell she was American. They stared at her, wouldn't move out of the way, called to her to come buy one of their handbags, or their fine silk scarves, or even the real!native! hand-carved goods.

Fu Ran would have thought that the stares would make

her crocodile soul uneasy, but instead, she reveled in being *home*. Clan legends had always claimed that the Middle Kingdom was the birthplace of the crocodiles. Fu Ran believed it. Her crocodile soul swam easily through the foreign waters, content despite the crowds.

After Fu Ran had checked into her very American hotel—complete with doormen in Western style uniforms and a generic suite of rooms—she went directly Aunt Leeda's apartment. The manager of the building had refused to talk with Fu Ran when she'd called, claiming to not believe her when she said she was a relative.

Technically, he was correct—Fu Ran wasn't really a niece. Her ties to Aunt Leeda ran much deeper.

The apartment house itself was in a nicer neighborhood, one of the smaller *hu tongs*. Hibiscus, aloe vera, and well-trimmed pines grew in large clay pots that lined the alleyway, making it impossible for cars to drive along. The gray brick walls in front of the building sagged with age and poor construction. Oil stained the uneven stones of the courtyard, and at least two dozen scooters were parked inside the rusted iron gate.

The manager finally answered Fu Ran's call and let her into the two-story building. He complained bitterly about all the "relatives" Aunt Leeda had. Fu Ran just shrugged.

"We come from a big family," was all she'd tell him.

"Was she acting confused?" Fu Ran asked as the manager let her into the building.

"If she's a crazy person, you must take her," the manager told her quickly.

Fu Ran just sighed. He would obviously be of no help.

The hallways were dimly lit, and the dark red carpet had seen better days. But it was clean, at least. No garbage lay piled up outside of any of the doors, and Fu Ran couldn't smell any rot.

Aunt Leeda had a very small one-bedroom apartment at the back of the building, overlooking what had probably once been a garden but had been sold off and now faced a modern concrete wall. Her front sitting room had a table with two chairs and many, many potted plants, most of which were wilting and hadn't been watered in a week or two.

The window shade of her bedroom was still drawn, as though she'd just risen from a nap and hadn't opened it yet. Breakfast dishes lay on the counter beside the small sink in the kitchen. Other than that, everything looked neat and tidy, as if her aunt had just stepped out on an errand and hadn't come back.

There weren't any strange scents that Fu Ran could pick up, nothing that didn't belong here. Just normal smells, the bitter *bi xi* herbs that Aunt Leeda burned, the sweet almond cookies that she loved, the salt of the seaweed snacks she ate because she thought they were good for her. Plus her own scent, rich and full, musty in that old lady kind of way but still more vigorous than most.

Fu Ran also caught a trace of Aunt Leeda's crocodile soul, a cool thread running through everything else, with scales like steel and moonlit ponds.

She wasn't there, however, and hadn't been there for a while.

Fu Ran walked out of the building, out of the *hu tong*, and returned to the chaos of the busy street. She stood in the gateway from the small neighborhood and raised her nose to the air, scenting it. She didn't care that people stared at her. She could be doing the most mundane thing in the world and people would stare at her.

Finally, she caught the thinnest trace of her aunt's scent. There. To the left.

A familiar spike of adrenaline shot through Fu Ran, and she was off.

Not to save the world, no, but just an important part of it.

The corner looked familiar. Had Fu Ran passed it more than once? An apothecary stood on one corner, the windows shuttered against the sun and curious eyes. Racks of drying herbs hung from the ceiling, while glass jars filled the shelves, covered with vinegar eggs, huge bulbs of fennel, and mysterious white balls she couldn't place.

Across the street stood a small altar, not much taller than she was. It was round, with heavy bars surrounding unbreakable glass, holding a tiny statue of a local god, seated in a position similar to the Buddha's enlightenment mudra, cross-legged and fingers of one hand touching the earth. A garland of tiny red and white flowers wilted on the shelf in front of the statue.

The building on that corner was deserted, the windows and doors boarded up. It would be demolished soon, making way for perhaps another high rise, as the more modern buildings and waves of gentrification came across the city.

A noodle shop and a rice stand made up the other two corners, not competing, as one serviced traffic going north, the other, going south.

Fu Ran wished she could stop everyone, just for a moment. All the zooming scooters, the workers on their bicycles, the streams of tourists and shoppers, the old women strolling with their birdcages, the peasant women with their peaked straw hats and bundles tied to their backs, everyone.

Not because she was overwhelmed, no, but because Aunt Leeda's scent kept leading her here, then it would get tangled up in something, and Fu Ran would walk away again.

However, she was certain, now, that this was not the second, but the third time that she'd come to this corner.

Aunt Leeda had to be nearby. But where?

With a sinking heart, Fu Ran turned to face the abandoned building. She must be in there.

Had her aunt gotten confused? She complained about the dirt and dust of her native China all the time. She would never go voluntarily into such a dump. Fu Ran could smell the rotting boards from here.

Dementia wasn't unheard of in the clan, though it was very rare.

It was the only diagnosis that fit the symptoms, however. And the mysterious phone call, though Fu Ran hadn't been able to track down the original caller.

Fu Ran studied the building in front of her. Aunt Leeda couldn't have gotten through the front doors or windows. Maybe there was an opening in the back.

Had her aunt gone in there voluntarily? Was she merely confused?

Or had she been kidnapped?

Fu Ran's crocodile soul swam closer to her own.

If someone had done something to her aunt, they'd pay.

Though Fu Ran had sworn to do no harm as a doctor, this was different.

This was *family*.

LUKAS

L ukas didn't like China, not one bit. It was pure chaos, particularly after coming from the order of Germany and the hound court. There were too many people, too many sounds, too many smells, all coming at him and once.

He couldn't identify half the languages he heard in the street. It couldn't all be Mandarin, but some variants he'd never heard of. People stared at him as he walked down the street: Though he had black hair, it was long and curled. His skin was so white and he stood at least a half a head taller than most everyone.

Some of the scents were the same, the smell of roasting duck, the sweat of too many bodies. But there were too many unfamiliar scents as well, like the sweet incense from the handbag shop he'd just passed, and the bitter herbs from the apothecary next door.

Hamlin, Lukas' hound soul, stayed pressed up warm against Lukas' side, as if he was guarding him.

And maybe he was. His guardian hound tended to take his position seriously. He'd kept Lukas safe for many years while he'd been trapped as a dog, unable to take human form without the shadows attacking him.

Still, Lukas felt he'd had to come here, to China. Mei Ling had gone missing. She'd been one of the crucial components during the fight of the shadows, one of the great warriors who'd helped defeat them.

If the reports Lukas had received were accurate, she'd been missing ever since she'd returned home from Seattle and the battle with the shadows.

Lukas should have checked on her sooner. He felt guilty about that. He owed her a great debt for her aid in the battle.

His excuses included that he'd needed more time alone to learn how to be human, and that he'd spent much of the summer with Oma, his grandmother, watching her slip away until she'd finally passed the month before.

At least Lukas hadn't had to worry about becoming the next king of the hound court. His cousin Oscar had been trained for the job when Lukas had been "stolen" by Rudi, who protected him from the shadows and all those at the court who'd been corrupted.

Mei Ling's house was old, possibly ancient. Then again, she'd been old as well. It was hidden in a tiny alley, though still close to one of the main streets. It smelled musty when Lukas arrived, as if it hadn't been opened in months. There was a lingering scent of incense that made Lukas shiver. Had it been burned for the dead?

No food was rotting in the kitchen, though there were many jars of spices and herbs that Lukas was curious about. He was still trying to get the hang of the purely human art of cooking. Maybe before he left he could do some experimenting. He didn't care that much for Chinese food, the time Rudi had taken him to a restaurant: It had been far too spicy for him. Maybe he could learn to cook his own, though.

Just inside the front door, to the right, was a library. Mei Ling's scent lingered there. She'd obviously spent a lot of time there. It had a very comfortable looking chaise lounge in the corner, with a light hanging just above it, probably perfectly placed for Mei Ling. She demanded that sort of comfort.

The books were in Chinese, French, and English, probably the languages Mei Ling was fluent in, though it wouldn't surprise Lukas if she spoke with some competence in half a dozen more. There were other, musky smells coming from the couch that Lukas politely ignored.

The narrow staircase leading to the first floor was lined with artwork: abstract paintings that were done in a Chinese watercolor style. That might have been a peach smeared across the canvas, and the next, watery pine trees.

They made Lukas' head hurt. Art was, again, a purely human thing, something he'd never learned or developed an appreciation for, since he'd spent most of his life trapped in the form of a dog.

On the first floor Lukas wound his way through the various rooms. Mei Ling's bedroom was again obvious. She'd unpacked all her clothes from the trip to America. Her silk blouses and beautiful slacks had made it to the dry cleaners, even. But they were still in the bags the cleaner had returned them in, and hanging on the door, not in the closet.

So Mei Ling had made it home. Then she'd vanished.

But to where?

No one in the crocodile court knew. Or cared, really. Mei Ling had been a wild one, raised outside the families. Lukas hadn't been able to get any answers from them.

They'd been almost as bad as the vipers, answering all his questions with more questions.

Lukas couldn't imagine that. To be raised outside the clan? The ravens killed the outsiders, the ones who didn't come in. Or at least they had, until Peter had taken over. The hounds, too, were very persuasive about being part of the clan, or at the very least, making regular pilgrimages to the court.

Of course, the crocodile clan had watchers, like all the clans. Maybe they'd just kept a better eye on her.

But they didn't know where she was now. And Lukas had a twisting feeling in his gut that said she wasn't there anymore, not just in China but on this earth.

What had she met that would have been strong enough to take her? Yes, Mei Ling was old. She was also strong and wily.

Lukas did a cursory look through the rooms on the top floor. He'd blanched when he realized that this was where Mei Ling had kept her "girls."

She'd been a madam. He'd forgotten that. And though she didn't use drugs to keep her girls under control, she had used magic to drain them of their will so they'd stay docile. She probably had been picky about the johns she let near her girls—none of the rooms had the smell of blood.

But the despair was still pretty thick up there.

Mei Ling had once told him that the shadows had started attacking her girls, which is why she'd gone to the hound court in the first place.

Lukas tried to tell himself that the hopelessness he still scented in the air had come from the shadows and not the girls.

He'd never been good at lying to himself, though.

VIRMAL

Virmal didn't relax until the driver passed through the gates of the tiger clan complex. It wasn't that he believed anyone would be so foolish as to attack them in the streets of Old Delhi, but still, he felt safer here.

The long curving drive wound up the slight rise. Palm trees lined the edges, the drooping leaves well maintained, tiny crystals and balls of wool hanging from them, adding layers of protection.

Half of the outer defenses had disappeared with the shadows. Virmal had been trying rebuild their magical protection and barriers, but he hadn't had the time or strength to do them all.

Was that how the soul eaters, those corrupted magicians, had come in? When the tiger clan's defenses had been the lowest? Or had they come earlier, when the court was tainted with shadows?

"Should we hang this on the outer gate?" Virmal asked Harita as he got out of the back of the motorized bike, taking the mirror from her before helping her down.

"No, I think we should first put it near the sick room," Harita said.

"According to that magician, that won't help," Virmal replied, unable to keep the growl out of his voice.

"Surely you don't think we should believe everything he said," Harita scolded gently.

Virmal blinked as they stepped from outside to inside, the cool entranceway dark and inviting. It wasn't cool because of modern air conditioning, but because the stone walls were so thick and the building itself had been cleverly designed to keep the more important rooms shaded.

The entranceway itself was round, like a tower, and two stories high. Staircases lined the walls along either side, with arrow slits set at strategic places. Tapestries hung from the pale yellow walls, showing ancient victories of the tiger clan, as well as the splitting of the courts into the Indian and British versions.

The tapestries showing the British tea company meeting the tiger court for the first time had long since been removed.

"To the sick rooms, then?" Virmal asked.

Harita hesitated. Her attention seemed to be caught by one of the tapestries that showed the complex under siege. "You've explored the tunnels more than I have," she said slowly. "Are there tunnels directly under that wing?"

Virmal nodded. "That used to be the children's wing," he said. "Before it was made into the sick rooms. And the children were always protected."

"When was it changed?" Harita asked, turning toward him.

"Less than a year ago," Virmal replied. Was that when the infection had started? Had the magicians known somehow that the clan was about to get sick? Was that why the sickroom had been moved to that wing?

"Let's explore those first," Harita said. She'd taken two steps toward the door before Virmal reached out and stopped her.

"I will go first," he told her fiercely. If there were rogue magicians down in the tunnels they would have to go through him to get to her.

Harita merely rolled her eyes at him. "You won't see them coming before me," she told him as she fell into step behind him. "You might not even notice them."

Virmal merely growled and shook his head. She might be right. She usually was.

That still didn't mean he wasn't going into battle first.

LUKAS

Outside in the streets, just outside Mei Ling's house, Lukas tried tracking the scent of Mei Ling. It wasn't an easy task.

The smell of so many bodies was difficult enough to sort through. Then there was the layer of pollution from all the scooters, acrid and eye-watering. Underneath that were all the food smells, the burned bamboo leaves wrapped around rice and shrimp balls, the steamed buns with spicy pork in the center, the dark scents of black and barley tea.

But Lukas persevered. He wasn't a scent hound, or a sight hound, but a guardian hound.

And one of his own was missing. One of his warriors.

He would find her. And then deal with the ones who had taken her.

VIRMAL

The ancient wooden door leading to the staircase down to the tunnels creaked loudly as Virmal opened it. Musty air rushed out, dry and full of dust. It was cool there, cooler than the hall they stood in. And dark, like a hidden, shameful secret.

Virmal looked over his shoulder at his sister. She merely nodded as if she was impatient for him to get going. They still wore their street clothes, dull browns and beiges, the scarf for her hair wrapped around her neck.

There was no turning back. She'd go without him, he knew.

No lights sprang to life as Virmal crossed the threshold. He raised his hand and felt the tiny containers of magic that were still imbedded in the walls, once fueled by magic and shadows.

It was one more thing he'd have to see to, another part of the compound's infrastructure that needed fixing.

He pushed out a small thread of magic, dimly lighting up the teardrop crystals in the walls. He had good night vision, but even he couldn't see in the pitch black they were descending into. Plus, Harita needed the light to be able to see, though she'd never admit to such a weakness.

The stairs were steep and rough, cut out of stone. Smooth red bricks, perfectly aligned, made up the walls. The stairs curved around to the left, completing about half a spiral before they reached the tunnel. The ground there was covered in soft gray dirt that puffed up as Virmal stepped on it. He pushed out with one hand, sparking torches set up and down the tunnel.

The tunnel was round and squat, barely tall enough for Virmal to walk upright, while being wide enough for two people to walk down, side by side. The place smelled ashy, like a tomb. Stray spiderwebs hung from the curved brick ceiling. They couldn't see too far in either direction before the tunnel curved away. No insects had chipped away at the mortar, not even time had eroded the fit of the bricks.

Virmal stretched his senses out, trying to find something, *anything*, out of place. He wasn't about to take a single step farther down the tunnel until he knew what he was facing. Nor would he lead Harita into danger.

The tunnel that led back toward the main part of the complex was empty.

However, in the other direction, the tunnel that led out and eventually under the walls…something was there.

Virmal didn't see anything as he stalked over to the spot that he could only describe as *soft*, while the rest of the brick and walls was hard. He raised one hand to the spot, his fingers already transformed into claws.

The illusion covering the thing was strong. Virmal might not have noticed normally. It was well-disguised, hiding in plain sight, made to look like an imperfection in one of the bricks, a stray bit of gray mortar.

With impatient slashing gestures, Virmal ripped at the magic hiding the thing. Slowly, the gray covering bled away until Virmal looked at something that appeared to be a modern surveillance camera with a round gray-glass dome over it.

Virmal looked over his shoulder at Harita, wondering if she saw the same thing he did.

When he looked back, instead of the gray-glass dome, an eye appeared, bloodshot and searching. A human eye.

Which meant it probably belonged to one of those stinking magicians.

Snarling, Virmal attacked the thing, ripping it out of the wall. It came off easily enough, then started smoking in his hand.

Before it could burn him, Virmal threw the thing to the ground and stomped on it. The glass shattered with a satisfying *crunch*, leaving just a trickle of smoke behind.

"Well, they certainly know that we know something, now," Harita said dryly.

"You think I should have just left it there?" Virmal snarled at her.

"No," Harita said slowly. "But we'll have to be more careful."

"I'm always careful," Virmal boasted, though he knew that wasn't the case.

It didn't matter if they knew he was hunting them or not.

They were still all going to die.

LUKAS

It took most of the morning to track Mei Ling's scent to an abandoned building that was probably waiting for demolition, based on the signs he couldn't read but nonetheless recognized as construction signs.

However, the signs were old and faded. Maybe the company had gone bankrupt before they'd finished the project.

The other corners in the busy intersection held an apothecary and two restaurants. He hoped he could explore them later. Plus a statue stood encased in a golden cage in the street, the smell of incense clinging to it, despite the honking scooter traffic that rushed by.

There wasn't an easy entrance to the building from the front. Not with all these people around, at any rate. If the street were empty, possibly he could break through one of the boarded windows.

There were too many witnesses though. He had to fit in, well, as much as he possibly could. Everyone still stared at him, pointed at him, called to him about their shop and how he should come and look. He couldn't just disappear, no matter how much he might want to.

Lukas walked down the side street next to the building, then up the small lane behind it. Tall concrete buildings rose on either side. Garbage piled up along the base of them, broken pieces of scooters and fractured pots with ivy still clinging to them. The smell of rotting garbage interfered with Mei Ling's scent for a moment, until Lukas grabbed hold of it again.

There was a broken window in the back of the building, leading to an abandoned courtyard. After looking up and down the empty alley, Lukas slipped through, avoiding the broken glass lining the bottom like a toothed gate.

The scents of rotting wood and molding plaster walls flowed over Lukas. He waited for just a moment while his eyes adjusted to the darkness, glad he did when he saw the huge holes in the floor. Cobwebs gathered not just in the corners but were strung like dangerous traps between the empty posts.

Lukas guessed that this had been someone's flat, once. The very, very faint smell of children still lingered, maybe laughing in the playroom, running in and out of the courtyard playing tag.

But that had been a long time ago. Now, water-stained drywall remained, the mold forming patterns, a type of Rorschach test Lukas would never pass, having spent too much time as a dog while growing up. Torn-up newspapers, food wrappers, and stained plastic bags lay blown along the bottoms of the remaining walls, like a barrier of garbage.

Lukas cautiously walked across the floor. Other footprints marred the dust that had formed. Some were smaller, probably women's prints, while others were larger.

Who else was here?

Lukas raised his head and brought Hamlin closer.

There was magic at work here. Something, no, some*one*, was deliberately hiding their scent.

Or at least trying to.

If Mei Ling had been here, it hadn't been through her own will.

Lukas abandoned caution. Whoever was here probably already knew he was here as well.

It didn't take much to bring Hamlin closer, to change into his hound warrior form. He pushed down on the sharp spike of panic he felt when his body started to transform. He'd been stuck for so long in one form, it was difficult for him to trust that he'd be able to change back into human again.

He had to trust Hamlin, though.

Lukas was glad he'd worn a loose T-shirt that morning. It now strained against all the muscles that he gained in his chest. He knew that his face was more doglike, now, like Hollywood's depiction of a friendly werewolf.

But Lukas wasn't friendly at all. His teeth were sharp enough to rend flesh and clothes. His clawed hands were strong enough to rip through soft metal. Under his bristling fur was bony armor that could deflect a casual blow from a sword. His legs ended in paws with thick pads that could easily walk over glass and not get cut, plus more claws.

Then Lukas ran up the stairs, taking them two at a time. They were surprisingly solid, another thing that told him this was a trap.

It didn't matter. He and Hamlin could fight and win against mere humans.

They'd survived much worse.

VIRMAL

Harita insisted on hanging the magician's mirror on the spot where the eye had been in the tunnel. "It will stop them from coming back into the compound."

Virmal didn't point out that if the soul eaters had made it that far into the compound, they probably already had a key to the front gate, figuratively speaking. He still did as she asked, holding the mirror against the brick, then melting the brick slightly and hardening it again immediately to hook the wood to it.

The mirror hung there, black and bulbous against the dark brick. It still didn't *feel* very magical. Just a single thread of magic meant to hold the mirror together.

Virmal experimented, casting a deliberate thread of seeking magic through the mirror, trying to find the next tunnel beyond this one, the one that he knew lay parallel several meters beyond this one.

His spell came back to him, reflected.

Maybe there was more to this mirror than it seemed. Because if he threw out the same line just a few inches from the center of the bulbous reflection, the spell wasn't returned, and he found what he sought.

"We should go back and see Ekanga," Harita said as they neared the door to the sickroom, where Aunt Parita and the others of the tiger clan who just couldn't seem to get well had gathered.

"No," Virmal said automatically. He couldn't help it. There was something *off* about that magician, something that bothered him, that he just couldn't place.

When Harita raised one perfectly arched eyebrow at him, Virmal shrugged. "I didn't like the way he looked at you," he lied.

Harita's trilling laughter washed over him. "Oh, brother. He wasn't interested in *me*. There's a chance he was interested in *you*, though he can't really do anything about it."

"What do you mean?" Virmal asked. He *hated* it when Harita knew more than he did.

"He's a eunuch," Harita explained.

"Really?" Virmal asked, shocked. Why would a man do that to himself? Or had someone done it *to* him, for his preferences?

Harita answered the questions he hadn't asked. "According to what I read, he emasculated himself in order to focus better on his magic. He really is a powerful wizard."

"He's still a magician," Virmal said. While he knew his sister would object to killing all the magicians, Virmal still considered it a possibility.

Harita merely rolled her eyes at him and opened the door to the sickroom.

The room itself was actually one of the longer halls. It had been a schoolroom, once. It was on the interior of the complex, without windows or distractions. Virmal remembered coming here once a year to learn the recitations of the tiger clan, chanting along with the girls, always off in his own corner to minimize the challenges the girls would throw at him.

Small wooden charms that brought calm to all who entered hung from the tall ceiling. Colorful murals covered the walls: rainbows stretching over the River Ganges, brilliant red and yellow flowers intertwined with dark green jungle trees, both a sunrise and a sunset over the seas.

An altar to the Asvins, the twin gods of medicine and healing, had been set up in the corner closest to the door. The smell of incense barely covered the stench of decay that flowed from the infected women. Fresh strings of white jasmine flowers had been hung from the golden statues, while bowls of pure water sat at their feet.

A dozen beds had been set up where there had once been long benches and desks. Each bed had its own white curtains around it, giving the women some privacy. At the far end of the room were couches and lounging chairs, set in a circle, where the women could gather.

All the aunts seemed to be gathered together on the couches that afternoon. That was a good sign. Sometimes, when Virmal had come in, all the aunts had been sleeping or napping and had been hard to waken.

Still, he hesitated. What was he supposed to do now? How could he accuse them of being infected, when they still didn't even believe him about the shadows?

Ekanga had mentioned something about them losing their memories. He could start with that, asking them about the past and what they remembered.

Harita preceded him along the aisle that separated the beds along the walls, calling out cheerfully, "Hello, aunties!"

Virmal kept his smile pleasant, though he felt like grinning. He knew they hated being addressed like that. But there was very little they could do about Harita. She wasn't part of the tiger clan, not officially. Just family, as far as Virmal was concerned.

Aunt Parita rose from her couch. White-gray haze covered her eyes, as if she'd developed cataracts. Red touched her cheeks, making her look fevered. She'd drawn her hair back into a severe bun, every hair in place. A *bindi* of a tiny golden sword glowed in the center of her forehead. She wore a navy blue blouse under her gold and blue sari.

"You've always been too smart for your own good," she purred.

Before Virmal could warn Harita, Aunt Parita's hand and arm changed into tiger claws.

Casually, without warning, Aunt Parita slashed Harita's neck, slicing open the jugular. She grabbed hold of Harita as she started to crumple, then tossed her to the side.

"You know too much too," Aunt Parita continued.

Virmal froze, shocked by his sister's death. One minute she was standing there beside him, and the next…

Claws and fangs erupted out of Virmal's skin. Fur and tough hide sprang up, covering his human skin, setting it on fire. The world turned black and white, Virmal's vision tunneling.

Normally, Virmal made an easy transformation from human to warrior, his tiger soul gently stealing over him.

But Virmal's tiger soul was angry.

Not because she'd particularly cared for Harita. His sister was merely human, after all.

But Harita had been in *her* charge, part of *her* family. Her clan.

And she'd failed her duty.

All of the aunts suddenly growled together, a noise that Virmal returned, with prejudice.

Even if he could get past his aunt, go to his sister, he couldn't cure Harita, or stop her bleeding. He was too late. Aunt Parita had used expert precision in making her cut.

"I'm sorry," he whispered to Harita, glancing at her once. She lay there with blood pooling around her head, eyes open, mouth gaping.

The better half of him had already passed on.

Virmal growled again. He had to survive, at least for a while, though he knew it wouldn't be long before he joined her.

But for now, he had to avenge her.

FU RAN

Fu Ran was curious when she saw the tall American boy slip through the side window, entering the abandoned building ahead of her.

What was he doing? She'd never seen him before, but she knew he was clan. Not crocodile, no. The movement of his clan soul was different. He sparked, the difference there and gone, as though a roaming spotlight had struck him for a moment, then moved on.

That was the sign of either a hound or a tiger. As he was male, that meant he was probably a hound, not a tiger.

What did he want? Who was he after?

Had the damned hounds betrayed them, like the ravens so long ago? Did they have anything to do with the disappearance of her Aunt Leeda?

He was going to have some very serious questions to answer. And soon.

Fu Ran followed the boy inside. The stench of the place made her eyes water. However, the more critical side of her brain told her that the smell seemed...excessive. She was used to bad smells—she worked in an ER with people who had gangrene. This was so much worse.

How could that be?

Though Fu Ran couldn't detect any magic in the scent —she'd never been the most magical of the clan—it still seemed suspicious to her.

So much scent was probably covering up something else.

It didn't surprise her when she saw the hound change shape, into a hound warrior, half human, half great hound, then go running up the stairs.

He'd probably detected that there were other people there as well.

Whoever he was chasing was in for a surprise.

Fu Ran brought her own sister soul closer, changing into her warrior form. The room went gray as color ran away from the world. Her snout pushed forward and sharp teeth jutted from her mouth. Muscles rippled across her chest and her legs grew more powerful. Claws developed at the ends of her feet and hands, and her skin turned green and covered with scales.

Then she followed the boy up the stairs.

Might as well make it a party.

ARIEL

Ariel couldn't believe that she'd missed Lukas at the hound court. At least she hadn't made it all the way to Germany but just to Chicago.

Now, though, instead of flying east, she was gonna fly west.

To China.

She left a message with Rudi, letting him know her plans. She even gave him her phone number, if she'd remember to keep her phone charged.

She was getting mighty tired of airports, though.

Luckily, the clan had funds Ariel could tap into. And first class was just the way to go. Hell, she'd rarely stayed at hotels that were as fancy. She didn't get the foot massage that went along with the flight, but it was a near thing. Maybe the trip home.

Ariel stepped out into the heat of the late summer in China.

Holy hell. It wasn't that it was hot. She was used to hot.

But the *people*, ten thousand at least in this street

alone, all going along their own way. The noise was just as incredible, with hundreds of different conversations going on, most of which weren't in English. All Ariel spoke was English, some French, and some Cajun, though she didn't think that would help her here.

Gret wasn't doing much better. She didn't like the noise or crowds. At least the heat reassured her.

Ariel kept telling herself that it was just like a big Mardi Gras. Only a *really* big Mardi Gras. That took over most of the city. She could get by in crowds like that. She'd spent more than one night cruising Bourbon Street.

She could get through this crowd.

Ariel first went to the hotel that the boy had checked into. Figured it was a fancy place, all clean and Western looking.

On the one hand, Ariel could understand wanting a bit of calmness, a bit of home to escape to.

On the other hand, where was the fun in that? She'd have to find her a proper dive to stay at, at least for a few nights.

It didn't take long to catch hold of the boy's scent, leading from the hotel and away. The trail led first to some of the older parts of town, where there were few foreigners and Ariel stood out even more, then back to a more developed area.

The thing that kept distracting Ariel was the food. It all smelled fabulous. There were so many things she wanted to try. The eel that was killed and cooked fresh, right there, with noodles in some kind of hot sauce. The sweets stand that had milkshakes made out of avocado. The wine shop that had little pots of sweet plum wine.

Ariel would make Lukas take her out to eat later. After she found him. After he agreed to help her revenge her clan.

There was a corner with shops on three sides and an abandoned building on the fourth. A cute little altar stood in the street. Lukas' scent was strongest there. If Ariel thought about it, she could also track a thread of Mei Ling as well. But it was an old scent, not recent.

The stink of magic was all new, though.

Had that boy gone and gotten himself into trouble? Ariel was just gonna have to go save his butt again, wasn't she?

Ariel went into the shop, finding a box of salt. If it was the magicians she was going after, she was at least going to have something to fight them with.

Gathering Gret close at hand, Ariel slipped into the side alley, then through the broken glass window.

No blood was in the air, but magic hung there, thick and heavy. It enhanced Mei Ling's scent, along with some others. The smells of garbage and rot were also thick, overlaying all the magic.

Those damned magicians sure were trying to hide the fact that they were just up the stairs, lying in wait.

Ariel knew it was going to be another fight. She'd nearly not gotten out the first time. Aunt Mabel had had to help, and then blow the place up after Ariel had left.

Damn it!

Was the boy even there? Ariel couldn't honestly say. It smelled like he was. But the place smelled as though half a dozen members of all the different clans were there.

It was likely to be a trap.

Ariel still took another step into the room, toward the stairs, when a figure stepped out of the shadows.

It was a Chinese woman, short and round. She looked peasant-ish, with black hair that stuck out from under her hat like straw. Ariel could tell that was magic too, that she was actually much more beautiful than she appeared to be.

The freckles across her nose were real, but that was about it. Her clothes were rough, an ill-fitting shirt and long pants, with sandals.

She wasn't human, either. It took just a moment for Ariel to identify her as a member of the crocodile clan.

"Don't go," the woman whispered in clear English. She looked over her shoulder suddenly, as if afraid someone would hear.

"Is there anyone upstairs?" Ariel whispered back. Now that she was closer to the stairs she could hear scuffling from above her head.

"No one you want to meet," the woman told her.

"But my friends—" Ariel started, gesturing toward the staircase.

"Are already dead," the woman said firmly

Horror filled Ariel's stomach. Not Lukas too. All her family, and now her friends? What the hell was she supposed to do now?

Ghost fingers of magic suddenly pricked at Ariel's back.

Damned magicians were trying to get into her head again. She made a warding gesture and they abruptly pulled back. She ripped open the box of salt and threw it in an arc of white toward the bottom of the stairs.

That at least got the revolting fingers out of her head. But only for a while, she suspected.

"Time to go," Ariel told the woman. She wasn't about to face those damned magicians again, not on her own. She wouldn't make it out alive this time, she knew.

Ariel darted forward, grabbed the woman's hand, and started dragging her toward the open window.

"I can't!" the woman said, panicked.

"You ain't like them," Ariel told her as she pushed her toward the window.

"But...I'm a watcher! I'm supposed to watch!"

"And they're about to eat your soul," Ariel pointed out. She couldn't save the damned hound, but maybe she could save this crazy crocodile.

When the woman wouldn't go through the window, Ariel went first, then reached back through and tugged at the woman's hand again.

The woman resisted for a moment. Then she shivered and shook herself, giving Ariel a very wide crocodile grin. "They won't catch another clan soul this time," she said.

She climbed out of the window as if it were a rock she was stepping over. "Come," she said, slipping out to the alley.

Ariel paused. She really should go back, check on the boy. At least note the place so the hound court could come and get his body.

What if he wasn't dead? What if they'd just taken his soul and now controlled him, like the damned soul eaters had done to Aunt Mabel?

Ariel shivered. She didn't want to have to fight him too.

At least not yet.

Leave the battle to fight another day.

Instead, she followed her new ally out into the streets. She was a native, right? A local?

Maybe the woman from the crocodile clan could at least recommend someplace great to eat, where Ariel could have a drink and mourn the death of her friends, as well as start planning her vengeance.

LUKAS

SMACK!

Lukas shook his head. What the hell had just happened?

He wasn't running anymore. In fact, he couldn't move.

A net of magic, expertly strung, had snagged him at the top of the stairs.

Hamlin bit at the ropes holding their body, but no matter how fast he moved, they kept growing back. Both Lukas and Hamlin thrashed, hard, but they weren't strong enough to break free. He howled loudly, though he knew he had no backup, no one to come to his aid. The way the sound dropped, muffled as soon as he finished, told him that no one would be able to hear his cries either.

There were at least eight magicians in the room, all working together. Their sticky fingers were trying to peel apart his defenses.

They were aiming for his soul.

However, Lukas had endured the shadows. Not fought them—he could never fight them. He could only endure, encase himself in his disguise, hide his scent, his human side, his very being, until finally the shadows had done their worst and he could break free.

So Lukas hunkered down, sliding his consciousness deep inside himself, walling up the outer parts.

He could sense the magicians' surprise. They'd never encountered defenses like his, had never met anyone like him before.

Of course not. He was the guardian hound, the only one of his kind for the last five generations of the hound clan.

They'd break through eventually, he knew. They were already tearing at his outer defenses, trying to find a way into his soul.

While they dug, he had to find a way out.

Or else he'd die here, after having survived so much.

FU RAN

F u Ran was surprised to find the hound warrior just hanging limply from the web the magicians had built. What was he doing? Why wasn't he fighting?

Stupid hound.

The eight magicians hadn't been expecting her as well. They weren't prepared.

Fu Ran immediately started her attack. She knew better than to aim for the ones on either end of the half-circle in front of the hound. Those would be the lesser beings.

Instead, she went for the one in the center, a tall Chinese woman wearing elegant pearls and a beautiful blue silk *qipao*. She looked like an actress from the fifties, with her eyes done up almost like a cat's, her hair piled up on top of her head in loose rings and curls.

She laughed at Fu Ran as she attacked, easily pushing aside Fu Ran's jabs toward her heart, blocking her strikes.

How was she doing that? She was merely human. She shouldn't have the speed or power of one of the clan.

But she did.

Had she been the one who had taken Aunt Leeda? Had

she stolen Aunt Leeda's power? Or some other poor victim?

The woman appeared to not even be making an effort. She started attacking now, throwing a punch to Fu Ran's head that she barely blocked, doing a sweep with her legs that Fu Ran tripped over and barely righted herself from in order to duck the next attack.

It had to be magic. Not the woman's natural abilities. But how did Fu Ran defeat her?

Again, questions. And no time for answers. Just fight, with the chances of winning diminishing with every step.

VIRMAL

Virmal knew the rest of his aunts wouldn't wait to attack him. They'd be on him as a group in moments. He had to fight *smart*, as Harita had always told him.

His sister. His twin. His better half.

She was gone.

Time for the one who'd killed her to die.

Virmal refused to recognize the tiger warrior in front of him. This was no longer his aunt. This was an enemy. *The* enemy.

This had once been a room of teaching, where children learned about the clan and its glorious history. The murals on the walls mocked him with their colorful portraits of sunrises and rainbows.

Time to do some more teaching, to show these damned magicians that the tiger clan could still take care of its own. No matter what that meant.

Virmal reared up on one leg and slashed out with the other, kicking high at his opponent's face. It wasn't a traditional fighting technique, but one he'd learned in England, when sparing with humans.

She jerked back in surprise, but not far enough.

Virmal drew first blood.

Normally, that would have been enough to end a challenge.

Not now.

The others roared their displeasure.

Too bad.

Now, Virmal attacked, clawing at his opponent. (Not his aunt. Never again would he consider this his aunt.)

She blocked. He followed the motion downward, then came back up with a sudden twist, grabbing her arm, another non-traditional move. She slashed at him, but he was still able to use his greater strength to fling her across the room, behind the lounging couches, hard enough that she hit the wall with a loud *thunk* before she slid to the floor.

Then the others attacked.

Virmal whirled as he'd seen Peter the raven warrior do, flaying his opponents with razor-sharp feathers. Virmal used his claws, his teeth, his strength, pushing the others back.

He was outnumbered.

But they weren't fully themselves. More than once when one of his opponents raised their hand for a blow they'd hesitate.

Virmal didn't allow himself to pause. To think.

Only to kill.

One by one, his opponents stopped attacking as they dropped to the ground, faces and necks slashed, bones shattered.

Finally, the last fell. Virmal stood for a moment, panting. The taste of blood, normally sweet on his tongue, sickened him. The smell of decay overwhelmed him, the bodies of his aunts already putrefying.

Bile rose and he couldn't help but vomit up the contents of his stomach.

He stood shaking, his entire body trembling. He was badly hurt, clawed on neck and shoulder and chest. His right foot wasn't working right—he could barely put any weight on it.

Finally he was able to go over to where his sister lay, dropping to his knees beside her.

She lay perfectly still, her eyes still open wide in surprise.

She'd known too much. She always had. She'd been able to help all of them fight the shadows with her simple recipes. Now, she'd died because of her constant curiosity.

Curiosity killed the cat.

Virmal couldn't help the hysterical laughter that bubbled out of his chest.

Or the tears that streamed down his face.

He struggled to pick her up, to stand. She couldn't lie here, not with her enemies slain around her. She shouldn't remain stained with their blood.

But Virmal was only able to stagger a meter or so before he fell again, his grief overwhelming, the pain of his loss and his injuries too much.

Howling wouldn't bring anyone to help, but he still did, voicing his grief in loud, undulating calls.

Virmal didn't just express his grief though, the loss of his aunts, his sister, his life.

He was also declaring his revenge on the ones behind her death.

LUKAS

L ukas felt the web holding him weaken. He sagged closer to the ground. His body automatically struggled harder, without him having to think about it or come up from his hiding place.

There was another woman there, fighting. A crocodile? What was she doing here? The other magicians had all turned their attention to her.

No wonder the web holding him was weakening.

Now, if only he could get loose. He didn't have any magic of his own, just the ability to hide himself and endure.

Beyond the fighters, in the corner, lay a pile of clothes. Several piles, actually.

That was where Mei Ling's scent was coming from. They'd taken her clothing—possibly the last thing she'd been wearing—and had put them here.

Had she, herself, ever come into this building? Lukas couldn't tell. He hadn't scented any blood in the air.

The crocodile was scratching the floor with her claws. What was she doing? Getting ready to spring?

She slipped to the side, avoiding the next attack neatly.

The magician moved to the left, stepping right into the section where the crocodile had been scratching.

And her foot went straight through the floor.

Instead of turning and attacking, destroying her enemy, the crocodile turned and ran.

Directly toward him.

Lukas braced himself as she tackled him, the pair of them flying through the air backwards, tumbling down the wooden stairs. Lukas struck his back, his side, then his head as they fell.

But he didn't cry out. Didn't mind, really, though the room darkened for a moment. At least those damned magicians were out of his head.

As soon as he could, Lukas stood, shifting back to human form. "Come on!" he said, reaching out his hand for the Chinese woman who still lay on the floor.

What was that? Salt? Where had that come from?

She ignored him and leaped past, heading for the window that Lukas had slipped through earlier. He followed her, the pair of them reaching the street moments later.

"This way," she directed, heading east down the sidewalk, quickly crossing the street, darting down an alley, then through another lane, back and around.

Lukas knew he could find his way back to his hotel, as well as to Mei Ling's house—he'd marked their scent and could track them down. But besides those two markers, he was utterly turned around.

Was she a native? She certainly looked Chinese. But there was something about her, the way she held herself, or how she didn't press as closely to those they passed, that told him she wasn't.

They ended up in a little tea shop off an alley that he

hadn't even known was there. It was on the first floor of an old wooden building. Regular apartments were on either side, with concrete yards blocked off by high walls, full of potted tropical trees and plants.

The tea shop smelled of old tea, sunk deep into the wood. Instead of Western style tables and chairs, all the tables were low and long, strung across the floor, maybe a dozen of them. Pillows lined the sides, stained with tea and smelling of mold.

Along the back wall were burners with huge pots of water boiling. It wasn't a cheery Western restaurant—Lukas wasn't even sure there were electric lights.

But no other customers had come in, and the woman running the shop didn't seem to be in any hurry to make them leave.

The woman he was with ordered them…something. Lukas assumed it was some sort of tea.

The server came back with a steaming pot and two cups that looked as though they'd been serving tea since sometime in the previous century. The pottery was old and cracked, and at one point had probably been white. Now, it was a beige color. But they were clean.

The tea was sharp and bitter, dark and black. Lukas could already feel his eyes widening as the caffeine hit his system.

He'd rarely had anything caffeinated, and he knew he might not sleep tonight, just from a few sips.

Possibly not the following night either if he drank more than one cup.

The woman kneeling across the table from him finally looked up, piercing him with a sharp stare.

"Who are you? And what were you doing there?" she asked in pure English, with an American accent.

The old woman server in the corner looked sharply at them.

"*Sprichst du deutsch?*" Lukas asked in return.

"*Ja*," she replied, continuing in that language.

When Lukas didn't add more, she asked, "Well?"

Lukas nodded. She did deserve something from him, as she had saved his ass.

But he'd been trained by Oma, his grandmother, to keep secrets, his entire life.

He would tell her some things, but no more.

Not until he heard her story too.

山山

Li Li's heart pounded as she wove her way down a smaller street. The sides of the street were a little less crowded, not as many people pushing against her. The air was bad, of course, with the number of scooters whining along in waves. There weren't any sidewalks—this wasn't a tourist part of town. Even over the horrible pollution came the tantalizing scents of garlic and rice.

No matter how many people were around them, separating them, Li Li knew that the girl she'd saved (saved!) still followed. Of course, there were gasps from some of those passing by. They'd probably never seen someone so black before. Or with such unusual hair! Dreadlocks had never been popular in China. The girl was straight out of a Hollywood movie.

Li Li's twin soul could feel the *otherness* of the girl, that wasn't obvious to the gaping Chinese peasants around them. The girl was from the boar clan.

However, that wasn't what made Li Li's heart pound so. It wasn't what made her whole skin tingle. It wasn't why she kept wanting to look back over her shoulder.

She had *acted*. She hadn't just watched. She'd had her eye on the trap set up by the soul eaters for a couple of months, now, horrified at how the defiled magicians were taking those in her clan.

The elders, of course, cautioned that they should wait. They couldn't afford to draw attention to themselves. They needed to be patient, figure out who and what the soul eaters were, then find a way to defend themselves against them.

All the while, the soul eaters grew stronger, stripping the powers from their fellow magicians as well as from those of the clan that they caught.

At least half a dozen had been trapped and sucked dry. Li Li assumed that the scents drew them, the ones who had been lost before them. Their clothing was left behind so that when someone came looking for them, they'd also be drawn into the trap.

When the hound boy had changed, Li Li had nearly acted then. It wasn't because he was clan—Li Li wouldn't necessarily move to save another of the clan. She was merely supposed to watch.

This boy, though, was different. She hadn't seen many of the hound clan. She'd read descriptions of the hound warriors. This boy seemed very different than what she'd read. His hound form was exaggerated, the ears and nose out of balance with his large, overset blue eyes, instead of being a perfect blend of hound and man. She'd have to look up his breed later, see if she could find it.

However, several decades of inaction lay heavily on Li Li. She couldn't move from her corner, couldn't stop him from going up the stairs, couldn't halt the decimation of his soul given the loud howls.

A young American crocodile had followed him. Would she be caught too? The sounds of the battle had raged above Li Li's head. She wanted to go look, but she could only wait.

When the young boar had come in, Li Li had finally had enough. Not a third young person. Not in one day. She couldn't let another one from the clans die.

Even if this was a boar, not from Li Li's clan.

Li Li had *acted*. She'd warned the boar away before she'd been killed too.

Now what was Li Li going to do? She'd never acted before.

And some deep, dark spark in both of her souls didn't want to go back to just watching again.

YVETTE

Yvette sat quite still in her hotel room in Germany, still cataloguing what she'd lost, what she could regain. The hotel was in the old part of Hamburg. Lace curtains hung across the window, keeping the room in shade. The tile bathroom in the corner still smelled of the vinegar used to clean it. Under the window ran a long radiator, the white paint covering what used to be beautiful swirls and designs pressed into the metal.

There were things Yvette remembered, like when she'd first seen a radiator like this one, in the village of Lamoura, when they'd gone from just stoves heating the houses to radiators. The smell of wool socks baking on the radiators in the winter. The fancy wood and metal covers that the youngsters in the 50s started putting over the radiators, hiding their elegant curls to make them more practical, to have more space. To the newest adults, who took off the covers, revealing the scrollwork again.

There were some things that were lost forever. Like most of her memories of Mama. Mama had called up ice for them once, during the heat of the summer, but then what had they done with it? Snow weasels lived on the mountain, that would come for Mama, but how did Yvette call them? The rug she'd destroyed, along with her house, had been from Mama, but when? That rug had been important, but how had she used it?

Yvette found tears running down her face again, and brushed them away angrily.

Tears wouldn't help her.

Getting back at the damned bastard soul eaters who called themselves demons wouldn't really help either.

But stopping them, so they didn't attack others? Ah, that was a cause she could get behind.

And Indukala Khushi Deshmukh. At least Yvette hadn't forgotten her name, or her sacrifice. Her Arthur, as it were.

Soon, Yvette would have to make her way to the tiger court. They were in India and someplace else.

Try as hard as she could, Yvette couldn't remember where else the tiger court reigned.

At least her winds hadn't all deserted her. Yvette called up first one, then another. The quiet winds, the tickling winds, the winds that teased desert sands in the night.

They could tell her things. Fill the empty spaces in her head, create new memories for her.

But she'd never regain what she'd lost. Even if she lived through the change of the next century.

And for that she mourned, her winds whisking her tears away.

FU RAN

"I don't know your Mei Ling," Fu Ran said as she sipped the last of her tea. It had grown bitter as it cooled, refreshing and awakening her tongue.

The boy shrugged. He looked so out of place, there, in the ancient tearoom, so tall and pale and other. He had black hair, but it curled, and his eyes were blue.

"Those magicians had her clothing in the room," Lukas said. "That's how I tracked her, and her scent."

Fu Ran nodded. "That was probably why I found the scent of my Aunt Leeda there as well. It was a carefully baited trap. They probably take the clothes of all the victims, so they can draw more in."

Who had called her when she'd been in America? Told her to come and save her aunt? Had it been the magicians, hoping to entice her into their trap? Or had Aunt Leeda survived for a while after their attack?

"Were the magicians stealing your powers?" Fu Ran asked. That had been the only thing that she could think of, why the mere human she'd been fighting had the power of the clan.

The boy shrugged again. "They were trying," he said. "But I have better defenses than most."

"Really?" Fu Ran asked. The boy didn't seem special at all.

Lukas stopped himself before he shrugged again. He glanced around the mostly empty teashop before he leaned further across the table, speaking barely above a whisper.

A human wouldn't have been able to catch his words. But Fu Ran wasn't fully human.

"I am the guardian hound," Lukas said. "We just defeated the shadows that have plagued us for generations."

Fu Ran could tell that he expected her to be impressed by that. But she'd never heard of the shadows before. Or a guardian hound.

Still, he thought he was different. Something special. Then again, so did most boys.

"So what can you tell me about those magicians?" Fu Ran asked. She needed information. She realized that she was approaching this as if the group was a disease. What was the most effective way to defeat the infection?

"They wanted to steal my soul," Lukas said.

Fu Ran didn't bother hiding her disbelief. Souls were as important to this as those fake herbs that quacks sold poor patients who couldn't afford to go see a doctor.

Then her own crocodile soul nudged at her, gently.

She did have a soul, two actually, one human, one crocodile.

Maybe she should have a more open mind about such things.

"Steal your soul, steal your powers?" Fu Ran asked.

"I believe so, yes," Lukas replied. "We need more information about them."

"I was just thinking the same thing," Fu Ran said.

Would the crocodile sisterhood know more? Who could she talk with?

"I don't know anyone else here, besides Mei Ling," Lukas said. "All my contacts are either in Germany or America."

Fu Ran nodded. That made sense. The boy was obviously from America, and the hound court was in Germany.

"I'm only here for one more day. Then I'm going back to Germany," Lukas said. He paused. "You could come with me. Combine our search. Our efforts."

Fu Ran hesitated. She should stay here, in China. Since this was where they'd been attacked, where her people were.

"Some contacts?" Fu Ran asked. Or was the boy sending them both on a wild goose chase. "You mean, like someone at the hound court?"

Lukas snorted. He seemed more amused by that than she would have thought. "You could say that," he drawled. "I am a prince, you know," he added very softly, almost to himself.

Fu Ran looked more closely at him, intrigued. She was going to have to hear more about that later.

"Okay," she said after another moment. "We'll combine forces for a while. Let's go to my Aunt Leeda's house first, see if there's anything more there. Then I need to contact the crocodile court, see if anyone knows something."

She wasn't promising to go with him, to leave China. But it did make sense to at least combine their efforts for the time being.

Lukas nodded slowly. "My friend Mei Ling is dead, isn't she," he stated quietly.

Fu Ran felt her heart lurch. "And my Aunt Leeda as well," she said.

They were both quiet for a moment before looking up. Fu Ran was certain that her own look was at least as fierce as Lukas'.

Words echoed between them, that they didn't have to speak out loud, knowing exactly what each other was thinking.

And they'll pay.

ARIEL

Ariel pushed back her bowl and smacked her lips. Man, that had been some good food. It wasn't like anything else she'd ever tasted. It certainly didn't taste like Lu Man's Chinese Kitchen back home. Nope, the real stuff always tasted better. She knew that, based on how disappointed she generally was anytime she'd gone and tried a "real Southern home-cooked meal" at a restaurant.

It was generally "Southern" by way of Manhattan or some such nonsense.

This food hadn't been like anything Ariel had ever tried before. The rice had been better than what her Aunt Sophie made, and her aunt made a mean cup of rice. But it had been fluffier here. The cook had added something to it, too, like how the Japanese did to sushi rice.

It hadn't just been the rice, though. There'd also been the fish, grilled and spiced perfectly, the flesh white and flaky. Next to that, some kind of long greens, probably seaweed, with just the right amount of bitter. The soup had been sweet without being cloying, with long strings of egg swimming in it.

Ariel had been in hog heaven, eating her way through dish after dish to ease her heart.

The restaurant was fancier than what Ariel had been expecting, with white linen tablecloths, heavy silverware (for her) and ivory chopsticks (for Li Li). There were only a dozen or so tables, mostly occupied by businessmen in their suits, all talking business. The walls were covered in hanging scrolls filled with Chinese calligraphy—poems, Ariel would bet. No pictures, not even a red star hung anywhere she could see.

All the water came in sealed bottles, so Ariel could drink it, as well as the sweet plum wine, served in fancy crystal glasses. The waiters wore starched white shirts with black bowties and spoke in hushed voices, their eyes low. Ariel figured it was a sign of respect, though she didn't get it. She'd rather share her meal and her joy with everyone around her than be fawned over.

However, not even the businessmen spoke loudly in this place. The waiters all shuffled their feet, adding to the quiet. If the food hadn't been so divine Ariel would have felt oppressed by the place.

Li Li, the watcher, had seemed happy to take someone out to eat, to share a meal. She hadn't talked much, something Ariel appreciated—food first, so it could be properly appreciated, then business.

Because they did have some business to take care of.

"So you're a watcher?" Ariel asked after the plates were carried away and the tea had been served.

Li Li nodded cautiously. She was a mousy thing, or at least seemed that way sometimes.

But mice also had claws and teeth and would come out fighting if they were cornered.

And this Li Li wasn't just a mouse. She was clan. A crocodile.

Ariel knew some crocodiles from the swamp. Not clan, no, real ones.

They weren't anything to be messing with.

"You find the wild ones for your clan, right?" Ariel knew the boar clan didn't have too many watchers, not like the hounds or the birdmen. Her sisters were more casual about the whole thing. Plus, a boar would almost always find their way home, wild or not. Every two or three years someone would show up out of the blue, drawn to the plantation.

Kids from the boar clan stayed better hidden than some of the others, despite their impulsive reputation. So it wasn't like a watcher could find 'em if they'd decided to stay hid.

Where would they go now that the main house had been destroyed?

Ariel couldn't think about that now. Or if she did consider it, it could only be for it to help fuel her revenge.

"Many families were split apart during the revolution," Li Li said.

Ariel didn't know Chinese history well enough to know which revolution Li Li was talking about. She also figured any revolution would do that kind of thing. Maybe it made sense for the crocodile clan to have watchers in their main birth place.

"How long you been watching that trap?" Ariel asked. She knew that she was going to have to be doing all the asking, as Li Li probably wouldn't volunteer that it was her birthday even after they'd already presented her with a cake.

"Two months," Li Li said.

Ariel gave a low whistle. "What do you know about the soul eaters?"

Li Li seemed surprised that Ariel knew what they called themselves.

"They attacked my clan," Ariel admitted. She took a deep breath before she growled any more. It still made her see red. Aunt Mabel. Aunt Belle. Who knew how many others?

That got Li Li's attention. "They've grown bold," she said. "And powerful." She paused, then asked shyly, "How did you get away?"

"Killed the lead one of the pack," Ariel said. "They weren't expecting a warrior."

"Ah, like the ravens, not all your clan are warriors?" Li Li asked.

Ariel hadn't realized that about the damned birdmen. She'd have to ask Peter later.

Was Peter still all right? He hadn't been hanging out with Lukas, had he?

She would have to call him. She reached for her phone. Damn it! Where was it? Had she left it on the airplane, charging? She was gonna have to buy a new one, get the number transferred.

After a moment, Ariel realized that Li Li was still waiting for a reply. "Oh, everyone in the clan can become a warrior. They just don't practice like some of us."

"Fascinating," Li Li said. Then she asked, "Did just killing the leader help you get away?"

"No," Ariel admitted. "They still had their fingers in my head. Tearing at my brain. My memories. My aunt helped me. Threw cornmeal and cayenne into my face. Then salt."

"And she used cold iron, too, didn't she?" Li Li asked.

Ariel thought back. Aunt Mabel had had an iron frying pan that she'd used to gather up the things to throw at Ariel. "Why's that important?"

"They…they think of themselves as demons," Li Li said.

Ariel scoffed. "They're human," she said.

"But their magic reacts to certain things. Like salt. And mirrors."

"Mirrors?" Ariel asked, surprised. Did she just have to carry a big damned mirror with her for the next time she battled the damned magicians?

"Not like the *ba gua*," Li Li said, pointing at the doorway to the kitchen.

Ariel saw an eight-sided wooden piece hanging above the lintel, about the size of her palm. Red lines of different count and length were painted on each side. The very center held a tiny mirror.

"That's supposed to keep demons out?" Ariel asked. Not that she'd ever met a demon. Those damned shadows had been bad enough.

"In Chinese tradition, they are," Li Li said. "But the soul eaters aren't affected by them. There's a different type of mirror, though, that magicians have, that the soul eaters can't stand. If a magician has one of those types of mirrors hanging outside their house or their workshop, the soul eaters leave him or her alone."

"Huh," Ariel said. "What's special about that?"

"Demons can't stand the sight of their own face," Li Li explained. "But you can't see anything in the dark mirrors. They're curved, too," she added, cupping her hand to show Ariel. "They come in an eight-sided wooden frame, but there's nothing magical about them."

"Do we need to get some?" Ariel asked seriously. She was damned tired of feeling those magicians inside her head. Made her want to go take a long hot shower or something.

"I don't know," Li Li said. "They seem to work for other magicians. But would they work for clan?"

"So what are we going to do about the damned soul eaters?" Ariel said after another pause. "They came after my clan. They'll go after yours, soon. They've got that damned trap set up and are gaining strength."

"I'm just a watcher," Li Li said.

"You saved me," Ariel told her.

"I didn't want another to die," Li Li whispered in return. "Like the hound. And the crocodile that went after him."

Ariel felt her back stiffening. It was just a damned shame about Lukas.

Stupid boy.

She was just going to have to avenge him too.

If only she could figure out how.

YVETTE

Yvette swallowed down her bitter words as she left her audience with the hound king. Though she might not remember everything she once knew, she knew better than to tell him what she was actually thinking.

Fool.

The king had addressed her from his throne, looking like a businessman playing at royalty in his bespoke blue suit and red power tie. His once black hair was shot through with gray, and his blue eyes had faded. The stone dogs that stood on either side of the throne looked more fierce.

But the hounds were still recovering from the shadows, their magic weakened now that the shadows were gone.

Didn't he understand that meant he and his clan were more vulnerable than ever?

Yvette strode down the marble hallway, away from the throne room, determined to head immediately back to Hamburg, and from there, to India and the tiger court, though she expected she'd have the exact same greeting there.

The tigers had been even more corrupted by the shadows, and so were even more vulnerable.

She needed allies. She couldn't fight the soul thieves, those corrupted magicians, on her own. She refused to call them demons. They were children, nasty and spoiled. She'd take them over her knee and spank them if she thought it would do any good.

"Excuse me."

A gentleman with salt-and-pepper hair stepped out of the shadows and drew up closer to her. He'd obviously been waiting for her. He had sharp features and a permanent twinkle in his brown eyes, as if there was always something about life that amused him. He wore a nice dress shirt with jeans and a jacket, American business casual.

"Yes?" Yvette asked frostily. She didn't have the patience to deal with another fool today.

Perhaps the soul eaters had stolen that from her as well. Though if she was honest, she'd never had that much patience for others, which was why she'd lived by herself on the mountain for so long.

"I am Rudolf Von DeWhite," the man said, clicking his heels together and bowing his head, like an old fashioned gentleman.

"Madame Lyon," Yvette replied, not giving a curtsy, but still dipping her head.

She hadn't shrunk with age, and was still taller than most women, even these youngsters with their better health and diet. This man at least came up to about her nose.

"Call me Rudi," the man said. "May I walk you to your car?"

"I will need to call one, actually," Yvette admitted. While she could still drive, particularly these modern cars that practically drove themselves compared with the original automobiles that she'd once known, she didn't trust her memory enough.

What if there was some gap that only exposed itself while she was hurtling along at 100 kilometers an hour?

"Let me drive you," Rudi said. "Please. It would be my pleasure." He glanced over his shoulder, then dropped his voice to a whisper. "I'd like a good excuse to get out of here for a while."

Yvette hid her smile. This Rudi seemed to find the atmosphere of the hound court as cold and oppressive as she did. "You may call me Yvette," she said as they left the grand front hall and stepped out into the late summer day.

The sky above them held thunderclouds, and the winds carried their usual gossip about the nearby hills, how many guards the hounds had around the palace, the training exercise the younger hounds were going through, the steaks the cooks were cooking for dinner later that evening.

"You know, you seem very much like a hound when you do that," Rudi commented.

"Excuse me?" Yvette asked, surprised. Had she completely forgotten how to be with people? Though it wasn't as if she'd ever had a lot of practice.

"You scent the air like a hound when you step into a new place," Rudi explained.

"Thank you," Yvette said, recognizing the compliment when she heard one.

Rudi didn't say anything more until he'd taken her to his car—a rental, but a nice one, with the front seat pushed all the way back so Yvette didn't feel as though she was folding herself in half to climb in.

Rudi gave her a grin. "My…charge is probably as tall as you are."

"Your charge?" Yvette asked.

"Lukas," Rudi said.

"The hound prince who defeated the shadows!" Yvette exclaimed. "I didn't know he was here."

"He isn't, now," Rudi said. "Though he was here. But a friend of ours is in trouble, and he went to help."

Yvette heard a complicated combination of emotions in the man's voice. Pride that his ward had gone off on his own to help. But pain, too, at being left behind. As well as fear, both for his ward and possibly for himself.

"Is this friend a magician?" Yvette asked.

Rudi gave her a sharp look. "No," he said slowly. "But she knows a lot of magicians. She knows a lot of people, and a lot about a lot of things."

Yvette nodded her head. So had she, once. "Is there a chance that the soul eaters may have gotten her?"

"I don't know," Rudi asked. "She was tough. Crocodile clan. But old. And she'd just survived the battle with the shadows."

"So vulnerable. Like your court," Yvette said.

Rudi nodded unhappily. "Though the tiger court will be more vulnerable," he pointed out.

"I shall go there next," Yvette told him. "The hound clan was closest." She wouldn't tell him about her debt.

"Will they listen to you?" Rudi asked as they drove through the corridor of pines that helped hide the entrance to the court.

Yvette shrugged. It didn't matter, not really, if they listened to her or not. She owned Indukala Khushi Deshmukh a debt.

"Do you have to leave right away?" Rudi asked.

Yvette knew better than to think he was propositioning her. She was old and forgetful, not stupid. "No, not right away. Why?"

"Lukas will be returning in a few days," Rudi said. "I think…I think you should meet him."

Yvette nodded slowly and said, "All right." The hounds weren't known for their foresight. The vipers were the clan best known for that.

But hounds had good instincts. It was part of what made them hounds.

And Yvette needed allies.

Maybe the trip to the hound court hadn't been a complete waste of time.

CARLOS

Carlos debated calling the police, telling them about his apartment just before he left, reporting that an infamous thief lived there. His reasoning was that the police would at least watch his place closely while he was gone if he reported it. They'd question everyone who came and left, and perhaps leave it intact, as a trap.

But Carlos wasn't sure when he'd be coming back. Plus, if he was honest with himself, he'd have to admit that the police weren't that smart. They'd just strip the place of its goods, keep half of them for themselves instead of returning all of it to the good law-abiding citizens of Mexico City, and then encourage his landlord to rent to someone more upstanding.

So he left with merely a small pack on his back, converting the watches and gold he already had acquired to quick cash. He got lousy rates, of course—he was in too much of a hurry to go bargain hunting.

No one waited for Carlos at the airport, which surprised him: He had imagined that his corrupted brothers might have flexed their considerable influence to stop him from leaving the country. Then again, he did travel under names they didn't know.

Still, Carlos didn't breathe easily until the plane took off. The three glasses of the best champagne first class had to offer didn't hurt.

Germany was cold, as Carlos had expected. He'd used his layover in Amsterdam to good use, and at least had the clothes.

The guards didn't bother him or even search him, just waved him through customs. Carlos didn't know whether to be relieved or offended. Maybe he didn't match the profile of a drug dealer, unlike the poor solo woman traveler who was directly behind him. Or maybe it was the passport and name he used, that of a well-connected businessman.

Carlos knew better than to try to drive himself to the hound court. Of course, he knew how to drive a car. He never did, though. He hadn't been bothered by a vision in a while, but he wouldn't risk injury to himself by trying to drive through one.

Carlos found himself walking by all the taxis waiting so orderly and patiently outside the airport. He wanted to stop. He'd thought about stopping more than once.

He didn't, though. That wasn't what he was supposed to do.

It was a strange vision riding him. He didn't feel ghostly fingers trying to direct him, as he'd felt when he'd left the temple. The vision didn't control him, not like how the soul eaters had been controlling the father or the other zombies. He could have taken a taxi.

It just wasn't necessary.

A bit past the taxis, further down the curb, was where passengers were dropped off and picked up. A long black sedan waited there, the engine purring like only a well-ordered German machine could.

Carlos abruptly longed for a wrench to throw into its engine, to disrupt all the smoothness he sensed there.

The young man waiting at the curb looked up and smiled at Carlos as he approached. "We've been expecting you," he said with a broad smile.

Carlos pulled back stiffly. Who had been expecting him? Who was this stranger? Carlos sniffed the air, and caught the faint trace of wet dog.

One of the hound court?

Carlos narrowed his eyes and studied the boy, who stood quite still and calm. Perhaps he was used to such examination. Carlos didn't see anything directing the boy except his own will and intentions.

The vision riding Carlos prompted him to step forward, into the car, and to go with this young man.

Was it safe? Or was it a trap?

Carlos would never know if he walked away.

山山

Li Li had never interacted with one from the boar clan before. Ariel was very different from her own people, very brash, very loud. But that might have been because she was an American. She exclaimed loudly over the beautiful red-clay roof tiles of the clan compound, the way the corners of the buildings tilted like a smile, how graceful the pond in the center was, asking loudly about whether the carp were good eating.

Li Li felt quite exhausted just listening to her. She had no idea that one could be an adult and still say every thought that came to one out loud.

Still, Li Li figured it was best that her new friend come with her to the compound, to visit the elders of the court, to tell them what she'd seen. Li Li hadn't been to the court for a while: she didn't interact much with them.

The elders might never forgive Li Li for taking action as she had. A watcher, well, watched.

And though Ariel was as different from her as a car was from a horse, she still felt as though they were kin.

Aunt Qe Nu was not the eldest aunt in the crocodile

court. But Aunt Ryo Hu had been sick recently, feeling her age, and Li Li hadn't wanted to wait.

Aunt Qe Nu agreed to meet them in formal Hall of Greeting on the compound. It was a long hall with beautiful lattice walls that let in the dappled sunshine. At the far end of the hall stood a tall, skinny altar that held a silver bowl of rice and a fine blue porcelain vase holding two bright yellow chrysanthemums. Next to them lay braided pieces of straw, shaped to form a long foot and claws—a representation of the crocodile clan.

Did the boar clan have similar altars? Li Li found that she longed to ask as she stood beside Ariel. They both had changed into much nicer clothes. Ariel had even taken Li Li's hint and had covered herself up, wearing a loose red and white blouse over a pair of modern black jeans. She didn't have anything other than her boots to wear, but she'd at least agreed to take them off at the door and stood in mismatched socks, one plain white, one striped.

As they drew closer to Aunt Qe Nu kneeling behind a portable tea table, Ariel grew stiffer. Was she frightened? Li Li suspected she was, based on how Ariel's breathing had also changed. There wasn't anything Li Li could say to the boar warrior, however, to assure her that there was no danger.

"Please, sit, have tea with me," Aunt Qe Nu said graciously, indicating the pillows on the other side of the tea table.

Ariel looked at Li Li and shook her head. Did she want to leave? That would be the height of disrespect.

"We can only stay for a short while," Li Li told her aunt. Hopefully that would mollify the boar warrior and she wouldn't shame herself.

"I understand," Aunt Qe Nu said. "Your friend has to be leaving soon, doesn't she?"

"That's correct, ma'am," Ariel said. "I need to catch my plane and head back to the United States."

Li Li had never heard the boar warrior speak so formally before. Her accent had greatly diminished as well.

"Then let's enjoy the time we have, shall we?" Aunt Qe Nu said. "Please, sit. Break bread with me."

Ariel paused for long enough that Li Li wondered if she'd refuse. Finally, Ariel gave Aunt Qe Nu a wide, pasted-on smile. "Why, bless your heart," she said as she smoothly sat. "What are y'all serving?"

What was going on? It was as though Ariel had just become a different person, one Li Li had never met.

Li Li would have to watch carefully to see what was going on with her friend.

"How long have you been here in the Middle Kingdom?" Aunt Qe Nu asked as she poured from the beautiful blue-and-gold porcelain teapot. The smell of rich black tea wafted out. There were also elegant rice crackers arranged artfully on a platter between them, with slivers of rolled cucumber held in place by strategically placed dabs of either black or red bean paste.

"I been here for a few days," Ariel said. "It's been marvelous. All the people! I swear, your everyday streets are more crowded than a Mardi Gras on a fine day in April."

She went on to talk about the temple she visited, the fine scrolls and paintings, the children riding a mechanical panda in the park.

Li Li wondered when Ariel had had time to see and do all those things. She sounded like a tourist brochure.

Ariel accepted a rice cake and put it on the small plate beside her as she continued to talk. If Li Li hadn't been watching carefully, she would have missed Ariel crumbling up a tiny bit of it then hiding it in her pocket.

But she never tasted it, just made it look as though she had. And she never took a sip of her tea, either, just brought it to her lips then put it back down again.

"Now, listen to me, just blathering on!" Ariel said after a bit. "I'm sure y'all have much more important things to attend to than to entertain me."

"It's been my pleasure," Aunt Qe Nu said, though Li Li could tell that she had her polite face on. Something bothered her as well. Li Li hoped it hadn't just been Ariel's blathering talk.

Aunt Qe Nu's eyes shifted just then, for a moment looking glazed.

Li Li kept her own expression placid. What had she just seen? Had it been anything? Or just a trick of the light?

"Was there something you needed? Some other reason for your visit?" Aunt Qe Nu continued.

"Well, as a matter of fact, ma'am," Ariel said, leaning a bit closer and lowering her voice. "I've been looking for a friend of mine. From the hound court."

"He hasn't come to call on me," Aunt Qe Nu said. "We have no formal relations with the hounds."

Li Li nodded. She'd already told Ariel that. Why was she asking about the boy she'd been following from the hound court?

"That's what I figured," Ariel said, leaning back. "But I had to ask. I suspect he's already left and gone back to Germany."

"Such a shame, to come all this way for nothing," Aunt Qe Nu said.

Li Li didn't understand the currents swimming through the room. Aunt Qe Nu seemed relieved that Ariel hadn't asked more. Was she hiding something? Was there some problem between the hound and crocodile courts?

Ariel seemed relieved as well. "That's just the way things go, sometimes," she said with a shrug. But she didn't sound as if she was disappointed.

"How did you meet Li Li?" Aunt Qe Nu asked.

There. That strange change in her eyes. Was there a reflection somewhere that Li Li hadn't noticed? A light flashing on and off?

Li Li felt her own back stiffen. She hadn't said anything about her precarious position to Ariel, hadn't mentioned that she'd be ruined as a watcher if her clan thought she'd acted, rashly or not.

"I followed her," Ariel said. She gave a sly grin to Li Li. "Wasn't easy. She's real good at sliding into the shadows, you know?"

Aunt Qe Nu beamed. "She's one of the best. I'm surprised you were able to find her at all."

"Boars are good hunters. As good as the hounds," Ariel boasted. "Maybe better."

Li Li doubted that was the truth. The hounds were well known for being able to track a scent across countries.

Then again, Li Li had watched more than one hog get raised. They were smart—possibly smarter than dogs. They also had a great sense of smell.

Maybe Ariel wasn't completely lying after all.

"Any who," Ariel said, pushing herself to standing. "It's time we skedaddled. Thank you very much for your time, ma'am," she added with a deep bow.

Li Li followed her, standing in surprise. It was on the edge of rudeness for them to be leaving so quickly.

Then again, Ariel was an American. What did they know of manners?

"You'll have to let me know what you see later," Aunt Qe Nu murmured. "If you find what you're looking for."

"Yes, ma'am," Ariel said. She gave another bow then quickly left the room.

"Li Li," Aunt Qe Nu said softly as she turned to leave. "Watch her. And report back soon."

"I will," Li Li assured her aunt. Then she quickly hurried out of the Hall of Greeting, blinking for a moment in the bright sunshine, seeking Ariel.

The boar warrior was already at the gate, waiting impatiently to leave.

What had that been all about? Why hadn't Ariel asked about the soul eaters? What was going on?

Li Li didn't like how unpredictable Ariel had become.

She also hadn't liked the undercurrents with Aunt Qe Nu, as if she, too, had more secrets to hide. Or the strange light that had come to her eyes.

Li Li vowed to watch them both.

FU RAN

Fu Ran left Lukas at his hotel after an afternoon of fruitless searching. Aunt Leeda's house didn't hold any clues, neither did Mei Ling's. She promised him that they'd meet for breakfast, but she would break that promise in a heartbeat if something more important came up.

Lukas had some interesting theories about the soul eaters, how they were attacking now that the shadows were gone. Fu Ran had been rather impressed that he'd been the one leading the attack against the shadows.

That still didn't make him clan, or rather part of her *shizu*.

Fortunately, he'd seemed to realize that, and had treated her as a friend and nothing else. It had been a relief to actually be able to work with a man, a colleague of sorts, without worrying about when he'd start hitting on her.

The compound of the crocodile clan felt like an oasis away from the bustling streets. It was set up in the old manner, with several halls in the center of the large square and rows of residential rooms along the edges. An old pond sat at the very heart of the complex, filled with grandfather goldfish longer than her arm.

Tall pines, twisted in elegant spires, lined the walkway from the round entrance to the Hall of Greeting. Fu Ran was pleased that someone from the court had agreed to meet her in the next hour. In the meanwhile, she ambled across the courtyard, visiting the shrine to *Gan Ou*, the lady of mercy, in the corner, then making her way back toward one of the smaller gardens set up behind the Hall of Ancestors.

Fu Ran paused when she heard voices coming from the garden. Should she not go in? Wait until it was empty?

Everyone had been so friendly so far. Fu Ran took another step forward, then froze.

She must be mistaken. That couldn't be the same businesswoman. The Chinese one, with the pearls.

But it was. Fu Ran recognized her. Deep in her bones. Her crocodile soul slid much closer to the surface, ready to protect her.

It was one of the magicians from that morning, who had attacked Lukas and her. One of the soul eaters.

Fu Ran didn't know the older woman who sat with the magician. But she wore a badge of power, over her heart.

Was this Aunt Qe Nu, who was supposed to meet with Fu Ran later?

Slowly, the older woman closed her eyes. The magician gave a triumphant smile and leaned over to whisper in her ear.

Fu Ran abruptly turned and walked away, out of the compound.

The crocodile court was corrupt. Her aunts. Her *family*.

The familiar rush of adrenaline overtook her, but it would do no good. She couldn't go back and fight them all. She had to assume that the disease had spread too far, too fast. She was alone here, and there wasn't anyone she could trust.

It seemed that she might be going to Germany after all.

ARIEL

Ariel couldn't help the shivers she had as they left the crocodile compound. She kept expecting to feel the sticky fingers of those damned soul eaters in her brain. Damn it! She should have insisted that they get a box of salt. That was next on her list. After they got her a new phone.

Aunt Qe Nu, or whatever the hell her name was, wasn't really herself. She was infected, like Aunt Mabel had been. Not in control.

It was much more subtle than Aunt Mabel's possession. Most of the time, she'd been talking to a leader of the crocodile clan.

But then her eyes…her eyes changed. One of those damned soul eaters would take over, acting as a puppet master.

Had Li Li seen that? She was a watcher, after all.

Ariel knew that Li Li wouldn't have seen the golden net around Aunt Qe Nu's head, sticky, like a spiderweb. Only a boar would see that kind of magic. The shadows had never been able to trick Ariel either—she was too much of the earth to fall for simple illusions.

It had taken Ariel a few moments to work out what the hell she was seeing. Why Li Li hadn't seen it, wasn't commenting on it. Probably none of the crocodile clan could.

Ariel had thought about going straight back to her hotel, right that moment, but then decided against it. They would expect her there. While Ariel was good at seeing magic, she had no protection against some kind of scrying spell. And who knew what kind of non-magical cameras or microphones had been placed in her rooms?

She tried to keep herself from growling out loud. They needed to get someplace crowded, where it would be difficult to track them.

That damned aunt had known about Lukas, known that he wasn't there anymore, that he'd been killed. Had she taken part in it, feasting on his brain? It made Ariel sick just to think about it.

Ariel saw the signs for a youth hostel and massage parlor just up the street. Better than nothing. She walked in, then reached back and put her arm around Li Li's shoulders and drew her close. "Follow my lead," she whispered.

Then she brought the pair of them up to the desk, giggling. "Howdy!" Ariel said loudly as she walked up to the desk.

The girl waiting there was skinny thin with long straight hair, as well as a puckered expression of disapproval that would probably break her face someday.

"Y'all got a room for the night?" Ariel asked loudly.

The girl sniffed, looking down her nose at them.

"The last place didn't work out too well," Ariel added. She pulled out her wallet and laid a hundred-dollar bill on the counter. "Did it?" she said, turning her head deliberately away from the girl and looking deeply into Li Li's eyes, resting their foreheads together.

Just breathe, she tried to tell the watcher. They needed someplace closer to the ground, someplace the precious aunts of the crocodile clan wouldn't bother looking. Someplace where there would be so many scents, it would be difficult to track them.

When Ariel turned back to the desk, the bill was gone. A key rested in its place.

"Thank you!" Ariel called, snatching it up with one hand and taking Li Li's hand in the other.

She raced up the stairs. The girl at the desk wouldn't be able to describe them. She'd been too ashamed to look them in the face. All she'd remember was a dark American and a shameful Chinese girl.

Good.

The room was about as crappy as Ariel expected. The door cleared the end of the bed by merely an inch. She wasn't about to take her boots off—the carpet crunched under her feet. A cracked porcelain sink dripped in the corner, the rust probably holding it together. Dim sunlight came through the dirty window, making it seem as though it was foggy outside.

And Ariel wasn't going to look any more closely at that bedcover than she had to, or the stains there.

At least Li Li finally seemed to have reached her limit. "What is going on?" she demanded. "Why are we here? Why didn't you ask Aunt Qe Nu about the soul eaters? Why did you talk about the hound prince instead?"

Ariel sighed. Now came the hard part.

"Your aunt's not really your aunt anymore," Ariel said softly. "She's being controlled. By the soul eaters."

YVETTE

Yvette tried to like the hound prince, this Lukas, when she met him. He was tall, as tall as her, with shaggy black hair that hung constantly in his blue eyes, and gangly arms and legs that he was still getting used to.

But he was so young, so earnest. He didn't have the patience that age brought. Just being around him made her exhausted in short order.

Rudi had insisted that they eat at a German restaurant that had been a pub for centuries. Yvette cringed at the hokey music they played. She'd been around long enough to know what German folk music actually sounded like, and it wasn't this.

The dark, aged wood that made up the walls were covered with stuffed glassy-eyed deer heads and plump pheasants, as well as stiff portraits of people long since passed. It was dark in there, the torches long since electrified, but still barely lighting the room. Uneven stones covered the floor.

They sat at a large round table in the corner, with two chairs left empty. Yvette assumed no one would be joining them, as Rudi had only specified a party of four when they'd come in.

The only thing that kept Yvette there was the scent of freshly baked bread that filled the restaurant, laced with sauerkraut and sweet mustard.

Lukas had brought a friend, a girl. She was of the crocodile clan, Chinese-American, and just as impatient and young. Fu Ran was obviously Chinese, but Yvette didn't try to address her in Mandarin.

When the first waiter came to serve the table, Lukas smiled at him in a way that told Yvette that the girl was not a girlfriend, and never would be. Rudi didn't appear to notice. The girl was oblivious as well.

Yvette felt pleased that finally she had another secret, more knowledge that was special.

The cider was excellent, well-crafted and tangy. It suited the perfectly spiced bratwurst that Rudi recommended she try. The conversation was stilted, none of them allies or even comfortable with one another.

Yvette still wasn't sure why Rudi had arranged for their first meeting in such a public place until a short, dark young man was also directed to their table.

"I am Carlos," he announced expansively. He had a calculating gleam to his eye that Yvette knew marked a con man. Rudi stiffened beside her.

Oh, this was going to be fun.

The hounds sniffed the air, none too subtly. Yvette turned her gaze to this Carlos, who stood there patiently, seeming to enjoy their scrutiny. He wore a navy-blue sweatshirt from the Amsterdam airport, a black fleece vest, and jeans. He was wiry in a way that spoke of too many missed meals. His black hair was stringy and he needed a shower. His cheeks were scarred and pocked with acne. Dark eyes stared out from under a heavy brow.

Yvette smiled further when she realized that he was from the viper clan. The spark of his snake soul glided comfortably around him, lazily turning, also not hiding.

Interesting. Had he foreseen their meeting and come to join them? She'd only met a few of the viper clan. She was looking forward to getting to know this Carlos.

Though she'd always keep her hand on her purse around him, something these children would have to figure out for themselves.

"Please, won't you join us?" Yvette asked him in fluent Spanish.

"Thank you," Carlos replied in English, sitting down easily in one of the two open chairs.

"How can we help you?" Rudi asked formally. It was good that he was on his guard.

It probably wouldn't help.

Carlos gave an expressive shrug. "I believe we're here to help each other."

"Really? Help with what?" Lukas asked.

Yvette was impressed. The boy had vulnerable and wide-eyed innocence down pat. He looked as though he was completely clueless, as though they hadn't been meeting to talk about a great threat.

Perhaps he wasn't as naïve as she'd first thought.

"The ones who steal will and soul, who make zombies of the most powerful," Carlos replied. He turned deadly serious. "The ones who have attacked the viper clan."

Yvette's stomach churned, a cold knot forming in the middle of her chest. The corrupted magicians had attacked the vipers? Who else had they gone after? Why were they attacking the clans first? Or were they also attacking magicians, who were wide-spread and not organized or easy to find?

Yvette's winds hadn't told her of any other attacks. Were they being fooled? Or hadn't there been any?

"Did you foresee us meeting here?" Fu Ran asked eagerly.

"My visions did not lead me here," Carlos admitted. "They merely foretold the zombies, the soul eaters."

"Then why are you here?" Rudi asked, surprised.

"I brought him." A young woman with blonde curls and brown eyes stepped up to the table. She wore nice enough clothes, looking like a secretary in her neat blouse and black pencil skirt.

"Greta!" Lukas exclaimed, standing up, then rushing over to hug her.

When they were that close, Yvette could see the family resemblance. A sister, probably, older. She'd lived hard, or been sick, her skin papery and pale.

"I don't have Oma's gift of visions," Greta said as she took the final seat. "But I still have dreams, occasionally. Like Oma did."

Interesting. She was fully human, not even a magician as far as Yvette could tell, though she wore more than one magical charm: her necklace, her bracelets, and something else hidden in her pocket.

Yvette knew of other humans who had dreams and visions, some of them foretelling the future, though most just plaguing the bearer. One had even sought Yvette out, assuming that she could be taught more magic. The seer had left disappointed but not deterred, determined to go find the right teacher who could help her.

"And she dreamed of me," Carlos purred. He gave her a possessive smile.

Yvette was glad that he didn't reach for Greta's hand or she might have had to slap him herself. The girl was vulnerable and not able to defend herself against such a one as Carlos.

The conversation flowed much better now, with Carlos telling tall tales of his travels, making even Fu Ran giggle. He flirted with everyone, including her. He seemed to know enough to leave Lukas alone, though.

Finally, after the coffee had been served, it was time to talk about what had brought them there.

Carlos had had visions of the coming attacks, though the vipers had mistaken his visions, assuming that he'd been foretelling the shadows.

That made sense to Yvette, as well as the others. The shadows had been a more obvious threat for decades.

Fu Ran and Lukas told of their time in China, and the attack there.

Finally, it was Yvette's turn.

"Make no mistake," she started. "I am old. I was born before the *fin de siècle*, in the previous century. I celebrated with Mama, watching the fireworks."

Rudi's eyebrows shot up at that. Carlos raised his glass of port in salute to her. The other children all looked at her wide-eyed.

It was good to know that she still wore her age well.

"Before the attack of the rogue magicians, those who call themselves the soul eaters, I was powerful. Some had said I was the most powerful of all the magicians." She shrugged. It had never mattered, before.

"They took my power. My knowledge, when they attacked. I still don't know all that I've lost," Yvette told them honestly. She continued to stumble across holes, pockets of frustration where once she had *known*.

"I only got away through the help of a tiger warrior. And by blowing my house up." Yvette paused, taking a sip of her coffee, remembering what she could of her sanctuary. The way the sunlight danced in the back garden when the winds blew the trees. The smell of fresh baked trout that she'd called from the stream not even an hour before. The sound of softly falling snow as it covered the lane, hiding her.

"You defeated the shadows," Yvette said, addressing the hound prince. "I need your help destroying those who are now hunting me. And, from the sounds of it, the other clans as well."

"I don't know what to do," Lukas admitted. "The shadows…Oma, my grandmother, had visions of them. Plans. She hid me for decades and prepared Rudi, others, to fight them." Lukas paused. "If she had visions of the soul eaters, she probably mistook them for the shadows, like the vipers did."

That wasn't good enough. "We need to find out where these rogue magicians are. Wipe them out," Yvette said deliberately, trying to appeal to the warrior nature of the clan members.

"What do they want?" Greta asked.

"Power," Carlos answered. "Control. They want to be the puppet masters behind all of the world's leaders." He told of his worst visions of the world, where no one had free will anymore.

"They also want knowledge," Yvette added. "They eat it, like candy, then go looking for more." She paused. She'd considered this for a long while, and thought it to be true. "When they attacked me, they used powers that weren't their own. Clan powers," she added.

Silence descended over the table for a moment while they all considered the ramifications of that.

"Why are they attacking now?" Fu Ran asked.

"Probably because the shadows are gone," Rudi said. "They don't have to share power, anymore."

Yvette shivered. The damned shadows had been bad enough. They could almost be forgiven for wanting to destroy the earth—they had been alien, after all.

These soul eaters? Were humans, and stupid enough to want to soil their own nest.

"You blew your house up," Rudi said, nodding toward Yvette. "Your clan's magic helped you escape," he added, addressing Carlos.

"And we ran," Lukas admitted.

"We wouldn't have gotten out of there alive if we hadn't," Fu Ran pointed out.

"We need to check with the other clans," Yvette said. "See if they've been attacked. The tiger clan will be the most vulnerable. Followed by the hound clan," she said pointedly.

Carlos looked at each of them. "I can see the zombies," he said slowly. "None of you are controlled by the soul eaters."

"For now, that will have to do," Rudi said decisively. He turned to Lukas. "We should check with Ariel. See if she knows anything."

"That is the boar clan woman who helped you defeat the shadows, isn't it?" Yvette said, pleased that she remembered, but also wondering if there was a chance that she'd get to meet her, another of the warriors who stopped the shadows.

"How do you know that?" Rudi asked, clearly surprised.

Yvette laughed at them. "*Monsieur*, I have told you already. I am old. I know things, despite the greedy ones who have robbed me."

"Do you know how to make one of those mirrors?" Carlos asked. "The ones that stop the soul eaters?"

Yvette shook her head. "I had one. For years. I had no

idea that was its purpose. The rogue magicians didn't attack me until after it had broken."

Greta spoke up. "I think we need to figure out how to make those mirrors," she said.

Yvette nodded slowly. She'd set her winds already to find out, or at least to find someone that knew, but they hadn't returned with anything useful. She blinked when she realized that everyone had turned to look at her.

"Me?" she asked, surprised.

"You're the only magician here," Fu Ran pointed out.

"I have been trying to find out how they're made," Yvette told them.

"How?" Lukas asked. He appeared to be merely curious, but Yvette had noticed how he'd listened much more than talked all afternoon.

The boy was more clever and sly than he appeared.

Maybe she could like him after all.

"The winds," she admitted finally. "They bring news to me."

Rudi gaped at her. "You're the magician of winds?" he asked, shocked. Clearly he'd heard of her.

Yvette shrugged. "I used to be. Now, I'm an old woman with a broken mind and an impossible quest."

She paused afterward, listening to the stunned silence around the table. She was glad she'd shocked them, startled them.

This wasn't some grand quest or adventure they were all about to go out on.

People had already died. And before the end, there would be many more deaths.

If only these children would listen and learn.

Before it was too late.

LI LI

"You are wrong," Li Li told Ariel harshly. "The soul eaters have not corrupted my clan."

It was bad enough that Ariel had brought them to this place, with the rotting fish stench from the restaurant next door and the cheap hashish that the youngsters smoked one room over. Li Li did grudgingly admit that it was a clever move. The rest of her clan would never think to look for Li Li in such a place as this. Even if they tracked her here, they'd assume that she merely passed by, or just entered the lobby. They never would have expected her to stay.

They had no idea of the places she'd gone, following scents and trails. Places much worse than this.

"I'm sorry," Ariel said. And she really did sound sorry. "But I can see it. It's like—golden threads. A web around her head."

"You must be mistaken," Li Li replied. It was true that the boars saw things. Better than any of the other clans. But this still couldn't be right.

Ariel shook her head. "Look, I don't know of any way to prove it to you. But she's not herself. Not fully."

"Then we watch," Li Li said firmly. "We watch the compound. I will watch my aunt. See if what you claim is true."

"We don't have time," Ariel growled. "The soul eaters are gaining strength. What if they take more people from your court, aunts you coulda saved if you'd moved faster?"

Li Li shook her head. "People get lost all the time," she said softly. "Life isn't fair." That was something she'd learned when she'd been eight years old and the Cultural Revolution had taken her parents.

Ariel peered closely at her. "All right," she said slowly. "We'll wait. We'll watch. But only for three days."

"Then what?" Li Li asked.

"Then we need to act. To move. To do something about them," Ariel said.

Li Li shivered. That wasn't in her nature. She'd never been taught action.

Maybe, though, it was time to learn.

VIRMAL

Virmal hadn't healed. His face still bore bright scars, his body ached, and his right leg could barely support his weight.

Plus, he'd never recover from the death of his sister.

Luckily, the other aunts didn't immediately turn on him when they came to the sickroom, found him covered in blood and the rest of the aunts dead. Someone had placed a camera in the room so that they could more easily watch the sick ones. Playing back the tape enabled them to see the aunts kill Harita without provocation, then turn and attack Virmal.

They were shocked and dismayed, another blow to the court that Virmal wasn't sure they'd recover from.

He still replied to the email that Lukas sent, still agreed to a Skype chat.

They would see his physical wounds. His greatest loss, too, if they looked closely enough.

Virmal held himself stiffly in front of the great computer monitor, looking directly into the camera at the top of it. These people were not his enemies. They'd fought together.

But Virmal couldn't trust anyone, now.

Several people were on the chat, each with their own window. Virmal knew that Rudi had set it up and secured the connection, so that no one could listen in.

Virmal stiffened further when he realized he didn't know three of the faces.

"Who are these people?" he demanded, staring directly at Lukas.

The boy seemed flustered. "Carlos, from the viper clan."

Virmal assumed that he was the man with the pocked skin and sharp features.

"Fu Ran, from the crocodile clan."

That must be the Asian woman. Pretty enough, if you liked them hard and energetic.

"And Yvette. A magician."

Virmal cut the connection immediately.

Were Lukas and the hound court already infected? Why would he allow a magician into this conversation?

The computer buzzed. Rudi was probably trying to reconnect the call.

Slowly, Virmal clicked the button to allow the call to continue. "What is she doing here?" he asked immediately. "Magicians are not to be trusted."

"She isn't a soul eater," Lukas assured him.

"How do you know?" Virmal challenged. He refused to look the woman in the eye. He wouldn't give her a chance to infect him.

A part of him knew he was being overly paranoid. He could hear Harita point that out, knew that she'd be rolling her eyes at his precaution.

But Harita wasn't actually there anymore.

Because of the damned magicians.

"I know," Carlos said. "I will vouch for her. Will that be good enough for you?"

Virmal paused, considering. The vipers were the ones with foresight. Perhaps this woman had a place in the future.

"All right," Virmal said grudgingly.

Rudi spoke up. "Where's Harita? Will she be joining us on another line?"

Virmal opened his mouth than closed it again as the grief struck him anew. For a moment, he found it difficult to breathe.

He was going to have to say the words out loud. Again.

"Harita is dead," he finally announced. "Killed by the soul eaters."

Technically, that was the truth. Though it had been Aunt Parita who had killed Harita, she never would have done so if she hadn't been under the influence of the soul eaters.

"Oh, Virmal, I'm so sorry," Lukas said sincerely. "What happened? I'm assuming it was a great battle, given your injuries."

"It was," Virmal said stiffly. "The soul eaters had taken over much of the tiger clan, those who'd been weakened by the departure of the shadows."

"You have my deepest sympathies," Carlos said. "Our priests, too, have been infected."

Virmal blinked, surprised. The damned soul eaters had gone after another court?

They all needed to die.

"What about the hound court?" Virmal demanded. "Are they still true?"

Rudi replied, "Some are. Some aren't."

"The crocodile court is infected," Fu Ran said.

Lukas seemed surprised by that. But he added, "We've probably lost Mei Ling. And we haven't been able to get in touch with Ariel. Or any of the boars."

"Their main plantation was blown up last week sometime," Yvette, the magician, added. "A great fire."

How did she know? Did they trust her information? It didn't appear to be a surprise to any of those on the call. "And the ravens?" Virmal asked.

"Peter says they've steered clear. Then again, they have gone through a recent purge," Lukas said dryly.

Virmal nodded. Since Peter had taken over the raven clan, more than one of the old regime had made the mistake of challenging him.

And dying.

"So how do we stop them?" Virmal asked. "Or do we go ahead and kill all the magicians?" he added, staring directly at Yvette, challenging.

He still considered a possibility.

"They have attacked me as well," she told him softly. "Taken more from me than you'll ever know."

"They took my sister," he growled at her. "My better half. My human soul."

"I want revenge as much as you do," Yvette told him. She paused, then added, "Do you know Indukala Khushi Deshmukh?"

Virmal hesitated, then nodded. One of his cousins, though he'd never really interacted with her much. She was older than he, and had been very cruel. He'd stayed away from her as much as he could when he'd come to visit the court.

"She came to see me. More than once," Yvette admitted. "The first time when she was infected by the shadows. She couldn't cross my borders, then. The last time, after the shadows had been defeated, she came again.

The soul eaters probably followed her." The older woman paused, then added, "She's dead. She died so that I could escape and avenge her."

"I will avenge her," Virmal told the magician sternly. Who did this human think she was, taking on such a debt for the tiger clan? They would see to their own.

"*Non*," Yvette told him sternly. "The debt is mine, not yours. I have already killed those directly responsible. And I will kill the others as well."

Though Virmal didn't want to like this magician, he found he was developing a grudging respect for her.

"So how do we stop them?" Virmal asked. That was one of the reasons why he'd accepted Lukas' invitation to talk. While he could involve all those in the tiger clan, they were still weak. Many would die.

"We set a trap," Yvette said. "We bring the strongest of them against the strongest of us. We weaken them, weaken their minds. Steal from them."

"How do we bait them?" Rudi asked. He seemed as perplexed as the others. "What do they want?"

Yvette's laugh sent chills down Virmal's spine. It sounded eerily familiar, like the laugh he'd given that morning when he'd almost sent the breakfast tray back because it contained grapefruit, and Harita hated grapefruit.

When he'd remembered that she was dead, he'd laughed, just like that.

"Me," Yvette said softly. "I'm considered a great prize among them. They want my knowledge."

"And what will we do once we've drawn them out?" Virmal asked.

"Destroy their magic," Greta proposed.

Virmal nodded slowly. That would be better than killing them all. Maybe.

"How?" Virmal asked.

"We send it through the mirrors," Yvette responded.

That made sense to Virmal. But…"I suppose you're the one to make the mirrors," he said sourly.

"With help," Yvette said. "There's a magician in India—"

"Named Ekanga," Virmal finished.

The perfectly arched eyebrow that Yvette raised reminded Virmal too much of Harita. "I'll get his number for you," he growled.

He didn't want to go back and visit that damned magician.

Then again, maybe Ekanga would be stupid enough to attack Virmal. Give him the excuse he needed to kill the *dhayana*.

"We'll meet again tomorrow, same time," Rudi announced.

"We're all so sorry for your loss," Lukas added, his dark eyes sorrowful.

Virmal snorted. "Don't be. Feel sorry for those who did it." He cut the call before anyone could say anything else, could remind him of his heart's greatest hole.

He didn't care, really, what happened to him after the battle. He'd kill, and probably be killed.

That was fine with him. He was already dead.

ARIEL

Ariel and Li Li camped outside the crocodile compound, having tea at a noodle shop just up the street. The owner knew Li Li and didn't bother them. They sat at a cheap wooden table that would get folded up every night and brought inside the store. The chairs were made from wooden slats that bit into Ariel's thighs. The tea was bitter, though Li Li seemed to enjoy it.

They had a good view of the round door that served as the main gate to the crocodile compound. Anyone looking at the complex from the street would think that many separate houses lined the block. They were just fronts, hiding the courtyard inside.

They watched in silence, something Ariel wasn't great at. But she didn't want to disturb Li Li, knew that she made a much better watcher.

Huge crowds of people came and went down the busy street. There were more people in Beijing than in all of Louisiana, she'd bet. Even during tourist season. Rich people in well-made suits. Poor people in drab clothes and straw sandals and hats.

It was mid-morning when Li Li reached across the table and touched Ariel's arm. "That woman," she said. "The businesswoman. She's a magician. My eyes keep sliding off her."

Ariel raised her nose to the air, trying to find her scent. But there were too many interfering smells, from the tea on the table, to the cabbage the old woman carried in the bowls hanging from her yoke, to the pollution that always hung around.

"Come on," Ariel said, standing.

They slid after the woman. She wore a beautiful, blue silk Chinese-style dress with a strand of pearls around her neck. Ariel could tell they were old and expensive: probably cost more than her bike at home.

Ariel knew better than to give Li Li a triumphant grin when the woman entered the crocodile compound without even slowing down.

It was more difficult to follow the woman once they went inside. Ariel followed the magic the woman gave off more easily than the woman herself. She had a damn distraction charm or something. Ariel didn't find her eyes sliding off so much as she kept finding herself wanting to look at other things, like the tall, twisted trees in the pots that lined the walkway, the red banner waving gently on one of the buildings, or even suddenly finding her stomach rumbling when the smell of fish and garlic wafted by.

Fortunately, they didn't have to follow the woman for long. Tall hedges set off the back gardens from the rest of the courtyard, each with their own doorway cut into the greenery. The woman slipped through one of those, into a side garden.

Ariel paused in the gateway. Li Li pushed in front of her. The watcher's face could have been cast in granite for all the emotions it showed.

Ariel took one step beyond the gate, then backed up immediately as Li Li came barreling out.

Li Li walked directly out of the gate of the compound then up the street, past where they'd been sitting.

Ariel followed, giving the watcher the time she needed to get herself back together.

Finally, Li Li led them to a large, open park. It was filled with tourists and loud children. Li Li led them to a small stone bench hidden under the trees.

Li Li sat down and stared out at the trees. Her look was harder, now.

Ariel wasn't sure what was going on in the young woman's head, but whatever it was, it weren't pretty.

Finally, Li Li spoke.

"That—that—that *magician* was sitting next to Aunt Qe Nu. In the garden. Bespelling her."

"I'm sorry," Ariel said. And she was.

But at least Li Li would now believe her.

"We have to stop her," Li Li said fiercely. "We've got to free my aunt."

"Got any suggestions on how to do that?" Ariel said. "'Cause I'm all ears."

Li Li nodded. "We must kill the magician."

"Okay," Ariel said slowly. It wasn't that she was opposed to such action. But did Li Li really mean it?

Had the mouse found her claws?

"We will track her," Li Li said. "Study her movements. Find her alone. Do away with her."

"Have you ever killed someone before, sweetheart?" Ariel asked gently.

Li Li turned and blinked at her, as if seeing her for the first time that morning. Hesitantly, she nodded.

"All right then," Ariel said. "Let's do this thing." She

wasn't about to get in the way of a mouse who suddenly wanted to roar like a lion.

VIRMAL

Virmal didn't want to go back to see Ekanga.

He wanted to stay in his rooms and grieve, to mourn for the loss of his sister and the elders of his clan. His people had been struck a double blow: First, the shadows, stripping them of their humanity and tainting their souls, giving them false powers in return, and now, the soul eaters decimating his clan's elders.

He wasn't the only one who now considered killing all the magicians, everywhere in the world.

It wouldn't be possible to hide so many deaths. The clans would end up stepping out from the shadows, acknowledging their own existence and asking the humans for help.

Virmal had never contemplated such an action before. As a boy, Grandmother Irita had put the fear of the clan into him. He knew just how fast he would have been killed if he'd breathed a word of his abilities to anyone, even hinted at it.

Plus, anyone he'd told would be just as dead.

But this was a new world, full of openness. Even in India. The possibilities excited him.

The old ones would have all counseled patience, and the importance of staying hidden.

They were all dead.

Before the tiger clan struck out, they needed more protection.

They needed more of the mirrors that turned away the soul eaters' magic.

The streets hadn't changed since the other day when Virmal had driven along them with Harita. He knew this. But it felt to him as though a dust storm had come up during the night and coated everything with a thin drab film. Not even the statue of Ganesh dancing on the corner sparkled anymore: The strings of white jasmine flowers hanging from his arm looked spoiled; the red paint outlining the lotus on the bottom of his upturned foot looked like blood; and even the flames of enlightenment dancing around his head had dimmed.

The driver of the motorcycle cab brought Virmal to the same spot, directly across the street from the magician's workshop. More discarded plastic bags and wrappers lay piled at the base of the walls of the shacks that lined the street. A young woman walking down the street, carrying an infant on her hip, swayed as she walked, as if the heat had sapped her strength and her youth, making her face frighteningly skeletal. Nothing green grew here: Even the plants in the pots outside the doorway to Ekanga's workshop seemed brown.

It took Virmal a moment to find the mirror still hanging in the mast tree to the right of the entrance.

As far as he could tell, it was the same. The wood hadn't cracked. The painting hadn't been chipped off. It still reflected back any magic Virmal sent at it, and subtly altered his divining spells.

So the magician probably wasn't corrupt, or in league with the others.

Ekanga had still better watch himself, or he'd end up as dead as all the others. Sooner, rather than later.

ARIEL

Ariel was surprised when Li Li suggested that they start their hunt at the trap that the soul eaters had laid, where they'd first met.

Seemed the girl had some good hunting instincts.

The damned magicians still had the trap going. They'd cleaned up the salt that Ariel had thrown on the first floor.

Ariel had another box of it in her bag, just in case.

The magicians didn't draw anyone in that morning. That was just as well, because Ariel damned sure wasn't about to let someone else die.

The only person who showed up that afternoon was the woman Ariel and Li Li wanted to track.

When she left, Ariel and Li Li followed her, though she was still difficult to see, and hard to follow.

However, her personal driver was human.

And unprotected.

Arrogant bitch hadn't thought to give him any kind of charm. He probably wasn't a person to her, but merely a tool.

Ariel had met too many rich folk like this woman, who

thought because they were powerful that they were the only ones who needed protection and not those around them. That somehow just their aura of specialness was enough.

She was about to learn just how wrong she was.

Li Li followed Ariel's lead, though she still was a hesitant thing. Ariel figured that was because she'd been watching for so long, not used to doing. Though she'd been the one who'd suggested killing the magician, she still just wanted to watch.

However, it was time to act, now.

The magician lived in a gated community in one of Beijing's suburbs. Two- and three-story townhouses took up block after block, with pristine yards and perfectly trimmed trees. The houses were all made out of wood, painted either white or beige. The whole place looked like it had been transplanted out of Generica, USA. Gave Ariel the creeps.

Fortunately, Li Li had some kind of concealment magic. Ariel's clan never bothered learning that kind of thing. Illusions didn't work on any of the boar clan, so why bother to learn how to do any?

Ariel could see right through Li Li's disguise, as well as her own. It still amused her, though, to think that she now appeared like a Chinese gal, complete with pale skin and long straight black hair instead of her dreads.

The magician seemed to do most of her work in the late afternoons and evenings. Ariel didn't know for certain, but she'd bet that the bitch just lounged around in the mornings, drinking her tea and reading her paper, instead of being up at dawn and working like most people Ariel knew.

The only time she got up early was when she went into

the crocodile court. At least Li Li hadn't seen her interacting with anyone else.

However, Aunt Jia Di, the actual head of the clan, was reported to be sick and had taken to her bed. Li Li couldn't get in to see her, which was worrisome.

But not something that Ariel could spend too much brain matter on, not at present.

Instead, Ariel spent her time studying the house, looking for magical traps. She found only a few, though one was a doozy—it worked like quicksand, and the more magic you poured into it, the more it took.

What would happen to a boar or a crocodile if she got caught in something like that? Would she be stuck in some in-between state, helpless as her warrior soul was drained from her? Or did souls go beyond mere magic, and would she be able to change and escape?

Ariel sure wasn't about to find out.

It didn't take long to plot a course through the backyard to the house. The back held fewer traps than the front, which didn't make any sense to Ariel. Was the fool only expecting attacks from the front?

Or were snares hidden there that even Ariel couldn't see?

VIRMAL

E kanga's room was still just as messy as it had been before. Several yards of bright blue-and-yellow cable cord had been added to the table, along with stacks and stacks of used paper coasters.

"Ah, my friend!" Ekanga said in greeting as Virmal came in. He wore the same dull brown robe, his bald head gleaming in the artificial light.

Virmal wondered again why the room was so sealed by magic, as if a single wind couldn't get in. Was it so that none of Ekanga's energies and magic would leak out and harm his neighbors? Or was it to protect himself from the other magicians?

"I didn't expect you to return so soon!" Ekanga continued. "And without your lovely sister? I hope there's nothing wrong."

"She's dead," Virmal managed to croak out. It was still so hard to say the words, like every recitation of them scored another furrow in his soul.

Ekanga grew very still, like prey before a hunter.

Virmal's tiger soul growled softly, pleased.

At least the magician recognized the precariousness of his position. A wounded tiger would kill even those trying to help her.

"I cannot express how sorry I am, Virmal," Ekanga said slowly. "Please. How may I be of assistance to you on this terrible day?"

Virmal nodded sharply, reining in his grief. "We need more mirrors," he said. "And the knowledge of how to make them."

Ekanga looked thoughtful. "I know that the tiger clan is the most magical of all the clans. But I doubt that even your people possess the necessary magical skill. Your magic is different. It comes from your soul. You don't intertwine the physical with the metaphysical, at least not in the same way."

"We need more of the damned mirrors," Virmal growled.

Ekanga shrugged. "I would teach you if I thought it would be useful, my friend. Truly, I would. Your sister was a delightful woman and a decent enough bargainer." He paused and shook his head. "I am very sorry. But the mirrors really are that difficult to make. The only ones I know of who have succeeded in making them are magicians of the highest order."

"So you have none and you will not help us," Virmal said. Good. Maybe he could kill a magician that day.

"I didn't say that," Ekanga said hastily. "I may have access to two others. I will have to check. As for learning how...do you know of any other magicians who could make the mirrors for you?"

"Perhaps," Virmal said, unwilling to give up any information to a magician. Even another magician's name.

Ekanga blinked, then shook his head. "You do not have to tell me, my friend. Here, I will make it easy for you."

Ekanga gave Virmal his contact information. It surprised Virmal how many social media accounts the magician had, including business accounts.

Virmal felt old, suddenly. He wasn't as connected. He'd never felt the need. Then again, he'd had Harita, and Harita had had all of those things.

He suddenly felt unmoored in the world.

He wasn't sure how to reconnect, or if he even would try.

Li Li

Li Li's heart raced as she and Ariel easily sprang over the back fence. It had been made to keep out humans, not their kind. Li Li didn't agree with Ariel that it was merely arrogance on the part of the magician, but because all the fences were that tall: It was more important to fit in. The arrogance came in with thinking she could protect herself just with magic, without any other defenses.

The yard itself was pristine, a miniature formal garden. A small stream trickled from one end to the other, with an equally small stone bridge crossing it. In one corner tall blue-glazed pots held exotic trees, lemons and oranges, that needed much care and had to be moved inside for the winter.

A round table under a large red umbrella stood in the other corner, on a stone patio. They'd never seen the magician use it. Like much of the rest of the yard, it was merely for show.

Li Li thought it sad that the magician lived such a solitary life. No friends had joined her for a meal during the entire week they'd followed her, no family had called. It was merely work and magic for her.

So focused. But for what?

Li Li carefully followed in Ariel's footsteps as she walked across the yard. The boar's eyes were a brilliant gold and tusks had formed from her lower jaw. She was still mostly human, still walked upright with smooth skin. Li Li found it fascinating. Her clan could also change into a partial state, but they appeared much different, with shimmering scales forming first, covering their skin.

The door to the townhouse had always been their greatest challenge. It was much stronger than it looked, reinforced with steel and magic.

That was, until Ariel pointed out that they didn't actually have to go through the door. Most people put their money in the obvious portal, while ignoring the easily accessible windows beside it.

Ariel paused and looked back at Li Li.

Li Li gulped. Then nodded, a thrill running through her.

They were actually going to attack.

Li Li hastily put up a sound-deadening spell.

The acrylic cracked and broke out of the frame with a single mighty punch of Ariel's fist.

Was the magician really that arrogant? That she wouldn't put additional protection on such an obvious opening?

Ariel was already leaping through the window. Li Li jumped in behind her.

They had to move quickly, now. The magician knew they were there.

Would she call for help? Neither of them expected her to. She was too solitary, possibly too arrogant as Ariel had proclaimed, to call anyone to come to her aid.

Li Li hoped they'd guessed right. Otherwise, they'd both be dead shortly.

YVETTE

Yvette carefully read the instructions back to Ekanga that she'd copied down in her long-hand cursive. She didn't trust him to send her everything: Knowing him, he'd go into far too much detail on some parts and just assume she had knowledge in other parts and not put in enough steps.

She'd always thought of him as a blowhard, useful, but going on and on about trivia that no one cared about but him.

Still, the process he'd recited to her seemed not easy, but not horribly difficult. It was both complicated and complex, with many steps. braiding together three spells while maintaining focus and using her will to bend the mirror. Certainly not impossible.

Rudi had set up a computer for her in one of the smaller guest rooms overlooking the back gardens. It was lovely, with many flowers and trees. Her winds had told her all about the compound, the classes with the boys, the training exercises they went on in the woods.

It all made her homesick, the order and discipline. She

longed for her lazy days on the mountain, her untamed garden, Mama's lavender mingled with her roses.

All her plants were probably dying without her care. The roses would all be gone by winter, as she hadn't covered them yet.

Yvette pulled her attention back to the Skype chat. That sort of inattention was likely to get her killed.

"What else can you tell me of these soul eaters?" she asked.

Ekanga's eyes widened with surprise. "I would have thought you'd be able to instruct the rest of us about them."

Yvette shrugged. Normally, that would have been the case. "They evade my winds," she said, peeved. "I'm not quite sure how."

Was it knowledge that she'd once had, that had been taken from her? She didn't think so. She didn't feel any kind of hole in her mind surrounding the soul eaters.

"Do you think that could be because of the nature of their magic?" Ekanga asked.

"No matter what they claim, they're still human, not demons," Yvette said dismissively. Surely Ekanga knew better than to believe what those children said.

"They are human, that is true," Ekanga said. "But the very nature of magic supports more than one source of power. Think about the clans. Their magic comes from a different place than ours."

Yvette considered the implications of that. Generally, her winds could readily identify magic, be it clan or magician, even those strange snake charmers in America and the huntsmen up in Iceland. And they knew the shadows as well, once she'd learned what to look for.

Were there other sources of magic? Was that why the damned soul eaters had evaded her so far?

"Thank you," Yvette said sincerely. "You may be onto something."

Ekanga beamed at her, his fat face shining. "Thank you, *mademoiselle*. It is an honor to work with you, at least once."

"What do you mean?" Yvette asked. Surely news of their plan hadn't slipped out.

Ekanga gave a hollow laugh. "Like you, I have far too much knowledge, am too attractive a prize for the corrupted ones. I've made my peace. I expect them to be coming soon. Any time now."

They said their goodbyes, but Yvette stayed seated at her desk.

Was Ekanga right? Would the soul eaters come after him? Particularly since he did have the knowledge of how to make the mirrors? Or was he merely being his usual, overly dramatic self?

Yvette didn't know. But she did put in a call to Virmal, leaving him a voicemail, asking him to go and check on the magician.

Soon.

ARIEL

Ariel pounded up the stairs of the house, barely noticing the soft, thick rugs under her hooves, or the elegantly painted cream walls. The stairs didn't shake, despite her best efforts.

The mage still sat at her morning table. The paper was spread out before her. She wore a fuzzy white bathrobe, the kind that only the best hotels in New Orleans had.

"You'll pay for that," she said coldly. "As well as any other damage to my house that you cause. Now leave. While you still can."

A wall of *will* swept over both of them, strong enough to make Ariel hesitate.

But it wasn't the mage's true power, now, was it? It was something she'd stolen from someone else. And while she could use it, Ariel doubted it was as strong as the original version.

Ariel gave the best reply she could think of. She called Gret, her boar soul, to the surface, changing in a flash.

And attacked.

YVETTE

Yvette worked alone in one of the cold laboratories. Lukas' sister Greta was a scientist—a botanist—but her labs weren't happy gardens. They were sterile places with white walls and stainless steel tables, the floor a hard plastic that was easily scrubbed. Nothing flourished there, despite the racks of plants lining the walls, their green drained by the purple lights they sat under.

Still, Yvette appreciated the quiet the lab held. The mountain hadn't been truly quiet, not really—there was always the rustling of the pines, the call of the birds, her gossiping winds. Greta's laboratory held the quiet of industry, manufactured not evolved.

Needs must when the devil drives. Yvette couldn't remember when she'd first heard that saying. Had it been Mama? One of the master lapidaries? Or had it been Thierry, after he'd grown from the boy she'd known into a skillful gem cutter himself?

At one time, she would have been able to call up not just the saying in French as well as English (though hadn't she heard it first in English?). She would have been able to recall who'd said it, where they'd been, the time of year, even the time of day.

The holes in her mind frightened her more than Mama's bears had as a child. What was she missing? She had no way of knowing.

And no time to figure it out.

Lukas' craftsmen had prepared the frame for the first mirror, using the exact dimension that Ekanga had specified. That part had been easy, with very little magic necessary, just a simple spell to hold the wood and mirror together.

Now came the difficult part: Bending the mirror using nothing more than her fist and her will.

If she lost focus, if she discovered another hole in her mind while in the middle of the process, the mirror would explode and the shards would cut her badly, possibly kill her. She couldn't wear gloves, however, or any kind of protective gear beyond her goggles: This magic needed skin contact.

She still had to do this. If not for her own revenge, then for Tiger Lily Indukala Khushi Deshmukh.

It made her laugh bitterly when she thought about it. There was no single aspect of her great knowledge that was useful in this battle, no profound fact or spell. There were no esoterica that would help. Instead, it was merely the fact that she was old and knew a lot that, that she had a brain that held do much, that they wanted to plunder.

Some Merlin.

A standing frame in front of Yvette loosely held a sheet mirror, its dark back to her. It was a foot square. The hole in the frame was only three inches across. However, Ekanga had assured her that was correct, that the bending and magic would take up more of the mirror, thicken it, until she was left with a much smaller piece.

Here goes nothing.

Yvette started the spells she needed, a thread of bending, another of knowing, another of hiding. She chanted out loud, blending the three spells together, a line of this, a line of that, like a braid. She had to grudgingly admit they fit together well, better than she'd expected.

Magic whirled around Yvette, swirling like thunderstorm winds. The smell changed to Mama's lavender instead of cool metal. Yvette cupped the magic in her hand, then made a fist and drove it into the back of the mirror.

The glass started to bend, slowly. Excited, Yvette pushed harder, sinking her fist into hard substance.

The strain made her arm shake. Yvette poured everything into the single point of her middle knuckle. Sparks flew and the mirror began to shrink.

This was going splendidly. Relief suffused Yvette.

Time for the next part.

Yvette added a thread of a fourth spell, part of a web, to drain away the seeking spells that touched the mirror, draw them out and away.

The mirror exploded.

Instantly, without thought, Yvette called winds to shove the shards away. The tinkling of breaking glass filled the quiet space, followed by the sound of Yvette's harsh breathing.

Slivers of mirror lay scattered before her, spread all the way across the floor. She brought up her hand to examine it critically. At least a dozen pieces of glass were embedded in her skin.

Yvette sighed as she took stock. The frame was still solid, waiting for its treasure. They had a dozen pieces of mirror for her to work on. She was tired, injured, but hadn't come even close to exhausting her will.

Mama had always said she was more stubborn than the rocks of the mountain.

Hopefully that was still true.

Yvette called up a cooling wind as she plucked out the shards of glass from her hand. A quick search of the nearby desk revealed a set of surgical towels. She tied one across her knuckles as a makeshift bandage, then she carefully placed the next mirror in the frame.

Time to start again.

LI LI

The battle didn't take long. Li Li had meant to join in. It had been her idea, after all, to attack the mage.

Instead, she merely watched, fascinated and revolted.

It wasn't that she hadn't seen fighting before. But her clan weren't barbarians. They didn't fight to the death, unlike the ravens.

It was humans who were much more likely to wreak carnage, as she'd seen more than once in her lifetime.

The magician had been strong, strong enough that Ariel was bleeding from her chest and her hip.

But the magician's powers had been stolen, and not her own. Li Li had seen more than one opportunity that the magician had missed to take down her opponent.

Ariel now stood over the broken body of the magician, her long tongue snaking out of her mouth and licking the blood off her snout. The brown fur that covered her forearms was also matted with blood. Would she lick that off too?

The rest of the morning nook looked undisturbed, the magician's tea in the fine, pale green porcelain tea cup still cooling. A few errant drops of blood dotted the newspapers spread across the table, but that was the only sign that something untoward had occurred.

Who would the police blame for the magician's death? They would investigate—she'd been a powerful woman, with all the right connections.

Ariel appeared to be reading her mind. She delicately dipped one razor-sharp hoof in the magician's blood, then wrote across the wall, in English, "Death to the Magi."

"Put those assholes on notice," Ariel said. "You hurt me and mine, there are gonna be consequences."

Li Li nodded. It would also tell her the level of influence the magicians had over the local police. Would they be able to cover up the crime? Or would it be splashed all over the papers?

"Now, we need to go see if Aunt Qe Nu is free of their influence," Li Li said. She found herself strangely calm at the prospect.

Either Aunt Qe Nu would be better, and they would know a cure. Though not all the magicians would be so easy to kill, Li Li knew that.

Or her aunt wouldn't be. Then Li Li would be faced with a much more difficult choice: Find and kill all the magicians responsible, or possibly all the magicians, everywhere, as Ariel had suggested more than once.

CARLOS

arlos knew better than to disturb the great mage as she was working. He'd heard of her—most of the clans had tales of her great magic and long life. She'd always answer questions truthfully, unlike his clan who specialized in misdirection.

He hadn't seen her at the final battle, though he was happy to let that damned arrogant tiger believe so. He hadn't seen a final battle. Just the zombies and the puppet masters.

That should have worried him, but it didn't. The future was generally shy, like a blushing bride, not ready to be beheld or revealed.

Still, Carlos watched the laboratory carefully, waiting for some sign that he could go in. He sat in the sterile hall outside the room. How could the hounds live in such a place? No windows. No greenery. Just cold and stone and *discipline*.

He'd show them discipline. They had no idea how much practice it took to lift the wallets and money clips that he did.

At least the clan hadn't come looking for him. What was happening at the temple? Were all the priests infected? The jungle had saved him, he knew.

As the door *snicked* open, Carlos leapt to his feet. The mage stood there, scowling at him. "What do you want?" she asked in her native French.

It was amazing how this proud woman made even a simple phrase like that sound like an insult.

Then she swayed, and Carlos realized she was injured. "*Señora*, please. Let me help you."

Tiny dots of blood covered her cheeks. Her hand was wrapped in a blood-soaked cloth. The front of her shirt sparkled with the shards of glass imbedded in it.

Yvette gave Carlos a sharp nod. He was at her side in an instant, one arm under her shoulders, supporting her as she sagged.

"Three mirrors," she whispered hoarsely.

Carlos glanced back at the laboratory. There was glass everywhere, tiny slivers of mirror, many speckled with blood.

It looked as though a party had gone terribly wrong.

Yvette limped as they walked, letting Carlos take more and more of her weight.

"How many more mirrors to go?" he asked as he led her to her rooms, just down the hall. She'd insisted on staying in a hastily converted office instead of the main living quarters of the court.

Carlos understood why, now. He wouldn't want to be seen in the state she was currently in, trying to fend off questions.

"None," Yvette said. "Need more mirrors."

It took Carlos a moment to figure out what she meant. She'd broken nine of the twelve mirrors, and only managed to make three.

No wonder she was so exhausted. And so bloody.

The door to her room was open. Either Yvette didn't have anything worth stealing, or she assumed no one would dare.

Or perhaps her winds had opened it for her.

It was another windowless place. A bed had been shoved up against the far wall, sandwiched in by a tall, four-drawer, black metal filing cabinet at the foot. A few toiletries sat on top of it. Abstract artwork of large orange and red circles balanced on thin black lines hung on the walls. Another door stood open to the left—a bathroom, with toilet and sink.

Carlos helped Yvette sit on the bed, then went into the bathroom. He wet one of the washcloths he found there, then grabbed the empty waste basket and filled it with water as well.

It surprised Carlos that it didn't bother him to kneel next to Yvette, to tenderly wash her hands and pick out the remaining slivers of mirror. To wipe her fevered brow and clear the blood off her face.

She needed a shower to wash the slivers out of her hair. Or maybe she could call some delicate winds to remove them, after she'd rested.

Carlos wished for a moment that he could tell the fathers about this work, that they hadn't been corrupted. Would they believe that Carlos had been able to humble himself, to merely serve?

As little as two weeks ago, Carlos might not have believed it either.

But while his visions had led them all to this point, for the first time, Carlos also realized that events had grown bigger than just him. He was an important part of their plan, but just a part. The team had taken on more significance than just the individual players.

It felt odd, but good.

The water in the wastebasket held enough blood by the time Carlos was finished that he could no longer see the bottom of it. But Yvette seemed to be breathing easier. She'd swayed while he'd worked, barely able to hold herself up.

Now, she was curled on her side, sleeping peacefully. She looked older, much older, now. Her skin had that paper quality to it that the truly old get, as if age had worn it away from the inside. A blue vein pulsed near her temple. Wrinkles marred her broad forehead.

Carlos said a blessing over her sleeping form, then went to find the others.

They'd have to hear about her success, not her failure.

Someone would have to be sent to clean her laboratory.

And to stock it again with more mirrors, because even Carlos knew that she'd insist on trying again.

ARIEL

A riel waited at the noodle shop just up the street from the crocodile compound while Li Li tried to assess Aunt Qe Nu's health. The afternoon was warm and the pollution hung heavy in the air, a sickly orange cloud that floated just above the buildings. It made Ariel shiver, though she knew that the pollution was just that, and not the shadows.

She found Beijing fascinating, though she was already tired of the crowds. Li Li had taken her to the *best* places to eat. Still, she was getting tired of rice, something she never would have expected.

At least she'd finally gotten a new phone. Now all she had to do was program it, figure out how to get her contacts.

Li Li wore what Ariel called her determined face—the one showing almost no emotion.

A tiny bit of despair leaked around her mask, however.

"She's taken to her bed," Li Li announced without sitting down. "No one is allowed to see her."

Ariel nodded, not surprised. "Like Aunt Jia Di?" The head of the crocodile clan had taken to her bed recently as well.

Li Li nodded slowly. Obviously, she'd made the same connection. "Exactly the same," she said softly. She sat down on the folding wooden chair, hard, her shoulders slumping. "What are we to do?" she asked.

"Kill all the magicians?" Ariel suggested with a smile. She wasn't completely joking. It seemed to be the most obvious solution.

Li Li shivered. "There must be another way," she stated adamantly.

Ariel sighed. She wasn't sure how the crocodile court worked. The inner circle of the boars settled things behind closed doors, over sweet tea and hours of conversation.

Sometimes, though, that didn't work, and a challenge would be issued.

"Can you make a challenge?" Ariel asked. "Accuse the court of being corrupt? Aunt Qe Nu and Aunt Jia Di?"

"I can," Li Li said slowly. "But I have to have irrefutable proof. Unsupported claims get—well, there are consequences."

Ariel wasn't sure what that meant exactly, but she wouldn't be surprised if the person making the claim died. "I'm not sure how to bring them proof. Not unless we hogtie one of those magicians and bring them with us to the court."

"If I call a gathering, can you identify all those who are corrupted?" Li Li asked.

"I can," Ariel said. She'd been practicing seeing the magicians' webs all week while they'd been watching the woman.

"Good. Then I will call a hearing."

Ariel wasn't certain what the Chinese equivalent of *and may god have mercy on our souls* was. If she had known, she still might not have said it out loud.

Was it really their souls that needed protecting? Or the corrupted ones?

VIRMAL

The mirror outside of Ekanga's workshop was missing.

Virmal's stomach turned. He was too late. The soul eaters had gotten here first.

The limp mast tree still stood in its pot, the branches drooping. The opening to the workshop still looked dark and ominous. Virmal couldn't see anyone watching. He sent seeking spells up and down the street, looking for any spare trail of magic.

Nothing but ordinary poor people going about their business.

It should have occurred to Virmal that Ekanga was in danger, particularly after helping so much. The soul eaters would go after him.

It wasn't as if Virmal would have invited him into the compound of the tiger court. But maybe he could have done something more, given him some sort of guard or protection.

Virmal nearly drove away at that point; however, he

wanted to see what had actually become of Ekanga's workshop. Did anything of value remain?

Then he realized that the spells making the corridor seem so dark were still working. That meant Ekanga was still alive. He quickly rushed into the corridor.

The smell of blood lay heavy in the air.

At the end of the dark hallway the six-panel door stood ajar. Magic leaked out around the edges. Bright lights burned in the room. Junk still lay heaped everywhere, even strewn across the table, now.

There, to the side, lay Ekanga, face down.

Virmal rushed to the magician's side, kneeling down in the cold blood, then turning the magician over gently.

The magician didn't have long. His heartbeat was thready and weak. Virmal didn't have any magic that would save him, either. The clan had never bothered to learn any kind of healing spells.

"What happened?" Virmal asked.

Ekanga's eyes fluttered open. They were covered in cataracts for a moment, then cleared slightly. "The soul eaters found me. Yvette told them how."

"The mage of winds?" Virmal asked. He *knew* she wasn't to be trusted.

"See how everything has been blown down?" Ekanga asked weakly.

Virmal looked at the shelves. There *was* a cant to a few of the shelves, as if the items had been knocked over by a great wind.

"Why would she do this?"

"Power," Ekanga wheezed. "Never trust her. Never trust a woman."

Ekanga faded fast. His breath grew ragged. Had he willed himself to stay alive until he'd delivered his message?

The magician's eyes suddenly cleared more. He blinked, as if he were surprised. His mouth gaped as he struggled to speak again.

"What is it?" Virmal asked, leaning even closer.

"Never trust…a magician," he whispered.

His heart stuttered, then ceased to beat.

Virmal stayed where he was, kneeling beside the body of Ekanga for long moments.

He'd heard the warnings from Lukas and the others, the signs to look for regarding possession.

Had Ekanga been himself? Or had one of the soul eaters been controlling his words?

It didn't matter, not really.

Virmal would never trust a magician.

Li Li wasn't sure if she was pleased that the assembled clan was treating her gathering like a party. The women stood in groups, chatting and laughing, hugging old friends. It had been a while since the clan had gathered together—possibly too long.

They met in the assembly hall that was sandwiched between two long rows of sleeping rooms. The room itself had been built in the Fifties and showed its age with the buzzing fluorescent lights, the browning textured ceiling tiles, the linoleum floor that was designed to look like marble, and the very narrow windows, giving the place a closed-in feeling.

At least the scrolls painted with beautiful watercolors had been maintained, showing peaceful waterfalls, ponds, and rivers.

It was time that they redid this hall, made it someplace where the clan would want to gather.

Li Li stood alone on the stage at the far end of the hall. It was plain wood, poorly constructed, with gaps between the boards. A microphone stood beside her. Li Li felt drab and out of place among these women. They dressed in fashionable shirts and jeans, or skirts and blazers, or even traditional Chinese dresses, with impeccable makeup and hairdos.

While Li Li had never cared about her hair or practiced with makeup. She'd chosen all her clothes so she'd never stand out.

Maybe it was time to update her closet as well.

Ariel stood out, dressed in a tight T-shirt that had pictures of Mao done in four different colors like that soup can painting, tight jeans, and her black boots. Her dark skin and dreads made her an exotic beauty, rough and solid among the flitting butterflies of Li Li's clan.

The other women politely ignored Ariel, as she hadn't been introduced, yet. They still watched her carefully, each group circling near enough to be able to see her closely at least once.

Ariel and Li Li had worked out some hand signals so Li Li had a rough idea of who in the crowd was affected and who wasn't. It frustrated her that she couldn't see the magic like Ariel. But she recognized the behaviors, the glassy stare that came between animated conversations, the way a woman's body might suddenly jerk and steer her away from the direction she'd been walking.

If only they had more time! Li Li wanted to watch more, to be certain. She wasn't used to having to make snap decisions about who was infected and who wasn't.

But there was no time. The disease was spreading, and soon, all the leaders would be controlled by the soul eaters.

Li Li had to act now. She wiped her sweating hands on her thighs and stepped behind the microphone.

"Hello?" Li Li said into the mike. "Hello? *Nin hau*."

That brought a laugh at least. Most of the women turned toward the stage, toward *her*.

Li Li gulped. She was a watcher. She wasn't meant to be *seen* like this.

"I am Li Li. I am a watcher for the *shizu*. And I am here to tell you that we are in danger of being corrupted from within," she declared, her voice growing stronger. "I have *seen* it."

"What have you seen?" a woman from the crowd asked.

Li Li recognized her as Aunt Zhen Yi. And also as one of the corrupted ones.

"There's a group of magicians—corrupted humans—who call themselves the soul eaters. They steal a person's memories, and possibly their soul. They live on the power." She wouldn't reveal that the magician could then use that person's abilities, at least for a while.

"Did you bring us one of those magicians?" Aunt Zhen Yi asked, glancing over her shoulder at Ariel.

"They have a trap set up in the city," Li Li said. "Where they've been luring not just the crocodile clan but others as well. They trap them there, steal their powers." Li Li paused, then added, "Doesn't each and every one of you know someone who has recently faded away? Dropped out of sight?"

A soft murmuring went through the crowd. It had been a gamble on Li Li's part to bring that up, but she was glad she had.

"Are you going to take us to this lair?" Aunt Zhen Yi asked.

Li Li was certain that it was already being dismantled now that it had been exposed.

And probably set up in a different place, a different part of the city, but that was a problem for another time.

"I will not," Li Li said. "Instead, I will expose those of the court who have already been corrupted."

Before Aunt Zhen Yi could say anything else, Ariel was suddenly behind her. The boar had partially changed. One strong arm wrapped around Aunt Zhen Yi's chest, bringing her tight against Ariel's front, holding her arms still.

Ariel's other arm, with its razor-sharp hoof, rested gently against Aunt Zhen Yi's jugular.

If she struggled or tried anything, she'd die.

The other aunts pulled back from the two.

Li Li knew that if she didn't handle the situation well, they'd both be overwhelmed and killed in short order.

"Watch her!" Li Li commanded. "Watch her eyes!"

For a moment, Zhen Yi's eyes glazed over, as Li Li had bet that they would.

"What do you mean?" Zhen Yi asked. "There's nothing wrong with my eyes. Let me go this instant, you fool."

That set some of the aunts murmuring more.

Aunt Zhen Yi wasn't known for her arrogance.

"That is not her talking," Li Li said sadly. "The soul eaters, the magicians, are her puppet masters."

"You are an idiot," Aunt Zhen Yi said. Her voice had fully changed, now. She was clearly no longer in charge.

"Lock the doors!" Li Li called out suddenly. "She is not the only one corrupted. Look at your neighbors, your friends, your allies. Have they not been themselves lately? Are they taking secret meetings? Do they have odd friends whom you've never met?"

Li Li's horror grew as the words came pouring out. She recognized them from her youth, from the revolutions she'd lived through. From Mao.

But the words kept coming. She couldn't swallow them down, even as her stomach churned, disgust filling her.

She'd finally found her voice.

"Beware the unbeliever! Stay true to your sisters, to the clan!"

The women began to separate, looking at one another suspiciously.

"Ya Dai! Mei Bao! Xi Yi!" Li Li called out the names of the women Ariel had identified.

The women separated out the ones who had been named, surrounding them. Gasps were heard as the guilty ones jerked or looked out with glazed eyes.

"You cannot stop us," Zhen Yi taunted. "There are too many of us."

Without warning, one of the accused started changing into her crocodile form, her claws glistening. She turned and bit the one standing beside her with her great jaws and fearsome teeth.

Li Li stood shocked. No challenge had been issued. No warning given.

Suddenly, the rest of the clan started changing. Great growls filled the room as sister attacked sister, claws rending bodies apart, scales no protection from multiple attackers.

Li Li watched in horror as her clan turned on itself.

And the ones responsible died.

ARIEL

Ariel considered the battle to be a tie, at best. The crocodiles had attacked each other, leaving her alone after she'd killed the creature she'd been holding. Plus, of the fifteen who'd died, only three of them had been innocent, at least as far as she could tell, with no golden web controlling their actions.

Maybe they had other secrets, or were disliked for some other reason. She knew that among her own clan there were a few aunts who might also have been killed in "friendly fire," just because of their general nastiness.

Ariel sat with Li Li in one of the closed-off gardens in the courtyard of the clan. The evening was full of the sounds of the city just beyond them, the tinkling of bicycle bells, the putter of scooters, the faint calls of the few birds who lived there.

Trees surrounded them, though not wild growing trees, but tame ones in pots, their limbs clipped and pretty. A stone waterfall trickled in the corner, with the statue of some goddess Ariel didn't recognize standing at the base of the shallow pond. The benches were made of carved marble, a red color that looked too much like blood for Ariel's peace of mind.

Along one side stood a row of bamboo trees, rustling in the slightest wind, their branches intertwined. They made a good hedge, though Ariel doubted she and Li Li were actually alone.

Li Li appeared to be in shock. Ariel wasn't sure what was the biggest part: that she'd spoken up in front of a crowd, or that she'd been believed.

All the killing that night hadn't helped.

It had finally been revealed that Aunt Qe Nu and Aung Jia Di had fallen into deep comas. None of the healing magic of the clan had been able to bring them back. The fact that they still jerked in their sleep when they should have been motionless lent credence to Li Li's claims that they, too, had been corrupted.

But what would bring them back?

"They must all die," Li Li said into the night air.

"Excuse me?" Ariel asked. Was she saying that her aunts must all die? Ariel did a quick scan of Li Li for any magical entanglements, but she didn't see any.

"The magicians. They must all die," Li Li declared. "To make up for the hurt to my people. To your people. For the good of all the clans."

"Okay," Ariel said slowly. Mouse really had found her teeth. "That's a lot of killing," she said, though she'd had the same thought herself. It would be difficult to hide so many deaths. The other aunts in the crocodile clan were already trying to figure out how to disguise the death of so many of their own.

The world was too connected for that many people to die unnoticed.

"And they won't all be as easy to kill as that first one was," Ariel added. "The magicians are all gonna be more cautious now. I doubt they'll be less arrogant—that might be built into their genes."

"I know," Li Li said. "But we have to stop them."

Ariel nodded. They did have to stop the damned magicians. "Maybe we should go talk with, I don't know, the tigers or someone. They have the most magic of any of the clans." Harita had been awesome, and even Virmal had turned out to be kinda cool, even if he did come across like a stuck-up prick sometimes.

"We will contact all the clans," Li Li said. "I will make sure of it."

"What if they all say no?" Ariel asked. "What if they say we have to bide our time, wait until it's right?" She'd certainly heard that before, more than once.

Li Li turned golden eyes toward Ariel. It was the first time she'd really seen the watcher's crocodile soul.

"We kill all the magicians anyway."

Three days later, Li Li sat in a neat room at the crocodile compound and listened to all the reports coming in. Even the ones that were written she still read out loud to herself. While she could read not only traditional but simplified Chinese characters, was a cadence to the spoken language that told her more than the words did.

The room was plain, with no calligraphy on the walls, no fine pottery on the shelves in the corner. Just a western-style wooden desk under a window covered in rice paper so the light that came through was soft and diluted. She sat on an old stool, upright and stiff.

Since the first time Li Li had seen the soul eaters operate, she'd always kept an eye on them. She knew where they lived, not just in Beijing but around the rest of China as well.

Spies went out and came back with news, some human, mostly clan. The soul eaters had many, *many* new recruits. Some had voluntarily joined, minor magicians who never had had much power. Some had been taken over and were merely puppets for the main group.

Hundreds of magicians lived in China—partly because there were so many people. Even India didn't have as many magicians.

As far as Li Li could tell, the soul eaters were strongest here. Had this been where they'd originated? She didn't know.

So here, in her homeland, was where the clans would have to attack.

The court had agreed with her assessment. Here was where the hammer would fall first.

FU RAN

F u Ran frowned as she sat back from the computer screen. Rudi had set up a secured connection for her to contact the crocodile court, or at least to respond to them when they'd called, trying to reach her.

Her hotel in Hamburg was quaint, a turn-of-the-century building with antique radiators and all marble bathrooms. The bed had an iron frame and a light down comforter. The windows all cranked open, and there was no air conditioning, of course.

It was that kind of quaint place that her parents loved. It made Fu Ran want to get out her nail polish and paint nasty words on the walls, just to shake the place up.

But Fu Ran refrained. Besides, there were too many other things to think about at the moment.

Like how the crocodile court had been cleansed.

And how they were now calling for the death of all the magicians.

Fu Ran hadn't bothered trying to counter the young woman's comments, or to tell her that other plans were afoot. She'd had a disturbing, fanatical gleam to her eye that Fu Ran didn't trust. It reminded her too much of the addicts she'd seen in the ER, the ones who fervently swore they were no longer doing shit, when their blood work told a completely different story.

Would their plan work? Would they be able to attack the magicians, drain them? Yvette swore the magicians were connected in a great web. Carlos agreed. If the plan worked, and they could suck enough power from a large enough group of magicians, they might be able to draw in all the other magicians connected. Could possibly drain them all.

Fu Ran felt her heart racing again, just thinking about it. It was a gamble, the greatest one of her life.

The knock on her door didn't surprise her. The crocodile clan had reached out to all its members to talk about this plan. So they'd also be reaching out to the other courts as well.

Lukas came barreling past her when she opened the door. "Did you hear?" he asked, already pacing from her bed to the window and back.

"Come in, won't you," Fu Ran said. "No, I'm not doing anything right now. Why don't you have a seat?"

Lukas at least had the grace to flush with embarrassment. "I'm sorry. Is this a bad time?" He suddenly stopped moving and held himself perfectly motionless.

His sudden stillness impressed her.

"In answer to your first question, yes, I heard. The crocodile clan wants to declare war on the magicians. All the magicians. They'll start by getting rid of all of those who reside in China."

Lukas nodded. "But the worst part of it? Is that they

know they can't hide all those deaths. They want to force the clans to come out. Into the open. To step out of the shadows. The tiger clan is already halfway convinced this is a good idea. Virmal…Virmal will never be himself again. Not without Harita."

Fu Ran nodded. What had happened to him truly made her sad.

However, his personal tragedy shrank when compared to everything else they faced.

"I can't believe that's what they're proposing!" Lukas finally said, the words exploding from him as he started to pace again.

"I can," Fu Ran replied quietly.

"Not you, too?" Lukas asked sharply.

"What do you mean by that?" She shook her head. "Never mind. Let me explain." She paused, weighing her words carefully. "I am *shizu*, from the crocodile clan." She drew herself up to her full height, aware that she barely came up to his mid-chest. "Make no mistake. I am powerful. Strong. And doubly hidden."

"How so?" Lukas asked, puzzled.

Good. At least the boy was listening.

"I know you had to stay hidden for years, hiding your human self. That wasn't easy to bear, was it?" she asked.

The boy grimaced and shook his head. It was obvious his experience still haunted him. He had that thousand-yard stare sometimes that made Fu Ran think of the veterans who'd seen too much death. It made him seem ancient.

While the rest of the time he acted like a boy half his age.

"As a woman, I am expected to be seen and not heard. For my beauty, or lack thereof, to be commented upon and judged. If I speak up, I'm a mouthy bitch who doesn't know her place." Fu Ran held up her hand when Lukas might have spoken up. "I know. I know. It's changing. Less so than you think, and certainly not as much in countries other than the United States.

Lukas gave a grudging nod.

"So let me repeat. I am powerful. I am strong. And I cannot do anything to show it. I must remain in the role set out for me by society. Do you understand why some in the clan, particularly the female-centric clans, may be agitating to break free?"

"There are reasons why we've stayed hidden," Lukas countered. "Do you think the humans will really accept that there are *others* living beside them?"

"I think the humans are more ready than they've ever been," Fu Ran replied. "Look at all the popular entertainment. The movies and books. It's all about the others around us."

"That's not the same," Lukas said sourly.

"True," Fu Ran said. "It would be a shock. And there would be a sharp reaction. But this is also not the dark ages. We have laws, now. At least in the US. Protection." She paused, then grinned. "And things like the internet, Youtube. They couldn't just hide us or deny us."

"It still isn't a good idea," Lukas said.

"I know you think so," Fu Ran said.

"And you?" Lukas asked. "What do you think?"

While it made Fu Ran pleased that he'd asked, that he'd actually listened and that he'd realized she hadn't stated her opinion.

"I don't know," she told him truthfully. "Would it be such a bad thing?"

Long after Lukas had left, Fu Ran continued to mull

the question over, trying to see all the advantages and disadvantages of the situation.

She'd never been one for that much introspection, however. She kept coming back to the same question.

Would that be such a bad thing?

LUKAS

Lukas ground his teeth in frustration. This was all taking so long! Yvette had only been able to make three mirrors at her first attempt, and merely two during her second.

He worried about her. None of the clans had much healing magic—being able to change into their true self healed most wounds. There were no other magicians Lukas trusted.

Lukas paced in the scent garden outside the castle. Hamlin, his hound soul, nudged up against him, trying to provide comfort. Lukas had had to wait *so long* when he'd been fighting with the shadows. Had to endure so much.

Hadn't it been enough?

Now, he was having to do the same again. Endure, and wait.

Squares of exotic grasses grew between the stepping stones: Kentucky bluegrass, African wild grass, even a grass unique to Ecuador. A low stone bench curved around the back. Just beyond, a fountain made of marble splashed.

And beyond that stood the woods.

Lukas raised his head and sniffed the air. He remembered those woods, training in them. The hound master would lay scents, trails for them to follow. Though Hamlin wasn't a scent hound, his nose was just as keen. He'd been just as good chasing rabbits as the sight hounds.

Hamlin pushed at him again. Longing flooded Lukas' soul.

He'd watched and waited long enough. Even if he couldn't do anything about the damned soul eaters, he could still act.

Lukas stripped out of his clothes and encouraged Hamlin to come to the surface. The change was easier than when he'd first become human.

A spike of fear always went through him, but it was more manageable now. He would always be afraid that he'd never be able to change back, that he'd be stuck in hound form again.

But there was joy in being a hound, a happiness that he'd never found anywhere else.

Hamlin gave a happy *woof* and bounded off into the woods, stretching his powerful legs as they gave chase to the wind.

It was good to remember what they were fighting for, too.

YVETTE

I t took all day, despite getting up at a horrid hour and driving like mad.

But Rudi got Yvette to the Alps.

They weren't *her* mountain, of course. But they were close enough, and she would just have to make do.

The air in the mountains was distinct, clear and crisp, despite the late afternoon heat. Thin ribbons of clouds stretched across the blue sky. Tall pines swayed just behind the outlook Yvette stood on. Rudi had parked the car a respectful distance away, giving Yvette some privacy.

He was younger than she, but still older than the rest of the children. He understood such things. He would have made a delightful companion if she'd been younger.

Such things were not worth contemplating. She was far too old, now. Possibly would have been too old for him even ten years ago.

No matter.

The winds sang to her, so far up above the rest of the world. Rudi had found her a beautiful valley to look down on. Steep-roofed houses in a picturesque village ranged to her right.

It wasn't Lamoura. She would never see her village again. She supposed she'd known that when she started her Quixotic mission.

Still. She missed the cobbled streets and the old, tiny, stone houses that had stubbornly remained, tucked in between the new tourist places. She could still smell the way the sun baked the cobblestones in the summer. Could still hear the trickle of water through the newfangled gutters as the snows melted.

The soul eaters had stolen many of her memories from when she'd been a girl. She could recall laughing like mad with her friend Thierry in the early spring sunshine, but she couldn't remember why. Or the taste of new cheese from the market.

It was time, however, to say goodbye to the rest. She might call up her winds again at a future battle, but the knowledge of them would be stripped from her as she did.

Lukas might talk of protecting her, but what did a hound know of defending one's mind? Even a guardian hound?

Yvette started calling up all her winds, her friends and truly her only companions for all her long years. The spring winds that brought the lightest of rains and carried the freshest of scents. The rough winds that made the pines in her front yard rustle and throw their needles to the ground. The late autumn winds that were heavy with the promise of winter snow.

And more, so many more.

Not all of them, though. There were holes in her mind, blank spots where winds had been kept.

It made her so angry that she couldn't remember them

all. That she could almost recall the soft touch of a summer breeze, only to not remember its name or how to call it.

She clenched her fists in frustration to stop herself from pounding the air.

Yvette called up as many winds as she could remember, letting them swirl around her like playful puppies, tugging on her long trench coat and running through her wild curls. She listened to their news of the horrible purge that had gone on at the crocodile court, the tiger court, and the boar court. Of the traitors still imprisoned in the cells of the hound court, the deaths of those at the raven court. How the vipers were still struggling to find the truth amid their corruption and their visions.

At least the jungle would help them, as they were starting to learn. The ones who didn't come back hadn't been true vipers after all.

Finally, Yvette let the winds go. She said goodbye to them, each and every one of them. Expressed her gratitude for all that they'd done for her, how they'd educated and entertained her.

Not that they understood what she said. They were worse than the children now attending her, thoughtless beyond their own needs. They'd never understand that she was gone, wouldn't miss being called, wouldn't even wonder where she'd disappeared to.

They had no thoughts of their own.

Yvette understood how selfish it was for her to come here, for her to insist on her goodbyes. It was just to soothe her soul before she died.

The winds didn't know or care.

When Yvette had finished, she took a final deep breath of the clean mountain air, knowing it was her last.

She wouldn't even remember the mountains if she lived past the end of the battle.

Rudi had promised to kill her if all that remained was a shell. She knew he'd keep his word.

Yvette returned to the car where Rudi still stood, looking every part the hound guard he'd once been, proud in his long blue coat, standing at attention. "Thank you," she said simply. She had no words beyond that.

"It was my honor," Rudi replied.

His voice sounded strange. Choked. What had he seen?

No matter. Maybe he would remember, and remember her, after she passed.

For the winds wouldn't.

RUDI

R udi opened the car door for Yvette and got her seated, tending to her as though she was a precious package, wrapping a soft blanket around her legs again. She was tired enough not to snap at his fussing, for which Rudi was grateful.

He wanted to do something for this magnificent woman. He was glad he'd brought her to the mountains as she'd requested, despite the long and tiring drive, despite the doubts that Virmal had cast on Yvette's trustworthiness.

Rudi was doubly glad that he'd been able to witness her magic.

He'd heard of the mage of winds. Not all at the hound court had, but Oma had instructed him about her. Oma had never gone to see the woman herself, but she'd told Rudi of those in the various clans going to talk with Yvette, ask her questions, in exchange for clippings to power her other magic. Though she never took much, and generally just wanted something of value in exchange.

Now Rudi understood why.

Rudi was the least magical hound in the entire clan. He had difficulty casting the most common of spells.

That also meant that casual magic slid off him. Some charms wouldn't work on him. It had made him a good guardian for Lukas, when the entire court was searching for the boy.

That meant that Rudi hadn't been able to actually see what Yvette had been doing. He knew she'd been casting magic, but exactly what, he never would have been able to tell. Her long, very fashionable trench coat had flattened against her front, then her back. Her gray curls had appeared to move on their own as fingers of wind traced through them. Little dust devils appeared by her feet, powered by currents that left him alone.

So he knew that she'd called some winds. Not a big deal.

His nose told a completely different story.

Oh, the scents her winds carried! They came from all over the world. The dank smell of the canals in Vienna, full of secrets and ancient wisdom. The scent of African savannahs and the spoor of gazelle, that made his heart pound. The warm smell of fresh baked baguettes from the finest of patisseries in Paris.

And more.

No wonder Yvette would be of such value to the soul eaters. He didn't know if they could eat the knowledge carried on her winds or not. Even so, she did indeed know a lot as she claimed, given how much the winds had carried to her just in the short time while he'd been watching her.

Would she survive the coming battle?

Rudi didn't know. But he vowed he'd protect her as much as he could.

And kill her body if the soul eaters took her spirit.
It was the least he could do.

YVETTE

Using two fingers, Yvette typed, starting a private chat with Yi Chan.

Can you believe the arrogance of these clans? They've threatened to kill all the magicians! All of us!

Yvette waited for his response. Yi Chen was more computer-savvy than she was, but Rudi had set up her system, swearing that to anyone snooping around it would look as though she was using a public internet café in Munich.

Finally, a message came in reply.

So good to hear from you! We heard you'd been attacked. Where are you?

Yvette narrowed her eyes at the screen. She was still at the hound court. She'd agreed to move to a better room, now that she'd made the mirrors—only half a dozen, when they'd hoped for two dozen or more.

They would have to do.

Now, it was time to set the trap.

Traveling.

It was more or less the truth. She'd be leaving for China, soon.

How did you get away?

The crocodile court had identified Yi Chen as one of the soul eaters. Was he asking that question to help his brothers and the other soul eaters? Or was he innocent, and merely trying to protect himself?

Yvette had no way of knowing. She didn't want the crocodile court to be right about Yi Chen. She'd always liked him.

Fools ignored the old knowledge that I have.

Which again was true. They hadn't bothered to disturb her knowledge of the internal combustion engine. How could that possibly be useful?

Yvette went on, boasting.

My knowledge runs much deeper than they could handle.

Would Yi Chen believe it? Her boast would seem normal—Yvette didn't believe in hiding her talents. It would make her irresistible to the soul eaters.

You have much to teach us, wise one.

That was odd. Yi Chen had never called her *wise one* before. Was it really Yi Chen on the other end of the invisible tether that connected them? Or was it a soul eater? Someone impersonating him?

Yi Chen had given the right passwords, all three of them. Plus failed the second one twice, as protocol demanded.

Maybe he was lost.

Yvette shook her head. Many were lost, including herself. She typed into the chat:

We need to fight the clans. Show them they can't just brush us all aside.

Yvette looked out the window over the back garden

while she waited for Yi Chen's response. He wasn't the only magician that she knew in China. However, he was one of the few who wouldn't suspect anything when she contacted him directly.

They were all far too paranoid now.

Or possibly, not paranoid enough.

What about those who attacked you?

Yvette nodded. A reasonable enough question.

The ones directly responsible are all dead.

She figured they'd already confirmed that.

The others I will deal with later. The clan is a more immediate threat.

Let him believe that she was dismissing the soul eaters that way. It was the best way to rile up an enemy—to merely laugh at their antics, not to cower in fear.

We should meet. You should come to us. There is strength in numbers.

Sadness washed over Yvette. This wasn't the Yi Chen she'd known. He would never have suggested a meeting in public. He was far too private a person. She'd only leaned his gender after a decade of communicating with him.

Yvette wasn't about to play along, though. That wasn't in *her* nature.

Surely you're joking. A large group of us together just gives the clans a bigger target. Haven't you learned anything from history?

The response came back almost immediately.

The internet isn't secure either. You're at a public terminal in Munich.

At least Rudi was as good as he claimed.

I will meet with you. And you alone. Not a large group.

Again, the reply came back quickly.

I can pick you up from the airport.

Yvette rolled her eyes at his eagerness. Did he really think she was that stupid?

No. We will meet in a private place. Outdoors.

He knew she used the winds as her main defense. If they met outside, she'd have her strongest defenses ready. It made sense for her to insist on meeting in this fashion.

A long string of numbers appeared on the screen. Yvette copied them down carefully in her longhand cursive that was no longer popular. Then she typed into the message window:

Three days, at noon.

That would give her a little bit of time. A small slice of breathing room.

She didn't have Mama's cheerful acceptance of her fate.

She needed the chance to say more goodbyes.

VIRMAL

Virmal waited by the exit to customs in Beijing. He knew that it would be difficult for him to find Yvette. He figured she'd be traveling in disguise. He also assumed that her magic was stronger than she let on. She might be old, yes, but she was also going to be powerful.

He didn't need to see her. He already knew what she looked like from the Skype chats. Besides, he was certain he could smell her magic coming from a mile away.

It surprised him when she walked right by him without him registering that the ancient woman who'd just passed was *her*. This magician that Lukas and the others had foolishly put their trust into.

She was *old*. There wasn't a flat plane that remained on her face: Every inch of skin was covered in wrinkles. Her gray and silver curls had thinned to the point that he could easily see the age spots on her scalp. She walked slowly, though without a cane, her back still straight.

It was only after she'd walked by him that his brain caught up with the fact that he hadn't seen her walk through the doors of customs, though he'd been watching everyone, tracking every single body carefully.

Virmal turned and hurried after her, trying to at least catch a scent of her trail. But nothing remained. All he could smell was the overpowering stench of the humans who filled this booming place, the rice they'd eaten and sweat out, the constant acrid pollution, the fresh paint on the walls trying to cover up how shoddily this place had been constructed.

Virmal rushed to the exits, nearly missing Yvette again as she walked through the doors ahead of him.

Her magic was very strong if he couldn't follow her. His eyes kept sliding off her back.

She walked directly to a private taxi. Had she called for it earlier?

Or had she already betrayed them to the soul eaters? Was the car actually driven by one of *them*?

Virmal wasn't about to do something as attention-getting as hopping in a taxi himself and commanding the driver to follow the other car. He had Yvette's itinerary. He knew where she was staying.

He'd just have to work harder at keeping an eye on her.

And then stop her, and the others, before it was too late.

CARLOS

Carlos woke on the morning of the big battle, knowing that it was his time to die.

He rolled over on the exquisite high-thread-count sheets of the soft bed, wondering. Where did this feeling come from? Was he corrupted? Afraid? Or was this real?

A band of light slipped through the drawn curtains to the east. The rest of the room was as dark as a tomb. No one lay beside him on the fluffy pillows: He'd turned down the girl he'd met in the bar the night before, though he'd been curious what her rates were.

While he'd trusted his own senses that she was what she seemed, the others would have disapproved. What if she'd turned out to be a soul eater?

Maybe he should have indulged.

Carlos waited for the bitterness to arrive. He was still a young man. He hadn't had his most important vision yet. He hadn't changed the world.

His name would never be written on the temple steps, above the other heroes.

The warmth of the covers comforted him. He found his

viper soul circling closer. He seemed placid as well, accepting of their fate.

They wouldn't kill him without cost. That much he knew. He would take out two, maybe three, before they'd get him.

Could his vision of the soul eaters be enough to mark his place in history? He had been the only one on the lookout for them. He'd seen the zombies when no one else had. He'd known they weren't the shadows, though none of his brothers had never believed him.

Maybe killing Father Pablo had been his fate. He shivered and burrowed further under the blankets. He didn't want to be remembered for that. He wanted to be known for his cleverness, his skills, though he didn't have many that were socially acceptable.

A stray thought came to him: Maybe it had been his relationship with Yvette, the great mage. He'd been the only one to stay with her those long days of making the mirrors. He'd been the one to take care of her when she emerged from her workroom, bleeding and beyond exhaustion. It had been a case of diminished returns: three mirrors the first day out of a dozen attempts, two the next, and only one the last day, before she'd declared herself done.

He had never known someone as stubborn as her. Or as arrogant. His people tended to go around obstacles, rather than attempt to go through them. Always deflect, slide, answer any question from an outsider with a question.

For all that she controlled the winds, she didn't resemble them: She was more solid than the mountains she talked of with longing.

She would be gone that day too, Carlos knew. It wasn't any foretelling, just common sense. No one would be able to survive the attack that was coming. Not even Yvette.

Carlos rose from his nest of blankets and flowed to the window, opening the shades and letting the sunlight in, filtered by the pollution that always hung over the city.

Then he did something he hadn't done since he'd been a boy: He knelt and prayed to the old gods, as he'd been taught. He thanked Q'ukamatz—Plumed Serpent—and Itzanam—Grandfather Iguana—as well as the nameless Christian god and his son. He thanked Saint Lonrad for the thick jungle surrounding the temple, and Saint Patrick for leading the viper clan to safety. He asked the gods to keep his feet on the Green Road.

He knew better than to ask them to keep him from the road to Xibalba—there was no path for him that day other than death.

VIRMAL

Virmal finally caught up with Yvette the next morning at breakfast. The hotel she'd chosen served a comforting English breakfast, complete with cold toast and strong black tea.

The dining room was open. All the patrons, with the exception of him, were white and generally older. All the servers were bored Asians. The little round tables all had stiff white linen tablecloths. The tables all had tiny cut-glass vases with delicate flowers in them. The china was good quality, and the silverware heavy.

It had an old-world elegance to it. As well as a stuffiness and stiffness that made Virmal long for the clutter of the tiger court.

Yvette turned and looked directly at him as she finished the final cup of her French press coffee. "You could come and join me, you know."

She spoke using a conversational tone, he was certain. But a wind carried her words directly to his ears.

Harita would berate him for being so careless. He'd had his own disguise in place. He wondered when she'd seen through it. When he'd sat down? Or after he'd spent his entire meal staring at her?

He hesitated to join her. Then again, what could this old woman do to him? Particularly in such a public place?

Virmal slowly sauntered to her table, as if he didn't have a care in the world, and he was doing *her* a favor.

The look she gave him reminded him of one of Grandmother Irita's looks, the one that warned that he should watch himself.

He stood stiffly next to her table even after she indicated the chair next to hers. "Please, won't you join me?" she asked in elegant French.

"Thank you," Virmal said, sitting smoothly.

"Should I order us another coffee? Or perhaps a pot of their most excellent tea?" Yvette asked.

"No, thank you," Virmal said. He didn't want to break bread with this woman.

Yvette sighed, obviously exasperated. "Young people. So impatient."

Virmal sat back, surprised. Did she mistake his intention? He was following her because he didn't trust her.

Any of the clan who trusted a magician was a fool.

"I lived during a time when enemies commonly met and exchanged polite words and ideas, seeing if they could convince the other to join their side," Yvette said as she sat back. "Some things were black and white, but many were gray."

"But that was if an enemy could be trusted," Virmal said, nodding. "At least for a little while."

"I see your point," Yvette said. "It's hard when friends can't even trust friends."

Without warning, her charm slipped away.

Had she done that on purpose?

Virmal suddenly found himself seated next to a woman who was still old, yes, but also very powerful. Her magic sat as comfortably on her as her hand-tailored clothing. She didn't look as though she'd been born in the previous century, but then again, Ekanga hadn't looked as old as he'd claimed either.

"Make no mistake," Yvette continued, her voice like iron. "I'm not sure I would trust me. I may have been compromised when I was first attacked."

She slipped her disguise back on as easily as one would slip on a ring.

"Then why shouldn't I kill you now?" Virmal asked. Since they were having a polite conversation and all. It made no sense to him that they would trust her.

"Because I'm your best bait for the trap we've set," Yvette replied.

"But who will the trap close on?" Virmal asked. "Us? Or them?"

Yvette took a moment to carefully examine Virmal, to really see him. He abruptly wished he had set up more of his own magical defenses.

Whoever underestimated this woman was a fool.

"That's up to you, now, isn't it?" Yvette said as she put down her cup and stood. "Whether you decide to live or not."

She turned and swept away, out of the room, before Virmal had a chance to respond.

There was never any question in his mind that he wouldn't survive for long after the passing of his sister.

But that was a private grief. It had no bearing on the upcoming battle.

Did it?

44

The attack of the clans against the magicians started at dawn. Li Li hadn't realized that she knew so much about organizing raids as she did.

But it made sense. She'd always watched, everything, everyone.

Learned.

She knew about people. Their hiding places. Their vulnerable spots. Their secrets.

It wasn't difficult to put that knowledge to use.

Tracking the magicians had been much more difficult. Powerful spells protected them now, distraction spells and fading spells and even masking smells that made them, at first glance, appear to be clan and not human.

Had they found them all? Li Li didn't know. As a watcher, she would have preferred watching and waiting and making better identification. Time they could not waste.

As it was, there would be some collateral damage, some innocents would be sacrificed.

Didn't that happen in every revolution?

It would be a shame to lose some of the friendly mages, those who weren't soul eaters, but they had to be certain. Just because a mage hadn't been seen with the soul eaters didn't mean that he or she hadn't been compromised.

The magicians in Beijing almost outnumbered the members of the crocodile clan. Ariel had called in some of her people to help. It had taken her a while to get her phone to work right, but they'd finally gone to a fancy store downtown that had taken care of everything for her.

They'd had a party the night before—loud and talking so fast and with such strange accents that Li Li hadn't been able to follow half of the conversations. They'd seemed happy to help, however, happy to get revenge on the ones who had killed Aunt Mabel and Aunt Belle and the other high powered aunts in the boar clan.

As Li Li had suspected, it wouldn't be easy to kill all the magicians.

Some of them were party officials—no one too high in the ranks of the party, but still, people with many human bodyguards. Others had taken the threat of the clans to heart and now traveled everywhere in groups, aware that singly they were much more vulnerable.

None of that would save them.

Li Li and Ariel hunted together, planning to take out one of the head magicians. He'd hidden himself away in a walled enclave. Armed human guards roamed the grounds. High-tech locks and magic protected the gates. The house itself was mostly underground.

They'd need an army to take it properly.

All they had were two clan warriors.

"If we do this, and do it right, we'll be legends," Ariel bragged as Li Li drove them through the pre-dawn light.

Their car looked like a high-class Mercedes, sleek and black as it dove through traffic.

It was much more than it seemed.

Beijing didn't sleep—waves of workers on their bicycles filled the lanes. Restaurants that served them, as well as those just coming off their shifts, were open. The office workers still slept, but they'd be rising soon to go jogging or do their Tai Chi in the park with the old people, one of the newest health crazes.

They'd timed their attack for the very end of the night shift of guards: Before the other guards arrived to relieve them, so the humans would be tired.

Like the other magicians, this one thought himself too important to protect his guards or to hire minor magicians.

It made Li Li as angry as Ariel, how badly they treated their workers. None of the revolutions and upheavals her country had endured had actually made much difference to the poor peasants and farmers.

But this time, this revolution, would change everything.

The magician had built his front gate carefully, a little off center from the main street. Also, the main street leading to the house was always full of parked cars, so it wasn't easy to get a running start.

Li Li didn't care about banging into any of the other cars, or damaging the vehicle they drove in. She floored it, thrilling at the way the great beast leaped forward, the loud rumbling noise from its engine the first sign of its true nature.

The guards didn't understand the nature of the attack. They didn't mass at the gate.

That was their first mistake. The arrogance of their leader had rubbed off on them.

As Li Li and Ariel cleared the last set of cars, the

guards realized something was wrong. However, they still assumed that it was just a nice Mercedes out of control, a car that would simply shred its tires on the row of spikes raising from the threshold and bounce off the gate.

No one bothered shooting at them.

Fools.

Only at the last minute did Li Li release the spell that disguised the car. The air around them shimmered as the vehicle transformed. The momentum they'd built up continued even during the change.

Now the guards realized they were in trouble.

The tank rolled across their barrier and through the gate as if there was nothing there. The guards belatedly started shooting. The bullets tinged off.

Li Li shook her head, deafened by the noise. She gave her crocodile grin to Ariel, who returned it with her own grin, her mighty boar tusks reaching higher as her mouth turned up.

The tank punched through the front door of the main building.

Li Li's heart pounded just as loudly in her chest. Not only because of the coming fight, no.

But because she was *acting*, once again.

No longer merely watching.

YVETTE

The stench from the landfill made Yvette's eyes water. She couldn't call up a strong enough wind, not in the private car she'd hired, to keep the smell away. She'd already known this was where Yi Chen was sending her, already knew it was a trap.

A raft of black workers' bicycles were lined up near the entry. Yvette knew they must be in desperate poverty if they came out here daily to rummage through the castoffs of the privileged. She grieved for them, vowing to send them a fresh wind, at least for today.

Garbage lay piled high close to the entrance, and grew to much taller heights. Trails led through the piles. To the far right, a large bulldozer stood, silent.

Maybe there was too much garbage for even its mechanical heart to withstand.

The driver didn't want to let her out of the car. "Ma'am, this can't be the right place," he said again.

Yvette continued to play the part of an ignorant heiress. "My husband left me this property," she said querulously. "I plan to claim it."

"You should check again," the man said.

"You should mind your place," Yvette told him haughtily as she opened the door to let herself out of the car.

Even the winds who came running to her could barely keep the stench away.

The driver looked at her, but then shrugged his shoulders and drove off.

It might have been easier to cast a spell on the man to get him to do her bidding, to merely drive her there and drop her off. But it wouldn't have been nearly as much fun. She'd still left him with a small forgetting spell, so he'd only remember the arrogant white woman, not her name or her face.

That should keep him out of danger. Saving an innocent's life wasn't much, and that one life wouldn't have much weight after the reckoning that would happen that day.

It still meant something to Yvette.

Yvette straightened up after the man had left. She tugged off her disguise charm and slipped it into her pocket as well. She had other tricks up her sleeve. Plus, she wanted the soul eaters to recognize her, to find her.

And just as the others would have to trust that this old woman had done her part, she'd have to rely on them to be the cavalry and come to her rescue. Though she didn't know if they were coming or not, or when, or even if they were in China. They'd left her out of all their plans on purpose, so that the soul eaters wouldn't be able to take the knowledge from her.

Even if they did come, she couldn't save all of them any more than she could save herself.

However, she wasn't about to die without a fight.

Yvette called up her winds, the strong ones that could

hopefully protect her from a physical attack. She pulled out a charm she'd constructed, made of twine, sunflower seeds, ivy and red ribbon, and put it in the palm of her hand. It looked like a child's attempt at a Christmas tree ornament, lopsided and prickly. Then she fed part of the strongest wind into it, trapping it there.

The wind whirled around her, angry, like a mini-cyclone. It was the best armor she could come up with.

The charm would only hold the wind for so long, before it blew itself apart. However, because the wind was contained in a charm, she didn't have to worry about the knowledge of the wind or how to work with it being stolen from her.

She slipped the charm over her wrist so she wouldn't drop it. Then she called up a seeking wind, instructing it to search out the particularly oily smell of the soul eaters' magic.

Yvette had finally figured out how the soul eaters had bypassed her winds, why it was so difficult to find out anything about them. Ekanga had been correct—they used a different strain of magic than most.

A particularly clever wind had managed to scoop up the scent of it and had eagerly carried it to Yvette. The magic had smelled dark and greasy, reminding her of the shadows.

No wonder these fools thought of themselves as demons—they used a magic that was horribly tainted. It came from a black place in the human soul, while Yvette had only known magic that came from light and air.

It had taken some practice, but Yvette had finally figured out the right winds to use for searching out the soul eaters.

Their scent was not difficult to find in the garbage dump. *Mon dieu*. There were so many of them.

Yvette almost turned back. But where could she go? She couldn't just steal one of the bicycles next to the entrance. The soul eaters were certain to have cars hidden around.

Even if she did get away, it wouldn't matter. She'd never be safe, as she'd known when she'd destroyed her house.

She didn't echo the sentiment that some in the clans had expressed. She didn't believe that all the soul eaters had to die.

She might yet play Merlin to them as well, teach them new tricks.

ARIEL

riel's shoulder still hurt where that one lucky son-of-a-bitch had shot her. She could still taste his blood. Probably had it all over her face.

Li Li had turned out to be a surprisingly good fighter for all her lack of training. Probably was because of her being a watcher. She hesitated more than Ariel, and that nearly got her killed. However, when she did strike, she used great accuracy to take down her opponent with a minimum of effort.

They'd gotten past the main building, into the underground maze of tunnels and rooms. They couldn't smell the magician—there were too many doors and fancy air filters between them and their prey.

They could still follow him, though. One of the crocodile clan had tagged the magician with a tracking spell that he either hadn't noticed or hadn't had the power to shake off.

It almost felt like cheating, tracking her prey with a little charm Ariel held in her hand.

Given the firepower of these assholes, though, she'd take every advantage she could get.

"How many bedrooms does this asshole need?" Ariel growled as they raced past yet *another* huge master suite with a round bed and red satin sheets, along with a hot tub in the room.

"The rich always need more," Li Li said simply.

"Ain't that the truth," Ariel replied. Dang. She was gonna have to talk with her aunts sometime about upgrading the new plantation house they'd agreed to build. The clan had never had a lot of money—they preferred good china to fat accounts—but still.

Not like they needed a gold-plated toilet. That was just excessive.

Finally, they tracked the magician down to a room. No idea how many guards were with him in there.

"You ready?" Ariel asked as she reached for the door.

Li Li grinned at her. She, too, was covered in blood, most of it not her own. Her golden crocodile eyes shone. Her scale armor had its own glow, and her long jaw and teeth gleamed. She'd broken more than one claw against the stupid armor of the guards—evidentially her claws weren't as sharp as Ariel's hooves.

It was only them.

And this battle would be the stuff of legends.

"Ready," Li Li said after taking a deep breath.

Would Li Li have nightmares about all the guards she'd killed? Ariel had no idea. She was aware that Gret, her boar soul, wasn't disturbed in the least.

And maybe that was the best reason for their plans to fail, for them to stay hidden in the shadows.

The humans would never accept the true bloodthirsty nature of the clans.

"Let's go, then," Ariel said as she used a borrowed machinegun to take out the hinges of the door.

Li Li would never forgive Ariel for what she was about to do.

And that was what Ariel's nightmares would be about.

YVETTE

Yi Chen stood alone at the top of one of the smaller piles of garbage, about a meter above the squishy path Yvette walked along. He wore a simple brown robe that flowed all the way to the ground, like what monks from ancient times wore, with long sleeves and a plain rope belt.

Yvette nearly snorted. As if that costume was supposed to put her at ease or something, since most of the soul eaters were as well dressed as she was, in her tight, tailored jeans and simple white blouse.

Pieces of plastic bags flapped at Yi Chen's feet. Flies and other insects formed dense clouds over the rotting mess, like a rolling wave of a filthy tide. More piles of garbage were strewn along the path, like some giant's marbles: some taller than the one Yi Chen stood on, some shorter.

Yvette couldn't possibly catalogue all the trash they stood on, though her winds tried: broken bicycle parts and faded tin cans, rotting rice and water bottles, Styrofoam peanuts and plastic wrapping straps.

The path up to where Yi Chen stood was clear, and as far as Yvette could tell, no one hid along it, waiting to ambush her.

Still, she went no further after she spotted him, and instead, waited at the bottom of the pile he stood on and looked up.

"*Bien*," Yvette drawled. "At least this is a private place. As well as outdoors."

Yi Chen beamed at her. She could tell the look was foreign to his face by the way his muscles scrunched up.

Her friend no longer existed, though his eyes were surprisingly clear and dark brown.

"We aim to please," he said with a sweeping bow.

"We?" Yvette asked, acting surprised and backing up a step. "I said I would meet with you. Alone."

"And so you are," Yi Chen said.

With a grace that wasn't his own, Yi Chen leaped into the air and floated down to stand beside her.

Yvette resisted the urge to roll her eyes at him. This wasn't some modern Hong Kong action flick with fighting monks and unbelievable wire work.

She was pleased, though, that he wasn't able to step close to her, as her winds whirled madly.

"You aren't alone either," Yi Chen said conspiratorially. "There are clan members following you."

Yvette gave a startled laugh at that. She hadn't known, not really, if anyone would be following her, or when they would arrive.

"*Mais oui*," Yvette said. "They don't trust me. Particularly that vulgar man from the tiger clan. He had the audacity to confront me at breakfast."

Would Yi Chen believe her? Did it matter? She was really just playing for more time, more breathing room, before the attack began.

The abrupt feeling of fingers lightly touching her mind was almost a relief.

She didn't have to play along nicely anymore.

"You really didn't know," Yi Chen said.

"Get out of my head," Yvette said with gritted teeth.

Just as abruptly, her brain was left alone again.

"Join us," Yi Chen said.

"Whatever for?" Yvette said. "So that I can steal more knowledge, knowledge that I didn't earn?"

"All knowledge is food," Yi Chen said solemnly.

Now, Yvette did roll her eyes. "*Non*," she said. "Knowledge is power."

And she threw the sharpest, most cutting wind at him, in an attempt to blow him to bits, knowing her effort would be wasted but too stubborn to not make the effort.

ARIEL

"Lightning bolts?" Ariel shouted at Li Li. "Who the hell has lightning bolts? Where did he steal that power?"

They cowered under the only cover they could find in the room, the splintered remains of a conference table. The magician stood, glowing and sparking in the corner while he gathered his power together for another blast at them.

"That can't be native," Li Li commented calmly, as if she were talking about a bake show on TV.

"Haven't seen any weaknesses about it," Ariel replied. Only their armor had saved them from the first attack, and their speed. But even as the asshole recharged they couldn't get close enough to attack.

Crack!

The wooden table shattered.

Ariel leaped to her feet with a growl and made yet another attempt to rush at the magician.

There was a blue barrier around him, though. It reminded her of the raven armor. She bounced off it, landing on her ass a few feet away.

Umph.

That was gonna be a big bruise.

If she survived.

Li Li also ran toward the bubble. But instead of trying to break through it, she paused and slashed her claws at it, trying to scratch her way through.

Her claws weren't as sharp as Ariel's hooves, though.

Ariel raced forward and did the same.

Screech.

The sound was worse than nails across a chalkboard.

But the armor cracked under the more subtle attack.

With a flurry of hooves, Ariel beat at the glass armor. More cracks appeared, racing across the top of the dome.

The magician looked up from his conjuring. Worry crossed his face, though he continued with his spell, drawing up another bolt of lightning between his two cupped palms.

Got you now, asshole.

YVETTE

Yi Chen had gone down surprisingly fast. For all his thoughtful consideration, his knowledge hadn't been that deep.

Or the soul eaters had stolen too much from him and not left him enough to protect himself?

It didn't matter. His head lay twisted at an unnatural angle, his robes bunched up around his waist, showing his well-muscled legs and filthy underwear that had once been white.

The almost familiar feel of someone else's touch in her mind had come back as the soul eaters left their hiding places, coming to surround her. They couldn't touch her physically. Her protective wind saw to that, though she'd already lost the knowledge of why it continued to whirl around her.

It was almost fitting, to find that garbage here amongst all the other castoffs. Yvette's winds kept the worst of the stench from her, but it still seeped in sometimes.

If she survived this battle she was going to burn everything she wore.

The first group that had attacked her had numbered merely six. There were four times that many, now. They all wore bespoke business suits and well-made dresses.

All of them focused on her. All ripping apart the knowledge she'd accumulated over the decades. They moved their mouths and licked their lips as they consumed everything she knew, growing fatter by the second. Her brain hurt as if it was being hammered by sticks.

They'd left her the bitterness though, of knowing how they were merely consuming her, bit by bit. They couldn't hold onto her knowledge. It was too broad, too deep. They couldn't hold all of her.

Plus, that had never been their intent.

The first of the clan warriors came roaring out of nowhere—a raven warrior. Yvette's winds hadn't told her that anyone else was nearby. He wore the glass armor of the raven's clan over his long wings and proud beaked face, with knife-sharp feathers instead of fingers. His feet were talons, sharp and deadly.

He slashed at the first soul eater he encountered. The magician fell like the garbage she stood on, as if he'd cut the strings animating her.

Then he froze as he was attacked, all his knowledge stripped mercilessly from him.

Yvette struggled to help him, to buffet the ones attacking him with her winds, only to find the knowledge stripped from her as soon as she called it up.

The warrior fell too quickly. How young had he been? Where had he come from?

She'd never know.

A viper appeared next. He was a pale yellow-gold creature, sinuous with powerful arms and legs, covered in shimmering scales. His fangs dripped with poison from his elongated head. She knew his claws were just as deadly, also tipped in poison.

Yvette couldn't remember his name. She had known him, though. She ground her teeth in frustration, telling herself that the tears that sprang to her eyes came from the pain in her head, not her aching heart.

She was surprised that she could still lie to herself.

The viper warrior took out another magicians, poisoning him with a lightning-fast strike of his head.

Yvette wanted to cheer. She threw burning magical fire at the next magician who came running up, who would have attacked the viper warrior.

The viper gave her a sharp nod.

Run! Yvette tried to call, her tongue tied up in loss.

The fool stayed.

The next magician to attack the warrior had fashioned a glowing wand. She struck at the viper warrior, however, she wasn't prepared for his speed, her arm slashed as she tried to defend herself from his quick attacks. He struck again, his claws finding hold in her skin as he tore her throat out.

But maybe that hadn't been her goal. She'd managed to keep the warrior in one place, hold him in the circle long enough for the soul eaters to get their own claws into him.

The viper warrior's eyes turned cloudy as he froze, his body shaking as if in a fit.

He dropped.

Yvette mourned. She would have given him a better death if she could have, much grander and befitting such a warrior.

Three more soul eaters came out of the shadows, completing their two dozen formation again.

Yvette shuddered as they renewed their full attack on

her. She struck out at them with what remained of her fire, her wind, her power.

And each of her tools was taken from her as soon as she used them.

There was something else the clan warriors needed to try. Something else they should do. A single clan warrior could easily take out all of these humans.

But they didn't remain themselves for long enough to make the attempt.

A tremendously large hound leaped into the fray. He was the size of a small pony, brindle-colored, with keen blue eyes.

He carried a bulbous mirror in his mouth. With a tremendous shake of his head, he threw it between the soul eaters so it landed beside Yvette's feet. Her winds immediately sucked it up, drawing it closer to her.

She *knew* this mirror. She'd touched it before. But what was it? What was she supposed to do with it? She grabbed hold of it with her left hand, looking at it curiously.

The tall male magician standing closest to her laughed. "You think those are going to protect you? Protect the clans?"

Yvette honestly didn't know what to think. She knew this mirror was different. Special. But how was it supposed to work? There was something about it…but the knowledge stayed buried in her head and she shied away from it, keeping it hidden.

The man purred, throwing his voice closer to her ear as he stole the knowledge of her winds from her. "Once we have you, we'll never let you go."

Yvette shuddered in revulsion. He sounded like every abusive boyfriend her winds had ever told her about. She shot a long, pure gout of fire at him.

He laughed at her again as the flame bounced off the shield surrounding him.

Suddenly there were ghost hands on her body, caressing her skin.

Yvette swallowed down her bile.

And still she attacked.

"This knowledge you're getting? It isn't really going to stay yours. Others will take it from you, as easily as you are taking it from me," she taunted. "I can still *see*."

She couldn't, not really. There had only been a flash here and there that unveiled the golden web that the magicians operated from.

A look of worry crossed the man's face, then was gone again, replaced by his greed. "You are wrong," he said simply.

Yvette snorted at him. Even as her head pounded with the pain of her great knowledge being ripped apart, even as her body was being violated, she still knew what she knew.

"You are a fool. The masters always take. You think you're feeding merely yourselves, but you aren't. The most tender bits, the *droit du seigneur*, are always reserved for those higher. You will only ever get the scraps until you've outlived your usefulness."

The man snarled at her in frustration. "You are wrong. We are all equal."

"Then who is pulling your chains?" Yvette gasped as a particularly nasty furrow was scratched across her soul. "Who is at the center of your web?"

Yvette had the strangest feeling that she hadn't been the one to say those words. It was as if she'd been conditioned, somehow, to fling this taunt at the height of the trap.

"None of your business," the man said.

But Yvette saw it. That cord of sickly light that trailed away from the man.

Was it enough? Would the others see the trail and be able to follow it back to the source?

"Enough of your questions," the man said. He reached through Yvette's winds and put pressure on her jaw, keeping her mouth from opening again. He couldn't crush her throat—he didn't have that kind of power.

Yet.

Yvette still laughed at him.

You are a fool, she thought.

From his grimace, that thought came through to him loud and clear, before he stole that from her as well.

VIRMAL

Virmal growled as the others they'd gathered together from the clans darted forward into the battle. *He* should be the one fighting. *He* had the most to avenge of all of them.

Yet, he waited, as the others had asked.

Towering piles of garbage surrounded him, confusing his sense of smell. He watched the battle through pair of high-powered binoculars. They'd been charmed significantly. They'd always show the truth and couldn't be misled. In addition, the optics now reached into the metaphysical realms. When Virmal augmented what he saw through the binoculars with own magical sense, he could actually see some of the magic being cast as well.

The soul eaters were like spiders, spinning sticky threads that sucked out the knowledge of their victims.

Just killing a few of them would never be enough.

He could make out close to four dozen soul eaters—many more than they'd anticipated. Every warrior who went in to do battle died, and died badly, their souls stripped from them.

Yvette still stood in the center of it, swaying under the constant attack. Virmal grudgingly admired her for that. It was like a lightning storm of power surrounding her, sneaking through her great whirling wind.

He still didn't trust her. Didn't trust any of the magicians. She would betray them in the end. He just knew it, though the others refused to see it.

Finally, the signal he'd been waiting for came. An arrow of light, like a lighthouse beacon, flashed, leading away from one of the magicians and back toward the city.

And though Virmal had positioned himself on that side of the battle, the flash still came and went too quickly for him to capture it in a mirror, about a meter to his left.

Damn it.

Virmal raced to where the flash had passed and tried to study the air, tasting it as best he could through the stench surrounding him. The magic that remained had an oily quality to it that coated his tongue unpleasantly, like rancid milk.

Once he had that taste, he knew he'd never forget it.

Unless one of the soul eaters got to him.

Virmal turned, unsure of what to do next. He had that scent. He had to find another thread of it, get his mirror between it and the sender somehow without breaking it.

There were too many scents. Too much going on. Too many conflicting types of magic as Yvette's magic was siphoned off and now being used by the others.

Virmal's tiger soul circled closer, growling at him, nudging him. She wanted to join the fight. Their friends and colleagues were getting slaughtered.

Virmal's hands holding the mirror grew into claws. It wasn't fair.

Suddenly, Harita's voice came to him. No, of course it wasn't fair. It had never been fair, him being born with a tiger soul and her without. Neither of them would ever be fully accepted by their clan.

But maybe it had been fate.

Harita had said those words to him so long ago, when they'd still been in college, their youthful idealism about changing the world vanishing as reality set in.

He'd scoffed at her then. He still wasn't sure he believed it now.

Still. He applied all his skill, all his knowledge, and all his ferocious anger to finding the next scent.

He could do this. He could beat the damned soul eaters at their own game.

Then join the slaughter.

LI LI

Ariel lay curled in the corner, where the magician's final blast had thrown her.

Li Li hoped the boar warrior wasn't dead, but Ariel wasn't moving.

She'd taken down the armor of the magician, though. Followed what Li Li had seen and broken through it.

Now, it was time to finish the job.

Li Li didn't bother casting some kind of holding spell on the magician. He might have magical defenses that she didn't know about. He lay flat on his back. Li Li sat on his legs, her claws digging into his arms, immobilizing him.

The magician at least had the grace to look scared, his eyes drawn to her dripping teeth. He still boasted, "It doesn't matter how many of us you kill. More will rise up, will take you and your clan. We are unstoppable."

"We will watch," Li Li promised. "None of you will ever have the strength to rise again."

"We are meant to be your masters," the magician continued. "To have dominion over beasts and humans alike."

Did the corrupted ones, these soul eaters, really consider the clan barely better than human?

It was time to end this.

Li Li reared back, ready to bite through his jugular, to drink down his blood like sweet revenge for all the aunts who'd been corrupted and already killed.

An iron arm wrapped around her neck, preventing her from biting.

"Wait," came Ariel's ragged command.

VIRMAL

Capturing that first ray of power had been almost impossible. Virmal felt like a pachinko ball dinging from one pile of garbage to the next, trying to get his mirror set up in time. While there were still three dozen of the soul eaters, the clan had lost every single warrior it had sent in to attack them. Only the boy had gotten out alive, but he'd gone in while in his monster hound form.

Finally, though, Virmal got one of the streaks to pass *through* the mirror.

The magic changed as it passed, growing stable and steady. One side was sickly yellow, like pus. The other was a brighter color, not cleaner, but much more powerful.

Damn it. Had Yvette betrayed them?

Or was this what the mirror was supposed to do?

Virmal didn't want to touch the garbage at his feet, but there was nothing for it. He jammed the mirror down into the crap to hold it in place, then piled more garbage around the base of it to hold it still.

Transforming his hands back to human and then to

tiger claws hadn't gotten rid of the filth. It matted the hair on the backs of his paws and gave off a sickly sweet smell.

But there wasn't anything Virmal could do about it. He just went and fetched the next mirror.

It was easier to place the mirror now that Virmal had a better idea of what to look for. The dark smell of the soul eater's magic coated all of him now, as if he'd rolled in fetid oil.

He wasn't sure if he'd ever feel clean again.

For the next one, the magical energy bounced off the mirror as he slid it into place, searing the wood and singeing the fur on the backs of his hands.

Virmal threw his head back in frustration and howled.

How the hell was he supposed to place six of these things? And would it be enough?

He couldn't give up though. Harita would mock him mightily if he gave up.

If she'd been alive.

Besides, until he'd done what he'd promised to do, he couldn't go and join the glorious battle, and give his all to help his friends.

Stubbornly, Virmal searched for the next thread of magic.

He could do this. Then he could go home, or to Heaven, which was the same thing.

LI LI

"What the hell do you think you're doing?" Li Li asked Ariel angrily.

She didn't let go of the magician. He still couldn't move, couldn't hurt them. The former conference room lay in pieces around them. Blasts of lightning and magic had punched holes through the plaster walls and wooden floor. The tables and chairs had all been blown to bits.

"You can't kill him," Ariel told her.

"Are you insane?" Li Li asked. She struggled, but only for a second, realizing a razor sharp hoof was pressed into her jugular.

If she moved, she died.

"I should have known," Li Li said bitterly. "*Never trust a boar in battle.* When were you compromised?"

"I wasn't, you silly bitch," Ariel snapped at her.

What right did Ariel have to get angry? She was the one who was ruining their plans.

"I did, however, change my mind when I learned you *lied* to me."

Li Li grew very still. While she normally wouldn't think twice about lying to someone in another clan, why on earth would Ariel accuse her of that?

Li Li hadn't lied about anything important. She was certain of it. "What are you talking about?" she asked as patiently as she could.

"She sees the rightness of our cause," the magician purred.

"Shut up," Li Li and Ariel said in unison.

"No, you lied when you let me believe my friends had been killed. On that first day," Ariel accused.

"I've never seen anyone escape that trap!" Li Li said. "How could I know they'd gotten away?"

"When y'all started planning this escapade, and talked with the hound court," Ariel replied. "The hound prince still lives."

"Oh," Li Li said. She *had* known that. She'd also known he'd been Ariel's friend.

And if she was truly honest with herself, she guiltily realized she'd liked having a co-conspirator. Someone who saw things the way she did, who listened to her and laughed with her and went out to eat with her.

She'd never had a friend before.

So she had always forgotten to mention to Ariel that her other friends were still alive, so she could selfishly keep the boar all to herself.

"I didn't learn about it until my aunts came to help your clan," Ariel continued. "That's when we decided to change sides."

Li Li suddenly realized that the boars had integrated themselves into the most important strikes, all the essential battles.

This betrayal was going on across the entire city.

"You see?" the magician crowed gleefully.

"We ain't joined your side, asshole," Ariel told him. "We've formed our own."

VIRMAL

Virmal snarled as he took out the first magician on the fringes of the group attacking Yvette. As he'd been setting up his mirrors he realized that the successful attacks were guerilla affairs—in, kill a magician, then out again. The faster he moved, the better.

The heaps of garbage made it more difficult to find the corrupted ones. Virmal couldn't rely on his nose to hunt his prey, and his eyes could easily be fooled by their magic. Instead, he had to use the magical touch that he'd been using setting up the mirrors, following the stench of their magic instead.

However, dropping the first magician wasn't nearly as satisfying to Virmal as he'd imagined it would be.

These were the arseholes responsible for killing Harita. He was getting his revenge, at last.

It still didn't feel right.

That wasn't about to stop him.

The next magician Virmal tracked went down far too easily. She didn't fight back at all, didn't try casting a spell at him. She didn't even have any armor. She stood there vacant-eyed, mouth agape. All he had to do was swipe his claws across her neck and down she went.

Were the mirrors working? Were they sucking the life out of the magicians, weakening them? Or had the magicians turned cannibal, and were they attacking their own? Drawing power from every available source?

Too late. Virmal hadn't kept moving. Something grabbed him, an irresistible force, wrapping around his arms and legs so he couldn't move.

"Here kitty, kitty, kitty," came a voice on the wind.

Virmal stiffened. That sounded like Yvette.

He turned his head. The invisible force carried him forward.

Yvette was no longer being attacked. Her winds no longer whirled around her. Instead, she stood perfectly still and proud.

She turned her face to him, the eyes covered in white cataracts. She still held the mirror Lukas had thrown to her at the start of the battle. A torn bit of red ribbon dangled from her wrist, like a leftover from a parade.

"Bad kitty," the thing using Yvette said. With a casual wave of her hand, she threw a bolt of energy and knocked over one of the mirrors he'd set up.

"Did you really think you could stop us with mere smoke and mirrors?" Yvette taunted as she took out another carefully placed mirror.

"I knew you would betray us," Virmal said through clenched teeth. "No magician can be trusted."

"Ah, but your clan is the most magical of them all. What does that say about you?" she asked reasonably.

To his horror, Virmal found one hand rising until sharp claws pricked his own jugular.

"Maybe you should show me," Virmal snarled. "You still hold a mirror."

"Oh." Yvette faltered. Her movements grew jerky as the hand holding the mirror moved first to the left, then the right.

How much of Yvette remained? Virmal might not have liked or trusted her, but he'd come to respect her.

He could hear her words again, from one of the meetings with the group, talking about how to stop the soul eaters. "They are arrogant," Yvette had said.

Virmal's back had gone up at how arrogant Yvette herself had sounded.

"They will dismiss the simplest of things, thinking that only a grand gesture will stop them."

Like a field of mirrors surrounding them will be the focus of their attack.

Not a single mirror held by one of their own.

Slowly, the hand holding the mirror rose, until it was directly between Virmal and Yvette, like a shield. Yvette drew back her other hand, as if to throw an overhand pitch.

A crackling ball of magic formed in the palm of the drawn back hand.

The mirror jerked again, as if someone was trying to move it out of the way.

But Yvette prevailed.

The ball of magic hit the convex side of the bulbous mirror with explosive force. Bright bolts of light ricocheted out, striking the magicians standing behind Yvette. From there, the pattern spread, bouncing off each individual to the next, and the next.

The mirrors Virmal had placed held. Massive amounts of magic and power channeled through them. They sucked magic from the magicians, weakening them.

The force holding Virmal disappeared as abruptly as it had appeared.

Finally!

Virmal turned to face his attackers.

But there was no one left.

The magicians were all crumpling to the ground as their stolen knowledge was stolen back, along with all their power and ability to do magic.

Not all of the magicians would die—too few to suit Virmal's taste.

However, none of them would ever be able to work magic again.

The mirrors started to buzz loudly with all the power they were accumulating. No one had been sure what would happen to them. Would they melt? Or would they explode?

"*Mon dieu*," came a soft exhalation.

Virmal turned back to see Yvette sway and then fall to the ground.

Damn it. He wasn't supposed to like her. Wasn't supposed to care about her or anyone else.

Virmal still found himself racing to her side.

Her face was pale and ghostly from all the effort she'd made, all the life drained from it. Her clothes were filthy and torn, as if she'd rolled in the garbage she now lay on. Blood trickled from her scalp.

But her eyes were her own again.

Yvette looked at Virmal clearly. "Live," she commanded him.

Virmal was too stunned to say anything. How could he?

"I couldn't save Indukala Khushi Deshmukh," Yvette said, her voice faltering. "Just as you couldn't save Harita. You must live for both of them."

Virmal shook his head mutely. That wasn't how it was supposed to go. He didn't want to live.

"Promise me," Yvette commanded him. "To honor all three of us."

Virmal couldn't. He couldn't find any words. He shut his eyes and lowered his head, as if in prayer.

He couldn't live without Harita. He didn't know how.

His traitorous tiger soul nudged him. *Maybe he could learn.*

Virmal opened his eyes. Yvette was fading.

"Now run," she murmured, her own eyes shutting.

Virmal looked up. The mirrors were whining now, vibrating in place.

Seemed as though they were likely to explode after all.

Virmal didn't want to leave Yvette in this place. The explosion would take care of all the bodies, either evaporating them or burying them forever.

He scooped her up as gently as he could, then used all his magical speed to flee the garbage heap before it was destroyed.

Yvette was long dead before he reached the edges of it.

He couldn't save her.

He could, perhaps, save himself.

L i Li helplessly watched. It had been what she'd been
trained to do all her life.

Now, at what she was certain was the end of her life,
she still watched. The ruined conference room around her
faded, as did her own aches and injuries, the taste of blood
growing stale in her mouth.

The magician she held immobile was…thinning. His
fat jowls shrank. He struggled more, but he was weaker,
she could tell.

"What's happening?" Li Li asked.

"The others found a way to drain these assholes of
their power," Ariel crooned. "Soon there'll be nothing left
but a mundane human. Oh, he might still have money and
influence. But his power'll all be gone.

Li Li blinked. How was such a thing possible?

"You lie," the magician snarled. "We're too strong.
There are too many of us."

"And y'all are connected, and interconnected," Ariel
replied. "The tigers have this saying, *Hurt one. Hurt all.*
And in y'all's case, that's literally true."

"What if they fail?" Li Li asked. It was a brave plan, and really, a better solution, to merely strip those responsible of all their magic.

Li Li felt Ariel's shrug.

"Then we get back to killing," the boar warrior said cheerfully.

Li Li wanted the plan to fail. She'd found her voice! She wanted to step all the way out of the shadows, to bring the clan into the light.

The fading magician before her told her otherwise.

"You are fools," the magician boasted when the process reversed itself for a moment. Suddenly, he seemed much stronger, much more capable.

But before Li Li could react, he shrank in on himself again. It was like a movie watching him age. They'd started battling a young man, no older than thirty.

Now, she held someone who was closer to eighty, and shrinking rapidly.

All the magic in the room died as the magician's power drained away. She'd heard that it never survived the death of the person who had created it. The charms in the corners and the protection runes on the walls all faded.

Finally, as far as Li Li could tell, all the magic was gone.

Ariel stepped back, releasing her.

Li Li slowly pushed herself to standing.

This wasn't the victory she'd planned on.

"Kill me," wheezed the old man still lying on the floor. "Please. I beg of you. Kill me now."

In a flash, Ariel had dropped to her knees beside him.

"To hell with you, old man," she sneered. "Don't you think my Aunt Mabel begged for the same thing after you'd taken her will and made her work against the rest of us? All the other people you stole from, don't you think they begged for the same thing?"

Ariel stood and backed away. Li Li could tell how much the boar warrior just wanted to attack, but she controlled herself.

"Live with it," she said as she turned and started heading toward the door.

Li Li stiffly followed after her former friend.

Was her betrayal so awful that Ariel would never forgive her? She didn't know.

But she, too, was just going to have to live with it.

PART FOUR
REBIRTH

VIRMAL

Virmal recognized the small crystals hanging like dewdrops from tall pines that stood guard at the entrance to Yvette's property. The tiger clan had agreed to oversee the land for all eternity, ensuring that it would never be developed.

Or found. Virmal would re-enchant the crystals with the distraction spells they once held, keeping the property safe from prying eyes.

The pine trees rustled as he walked up the lane toward her cottage. It was late fall. Snow covered the ground in a virgin blanket: His were the only footprints to be found. The air seemed hushed, expectant.

Once Virmal cleared the rows of trees, more footprints showed up. Bird tracks, squirrels, deer, rabbits, and other animals Virmal couldn't immediately identify had all walked across the yard, unafraid in the open space.

This had been their sanctuary for centuries. Virmal would work hard to keep it so.

The cottage was in ruins. The light coating of snow

couldn't hide how the roof no longer sat straight on its walls. The smell of smoke wasn't fresh, but still lingered.

Virmal didn't bother going inside. He wasn't sure what he'd do with the place—let it fall to pieces or try to rebuild it. He wasn't planning on coming back here often.

The reason for this trip was still in his hands: a small clay urn that held Yvette's ashes. Though she'd probably scoff at his gesture for the sentimental crap that it was, he also figured she'd be touched by it.

A tall stone wall stood to the right of the cottage. Virmal would have bet that the round-top wooden door had once been enspelled as well—possibly to make it invisible. Certainly to keep it locked, as it now pushed open easily enough.

The garden in the back was still wild and untamed. Tall roses shivered, naked against the snow. They were possibly too far gone. Virmal would have to get an expert up here to see. Snow made mere lumps of the rest of the plants. A greenhouse stood in the far left corner, frost covering the windows. Whatever had been grown in there was probably frozen as well.

Virmal tromped through the snow to the very center of the yard. He stood, unsure what to do next. He'd planned on sprinkling Yvette's ashes over her plants. All he'd do now, though, would be to dirty the snow.

A tickling wind brushed against the back of his collar, sending chills down his spine. A second wind suddenly pushed against his right arm, the one holding the urn. More winds sprang up out of nowhere, as if the calm afternoon had suddenly turned stormy.

But no storm clouds crowded the sky.

Did the winds recognize what he carried? He hadn't realized they had any will of their own.

Hesitantly, Virmal uncorked the urn and held it up.

A whirling wind raced around his arm and dipped into the clay pot. Ashes circled up, as if caught in a dust devil, then were spirited away.

Slowly, Virmal tipped the urn. As the ash spilled out it was whisked away, like an angry maid working to keep the snow beneath his hand pristine.

Finally, the last of the ash trickled out. The winds spiraled around Virmal one last time, as if saying, *Thank you*. Then the air stilled, growing as calm as it had been before.

Virmal looked over the dead yard. He felt as empty as the urn he carried. The winter would be long and harsh.

But come spring, he'd make certain that this garden lived again.

And maybe, so would he.

READ MORE!

Are you a traveler? Do you enjoy exploring strange new worlds, new cultures, new people?

Journey into the various lands envisioned by Leah R Cutter.

About the Author

Leah R Cutter writes page-turning fiction in exotic locations, such as a magical New Orleans, the ancient Orient, Hungary, the Oregon coast, rural Kentucky, Seattle, Minneapolis, and many others.

She writes literary, fantasy, mystery, science fiction, and horror fiction. Her short fiction has been published in magazines like *Alfred Hitchcock's Mystery Magazine* and *Pulphouse*, anthologies like Fiction River, and on the web. Her long fiction has been published both by New York publishers as well as small presses.

Find Leah's books on Knotted Road Press at (www.KnottedRoadPress.com)

Follow her blog at www.LeahCutter.com.

Read her essays on her Patreon, get free stories, and more! www.Patreon.com/leahcutter

Reviews

It's true. Reviews help me sell more books. If you've enjoyed this story, please consider leaving a review of it on your favorite site.

Come someplace new…

Are you a traveler? Do you enjoy exploring strange new worlds, new cultures, new people?

Journey into the various lands envisioned by Leah R
Cutter.

Sign up for my newsletter and I'll start you on your travels
with a free copy of my book, *The Island Sampler*.

I will never spam you or use your email for nefarious
purposes. You can also unsubscribe at any time.

http://www.LeahCutter.com/newsletter/

ABOUT KNOTTED ROAD PRESS

Knotted Road Press fiction specializes in dynamic writing set in mysterious, exotic locations.

Knotted Road Press non-fiction publishes autobiographies, business books, cookbooks, and how-to books with unique voices.

Knotted Road Press creates DRM-free ebooks as well as high-quality print books for readers around the world.

With authors in a variety of genres including literary, poetry, mystery, fantasy, and science fiction, Knotted Road Press has something for everyone.

Knotted Road Press
www.KnottedRoadPress.com